D0297699

THE BANGKOK SECRET

Books by Anthony Grey

AUTOBIOGRAPHY

Hostage in Peking (1970)

SHORT STORIES

A Man Alone (1971)

NONFICTION

The Prime Minister Was a Spy (1983)

NOVELS

Some Put Their Trust in Chariots (1973)
The Bulgarian Exclusive (1976)
The Chinese Assassin (1978)
Saigon (1982)
Peking (1988)
The Naked Angels (1990)
The Bangkok Secret (1990)

The Bangkok Secret

Anthony Grey

บ ช

MACMILLAN
LONDON

Copyright © James Murray Literary Enterprises Limited 1990

All rights reserved. No reproduction, copy or transmission
of this publication may be made without written permission.
No paragraph of this publication may be reproduced, copied
or transmitted save with written permission or in
accordance with the provisions of the Copyright Act 1956
(as amended). Any person who does any unauthorised act
in relation to this publication may be liable to criminal
prosecution and civil claims for damages.

First published 1990 by
MACMILLAN LONDON LIMITED
4 Little Essex Street, London WC2R 3LF
and Basingstoke

Associated companies in Auckland, Delhi, Dublin, Gaborone,
Hamburg, Harare, Hong Kong, Johannesburg, Kuala Lumpur,
Lagos, Manzini, Melbourne, Mexico City, Nairobi, New York,
Singapore and Tokyo

A CIP catalogue record for this book is available from
the British Library.

ISBN 0 333 53909 5

Photoset by Rowland Phototypesetting Limited
Bury St Edmunds, Suffolk

Printed and bound in Great Britain by
Billing & Sons Ltd, Worcester

Dedicated to
the real Tongkam, an ordinary working
elephant in northern Thailand – and all his wondrous kind
in Asia, tamed and wild

CONTENTS

PRELUDE

1946

The muzzle of the US Army Colt .45 pistol wavered slightly, then steadied. It was fully loaded and its safety catch was in the 'off' position. From a distance of only a few inches, it was pointing directly at the head of King Rama VIII of Siam.

The youthful king was stretched out flat on his bed in the heart of the sumptuously ornate Grand Palace compound. Although it was after nine o'clock on a June morning in 1946, a mosquito net of finest muslin was drawn loosely round the bed. The king was still dressed for sleep in a pair of blue Chinese silk trousers and a pale, loose tunic; the thin-framed spectacles he normally wore lay on the bedside table and his eyes were closed. In the sultry, debilitating heat of Bangkok's high summer, his face shone with the damp pallor of a slight indisposition.

Beyond the tall windows of the king's bedroom sunlight shimmered on the gilded, needle-sharp spires and towers of the world's most spectacular temples and throne pavilions. Curved roofs of saffron, green and crimson tiles crowned with mythical birds soared spectacularly above the square mile of formal courtyards and gardens. As always a mystical, dream-like hush broken only by the tinkling of hanging temple bells embraced the ancient precincts; they had been inhabited for almost two centuries by monarchs revered and venerated in the Hindu tradition as divine beings, living god-kings, the 'Lords of Life'. Under the gaze of giant demons, seven-headed serpents and fantastical statues that were half bird, half human, courtiers, attendants and visitors of all ranks were accustomed to move in a suitably reverent silence.

The nation's most sacred image, the Emerald Buddha, glimmered in the candle-light of the finest temple only a few paces from the bedroom where a finger was tightening around the trigger of the Colt .45 pistol. Carved from translucent green jade, the Buddha sits high on its own gilded throne guarded by a host of tall, standing Buddhas; each guardian carries the slender, multi-tiered golden parasol symbolic of Siamese royalty. According to legend, a bolt of lightning split the tapering golden *chedi* of a northern temple in the fifteenth century to uncover the sacred image. Transported south by elephant to the Grand Palace in later years, it had been linked inextricably ever since with the nation's security and well-being. Three times each year jewelled, gold-mesh garments are solemnly draped around the jade figure by the reigning monarch and as the Colt .45 exploded with a roar in the bedroom of King Rama VIII on that morning in 1946, perhaps the Emerald Buddha trembled violently on its gilded altar from the shock.

The bullet smashed into the king's skull just above the left eye. It left a jagged X-shaped hole in his forehead. Later, the spent bullet was found embedded in his mattress. Its passage through the brain suggested the king had not raised his head from the pillow in the moment that the pistol was fired. After a stunned silence anxious cries and the sounds of running feet echoed in the corridors leading to the king's quarters. Royal attendants, the king's mother and his eighteen-year-old brother Bhoomipol, who was to become the present King Rama IX, hurried into the room to find blood flowing from the wound. They saw the Colt .45 lying on the bed close to the left hand of the right-handed king. One spent cartridge had fallen nearby on the floor; only one round had been fired from the pistol.

Within minutes the twenty-year-old king, whose personal name was Ananda Mahidol, was dead. At once shock waves in the form of rumour, counter-rumour and speculation began to spread like wildfire beyond the white, fortified walls of the Grand Palace. The nation, known until 1940 as Siam but since renamed Thailand, was stunned by grief and disbelief. King Ananda had come to the throne as a boy at the age of ten in 1935, after the surprise abdication of the previous king. But, like his younger brother, he had been born abroad and they had wisely remained in Switzerland with their mother throughout the Second World War to continue their education. During his absence Thailand had been occupied by the Japanese Army and forced to declare war on Britain and the United States. Throughout these difficult years no king on whom the Thai people could focus their devotion had dwelled in the fairy-tale Grand Palace.

So King Ananda's return home from Switzerland six months earlier in December 1945 had seemed to signal a joyous end to these years of darkness and national self-doubt. Massive crowds turned out to cheer their shy young monarch and members of his family. For people whose Buddhist beliefs are mingled inextricably with primal fears about the invisible spirit world, seeing their own 'Lord of Life' walking amongst them once again after a decade of absence induced a wildly elated mood of relief and rejoicing.

But now only six months after his return that new symbol of hope lay dead in the Grand Palace, his brain pierced by a bullet. And there was no clear evidence to prove whose finger had pulled the fatal trigger – or why. Could it have been deliberate suicide? An accidental self-killing? Accidental manslaughter? Or, worst of all a planned and cold-blooded assassination?

The rumour-mongers in the alleys and temple courtyards flanking Bangkok's majestic Chao Phraya river retailed every possible combination on that first steamy morning. The more superstitious souls saw the hand of dark forces and malevolent spirits at work. They had struck in the most sacred sanctuary of the capital city that had been originally named Krungthep – 'The Royal, Invincible and Beautiful City of Archangels'.

A hasty official statement prepared on the first day asserted that the king's death had been an accident. Four months later a formal Commission of Enquiry concluded a preliminary investigation. The accident theory was then dismissed completely but the Commission could not find sufficient evidence to support a verdict of suicide or assassination. Suspicion, intrigue and political unrest flourished until late in 1947 a new government seized power through a military *coup d'état*, promising to solve the vital 'King's Death Case'.

The former prime minister fled abroad and immediately two royal pages and a court official were arrested and accused of conspiring to help assassinate the king. After trials and appeals lasting nine long years, in 1955 all three men were executed by firing squad. But the flimsy, conflicting evidence and the convictions were viewed with widespread scepticism in

Thailand and around the world. None of the executed men was ever accused of firing the fatal shot. As the years ticked by the mystery has continued to resist any satisfactory solution. Intermittently the unanswered questions have cast shadows of doubt and intrigue over the fabled spires and towers of Bangkok.

PART ONE

CHIANG MAI

THE BANGKOK SECRET

Chapter One

Without warning in the dead of night, the chilling, primeval scream-roar of Poo Tongkam, my biggest bull elephant, rang out suddenly through the blackness shrouding the jungle-clad mountains. Bouncing and echoing back and forth among the massive boles of the standing teak, the frenzied trumpeting woke me instantly in my tent. I was rolling off my camp cot on to the ground in a reflex action at the same instant that I came awake. Still reasonably fit and sharp-witted in those days, I was scrambling to my feet and pushing aside the tent flap even before my eyes were open because I had recognised the unmistakable, terrifying sound of 'musth'.

Muzzily I remember thinking that all my terrified Siamese camp coolies would immediately imagine that a great horde of *phii paa* – the malignant forest spirits of northern Thailand – must be pursuing and enraging Poo Tongkam. I little realised then how near the mark that sleep-muddled thought was to prove. For the local *kon song*, the native mystics and mediums who interpret such events, would eventually identify elements more sinister than familiar local spirits like the Lord of the White Hat and the Crystal Prince. The tormented spirit of a real, modern, flesh-and-blood monarch, they would say, had come terrifyingly amongst them.

But with the anguished *musth* roar of Poo Tongkam filling the darkness outside my tent, my mind at that moment was struggling to focus more on the living. When I pulled aside the tent flap, I realised that the terrible noise was coming from the direction of the Siamese coolies' camp lines. They habitually erected lean-to shelters thatched with palm leaves to serve as their quarters and I could hear the enormous elephant trampling and breaking these flimsy structures. Shouts and screams of terror were beginning to rise above the trumpeting of the frenzied animal as I ran across the clearing, buckling on my revolver belt.

By the faint luminescence of the stars I could see the great bulk of Poo Tongkam only fifty yards away. He was rearing and plunging madly among the trees, swinging his great head and his long tusks from side to side in a murderous frenzy. I could hear the broken chain which had secured him to a tree clanking and jingling in his wake. By then, I found later, he had already killed his mahout and two young coolies. Their lifeless bodies, smashed and crushed beyond recognition, were later found amongst the tangle of branches and demolished trees.

Other terrified coolies were fleeing across the camp in all directions. Prapoth, my headman, was bolting wide-eyed towards the ridge above my tent and I dashed forward to cut him off, grabbing him by the wrist.

'Come with me, Prapoth!' I yelled close to his ear. 'We have to try and stop him.'

Prapoth struggled frantically to tear himself from my grip. His mouth was agape with fear and his eyes were rolling. 'Let me go, please, Master! This is the work of a terrible *phii taay hoong*.'

'No, don't be afraid,' I yelled again. 'Poo Tongkam has only gone on *musth*. I saw the oil on his head this afternoon.'

All male Asiatic elephants at some time or other suffer these strange bouts of disturbance. Attacks of *musth* are invariably foreshadowed by the discharge of an oily secretion from a tiny hole in the elephant's temple. I had noticed a tell-tale trace of oil on Poo Tongkam's head earlier in the day and ordered his mahout to shackle him securely to a tree for the night with double chains. But because of his size – nine feet tall at the shoulder and one of the biggest elephants I'd seen in northern Thailand – he had obviously broken free without too much difficulty.

Gazing fearfully over his shoulder, Prapoth was still struggling to free himself from my grasp. 'Please, Master,' he whined in a low voice. 'It isn't normal *musth*. It is the *phii taay hoong* of the dead king who is tormenting the elephant. One of the

Royal Palace pages who served the king before his death has fled to hide in the next village. The *phii taay hoong* must have followed him here. Now we are all being punished!'

Wrenching himself from my grasp, Prapoth stumbled blindly away up the slope and disappeared among the trees. I knew that, according to the prevailing beliefs of the region, *phii taay hoong* were the ghosts of men and women who had died violent deaths. They were among the most feared of all the vast army of invisible spirits who have held sway over the forests, fields and villages of northern Thailand since time immemorial. Only the ghosts of women who died in childbirth were more feared because they had suffered nature's gravest punishment – death at a moment that normally celebrates joyous birth and renewal.

In the near-darkness with the chilling roars of the crazed elephant echoing all around me, it would not have been difficult to share Prapoth's primitive fears. During my years as a forest assistant in those northern jungles I had developed a healthy respect for local customs and lore. Without delving too deeply, I had concluded that these ancient superstitions belonged to another time. My conventional middle-class up-bringing in pre-war England, I conceded, had not equipped me to understand such powerful and archaic forces. In those days, I was content to leave it at that. But I had made it a personal rule never to scoff or show any scepticism about my coolies' beliefs and superstitions. Running on down the slope towards the turmoil, tugging my revolver from its leather holster, I had no time to reflect on the extraordinary claim that a tormented royal soul might be spurring my most powerful and most valuable working elephant to an orgy of unprecedented destruction. I had no way of knowing at that moment that the wild midnight rampage of Poo Tongkam would mark the beginning of a mystery that would return again and again to dog my life over many years.

 บ ช

1

'Where did you find my father's manuscript?'

The dark eyes of the English television journalist were bright with an inner tension when she glanced up from the mildewed page bearing the description of the rogue elephant's midnight rampage. Although the events of which she had just read had taken place more than thirty years earlier, the expression on her face suggested they had become as real and intense to her in the autumn of 1989 as if they had occurred only minutes before.

'I think it was brought down from the Shan hills by a caravan of ivory traders in this tin box.'

The short, burly Thai sitting opposite her spoke his English with a halting sibilance. He did not look directly at her as he gestured towards a dented box that lay open on a table beside his chair. Once it had been green, but its paint had largely flaked away and rust was crusted along its bevelled edges and around the hinges and clasps.

'When?'

The Thai shrugged, still without looking at her. 'I haven't been told that, Miss Hampson.'

'Who gave it to you?'

Outside the bare room the first sounds of a tropical storm were beginning to disturb the night. The shaded light bulb suspended from the centre of the ceiling flickered briefly once or twice, as though threatening to deny them its light. A few feet from her chair, closed french windows leading to a veranda rattled and strained at their flimsy fastenings under the urging of the strengthening wind.

'I was sent by somebody who wishes to remain anonymous at present, Miss Hampson – someone who perhaps once had dealings with your father.'

'A man or a woman?'

The Thai neither moved nor spoke. He raised his eyes once to look at her fleetingly but did not hold her gaze. Outside, the noise of the storm was growing louder; the light bulb began flickering again and the french windows rattled more noisily.

'Will you tell me then why you brought me the manuscript?'

'I know almost nothing of the reasons, Miss Hampson. I was just told to convey it to you.'

'How did you know I was in Chiang Mai?'

The Thai shrugged again, his face still expressionless. 'Chiang Mai is not a large city. The name of Adam Hampson was well known here before he disappeared . . . News travels quickly in Thailand. So the arrival of Miss Joceline Hampson, the well-known television reporter, would hardly pass unnoticed.'

Glancing down at the discoloured title sheet attached to the manuscript's first chapter which lay in her lap, Joceline Hampson read again the six words that had been typed with a fading ribbon: 'The Bangkok Secret by Adam Hampson'. She breathed in slowly, flicked over the page and read the first paragraph again. When she had run her eye down that page the first time, her hands had been shaking slightly and she had found it difficult to concentrate. The soft knocking at her door only minutes after her arrival in the faded hotel had alarmed her. Something in the tense, edgy manner of the dark-faced Thai clutching the tin box had heightened her unease. Without introducing himself he had unlocked the box and taken out a thin sheaf of paper from inside. After thrusting it into her hands he sat down and watched with a curious intensity as she began to read. 'Without warning in the dead of night, the chilling, primeval scream-roar of Poo Tongkam, my biggest bull elephant, rang out suddenly through the blackness . . .'

This time, because she knew what was to follow, the opening words seemed to take on a new, ominous vibrancy. The blue bush shirt and trousers she wore were damp with perspiration but despite the humid heat of the night a faint chill of apprehension climbed slowly up her spine. Looking up she found that the Thai had taken another thin sheaf of paper from the pile of mildewed manuscript visible inside the box. He held it wordlessly towards her, motioning with his head for her to take it from him. She hesitated, then reached out – but at that moment the french windows sprang open and banged violently back against their frames. A rush of wind filled the room with noise and a dozen loose sheets of paper blew out of the tin box. They whirled up towards the ceiling and only when the dark-faced Thai rose and secured the faulty locks on the doors did they flutter to rest on the polished teak floor.

Joceline Hampson stood motionless beneath the light, staring out into the darkness. The rush of damp air had carried the earthy odours of the jungle into the room and the wildness of the night outside alarmed her. She held the new sheaf of typescript absently at her side, her expression distracted and uneasy.

'Read on, now, please,' said the Thai quietly, collecting the scattered pages from the floor. 'Don't imagine it's the *phii taay hoong* – there's often a storm at this time of night.'

เดอะ บางกอก ซีเคร็ท

THE
BANGKOK
SECRET

Chapter Two

แอนโทนี เกรย

แบบ แอนเคน เวย

Poo Tongkam had already killed three native mahouts in his twenty-five years of life. He would fell an unwary man with a sudden lash of his trunk or a swing of his long, curved tusks, then swiftly crush the life from him on the ground with one massive knee. He had gored and savaged a dozen other lesser tuskers while on *musth* and as I ran towards him I feared for the safety of my eleven other working elephants that had been grazing or slumbering at their shackles between the river and the camp.

Male elephants are rare in the animal kingdom; they appear to go on *musth* at indeterminate intervals in the same way that many female animals come into season. Male camels are the only other animal known to behave in a similar way. Even docile male elephants become ill-tempered and unpredictable at such times. But those few rare males that show a savage temperament from birth are always especially dangerous when on *musth*. Why this should be, nobody who has worked with elephants really knows. It appears to be a primordial instinct to kill rivals before mating with a chosen cow elephant. But mating itself does not calm the bull elephant's frenzied blood lust. He remains wildly aggressive, ready to kill perhaps to defend his mate, until that mysterious trickle of oil ceases to flow from the hole in his temple.

Working Asiatic elephants of all kinds, male and female, are customarily decked with wooden bells because their natural movement is eerily silent despite their bulk; only those known to be savage are tagged with metal bells as a constant reminder to the humans working around them. Poo Tongkam's screams and trumpetings were mingled with the fast, frantic clanking of his brass bell and the jingling of his broken fetters so I had no difficulty in following him as he raged along the darkened jungle trail leading from the camp towards the river.

Despite the sense of terror which had seized the camp, a part of me relished the danger and the challenge as I rushed in his wake. My fascination with elephants had begun the week after my arrival in wartime Burma at the age of twenty. I was posted to one of the XIVth Army's elephant companies on bridge-building duties and almost immediately a feeling of exhilaration came over me. Working with the massive, but dignified and intelligent animals seemed to transform the ominous tropical forests into a realm of infinite mystery. The grandeur and nobility of the strength they exerted as they shifted and manoeuvred the great teak logs on land and in the foaming rivers captivated my mind. A strange infatuation with those jungles and the animals in them was born in those first few days and I wasn't surprised to find later that both the people of Burma and Thailand greatly revere the elephant – in particular the rarely found 'white' species. According to ancient religious texts and legends, the conception of the Lord Buddha involved a mystical white elephant with a trunk 'like a silver rope'. Carrying a white lotus in this fabulous trunk, the elephant was said to have entered the golden mansion where the Buddha's mother lay and, after circling her bed three times, smote her right side and appeared to enter her womb. Ever since, the white elephant – a kind of albino in our terms – has been seen as a holy messenger from heaven and the finding of such creatures in Thailand's jungles has always sparked off great rejoicing. My own infatuation with elephants was perhaps more practical from working day by day with them – but I have never lost that fascination nor been able to explain it satisfactorily.

It was strong enough to lead me back to northern Thailand as a civilian immediately after demobilisation at the end of the war. I quickly rose to become a forest manager for the Anglo-Siamese Teak Trading Company. By 1950 I had under my charge about a hundred elephants divided into a dozen groups in a teak forest that was the size of an English county. I insisted that my European forest assistants keep detailed temperament and behaviour records for all the elephants, ostensibly so that the business of teak logging could proceed with the utmost efficiency. But in truth these annotated life histories of my different elephants had long since become my private obsession.

The written files were the first things I would pore over on my arrival at each forest camp. I knew it was a standing joke among my forest assistants that I was fonder of elephants than I was of people. Whether that was true or not, because Poo Tongkam was the mightiest and the fiercest of all my elephants, I had gone straight to his records on arrival at the camp two days earlier. I had read and reread the entries made since my last visit to that region some nine months previously, feeling a curious sense of pride, both in details of the prodigious strength he exerted at work and his periodic bouts of savagery. I had noticed at once that he had not been on *musth* since my previous visit and as I sped along the river trail I suddenly found myself mentally reviewing his entire record with great urgency.

A second or two must have elapsed before I realised that my subconscious mind was working faster than my senses of sight and hearing. The clank and jangle of bell and broken chains that previously had been growing fainter ahead of me as the bull elephant rushed towards the river had become suddenly loud and were growing louder. Poo Tongkam, having scented me, had swung abruptly in his tracks and was now charging dementedly towards me along the narrow trail.

In that instant of realisation, I halted in my tracks too. Turning I began running steadily back the way I had come. It was not the first time I had been pursued by a charging elephant but as always I had to fight down my natural impulse to run too quickly. Poo Tongkam's front and back legs were still hobbled loosely and I knew from experience that I should be able to run at roughly the same speed as a hobbled elephant in near darkness. If I kept my wits about me and did not trip and go sprawling on the trail, I knew I ought to be able to stay just ahead of those wickedly curved tusks and the snaking trunk. More importantly, although I had become the enraged Poo Tongkam's hated prey, I had already won some limited control over him. With him bellowing murderously at my heels I could at least dictate the direction of his charge.

Elephants follow as much by scent as by sight. Some of my forest assistants, I knew, when pursued by their unstable, four-legged charges, had flung off articles of clothing at the trail-side. Stopping to trample a shirt, or helmet in their rage, the elephants had sometimes given a desperate quarry vital breathing space. I considered tearing off my shirt as I pounded on along the winding track, but I could remember no instance of Poo Tongkam being successfully distracted in the past by such a ruse. To my surprise the noise of the elephant's bell was growing rapidly louder behind me. If his hobbles had snapped I realised I might not have much time left for manoeuvre – or anything else for that matter.

Looking over my shoulder as I ran, I was able to catch a blurred glimpse of Poo Tongkam rounding a bend in the trail not far behind me. In the faint glow of the stars I could see his trunk was lifted and curled, searching sinuously ahead. Rocking and swaying, he was a bulky, ever-growing shadow and I caught a glimpse of reflected light gleaming in his maddened eyes as he shrieked and trumpeted his way along the narrow tunnel through the trees.

At a fork in the trail, I sprang off to the left, following a narrower path which led uphill. I hoped the overhanging bamboo and other trees would slow Poo Tongkam. I remembered that other trails joined up with this path beyond the ridge and I sprinted faster, hoping to be able to give the charging animal the slip at the point where the paths diverged. But as I panted up the hillside, I saw to my surprise a glow of orange light ahead. Coming over the crest of the hill I caught sight of a group of native people below me holding smoking torches. They were gathered tensely in a clearing around a termite hill where I knew small shrines to the Lord of the White Hat and the Crystal Prince had existed since time immemorial. Behind me for an instant the clank of Poo Tongkam's bell and chains died away. His trumpeting ceased and I guessed that he had halted uncertainly at the fork in the trail to scent the air.

I held my breath and in that sudden silence, the quavering voice of a *kon song* rang out, repeating an incantation over and over again. I could see by the flickering torchlight that a female spirit medium dressed in coloured robes was facing the shrine, her body taut and bent forward in a trance-like posture. Those around her began to beat small forest drums and ancient stone lithophones as she advanced towards the termite hill, holding in her outstretched hands a square platter made of bamboo and banana stems. I knew enough to recognise that the traditional *sia kabaan* ritual was being performed for the expulsion of an evil spirit. The tray, I could see, bore ritual straw dolls, leaf cups of boiled rice, garlands of jasmine flowers, a candle, joss sticks and a large clay figurine of an elephant. The *kon song* was making little circular horizontal movements with the platter in front of her face, all the time repeating her shrill incantation.

'*Let the spirit of the murdered king depart from us,*' she was shrieking in an imploring voice. '*Let the restless spirit leave us in peace!*'

The eerie cries echoed and re-echoed among the silent teak trees for a few moments. Then from behind me a new ferocious bellowing suddenly drowned the ritual. It grew louder with a terrifying rapidity and the urgent clanking of Poo Tongkam's bell and chains indicated that the crazed elephant was rushing swiftly up the hill path.

Below me, the participants in the ritual seemed to freeze. I watched their heads turn fearfully in my direction. I knew I had only seconds left and I ripped open my bush shirt and tore it off. The moment Poo Tongkam reached the crest of the ridge, he would see the torchlit clearing. The way to the termite hill shrines lay open through the trees. I half turned, waiting until the great head and tusks were upon me. At the last moment I lashed my sweat-soaked shirt across the eyes of the elephant, momentarily blinding him. I threw myself to one side in the same movement, trying to twist and tug the shirt downwards to impale it on Poo Tongkam's tusks. He reared up above me on his great hind legs, roaring in fury and pawing the air as I tumbled over and over down the slope among the boles of the teak trees.

ม ช

2

Joceline Hampson raised her eyes slowly from the manuscript. She stared across the room, scarcely seeing the face of the burly Thai seated opposite her. He appeared to have remained motionless in his chair watching her read but it took her several seconds to bring her mind fully back to the present. The french windows were still rattling under the buffeting of the storm and the light bulb continued to flicker intermittently. A small bamboo cane table, she saw with an inward start, had been wedged under the door handles to support the faulty lock. Only then did she realise that she had been so engrossed in her reading that she had not noticed the Thai move from his chair.

'Do you find your father's writing interesting?'

Joceline studied the Thai's features. He had a broad, heavy-jowled face with jutting brows which gave him an outwardly sinister air; but like most of his race his manner was quiet and gentle. 'I find the manuscript very interesting,' she said. 'Please tell me who gave it to you.'

'I'm very sorry. I'm not authorised to say.'

'What is your name?'

The Thai hesitated and a smile flickered across his dark face. 'Call me Surachai. That will be sufficient.' He fingered the top sheaf of manuscript inside the tin box, apparently the next chapter. 'But if you would like to read the rest of this, you must say nothing about our meeting to anybody else you meet in Chiang Mai.'

'Why is there a need for secrecy?' asked Joceline in a puzzled voice.

The Thai smiled as though in pity. 'Forty-three years may have passed since King Ananda's brains were blown out by a revolver bullet. But his death is still a taboo subject in Thailand. The mystery has never been solved. The present king succeeded to the throne after that terrible event. Thailand's kings have always been regarded by the people as divine beings. Those old habits die hard. So nobody ever speaks their thoughts aloud about the former king's death. Three palace servants were convicted and executed.' He shrugged and gestured towards the manuscript and the tin box. 'But still nobody really knows the truth. And your father's manuscript speaks of things never before discussed openly . . .'

'Why haven't the contents been made public?'

'Perhaps the manuscript has only just come to light.' The Thai shrugged again. 'Perhaps nobody had bothered to read it before. I don't know.'

'Did you know my father?' asked Joceline, watching him closely.

'No – I wasn't a friend of your father. But everybody in Chiang Mai has heard of the famous English *farang* who preferred the jungle and elephants to people . . . It came as a great shock to many people when he was found trampled to death in the mountains last year . . .'

'If the manuscript really is the property of my father, all of it should be handed over to me at once.' Joceline rose from her chair and walked purposefully towards the table on which the tin box lay open. 'My mother is dead. I'm his only surviving relation.'

The Thai reached out quickly and snapped the lid closed. 'Please, Miss Hampson, be patient. I believe the entire manuscript will be handed over to you eventually.' He paused significantly. 'When it is clear what use you will make of it . . .'

Joceline's brow crinkled in a frown. 'What do you mean?'

'You are a journalist – in television, yes?'

'Yes.'

The Thai tapped the closed tin box with the pudgy index finger of his right hand. 'Couldn't such information be of interest to television viewers? In Europe, in America – perhaps all over the world?'

'I can't tell from what little you've shown me.' Joceline paused, subjecting the Thai to a searching scrutiny. 'What do you want me to do? Promise I won't breathe a word of it to anyone?'

He smiled, revealing gold fillings in his teeth. 'No. It would be quite natural, wouldn't it, for a grieving daughter to publicise her dead father's dramatic discoveries? There would be no objection at all.'

Joceline sighed exasperatedly. 'Mr Surachai, I know little or nothing of Thailand or its politics. Up to now that hasn't seemed like a serious omission in my life. I've spent a lot of the past three years in Latin America making programmes. I'm very interested in human rights. I was in the backlands of Paraguay when the news about my father's death came through. I didn't know about it until I returned to London weeks later. But he had never played any significant role in my life. I have no memories of him whatsoever and I've never been sentimental about him. I was on my way home from Australia when I decided to come here merely out of curiosity. And the moment I walked into this room you knocked on the door. All this is a bit sudden and I'm very tired.'

'I apologise for hurrying you.' The Thai ducked his head in a deferential gesture. 'But it was most important that I speak to you first – before you saw anybody else in Chiang Mai who might have known your father.'

'Why?'

'Because nobody else here knows of this manuscript's existence – and you must not speak of it to anybody if you wish to read more.'

Again Joceline frowned in mystification. 'What are you trying to say?'

'That extreme care must be exercised.' The Thai stood up and, with a swiftness surprising in such a fat man, crossed the room to Joceline's chair. He plucked the first two chapters of the manuscript from the table beside her and returned quickly to his own seat. He opened the tin box, removed another set of pages fastened with a clip, then carefully replaced the first two chapters before closing the lid. 'It will not be possible for you to retain any part of this manuscript while you are in Thailand.'

'Why not?'

'It would be too dangerous for you.'

The light bulb which had been flickering with increasing frequency as the storm intensified went out altogether for a few seconds. In the sudden darkness the noise of the driving wind and rain outside grew perceptibly louder. She noticed then that the shutters and french windows were rattling and shuddering constantly. When the light came on again she was surprised to find the Thai standing beside her chair. He held one hand towards her, offering the latest batch of manuscript.

'Although you are tired, I think you ought to read one other chapter before we part, Miss Hampson. We can arrange to meet again before you leave Chiang Mai. How long will you be staying?'

'Only a day or two.' She took the sheaf of typescript from him. 'I have to hurry back to London to edit my Australia film.'

'Then perhaps we could meet again tomorrow.' The Thai pulled a small notebook from the top pocket of his shirt, wrote an address in both English and Thai script then tore out the page and handed it to Joceline. 'Shall we say at midday? You will be able to read more of the manuscript in comfort at this address.'

She took the slip of paper without looking at it. 'Mr Surachai, perhaps I ought to make one thing clear. I'm not a hit-and-run television news reporter. I make documentary films in depth. I like to spend plenty of time doing careful research and establishing reliable background information. If I can't be sure my film will stand up on the screen, it doesn't get made. So don't imagine I'll treat this manuscript any differently for sentimental reasons – even if it does prove to have been written by my father. Do you understand?'

The Thai, who had been concentrating hard on what she was saying, nodded and smiled uncertainly. 'Yes, I understand.' Then his eyes narrowed questioningly. 'Who do you intend to see here in Chiang Mai? Which of your father's friends?'

'I've made an appointment for tomorrow morning to see Arnold Davenport, the secretary of the Chiang Mai Foreign Cemetery Committee. He will show me my father's grave.'

'Mr Davenport will probably invite you to the Gymkhana Club. There you will meet all the British expatriates. But please say nothing of our meeting or the manuscript. It is in your own best interests.'

The Thai stood looking down at her, waiting for an answer. But she said nothing. Her eye had fallen on the next typewritten page and, reading on, she had become instantly oblivious to his presence.

เดอะ บางกอก ซีเคร็ท

THE
BANGKOK
SECRET

Chapter Three

The orange glow of the burning torches drew Poo Tongkam to the foot of the slope with a terrible, lumbering rush the moment he shook my shirt from his tusks. Like a moth drawn fatally to a flame, he thundered down through the trees and into the clearing, trumpeting madly. The shrieks and screams of the terrified participants in the ritual were added to the din as Poo Tongkam plunged amongst them; a moment later the termite hill exploded and collapsed under the furious onslaught of his flailing feet. The ornate, painted shrines to the Lord of the White Hat and the Crystal Prince disintegrated, showering the people with splinters and shards of wood.

Despite the closeness of the enraged elephant the female *kon song* stood her ground and stared fearlessly at him, still holding the bamboo platter and its ritual objects high in front of her face. The other participants had retreated to the safety of the trees, ready to leap to the lower branches if Poo Tongkam showed any sign of moving towards them. The elephant, after trampling down the shrines, turned in her direction and lowered his head slightly, readying himself to charge. He had fallen ominously silent and from where I lay among the trees I could see that his gaze was locked fixedly on the *kon song*. In her turn she was staring back unwaveringly at the elephant and in the sudden silence I could hear her voice rising and falling as she repeated her low, monotonous chant over and over again. *'Let the spirit of the murdered king now depart from us . . . Let the spirit of the murdered king now depart from us . . .'*

I scrambled to my feet and ran, bent low, through the trees towards the little clearing, making as little noise as possible. As I drew near, I slowed to a walk, then crept soundlessly on all fours over the last few yards, not wishing to break the electric tension which joined the animal and the *kon song* like a taut wire.

A low rumbling sound was coming from deep in Poo Tongkam's chest. I had never heard a noise quite like it before from an elephant and a sudden chill ran through me despite the heat. Poo Tongkam was walking slowly towards the *kon song*, lifting each great foot with a curious deliberation as he went; for all their slowness, his movements were more threatening than any charge I had ever seen him make. But still the *kon song* showed no signs of flinching.

One of her courageous assistants was continuing to provide light with a flaming torch at the edge of the clearing. By its flickering glow I could see that the *kon song* was intent on holding Poo Tongkam's eye as his massive bulk shifted towards her. With all my elephants I had kept up the practice, learned in Burma during the war, of appointing a spearman to assist each mahout. The spearman always stood watchfully by whenever the mahout climbed down and turned his back to fetter or unfetter his charge. Although the spear was always held at the ready, the animals were controlled largely by the steadiness of the spearman's gaze and I realised that the slender Thai female was attempting this kind of control. Instead of a spear, she held out only her ritual platter and its objects; as the elephant came to within a few feet, she began chanting faster. But Poo Tongkam did not stop.

The *kon song*'s body was shuddering with the intensity of the effort she was making and she held the bamboo platter suddenly higher, lifting it towards the rumbling elephant. As I watched I am perfectly certain I saw the straw dolls and the clay figurine move; they twisted and spun to face the huge animal, then continued spinning in another full circle before coming to rest.

For a second or two Poo Tongkam halted in his tracks, his great head and tusks swaying slowly from side to side. He was obviously scenting the motionless human female before him with his sinuous trunk. Then without warning he let out a spine-tingling roar and rose up on his hind legs. Still roaring menacingly, he moved nearer until he towered above her; in the glare of the torchlight, he looked like an avenging leviathan from the fetid swamps of prehistory.

'Stop him! Stop him, somebody!' shrieked an agitated Thai voice from the side of the clearing and the next instant one of my mahouts dashed forward from among the trees. 'It was my fault – I helped kill the king,' he screamed hysterically. 'That's why he's come here to haunt us!'

Wearing only a *panung* about his loins, the seemingly demented mahout, whom I knew only slightly, raced towards the *kon song*. He continued to shout with all his strength but before he could reach her side, Poo Tongkam crashed back on to all fours. A terrible scything movement of his tusks sent the ritual platter spinning into the darkness and felled the *kon song* in the same instant. Rearing and plunging, the elephant began to trample the inert figure on the ground.

Seeing that he was too late did not stop the mahout and he ran on, still yelling in a frenzied voice. Poo Tongkam reared up again, threatening to crush him too, and it was at this point that I drew my revolver and ran forward into the clearing. With my other hand I pulled from my trouser pocket a loose ball of raw opium wrapped in a palm leaf that I had snatched from the cotside box in my tent as I stumbled out through the flaps. As I ran I kneaded the opium frantically with my fingers to help release its distinctive smell, then tossed it in a gentle arc towards Poo Tongkam. It fell close to his feet but after a moment's hesitation he ignored it. The points of his long, curving tusks passed only a foot or two from my face as I bent to snatch up the Thai mahout with my left arm. As I turned away, I heard again the swish of those tusks passing close to me and I fancied I could feel the animal's hot breath on my neck. In the light of the single torch a tell-tale trace of *musth* oil was clearly visible on his temple. It had already trickled down beyond his left eye and into his mouth, giving proof, if any were needed, that he had indeed entered his most dangerous phase.

The sudden new weight of the mahout slung across my left shoulder unbalanced me and I stumbled and dropped to one knee as I tried to duck away into the trees. I expected in my turn to feel the sudden crushing weight of Poo Tongkam bear down on me, forcing all breath and life from me. But in the seeming age it took me to rise, I heard only the fearsome rumbling from deep within Poo Tongkam's chest. The sound continued without changing tone – but it came no nearer.

I dared not look behind me. The young mahout by this time was struggling hysterically in my grasp, shrieking incoherently and staring in terror behind us. Although I still clutched the revolver I managed to cover his mouth with my fingers to silence him. Then ducking low beneath trailing creepers and tall ferns I flung myself headlong into the surrounding undergrowth. When I had gone fifty yards and realised we were not being pursued, I stopped and looked back towards the clearing.

By the light of the fallen torch which lay nearby, Poo Tongkam was still visible; he stood swaying slightly above the inert body of the *kon song*, his trunk curling and uncurling slowly by turns. The rumbling sound had ceased and I had the impression that his eyes were half closed, although from that distance I could not see clearly.

I had heard during the war that courageous Burmese native women sometimes used opium to pacify rogue elephants. But I had never myself tried, until then, to use such a method. I had prepared the opium ball because Poo Tongkam was on *musth* but I had no idea what to expect. Then to my relief, as I watched, Poo Tongkam turned and moved slowly away among the trees in the opposite direction, leaving the clearing silent and empty.

The mahout was still struggling feebly in my grasp, making a low whimpering noise. Setting him on his feet, I grabbed him by the arm and urged him into a run towards the camp. Taking him straight to my tent I poured a stiff measure of Scotch whisky into a mug, sat him on a chair and urged him to drink. He was shaking uncontrollably and he choked on the strong spirit. Squatting on my camp cot opposite him I held him by both arms to calm him and looked directly into his face.

'What did you mean when you said you helped kill the king?' I asked him gently in his own language. 'Surely that can't be true?'

The young mahout's eyes were wild and dilated. He was still breathing fast and he stared back at me with an expression of uncomprehending shock. He remained transfixed like this for a minute or more, even though I repeated the question in a quiet tone.

He was taller than average but wirily strong and on looking closely at him I saw that he was light-skinned and had open, honest features. I guessed he was in his early twenties but, beyond the fact that his name was Jutulak, I knew little of him. He had been hired by a deputy headman some months earlier and I had not had reason to talk personally to him at any length until then. Because he continued shaking I slipped an old jacket of mine around him and patted his shoulder reassuringly.

'Thank you, thank you, Master,' he gasped at last when he began to recover some composure. Pressing his palms together, he bowed his head low over them in a *wai* of gratitude. 'Thank you for saving my life.'

I grinned and poured a little more whisky into the mug for him. 'There's no need to thank me. Just tell me now why you shouted what you did about the king.'

Although the shock was wearing off, Jutulak's expression became deeply troubled again. 'I thought everybody was going to die, Master,' he said at last in a choked voice. 'I had a dream last night. I told Prapoth and the village *kon song* about it. It seemed to be coming true. I thought the elephant maddened by the king's tormented spirit would kill us all . . . I should have remained silent.'

'But how on earth could you have helped kill the king?'

For a long time Jutulak gazed at me with anguish in his eyes. 'I swore a solemn oath in the temple never to speak of this . . . That's why I fled here to the north to hide in the forest . . . But you have risked your own life, Master, to save mine. So perhaps you deserve an honest answer.'

Again he fell silent for a long time, wringing his hands in distraction. Then he leaned towards me with a beseeching expression and spoke in a half-whisper. 'Please tell nobody what I say to you . . . I was employed as a mahout in the Royal Elephant Stables at the Grand Palace. I saw the king many times after his return from Switzerland. For some reason he took a particular liking to me one day when he inspected the ceremonial elephants. We were the same age, you see . . .'

He broke off in alarm on hearing a faint sound outside the tent. For a full minute he sat rigidly upright, listening fearfully to the faint night noises of the jungle. Then he gathered himself and turned back to me.

'I often saw King Ananda and his brother firing their pistols in the Tortoise Garden. They loved guns of all kinds. Most of all they loved target practice. Once I was invited to fetch and replace the targets – it was a great honour for me. When the war ended, my father had been given a pistol by an American soldier. I took it to show the king, to please him, when he next visited the stables. He smiled with real pleasure and showed such great interest that on an impulse I begged leave to present it to His Majesty as a gift. To my amazement and delight he accepted . . .'

Jutulak's voice faded to nothing and he buried his face in his hands. 'It was an American Colt .45. When I read the reports of the trial in the newspaper I knew at once – it must have been the very gun that killed our great Lord of Life.' His shoulders shook and he began to sob loudly. 'That's why his spirit has come here to hunt me down.'

'Perhaps you're mistaken,' I said soothingly. 'Perhaps Poo Tongkam is simply on *musth*. Nine years have passed, after all, since the king died.'

Jutulak raised his head sharply, the agony visibly intensifying in his face. 'Yes, nine years have passed, Master! But three courtiers were executed only last week in Bangkok. Although people never believed they were guilty, they were sentenced to death as accomplices of an unknown assassin . . .' He paused, wringing his hands in anguish. 'They were machine-gunned to death in the central prison – so can't you see, the king's spirit must be suffering new and terrible agonies . . .'

Until that moment I had been prepared to dismiss everything I had heard and seen that night as the product of self-induced hysteria. But it was late February 1955, and a week earlier I had listened to radio news reports from Bangkok announcing the 'King's Death Case' execution of two royal pages and a former secretary to the king. Amidst the flood of primitive superstition which seemed suddenly to have engulfed the camp, Jutulak's reference to contemporary events in the capital struck a curiously rational note and I sat staring at him, fascinated despite myself, by his curious logic.

'The king's spirit, you see, must have remained captive inside his earthly body for four years after his death because the cremation was so long delayed,' continued Jutulak in a strained whisper. 'It was finally released by the flames of the great funeral pyre in front of the Grand Palace five years ago – perhaps you remember that, Master.' He paused again, staring back at me. 'I believe the spirit of the king has been wandering in torment ever since . . .'

I sat back on my sleeping cot and slowly poured myself a generous measure of whisky. From my tent in the jungle I had indeed listened on my crackling radio to reports of the ancient and solemn ceremonies which had taken place five years earlier in front of vast crowds in the heart of Bangkok. I had been very conscious then of the historic nature of the occasion and had jotted down copious notes of what took place in one of my working books. I had always had a vague desire to write some account of the unique life led by foreign 'jungle wallahs' in Thailand, although then I had no suspicion that I should ever compile such an account as this. Those ancient cremation ceremonies had greatly fuelled my ambition to capture something of Thailand's essence to augment the account and I had collected as much detail as I could about the events.

Soon after his death in June 1946, I discovered, King Ananda's body had been bathed, bound and dressed in fine coronation robes and a crown. Then he had been placed inside a silver casket in an attitude of prayer. Later the silver casket had been bolted inside a vast, eight-sectioned urn of carved gold and raised on a multi-tiered catafalque in the richly ornamented Pavilion of Paradise at the heart of the Grand Palace. Shaven-headed monks in saffron robes had chanted unceasingly before the glittering urn for a hundred days while the elaborate rituals of the Chakri dynasty were observed.

But the four uneasy years of political turmoil which followed had delayed completion of the funeral ceremonies. The new monarch, King Bhoomipol, unmarried and only nineteen, had soon returned with his mother to the peaceful haven of Switzerland to finish his studies. His desire to leave Bangkok was perhaps understandable: in the wake of the 1947 military coup, Thailand became a terrorised nation dominated by the unsolved and long-drawn-out 'King's Death Case'. Although I had personally felt little effect of these changes in the northern jungles, forest assistants returning from visits to the company's headquarters in Bangkok told lurid tales of the fear that gripped the city. Vicious political witch-hunts, wholesale unpunished murder, high-level corruption and gangsterism under the notorious Police-General Phao Sriyond, popularly known as 'the Butcher of Bangkok', made life in the capital close to intolerable, they had said. Even two defence lawyers, acting for the Grand Palace courtiers, had been mysteriously murdered.

Because it brought some relief from this reign of terror, the announcement in 1950 that King Bhoomipol was to wed a beautiful, aristocratic Thai girl produced a great upsurge of rejoicing. After so many years of fear and hardship, the prospect of a royal wedding and the mystical rites of coronation induced a nationwide mood of euphoria. It had been necessary first to proceed with the murdered monarch's long-delayed ritual cremation and emotional crowds had flowed into Bangkok by road and river for many days before the ceremony. Even though I had been crouched over my radio set in a teak forest clearing hundreds of miles away, I had been able to sense the profound currents of emotion which the occasion stirred in the Thai people and I filled a whole notebook with jottings.

On the appointed evening the great, eight-sectioned golden urn was brought from the Grand Palace in a spired pavilion mounted on a gigantic wheeled chariot. Drawn by a hundred uniformed marines, its tiered, gilded sides, the radio reported, were inlaid with crimson dragons carved from wood and shimmering glass mosaics. By then the sun was beginning to set across the Chao Phraya river and after parading the urn solemnly around the crowded Pramane Ground, outside the palace walls, it was raised into a magnificent temple of teakwood and gold that towered above the throng.

King Bhoomipol appeared wearing the uniform of a Marshal of the Royal Guards and carrying a lamp of oil consecrated in the Emerald Buddha Temple. He lit symbolic candles beneath the urn, then solemnly prostrated himself three times before the pyre. An awed rumble of grief that was clearly audible on my radio in the forest clearing rose from the huge crowd. A volley of shots was fired by soldiers in salute, then ancient conch-shell instruments and flutes wailed in the following silence.

After the fire was lit, filling the darkness with its glow, every individual in the great crowd approached one by one through the long night to add scented sandalwood shavings and joss sticks to the flames. The radio had continued to broadcast from the scene throughout the night and I had found the simple ritual of each individual taking personal leave of their 'Lord of Life' intensely moving.

As I recalled those poignant moments I glanced across the tent at the frightened and exhausted figure of Jutulak. He had fallen silent, absorbed utterly in his own fearful thoughts; his face looked pale and pinched and suddenly, remembering the deep significance for all Thais of the solemn ritual surrounding their former king's death, I felt I appreciated for the first time something of the deep-seated nature of his fears. Yet at the same moment some instinct suggested that I had not yet been given the whole story.

'Jutulak, have you told me everything?' I asked him softly. 'Or is there something else that would help me to understand?'

For a moment Jutulak's face showed great alarm; then he began to shake his head, staring straight ahead, his features frozen in an unnatural grimace. 'No, Master, I haven't told you everything. There is more, much more . . . I should explain to you why I ran away to hide here in the northern jungles . . .'

His voice died away completely. He remained silent for a long time and I did not think he was going to continue. Then he spoke suddenly in a haunted whisper: 'I saw everything that happened . . .'

By then I was beginning to feel the strain of the night's exertions, and could not think immediately what he meant. 'What did you see, Jutulak?' I asked. 'Where?'

'In the Grand Palace! . . . In the king's bedroom! . . . I saw everything!' The whites of the young mahout's eyes became suddenly visible all around the irises and he stared wildly at me. 'Many lies have been told. Many innocent people are suffering in Bangkok . . .' Again a faint sound outside the tent made him break off. As before he stared agitatedly into the darkness beyond the front flap for several seconds before turning uneasily to face me again. 'Because of this knowledge, I am frightened for my own life, Master! I was so frightened that I persuaded my father and mother in Bangkok to do a terrible thing . . .' He paused and fell silent, staring out of the tent flap again, although I had heard no further sound.

'What sort of "terrible thing"?' I prompted.

'Every day that I left to go to the Grand Palace, I thought I might never return. I thought I would be murdered, too . . . Our house was on one of the *klongs* close to the Chao Phraya. One morning at dawn I saw the body of a youth who had drowned floating in the water below our home. I was shocked because he was about my age. Then because I was so desperate, I had an idea and hid the body. I pleaded with my father to help me in a plan to escape . . .' Jutulak shook his head violently at the recollection, as though overcome with remorse at what he had done. 'My father finally agreed because he was frightened too . . . When the boatman came to take me to the Grand Palace I pretended to slip and fell overboard fully dressed. I swam underwater along the canal and came up under another house out of sight. We faked my drowning and my father "found" the other body during the night and pretended it was me. They held a funeral very quickly. I hid in a nearby temple for a week, then ran away. I later became a monk in the central plains before coming north to the jungle . . .'

Jutulak began sobbing uncontrollably again and buried his face in his hands. I sat and waited patiently until he quietened. Then I tapped him on the shoulder.

'How were you able to see everything that happened to the king?'

He raised his head then and looked at me dully: his face was pale and drained of all energy. 'The king had often invited me to visit his living quarters. I think he was very lonely. Because he had grown up abroad he knew almost nothing about ordinary life in his own country. He asked me endless questions about *klong* life, about my family, about the people, about the Chao Phraya river and all that went on there . . .'

'Did others know about your visits to his quarters?'

Jutulak shook his head quickly. 'Almost nobody. I would go at quiet times. We used to make a light-hearted game out of my visits. If we heard anybody coming, he would laugh and make me hide until they were gone. I had many hiding places . . . his dressing room, the adjoining Buddha room, the study. There were two corridors leading to his quarters in the Barom-piman Hall, one at the front, one at the back . . .'

I stared hard at the young Thai; his eyes had a faintly glazed look, perhaps from shock, but I was suddenly suspicious. 'Are you sure you're telling the truth, Jutulak?'

'I wish I were lying,' he said in the same dull tone of despair. 'On that terrible morning I went early, as His Majesty had requested. I slipped into the building as usual by a small door at the rear without any guards seeing me. But the king didn't feel well. We talked for only a few minutes . . . When we heard footsteps approaching along the front corridor he waved me away to hide. I always waited obediently until he made a loud clicking noise three times with his fingers before coming out. I waited and waited . . . Nearly half an hour went by and I began to get worried. Perhaps he had forgotten I was there, I don't know . . . All the time I could see him and his bed . . . Then I saw the Colt .45. I was almost certain it was the one I had given His Majesty . . . I could not believe my eyes . . . it was like a terrible nightmare . . .'

I thought he would say no more when his voice died away again and for several minutes we sat in silence. Jutulak was staring glassily at the ground between us; he had become strangely stiff in his posture and I felt certain that further questions would not serve any purpose. But to my surprise he did continue at last, in a barely audible voice.

'The shot was deafening . . . It paralysed me in my hiding place in the dressing room. I went cold all over with fear . . . When the shouting began and people came running I closed the door and hid behind the long racks of His Majesty's ceremonial uniforms . . . I was there for many hours . . . Every second I expected to be found. But there was great confusion and panic and nobody searched the dressing room properly . . . When everything fell silent and I could see the bedroom was empty, I slipped out of the dressing room by a door leading into the back corridor. Shaking with fright, I went down a narrow back staircase and out into the Tortoise Garden without anyone noticing . . .'

I drew a long breath. 'Who was it that fired the Colt .45, Jutulak?'

The mahout's head was bowed and when he finally looked up, his eyes were still strangely glazed. 'I swore a solemn vow in the temple, Master. I can't break my vow . . .'

At that instant a sudden movement and the sound of a soft footstep by the open tent flap made us both swing round. Prapoth, my headman, was standing sheepishly in the doorway, his face strangely taut. For a moment he gazed back and forth between Jutulak and me and something in his demeanour betrayed that he had overheard at least part of our conversation. Jutulak stared at him aghast as the same realisation dawned on him.

'What is it Prapoth?' I snapped.

'The people of the village are afraid, Master,' he stammered. 'They wish to retrieve the body of the *kon song* from the ruined shrines. But nobody dares to approach the spot.'

I stood up, suddenly remembering the tragic outcome of Poo Tongkam's rampage. 'I'll come at once and retrieve the body for them myself.'

'Thank you, Master.' Prapoth nodded and moved aside to let me pass.

'Get one of the coolies to come and sit with Jutulak,' I said sharply. 'He's been badly shocked.'

Prapoth nodded again but he did not move. As I hurried out, the mahout and the headman remained curiously rigid in their postures, staring blankly at one another inside the tent.

บ ช

'Life in the teak forests was always . . . er . . . adventurous, to say the least . . .'

The florid, paunchy Englishman ambling at Joceline Hampson's side smiled uncertainly as their feet crunched lightly on the gravel pathway of the Chiang Mai Foreign Cemetery.

'Downright hazardous is probably a better way of describing it. A thousand things could destroy your health in the winking of an eye.' He paused and waved an arm vaguely. 'Hence the very real need for this establishment . . . The British teak companies and some American missionaries founded the cemetery in 1898. King Chulalongkorn, Rama the Fifth, granted us the land . . .'

Uneasy beneath the burden of his unavoidable escort duty, the current secretary of the Foreign Cemetery's Local Committee had seemingly set himself the task of distracting Joceline's attention from the sad moment that was coming closer with every step. Whenever a silence opened up between them he hastened to fill it.

'The first grave dates back to 1900 – a British major rode out of the jungle dying of dysentery. We think he might have been spying on the French in Indo-China . . . ' He flapped an arm towards different headstones. 'Black-water fever, that one; typhoid over there; this one "murdered by unknown assassins while journeying through the forest" . . . The jungle has been responsible for more than its fair share of those resting here.'

They passed a huge bronze memorial statue of Queen Victoria and he slowed in pantomime fashion to allow her to read the inscription. Attributed to 'loyal subjects of every race residing in Northern Siam', it expressed their 'deep reverence and affection for the memory of our late, gracious queen . . .'.

'Even Her Majesty knew something about the dangers of the

forest,' said Davenport jovially. 'She was shipped to Rangoon, and taken up-country by rail. That was in 1903. Native porters brought us this image of Her Majesty, bearing her on elephants through the jungles and across the rivers of the Shan states . . . '

Joceline nodded politely in acknowledgement, glancing over the orderly ranks of marble crosses and headstones towards the tangled green bulk of Doi Suthep, the massive, forested mountain that towered above the medieval walled town of Chiang Mai. The mountain had been the first sight she had seen on drawing back the curtains of her hotel room that morning after a long, restless night filled with vivid images from the manuscript. The contrast between the mountain's primitive wildness and the suburban neatness of the foreign, lawned cemetery was a telling reminder of the fact that Europe and the Orient had met in the mountain's shadow. Up there in the shimmering heart of the forests, fever, murderous natives and wild animals had inevitably claimed white-skinned victims. But after the strife, in shady parkland in the valley, the foreign dead were still arrayed with the dignity which the Victorians believed was appropriate to their European rank and civilised upbringing. In her uneasiness, Joceline found the incongruous formality of the cemetery vaguely comforting.

' . . . Despite the dangers,' Davenport was saying, 'many who come here will tell you that once the jungle gets into your blood, it's there for ever . . .'

Joceline's brow furrowed into a frown and she stared down at the neatly raked gravel of the path, struggling to gather her personal thoughts. It was not yet ten o'clock but the morning was already hot and hazy; the constant whine of cicadas in the avenues of planted trees was providing a shrill accompaniment to the shrieking of unseen birds and all these tropical sounds seemed to be amplified in her ears by the unnatural stillness of the cemetery. She was again wearing a tailored blue bush shirt and trousers, with low-heeled shoes; a bright, flower-patterned bandanna held her long, blonde hair clear of her face and a small handbag of soft navy leather hung from one shoulder on a long strap. In her right hand she carried a single purple orchid, her sole concession to the solemnity of the setting.

At a junction in the path she paused in front of a glass-fronted notice-board which had been set up in the shade of a spreading tamarind. It contained a yellowing, curly-edged 'Statement of Accounts' for 1987, showing a modest balance in hand, and a printed appeal for funds required for the cemetery's upkeep. Both notices, she saw, bore the signature of Arnold Davenport, her companion. After staring through the grimy glass, twisting the orchid distractedly in her hands, she fell into step again beside him.

'There's an old proverb they quote out here,' Davenport went on quietly. 'It says: "You can take a man out of the jungle, but you can't take the jungle out of a man . . ." ' He hesitated, as though suddenly unsure of whether he was saying the right thing. Looking hard at Joceline, he found she was still gazing expressionlessly along the path in front of her. Apparently reassured, he continued in a quieter voice. 'I think I'm probably right in saying that was true of your father.'

'Did you know him well?'

'I don't think anybody knew Adam Hampson well – at least nobody in Chiang Mai.'

Joceline looked sideways at the perspiring Englishman, whom she guessed was in his mid-seventies. He wore old-fashioned, horn-rimmed spectacles and an unruly shock of salt-and-pepper hair flopped over his damp forehead. The floridity of his complexion, she guessed, was probably caused by a mixture of heat and whisky, both endured over many years; as he walked he dabbed frequently at his forehead with a coloured handkerchief, tucking it back foppishly each time into the cuff of a crumpled, double-breasted blazer which she suspected he had donned with a striped tie especially for her benefit.

'Does that mean somebody *outside* Chiang Mai might have known him better?'

Arnold Davenport stopped and mopped his face again; then he flapped the red silk handkerchief approximately in the direction of the jungle-covered crags of Doi Suthep. 'Up there in some very remote hill-tribe village, I suspect there may be people who know more about your father than any of us down here ever will.'

'Why do you say that, Mr Davenport?'

He stopped and stared at Joceline in open-mouthed surprise. 'You really don't know?'

She shook her head impatiently. 'No, Mr Davenport, I don't. I know little or nothing about my father's life. I never had any personal contact with him. Nor did my mother after he left England to come back to Thailand. That was more than thirty years ago – before I was born. My mother told me only that she believed he lived modestly here in Chiang Mai. We understood he eked out a living somehow by teaching English at the university after the forests were nationalised.'

'Yes,' said Davenport slowly, drawing the word out. 'That's certainly true as far as it goes. But it doesn't go nearly far enough.'

'Did he spend a lot of time up in the mountains?'

'*Indeed* he did.' For several seconds Davenport stared searchingly at Joceline as though still unsure whether to believe her or not. Then he shook his head and smiled incredulously. 'He spent more of his life up there in the jungles than he did here . . . He would disappear for months, quite often a year or more – sometimes two. Nobody knew where he went, what he did or why. Then he would reappear to do a bit of teaching. We seldom saw him, even when he was here. He would stay in Chiang Mai a few days or a few weeks at a time. Very occasionally he would show up at the bar of the Gymkhana Club . . .' Davenport turned northward and gestured in the direction of a trim golf course and a group of colonial-style buildings that, like the cemetery, lay close to the Mae Ping river alongside the road to Lamphun. ' . . . But he never drank much and he never answered direct questions. He had an exceptionally easy way with him. Always humorous, smiling, affable.'

'Might he have gone into the forest to work with elephants, do you think?' asked Joceline suddenly.

'Oh, so you've heard something of his reputation in town, have you?' Davenport laughed. 'Locally he was quite a figure – more than he ever realised I think. *"The farang who loved elephants more than people."* That's what they called him. You've heard this expression *"farang"* – the Thai term of friendly abuse for "foreigner"?'

Joceline nodded quickly. She was looking expectantly at Davenport and her expression made it clear that she was interested only in the answer to her question. 'But is it possible he went to be with elephants?' she prompted quickly. 'Are there many working in the forests today?'

'There are still quite a lot of working elephants here in the north – and in Burma and Laos. At this minute they're dragging, lifting and carrying logs just as they've done for a century or more. Your father did occasionally turn up at the logging sites and the elephant training camps. He never seemed to tire of breaking in young elephants and teaching new mahouts – he seemed happy to pass on the benefit of his own great experience. Because of his knowledge he was respected by the forest people. He was always made welcome. I heard that sometimes he would stay a few days, sometimes several weeks. Then he would suddenly disappear into the jungle again . . .'

'What do *you* think it was, Mr Davenport, that always drew him back?'

The Englishman shook his head slowly, raising his shoulders and his eyebrows in an expression of puzzlement. 'It could have been an excuse, I suppose, but he once told me he was writing a book.'

Joceline swung round sharply to look at Davenport. 'What sort of book?'

'He didn't exactly say. I assumed it in some way concerned "things mystical". Your father seemed to become increasingly fascinated over the years with Thailand's ancient spirit mythology – and how it's all bound up with the nation's Buddhist beliefs . . .'

'Why did you assume that?'

Davenport screwed up his eyes in thought. 'I can't honestly remember. Maybe it was something he let slip. I formed the impression he was trying in some way to lay bare the Thai soul. Perhaps trying to explain why this enigmatic country and its graceful people have always cast such a spell over the Western mind.' Davenport paused and smiled ruefully. 'All the way from the dignified days of "Anna and the King of Siam" to the golden girls of Bangkok's modern massage parlours.'

'Did he ever show you anything he wrote?' asked Joceline, watching Davenport closely.

'Never.'

They walked in silence for a moment between the neatly trimmed lawns and well-tended graves.

'Didn't my father leave a will?' There was a faint hint of surprise in Joceline's voice, as if she was wondering as she spoke why she had never thought to ask such a question before. 'Or papers of any kind?'

'None were found, to my knowledge. Whenever I visited him at his quarters I always marvelled at one thing – I'd never known a man who had fewer possessions . . . I've been there once since his death – an Irish doctor who lives here, Patrick McKenna, gave him the use of a bungalow in the grounds of his house that had once been servants' quarters. But there was no sign of any papers at all.' He halted and closed his eyes, obviously summoning an image of the room as he had last seen it. 'No, just his old, battered typewriter and a few dog-eared books on Thai history, religion, animism . . . that sort of thing.' Davenport walked on in silence then stopped in mid-stride. 'Wait a minute. I do remember I once saw him locking some papers for safety into a box as I arrived. But there was certainly no sign of that box afterwards.'

'Was it made of tin?' demanded Joceline in a taut voice. 'And painted green?'

'It might've been . . . Yes, I think it was.' Davenport subjected Joceline to a searching scrutiny. 'Miss Hampson, may I ask how you knew that?'

'I think my mother must have given it to him,' said Joceline quickly, giving voice to the first thought that came into her head. 'I was curious to know if he had kept it.'

'I see.' Davenport smiled again, his expression sympathetic. Reaching into a pocket of his blazer he pulled out an envelope, extracted a faded black-and-white photograph and held it towards Joceline. 'I wrote to the former secretary of the Anglo-Siamese Teak Trading Company after getting your letter. He knew where the old files were and came up with this.' Davenport held the picture closer to Joceline. 'Your father was in his late twenties there I should think. Please keep it, if you'd like to.'

Joceline stared at the photograph but made no move to take it. Its subject was an engaging, confident-looking young man; his fair hair, trimmed short, was slicked down in the fashion of the forties and a smiling, clean-shaven face suggested he possessed a quick eagerness for life. Wearing an open-necked shirt and standing before a tent in a forest clearing, Adam

Hampson appeared to be a young man supremely happy in his element.

'It's very kind of you, Mr Davenport,' said Joceline evenly. 'But I should perhaps tell you I don't nurse any anguished feelings for my "long-lost" father. My mother married again whilst I was very young. I was extremely fortunate, I think. In every way my stepfather has always seemed like a genuine father to me.' She paused and looked up directly at Davenport, holding his gaze. 'The man in that picture became a forgotten figure in our family. He was rarely, if ever, discussed or thought about. He has never loomed large in my life. This may sound unfeeling, but he never seemed to have any great significance for me.'

'I see. Thank you for explaining that.' Davenport withdrew the photograph but did not immediately return it to his pocket. Instead he peered down at it himself as they moved off again along the gravel path. 'If you'll forgive so direct a question, may I ask then, Miss Hampson, what it was that made you come here?'

'Curiosity, pure and simple.' The crisp, unemotional tone of Joceline's reply caused Davenport to look at her sharply. But consciously or unconsciously she avoided his gaze. 'Since I was travelling back to Europe after filming in Australia, it seemed good sense to make a short stopover in Thailand.'

'I can see a clear family resemblance.' Davenport spoke quietly, almost to himself, glancing down again at the photograph. 'There's something distinctive in your father's expression that you share ... Some brightness in the eye.' He had stopped and again he held out the photograph towards her. 'Are you certain you wouldn't like to keep it? I'm sure Adam would rather you had it than me.'

Joceline did not answer. She was staring past the proffered photograph at a small, pillow-like headstone of polished grey marble. Neatly chiselled black lettering announced simply that it was the grave of Adam John Hampson. There was no trace of ostentation. The inscription merely said: *Died January 1989 In The Northern Forests That He Loved*.

Joceline remained silent, looking down at the epitaph; the small headstone rested on an unadorned rectangular slab of darker granite and the inexpensive masonry was incongruous amongst the ranks of larger tombs decorated elaborately with plinths and crosses wrought from shimmering white marble. As Davenport watched, he saw Joceline's gaze shift to the photograph he was holding out to her. She stood and looked at it for a long time, her face pensive; then without speaking she took it from his hand. In the same moment she knelt and placed the single purple orchid gently on the marble pillow at the head of the grave.

The atmosphere of quiet tranquillity which embraced the cemetery seemed to deepen; the whine of the cicadas and the screeching of the birds became subdued. Clattering *tuk-tuk* engines and the dull roar of heavy lorries rushing along the road to Lamphun still added their discordant backdrop of noise – but the heat shimmering above the graves seemed to muffle all sounds in the cemetery. Although Joceline stood up again almost at once, neither she nor Davenport broke the stillness for a minute or more.

'Perhaps this might sound strange to you, Miss Hampson,' said the elderly Englishman at last. 'But I still have considerable difficulty in believing that your father is really dead.'

'Why?' Joceline's tone was startled. 'Please tell me why.'

Davenport hesitated, his expression becoming faintly troubled. 'It could be that I got so used to him always turning up after those mysterious absences of his – no matter how long they lasted . . . Whenever I walk into the Gymkhana Club in the evenings I still find myself looking for him at the corner of the bar where he usually sat . . .'

Joceline waited for him to continue but Davenport remained silent. An uneasiness in his manner, however, made her pulse quicken. 'There's something else, isn't there?' she prompted quickly.

The Englishman plucked the damp silk handkerchief from his sleeve again and mopped his perspiring face comprehensively. 'I'm not sure there is . . . Perhaps nothing more than an old man's senile fantasies . . .'

'About what?'

Davenport tucked the handkerchief away and ran a finger round the inside of his limp collar to loosen it; within moments new beads of perspiration appeared on his brow and he sighed resignedly.

'When the report came in, local police were sent up into the jungle to retrieve the body. It was a two-day journey. Doctor

McKenna went up with the police party. A coffin was taken along and he alone made the identification. Because of the heat, the time that had elapsed since death, and the nature of the injuries, he ordered the coffin sealed on the spot. Burial took place here immediately on his return. There were a mere handful of mourners. Most people caught up with events only at a memorial service in the community church a week later . . .'

'So only Doctor McKenna identified the body?'

Davenport nodded, dabbing distractedly at his face again with the handkerchief.

'Do you have any reason to distrust his identification?'

'Not really . . .' Davenport's tone, despite the denial, betrayed some reservation and he eyed Joceline uncertainly.

'But what, Mr Davenport? There is a *but*, isn't there?'

A furtive look came into the old man's eyes. 'I've said nothing to anybody else. Perhaps I'm being quite unjust. I don't really know what made me say this to you. I think it was seeing that striking likeness in the photograph . . .' Davenport looked at her once more, then shook his head in a little gesture of confusion. 'Please forgive me and forget what I said. Put it down to an old man's suspicious mind – and the heat.'

'No matter how unlikely your suspicions might be, Mr Davenport, I'd like you to tell me about them,' said Joceline firmly.

He hesitated for a moment, looking uncomfortable. Then he cleared his throat self-consciously. 'Far be it from me to accuse others of what I'm guilty of myself, Miss Hampson. Many expatriates here fortify themselves against the climate with something out of a bottle. And I'm not saying that Doctor McKenna didn't know Adam Hampson as well as anyone here. He lived in McKenna's bungalow, after all. But the doctor is almost as old as me. And he had to ride a horse a long way through the jungle up there. He would probably have needed plenty of help from his bottle. The Chiang Mai police told him before he left it was your father he was going to identify. And wild elephants, when they attack a man, do not respect appearances . . . It perhaps doesn't add up to much – but it leaves room for doubt, at least in my mind . . .'

Joceline found herself staring down at the grave as she

listened. The single orchid with its fleshy petals of purple and white lay neatly on the stone pillow, bisecting her father's name. She still held his photograph in her hand and turning it face upward, she saw for the first time the faint likeness that linked them.

Suddenly, without reason, she was seized by an inexplicable feeling of apprehension; her head seemed to swim with the heat and the orchid and the photograph blurred before her eyes. She swayed slightly and she feared she was going to collapse melodramatically across her father's grave, clutching his picture. But then her firm resolve to avoid entrapment in feelings of false sentimentality reasserted itself; she clenched her fists hard and was relieved to find that the dizziness passed.

'I have another appointment – I must go now,' she said abruptly, turning away in the direction of the cemetery car-park where her taxi waited. 'Thank you for all your kindness. Please don't bother to walk with me, it's too hot. Stay here and rest in the shade for a while.'

'Who are you going to see?' Davenport called after her in a puzzled voice. 'Do you know anyone else here?'

Joceline did not stop to reply; waving her hand in farewell she hurried away across the sun-drenched cemetery, intensely aware of the growing heat. Once inside the air-conditioned taxi, she turned back to look over her shoulder. Arnold Davenport was still mopping his face confusedly beside the modest grave labelled with the name of the father she had never known. Despite the cemetery's English Victorian trappings, he seemed a forlorn, anachronistic figure; apparently abandoned to Thailand by the semi-colonial past, he stood alone and ill at ease with his doubts in the alien landscape.

*   *   *   *   *

As the taxi accelerated rapidly away across the Mangrai Bridge, heading north-west, Joceline began to realise that, like Arnold Davenport, she too was now racked by similar uncertainties. Inexplicably, in a matter of hours, the emotional barriers that had grown up since early childhood had been breached. Was the father, for whom she had always believed she felt nothing, now lying dead beneath the neatly tended lawns of Chiang Mai's Foreign Cemetery? Or could he still be alive somewhere up in the dense, dangerous wilderness bordering the Golden

Triangle? Were the doubts of the strangely old-fashioned Englishman in the cemetery really justified? Or might his mind, too, already be half pickled in whisky? She had no way of knowing any of the answers for certain. But these questions nagged repeatedly in her mind as the taxi sped up the snaking, tree-flanked road above the old moated city. She felt bemused that against every expectation a fundamental change was taking place in her feelings about her father – no matter how remote he had been from her, astonishingly, she was discovering, she did care.

Even when the taxi turned off the mountain road to bump along a sandy track leading into the forest she remained abstracted by her thoughts. After running alongside a fortified wall topped with spikes, the taxi stopped outside gates of solid steel that had been painted red. She was brought back fully to the present when a small viewing aperture scraped open, and she sat straighter in her seat. For a long moment a pair of narrow, brown eyes scrutinised the taxi and its occupants; then slowly the gates were swung apart.

Joceline had a fleeting impression of a stocky man in a dark uniform holding an automatic rifle in the shadow of the gate. Moving slowly, the taxi circled a lotus pool splashed with red and white flowers to draw up before a short flight of steps leading into a traditional teak house. A small, white-jacketed Chinese servant immediately ran out and opened Joceline's door. He motioned her politely up the steps just as the portly man she knew as Surachai appeared in the open doorway. Surachai smilingly inclined his head over his joined hands in a welcoming *wai*. When she responded with a similar gesture he turned and led her into the cool interior where big wooden ceiling fans spun noiselessly overhead.

In a simply furnished room, a thin sheaf of typescript was already laid out on a low table around which four elaborately carved teak chairs were positioned. A lacquer tray bearing a bamboo-handled teapot and small cups had been placed beside it. The Chinese servant hurried ahead of them to pour out some of the fragrant tea for her alone and when this had been done, Surachai backed away deferentially towards the door.

'Please continue your reading, Miss Hampson,' he said in a hushed undertone. 'For the moment there is nothing more important than that.'

เดอะ บางกอก ซีเคริท
THE BANGKOK SECRET

Chapter Four

แนะนำ แอนกก ะอน

Ten days after his murderous rampage I was straddling Poo Tongkam's massive neck, squeezing gently with both knees to guide him down a steep, muddy river bank. He moved with a sensitive nimbleness, testing the slippery ground carefully with each of his forefeet in turn before shifting his powerful bulk slowly towards the rushing water. As he descended, he held his head and trunk unnaturally high, fanning his great ears at the same time to ensure that I remained wedged in place behind the massive dome of his skull. Had he lowered his head, as well he might, I would have been forced to hang on grimly to his back harness with both hands to prevent myself slipping head-first into the fast-flowing torrent.

By this manoeuvre, without any prompting from me, he showed as much consideration for my safety as his own. Few elephants among the hundreds I had worked with up to then during eight years in the jungles of Burma and Thailand would have acted that way. Without any further urging from me, he waded fast and purposefully, belly-deep in the water, towards a growing tangle of teak logs from higher up the valley that were jammed ominously at a rock-strewn bend.

Heavy teak logs didn't always float in the shallow, sandy-bottomed jungle rivers of northern Thailand. It required heavy rain to cause a 'rise' before the logs, weighing anything up to three tons each, would move. There had been heavy, prolonged rain the previous night but it had not lasted and a 'rise', I knew from experience, always disappeared quickly if the rain was not constant. Every effort therefore had to be made to keep the logs on the move down the jungle creeks and tributaries. Otherwise they would not drift steadily into the main southward-flowing Mae Ping and Mae Yom rivers to continue their five-hundred-mile journey to the saw mills at Bangkok. Fines were levied on every log left grounded in the jungle creeks after the rainy season ended. The teak companies deducted these fines from the bonuses paid to forest managers, assistants and their camp teams, so breaking up jams and stacks was of vital interest to everybody toiling in the jungles.

Instinctively and from long experience Poo Tongkam knew what was required of him. Many ordinary elephants had to be urged into log-jammed rivers with repeated prods from the curved steel hooks wielded by their mahouts. But Poo Tongkam moved unhesitatingly and without fear towards the dangerous pile-up of teak. As I eyed the barrier around which the river was foaming white, I found it difficult to remember that the willing, courageous animal beneath me was the same one that had killed the two coolies and the female *kon song* such a short time before.

The two small *musth* orifices on either side of his head which had swollen to open and secrete the tell-tale oil had subsided and were now firmly closed. For ten days after his recapture I had kept him securely tethered and fed him sparingly to reduce his energy. Normally when an elephant killed a man there was a rush of volunteers among the other mahouts to be the first to ride him; male bravado and an opportunity to parade their courage usually overcame any lingering fear. But whispered talk of the involvement of evil spirits in the tragedy immediately had a sobering effect on the whole camp. As a result, none of the mahouts had come forward the morning following the rampage to help me recapture Poo Tongkam. He had been found grazing quietly in a plantation of sugar-cane and I decided to set an example by riding alongside him myself on a docile female. Climbing quickly into a tree overhead, I dropped firmly on to his neck to surprise him. I had been ready to exert all my strength in regaining control but to my intense relief he had reacted quietly and obediently and was soon fettered and tied firmly to a giant cotton tree.

Because the death of the *kon song* and the destruction of

the spirit shrines had deeply shocked the people of the nearby village, as a mark of respect I decided to move the whole elephant camp at once. I made a promise to the village headman to pay a sum of money in compensation to the *kon song*'s family, then shifted to a new site five miles higher up the mountain valley where already girdled teak was ready for cutting. I stopped all work for two days to allow time for funeral rites for the dead coolies. Then to counteract the atmosphere of growing apprehension that had descended on the camp, I ordered the immediate resumption of full-scale cutting and dragging operations, dawn to dusk.

Although I rarely rode elephants myself, I ostentatiously mounted Poo Tongkam as soon as it was evident his *musth* holes had closed and dried. With elaborate cheerfulness I led the way myself in dragging newly cut teak logs to the river, sometimes singing English music-hall songs, meaningless to my native workers, at the top of my lungs. The other mahouts and coolies worked dutifully but they were obviously subdued and lacked their normal cheerfulness. They eyed Poo Tongkam warily whenever he passed near them and they pointedly shunned Jutulak, who the morning after the tragedy had fallen into a strange, listless silence.

I erected a special tarpaulin beside my tent for him to sleep under and invited him to take meals with me – but he ate little and became progressively more withdrawn. In an effort to give him some reassurance I told him quietly that I would not endanger him by speaking of what he had revealed. But he did not seem comforted and constantly avoided my eyes. Eventually he became unwilling even to exchange formal greetings.

As I rode Poo Tongkam out into the river, Jutulak was sitting astride a young, vigorous tusker, one of a group of half a dozen elephants awaiting my orders at the top of the steep bank. I had asked if any of the mahouts wished to volunteer for the task of freeing the jam. But all had glanced uneasily at each other and remained silent. On seeing this, I had urged Poo Tongkam down the bank alone. As I neared the middle of the river I could sense that the watching mahouts were still as much afraid of Poo Tongkam as they were of the gathering dam of teak logs. If he were again to become possessed of an evil spirit while chest-deep in water before the log barrier, they seemed to be saying, it would be better if they and their elephants remained on the bank. In normal times my mahouts were eager volunteers and the thought struck me suddenly that perhaps they feared that evil demons had deliberately tangled the floating logs! Perhaps even now they believed that malevolent spirits were hidden deep in the heart of the stack, waiting to hurl themselves frenziedly at their victims amidst foaming water and crashing timber.

I tried to push these bizarre thoughts from my mind on seeing that the river was building up dangerously above the jam. The water was four feet higher than on the downstream side and Poo Tongkam slowed his pace as we reached the centre of the barrier. His trunk was searching constantly beneath the surface as he moved, testing the firmness of protruding ends. In my turn I scanned the jumble of timber, trying like the elephant to detect one vital column of teak that might be loosened to free the rest. In mid-river the hollow boom of down-rushing timber striking the rocks and stationary logs was almost deafening. Each giant tree-trunk that smashed into the jumble was thickening the stack, making it more dense and lethal if Poo Tongkam should make a mistake.

I watched intently, making quiet noises of encouragement as he wound his trunk around the submerged end of a long, thick log which lay slantwise across the front of the jam. At first it did not move at all. Poo Tongkam let out a bellow which rose to a high note of frustration, then released his grip. For a moment or two he stood looking at the intertwined logs and I sensed that this was the time to leave him to make his own decisions.

His head swayed from side to side, then, turning his whole body quickly in the water, he trumpeted twice and moved head-on towards the barrier. At the same time he curled his trunk into his mouth as all male Asiatic elephants do when preparing to charge. Leaning forward he pressed his huge forehead against the upper part of the log that rose above the water level. He paused as though gathering his strength, then threw all the weight of his massive body against it.

The log this time shifted perceptibly. In the same instant a long eerie screech escaped from the heart of the stack as the great trapped timbers scraped and pressed together. A fierce jet of water spurted high above the barrier, drenching me and

Poo Tongkam, but gradually the massive tangle settled and was still again.

I was controlling Poo Tongkam in the way I had learned from Burmese 'oozies' during my war service. I had removed my boots so as to be able to deliver gentle but firm prods and kicks behind his ears with my bare toes. Jabbing him simultaneously with both feet I shouted 'Yooo yooo!' to make him lower his head and slide his massive curved tusks under the slanted log. He did so obediently and when I shouted loudly again to urge him on, he lifted with all his strength.

This time the log came free with a loud crack. It shuddered for a moment, then rolled sideways. Poo Tongkam bellowed loudly in triumph and tossed his head, flinging the log from his tusks. It splashed below the surface, rose again immediately and slid past us, moving slowly away downstream. A new tumult of groaning broke from the stack and water began leaking through in several places along the whole length of the barrier. The shifting timbers sounded eerily like a thousand ancient doors creaking open on unoiled hinges. Suddenly from the bank I heard Jutulak and the other mahouts calling frantically; their elephants had begun trumpeting and I prodded Poo Tongkam quickly with my right foot, urging him to wheel and dash back towards the bank.

But on turning I saw why they were shouting so wildly. The flank of the log-stack nearest the bank had already buckled and broken first. A slew of two dozen logs had spun round the bend and was moving forward in a seething rush of white water beneath the overhanging vegetation. Seeing our retreat to the bank was cut off, Poo Tongkam half-reared up on his hind legs, trumpeting ferociously in a mixture of anger and surprise. Beside us I could see the centre section of the massive teak barrier was about to disintegrate. Poo Tongkam, realising this, dropped back solidly on to his four feet in the river and turned of his own accord to face the logs that threatened to sweep us both to oblivion.

With a deafening rumble like thunder, the avalanche of teak broke and swirled about us. Some logs, jammed well back from the wall, were catapulted high into the air above our heads, turning end over end and smashing into the river fifty yards downstream. Others, although twenty feet in girth, snapped like matchsticks as they rammed together. Sitting helplessly astride Poo Tongkam's neck amidst this maelstrom, I felt icily calm, certain that death would come to me in moments.

The first foaming wall of water almost swept me from my place but I hung grimly on to Poo Tongkam's girth chains at my back. By a seeming miracle, Poo Tongkam fended off the first flurry of logs that burst over us. Moving his great head with astonishing speed, he lifted and tossed most of the timbers aside with his trunk or tusks. Others buffeted his chest and shoulders but his massive strength rooted him solidly to the river bed and they bounced away.

The roaring noise filled my ears as a further solid wedge of logs rose and loomed above us. But then, amazingly, another elephant, bellowing as fiercely as Poo Tongkam, was suddenly at our side. The gleaming ivory of his long tusks flashed amidst the foam as he bent his head to help splay and part the logs crashing around us.

I caught a glimpse of Jutulak on the elephant's head, his face contorted as he shouted commands and urged on his charge. Through the spray and flying logs I saw that the rest of the half dozen elephants had also followed Jutulak's example and were charging bravely out from the bank. Formed by their mahouts into a rough line beside Poo Tongkam, they lunged this way and that with mercurial speed, fending off and diverting the logs with their tusks and snaking trunks.

For several minutes the frantic yells of the mahouts, the bellowing of the elephants and the booming roar of the hurtling logs merged into a single nightmare of noise. Then, as though its energy was mysteriously spent, the river suddenly appeared to relent; the rushing wall of logs shrank, then subsided altogether, and the surface of the river quickly became flat. Logs continued rushing downstream but now they were spaced evenly below us rather than above.

Gradually and with great care we edged the elephants to the side of the river. One by one they scrambled up the bank. In a level clearing we dismounted and inspected them for cuts and bruising. There was murmured praise on all sides for the exhausted animals but we did not otherwise speak among ourselves.

Poo Tongkam, unhurt and at ease despite the ordeal, was casually stripping overhead branches of their succulent leaves. I stood quietly beside him, looking out towards a distant forested limestone crag that rose sheer above the undulating valleys of deep, thrilling green. The smell of the moist earth beneath my feet and the great beauty of the dense jungle spreading into the infinite distance filled me with a sudden, wild joy. I felt heady, deliriously intoxicated with this vast gift of new life after staring death so terrifyingly in the face.

How long I stood there I do not know. With only part of my mind I noticed that a long caravan of mules and men, as small as ants in the far distance, was winding down a narrow jungle trail below the limestone crag. In normal times the sighting of one of these sinister armed caravans carrying contraband opium from Burma would have triggered an instant wariness. But in my mood of high exhilaration the train of mules was merely another detail in that glorious tropical forest landscape. I continued to breathe deeply, exulting in my good fortune. Eventually I turned away and went quietly round the clearing, patting each mahout gratefully on the shoulder. Harness was being checked and other routine tasks completed with a careful thoroughness. But I noticed that every man, like me, walked with a quiet air of elation.

I went to Jutulak last and took one of his hands warmly in both my own. He smiled wordlessly back at me. Without my saying so, he knew that he had repaid any debt he owed for the night of Poo Tongkam's rampage. By his bravery that day he helped forge a strong, enduring bond between us. What we did not know at that moment was that within hours horrifying violence would visit the camp again, deepening still further the mystery surrounding Jutulak and the death of the king.

บ ช

4

Joceline looked up sharply on hearing the scuff of cotton-soled Chinese slippers on the polished teak of the corridor. She was still holding the last sheet of typescript in her hand. She had been staring at its final paragraph, she realised, for several minutes.

The soft footfalls ceased as the white-jacketed Chinese servant appeared in the doorway. His face expressionless, he bowed slightly in her direction and made a brief *wai* with his hands. Then he advanced towards the low table and paused for a second before motioning for her to rise and follow him from the room.

But Joceline did not move. Half of her mind was still in the jungle clearing with the elephants and their mahouts. The tense drama of their escape had engrossed her utterly and she found herself pondering one haunting question over and over again: if the outcome of the attempt to dissolve the log-jam had been different, would she herself be alive? If her father had been drowned in March 1955 then she could scarcely have been sitting on the fringes of the same jungles thirty-four years later reading the manuscript. If Jutulak had really saved the life of Adam Hampson less than twelve months before her birth, he had also indirectly saved her life as well.

Other more pressing questions, the instinctive responses of an experienced journalist, seethed too in her mind. Who was behind those presenting her so clandestinely with the manuscript? What were their aims? Were they trying to use her for some obscure political end she did not understand? And had the manuscript really been written by her father – or was it false and unreliable? Since her first meeting with Surachai she had wrestled intermittently with these possibilities. Now her speculation about the direct effect of those distant events on her own life had heightened the feeling of tension which all the unanswered questions had sparked in her.

When she could no longer ignore the servant's unspoken invitation, she shuffled the pages of typescript into an orderly pile on the table. The Chinese immediately bent to gather them up. With an impatient gesture he motioned again for her to follow and led the way out of the room. Although the open windows were all shaded with slatted sunblinds, she could sense the bright midday hush of the surrounding forest beyond them. Her imagination, strangely heightened by her reading, registered an awareness of mouldering vegetation and the rank odours of large animals. In almost every empty room that they passed, the polished wood blades of the overhead fans stirred the hot, stagnant air noiselessly. To Joceline the whole house suddenly seemed eerily silent; the tapping of her own hard-heeled shoes on the teak boards of the shadowy corridor were the only sounds she could hear.

In front of her, the Chinese servant knocked on a closed door and waited a second or two before opening it. The room appeared at first to be enveloped in total darkness. Joceline hesitated, her anxiety increasing; then, on seeing that the gloom was relieved by two small candles, she stepped across the threshold.

Inside, she found that the two tiny flames illuminated a small Buddha figure, gilded and seated in the traditional, cross-legged posture in a wall niche. At first she thought she was alone and stood gazing uncertainly at the image. Then a sound at the far end of the long room made her turn.

'Your host apologises for the poor light in this room,' said the unctuous voice of Surachai. 'But as his identity is of little consequence in these matters, he felt it better not to burden you with any unnecessary knowledge.'

As her eyes became conditioned to the near-darkness Joceline was able to see the corpulent Thai. He was standing close to a desk behind which another Asian was seated. The man at the desk, she could see, was wearing a Western suit, shirt and tie, and wrap-around dark glasses. The faint light from the candles gleamed on his sleek black hair and white shirt-cuffs but his sallow face remained indistinct in the shadows.

'Your host who is Chinese invites you to be seated, Miss Hampson.' Surachai came forward and indicated a chair that had been placed against a wall. 'He wishes to know your reaction to the manuscript. Since he doesn't speak any English I will need to translate for you.'

Joceline sat down facing the desk. She stared hard at the shadowy figure but the man remained silent and unmoving. 'Before I say anything else I'd like "my host" to tell me what's behind all this cloak-and-dagger secrecy.'

'There is no need to be alarmed, Miss Hampson,' said Surachai smoothly. 'Everything will become clear in due course.'

'I hope so. But I would still like to know why everybody is behaving in such an underhand way.'

Surachai murmured a translation and after a short silence the seated Chinese gave his reply in the staccato cadences of their common language. When he had finished Surachai translated again.

'Your host says you perhaps know that Thailand's leaders now claim that the country is well on the way to becoming a democracy. But universal free speech, unfortunately, is not yet a well-established feature of our society. For instance, newspapers that print material regarded as harmful to the king or the royal family can still be shut down overnight. Individuals, Thai or foreign, can be imprisoned for even mild criticism of the royal family. At present an Englishman faces many years in jail for a casual, impolite remark about a princess overheard in a Bangkok restaurant . . . Therefore the utmost discretion is essential.'

'But why is my host so secretive about his own identity?' asked Joceline insistently. 'It casts great suspicion over the whole affair.'

'Your host wishes to make one thing very clear,' said Surachai, after translating and listening attentively to the reply. 'He has no direct interest in all this. This is not his house. He has many business interests in places such as Hong Kong, Singapore, Taiwan. He trades in many things and travels constantly. He must be careful of his reputation. In this instance he is acting merely as an intermediary . . . on behalf of friends.'

'It seems I'm destined to meet one intermediary after another,' rejoined Joceline in exasperation. 'Is there some kind of trade-off expected at the end of all this? Is my host expecting to make some profit as a middle-man?'

The shadowy figure shifted and straightened in his chair on hearing the translation. There was a long pause while he considered his reply. Once he moved his hands on the desk in front of him and Joceline saw rings of gold flash, reflecting the distant candlelight. When he spoke his voice took on a harder edge.

'The friends of your host wish the manuscript and the information in it to be put to the best possible use,' said Surachai, his voice echoing the new sharpness. 'It is only the beginning, as you already know. More sensitive chapters can be conveyed to you in London. Important additional information on the same subject can also be made available. No money whatsoever will be sought or expected. We only seek assurances about what use you will make of the material.'

'Before I give any assurances I'll want to know why I've been singled out to receive this material.' Joceline paused and drew a deep breath. 'This is my first visit to Thailand. It's not entirely unknown for people to try to plant false information on journalists ... especially on politically sensitive matters ...'

Joceline watched the shadowy outline of the seated man closely during the translation and his murmured reply. But she detected no outward change in his demeanour.

'Your host says the manuscript was found and brought down from the jungle about three months ago. Much debate has taken place about what should be done with it. Clearly it could not be given to journalists resident in Bangkok. There are other journalists resident in Singapore and Hong Kong who specialise in the affairs of South-East Asia – preparations were being made to approach them. Then providence appeared to take a hand. It was learned that you were visiting Chiang Mai to see your father's grave ... Because your reputation is well known, a decision was made to approach you ...'

'Where exactly was the manuscript found?' asked Joceline pointedly.

The anonymous figure absorbed the translated question in silence. Behind Joceline the tiny candle flames danced briefly in an unseen draught. The soft shadows in the room quivered for a moment then were still again. The silence lengthened and Joceline was thinking her question would go unanswered when the Chinese rapped out a terse reply.

'The manuscript box was found in a bamboo hut of one of the hill-tribe villages high in the jungle. A mule caravan brought it here. But that's enough questions! You must tell us now your reaction to what you have read. If we provided you with the full manuscript, what use would you make of it?'

'That depends on what it says,' replied Joceline. 'So far it is merely tantalising. There is no substantiation of what appear to be dramatic events. It might or might not be the start of a significant international news story.'

'The rest of the manuscript and the new material we will make available in London will confirm its importance,' said the Chinese quickly through Surachai.

Joceline sat back in her chair. 'If what you say turns out to be true, I will do what any responsible television journalist would do – investigate and present the facts in their true perspective in a comprehensive filmed report.'

In the near darkness Joceline saw the teeth of Surachai gleam briefly in a smile. But the posture of the seated Chinese did not alter. He spoke rapidly in an undertone to the Thai, obviously not intending all of what he said to be translated. She saw Surachai reach out to press a bell and moments later the Chinese servant entered the room carrying papers which he placed deferentially on the desk.

'When are you leaving Chiang Mai?' asked Surachai politely.

'At six o'clock this evening. I'm due to make a connection with tonight's direct Thai International flight to London from Bangkok.'

Surachai nodded, picked up two sheets of paper from the desk and crossed to her chair. 'I am giving you a short note written in our language. Also the address of a small Thai restaurant in London. Take dinner there. On arrival hand this note to the manager. It will provide confirmation of your identity for those who will contact you.'

Joceline took the sheet of paper without looking at it and stood up. 'When we first spoke, Mr Surachai, you said that you had been sent by somebody who'd had dealings with my father.'

The Thai smiled uneasily. 'Yes . . .'

'I'd like to ask my host when was the last time he saw Adam Hampson.'

The Thai turned back to the desk and translated the

question. In the silence that followed the twin flames of the candles illuminating the Buddha glinted suddenly in the lenses of the dark glasses worn by the anonymous Chinese. He appeared to have lifted his head for the first time and Joceline had the impression that he was staring intently at her. His delivery, when he replied, was guarded.

'Your host wishes to say that it is many years since he last had anything to do with your father,' translated Surachai. 'But he feels very honoured now to meet his attractive daughter. He says Adam Hampson's knowledge of the teak forests was very widely respected. He is glad that you have decided to investigate the matters mentioned in the manuscript.'

Joceline stood looking indecisively towards the shadowy figure behind the desk. His answer had been deliberately evasive but inside her head one further question was repeating itself over and over again.

'Is my father really dead?' she demanded, uttering it aloud at last in an intense voice.

The two candles were again reflected fleetingly in the shiny, blank lenses. In the voice of the Chinese too, Joceline detected the same guarded note.

'Your host understands you have already visited the grave of your father in the Foreign Cemetery,' said Surachai softly. 'And he therefore can only offer you his sincerest condolences . . .'

INTERLUDE

1950

A heavy gold crown studded with diamonds flashed and sparkled in the hands of King Bhoomipol. With a ritual slowness he lifted it above his head. Seated on a high, gilded throne in the Amarindra Hall at the heart of the Grand Palace on a May morning in 1950, he solemnly crowned himself King Rama IX.

Above the throne in the sumptuous crimson and gold chamber rose a conical, nine-tiered umbrella associated in Hindu tradition with mystical kingship. The crown, fashioned similarly in the shape of a tapering temple spire, confirmed that the bespectacled young man of twenty-three was Thailand's new Lord of Life. From that moment he held in divine trust for the duration of his reign the lives of the people, their animals, the land, the waters of the fields and rivers, and even the sky above them.

Brahmin priests chanted invocations for their gods to attend and bless the ancient ceremony. Beyond the ornate throne room in the palace grounds, ancient music was played and ritual silver trees were presented as offerings at the shimmering shrine to the jade-green Emerald Buddha. Soldiers fired a modern hundred-gun salute and in the courtyards of Buddhist temples across the nation, monks and peasants beat triumphal gongs.

That solemn moment combined all the powerful strands of Thailand's nationhood. Only seven hundred years earlier the slender, graceful minority 'Tai' tribe of southern China had been forced by its hostile Chinese hosts to flee southwards. They had trekked and trickled down into the greatest and most fertile rice-growing plain of South-East Asia. The powerful Khmer people with their magnificent temple capital at Angkor then held sway in the region. But after years of paying tribute, the Thais conquered the Khmers. In their victory they absorbed the twin religions of Hinduism – for the court – and Buddhism – for the people – which had become dominant with the earlier colonisation of the whole area by India. The Hindus had always believed that their kings were living incarnations of gods; when the Thai kings also embraced the Buddhist faith of their people, they bound the two religions closely together. The fierce aboriginal belief in a world of invisible spirits, which they had brought with them from China, also became fused inextricably in the mixture.

The nation's first capital was Sukhothai, founded in 1238. A second capital, Ayutthaya, set up fifty miles north of present-day Bangkok in 1350, endured for nearly four hundred years. Thirty-three successive kings reigned there and their supposed divine nature gave rise to strict traditions. No man or woman was ever allowed to touch a king, even if he were drowning: the penalty was invariably death. All subjects had to crawl on their knees in the presence of the monarch – as they often do today in modern Thailand. No 'divine' blood could ever be spilled. Therefore royal traitors and miscreants were thrust into silken sacks and beaten to death with perfumed, sandalwood clubs.

Horrifying though the modern death of King Ananda was in 1946, it was not without historical precedent. Of the monarchs who reigned at Ayutthaya during four turbulent centuries, one third were involved in assassinations or the murder of their rivals. The assassins included courtiers, brothers and a parent among their number. Public recollection of these facts of history inspired many modern rumours during the years following the death of King Ananda. In addition to the three men eventually charged with conspiracy, other officials, courtiers and members of the large royal family became the subject of intense speculation. The eventual trial and controversial execution of three courtiers in February 1955 did not end the speculation entirely.

These dramatic happenings in Thailand, however, were always overshadowed by greater events in Asia. Independence for India and the civil war in China, ending in Communist victory in 1949, dominated the world's attention during that period. The Korean War of 1950–53, then the French and American wars in Vietnam during the 1950s and 1960s, ensured that Thailand and its unsolved 'King's Death Case' always remained on the international sidelines. There were other historical reasons, too, why Bangkok retained an air of mystery in the world at large.

Alone in the region, Thailand had remained uncolonised by European powers. The first king of the present Chakri dynasty, King Rama I, established his capital at Bangkok following the sacking and destruction of Ayutthaya in 1767 by Burmese forces. Bangkok – meaning 'wild plum' – was then a village of Chinese traders on the broad Chao Phraya river. Around a maze of canals the first dazzling monasteries and palaces were built in imitation of Ayutthaya's former glories. One of King Rama's first acts was to command the execution of his predecessor, who had gone mad. The scented sandalwood club and the silken sack, in strict observance of tradition, were used for that purpose early in the life of the new capital.

The successors of Rama I, however, were astute enough not to cling too rigidly to the past. In time they welcomed British, American, French and Dutch specialists to Bangkok to help modernise their country. The army, government and the legal system were reformed with Western help; missionaries and teachers were cordially received in keeping with the principles of Buddhist tolerance; Western doctors and medicines were imported, trade was liberalised and treaty concessions were made so that no Western power could find an excuse to intervene by force. Shrewdly, all the benefits of European progress were obtained without knuckling under to foreign colonial domination. Most importantly to the Thais, the integrity and exclusivity of their own traditions – especially the monarchy – were successfully protected.

As well as welcoming foreigners to Bangkok, Thais began to travel abroad themselves, seeking education in Western ways. The culmination of this was the historic coup of 1932 which ended the absolute rule of Thailand's monarchs. All the royal princes were taken hostage and the king was forced to sign an ultimatum giving up his exclusive right to rule. Organised by zealous civilians and army officers who had studied in France, the coup was designed to establish full constitutional government through a National Assembly. But three uneasy years followed and in 1935 the monarch, King Prajadhipok, abdicated, protesting that power had passed to the military-backed leaders of the coup and not the people. The first elections revealed profound political apathy among the mass of the population. A similar electoral apathy continues to the present day. Military leaders have also continued to be the real power-holders ever since.

Prince Mahidol, father of Ananda and Bhoomipol, had gone abroad to study Western medicine in the 1920s. Ananda was born in Heidelberg, and Bhoomipol in Boston, Massachusetts – the only king, it is believed, ever to have been born in the United States of America. An older sister had been born in London. Their father, however, died before the 1935 abdication and Ananda became king that year at the age of ten. The news was broken to him as he lay in bed with a cold in the Avenue Tissot in Lausanne, Switzerland. A Regency Council was appointed to represent him and with the exception of one brief pre-war visit to Bangkok, Princess Mahidol continued to live in Switzerland with her children until 1945. Ananda and Bhoomipol therefore both spent their formative years in Europe studying at foreign schools and universities. Their companions and their cultural tastes during that time, not unexpectedly, became Western rather than Oriental.

Ananda's reign had been all too tragically brief. In contrast, the new, golden-robed king crowned Rama IX amidst great splendour in May 1950 would by 1990 become the longest-reigning monarch of the whole Chakri dynasty. More than any of his predecessors he embodied two worlds – the ancient Orient and the modern West. In Switzerland he had grown to like photography. He had also found delight in playing American jazz on clarinet, trumpet or saxophone. He had assembled a vast collection of jazz records from Europe, and in due course he would broadcast them regularly by radio from the palace to the light-hearted, pleasure-loving nation that saw no contradiction between near-divinity and human eccentricity in their monarch.

But on the solemn day of his coronation in the 'City of Archangels' in May 1950, the king's youthful face remained grave. The events of 9 June 1946 had begun a living nightmare for the entire royal family and the nation. The outcome of the unsatisfactory trial of the courtiers was then still uncertain. Furthermore, because of the tragic death of his brother, King Bhoomipol would not be seen to smile in public in Thailand for ten long years.

PART TWO

LONDON AND PARIS

1

'I doubt very much, you know Joceline, if the great, unwashed masses who watch television in Britain today even realise that Thailand still has a royal family . . .'

Nicholas Penhaligon's patrician features contracted into a little grimace of disapproval. He bent his long, angular body at the waist and brought his nose to within inches of the glazed porcelain features of a Chinese mandarin.

'D'you know what would happen if you put every single one of 'em on a psychiatrist's couch and played the word association game? You'd say "Bangkok" and ten million identical responses would come howling back at you – "massage parlours". And that, very definitely, would be that. Every answer thereafter, whatever you said, would be "pass".'

Penhaligon, an elegant figure in blue corduroys and a navy blouson, continued to gaze fixedly at the lifeless mandarin figure on its octagonal plinth. Absorbed in the decorative detail of the imperial courtier's silk gown he appeared to have forgotten Joceline's presence. He seemed oblivious also to the other visitors who were thronging the Long Gallery of Brighton's Royal Pavilion, commenting in awed whispers on the dazzling profusion of bamboo, silk and Chinese porcelain shimmering beneath fragile lotus lights and red-tasselled Cantonese lanterns in the mirrored corridor.

'We never make enough damned effort to get below the surface,' exclaimed Penhaligon. 'The Orient has always managed to exploit our foolish desire to drown ourselves in the exotic. Take this figure – it's Sino-Regency kitsch. An "export only" product made specially in Peking for our gullible royal forebears. No self-respecting Chinese emperor would have allowed rubbish like this within a hundred miles of the Forbidden City.'

'I bow to your expertise – but I confess my untutored eye

is wonderfully impressed. It's totally unexpected.' Joceline smiled and glanced at the blue groves of flowering bamboo painted on sunset-pink walls the length of the Gallery; porcelain pagodas and giant vases, jade elephants and bronze lions glimmered in illuminated niches on either side amidst chairs, tables and cabinets of silk and bamboo cane. At both ends of the Gallery, fine trellises and staircases of cast-iron had also been cleverly decorated to make it seem they were fashioned from the slender, supple wood that symbolised Asia. 'For some reason I've never felt drawn to visit Prinny's Royal Pavilion before. Who'd ever have guessed such Oriental splendours existed in common-or-garden Brighton.'

'At least I'm excused, then, for suggesting we meet here rather than at my shabby bachelor's quarters near the station,' said Penhaligon, straightening up and glancing ostentatiously at his watch. 'I hoped you'd forgive me. A group of Thai students are coming down from London on the train to see me this afternoon, you see. I'm meeting 'em outside here in half an hour. I shall work extra hard to make sure they don't share your enthusiasm for the Prince Regent's follies.'

Joceline smiled again. 'I very much appreciate your sparing the time to see me at such short notice. Everybody I consulted about Thailand in London said, "Don't do anything until you've talked to Nick Penhaligon at Worthing University." '

'Did they?' exclaimed Penhaligon, raising his eyebrows in an exaggerated expression of surprise. 'Did they indeed. How very flattering of them!'

'Some went further. Some said, "What Nick doesn't know about Thailand isn't worth knowing." '

'Hmmm, a very dubious statement. And then you discovered that "Old Nick" Penhaligon spends as little time as possible teaching South-East Asian history at Worthing and as much time as he can penning books nobody reads amongst the frivolous sea breezes of Brighton.'

He turned abruptly and led the way along the Gallery towards the mirror-faced double doors of the Pavilion's magnificent, domed Banqueting Room. Then he stopped in mid-stride, staring up towards the corridor's central skylight, as though struck by a sudden thought. Following his gaze, Joceline found herself looking at a great panel of emerald-coloured glass emblazoned with dragons, flowers and the image of the Chinese God of Thunder. 'Does your instant liking for all this vulgar chinoiserie mean you've already gone soft on "the mysterious Orient", Joceline? Have you decided to go ahead with this enigmatic project?'

'No, not yet,' replied Joceline without hesitation. 'I'm trying to be even more hard-headed than usual. I don't want my professionalism doubted anywhere in television because there's a hint of an emotional tie with my late, unlamented father. That's why I wanted an impartial assessment from you, above all else.'

'But from what you said on the telephone, you're going to keep this mysterious appointment at the unknown restaurant.'

'Not necessarily – if you advised otherwise I'd think very hard about it.'

Avoiding Joceline's eye, Penhaligon lowered his gaze and stared down hard at the floor as though contemplating the possible tangrams that might be contained in the geometric design of the red and gold Oriental carpet beneath their feet. 'I wouldn't think there's any particular harm in keeping the appointment to see what's on offer,' he said pensively. 'Have you got the slip of paper they gave you with the restaurant address?'

Joceline opened the capacious shoulder bag of maroon canvas which she carried back and forth each day to her film editing suite in West London. While she was searching for the slip of paper given to her in Chiang Mai, she sensed that Nicholas Penhaligon was subjecting her to a close head-to-toe scrutiny. As usual when engaged in editing work, she was casually dressed: faded, comfortable jeans, soft-soled shoes of white leather and a blue candy-stripe blouse. When she looked up, smiling at him, with the paper in her hand, Penhaligon still seemed to be studying her – but with a disinterested expression in his eyes that was devoid of male challenge.

'Yes, that's fine,' he said, reading in an instant the half dozen lines of Thai script that to Joceline were as weirdly impenetrable as Arabic or Cyrillic. 'It's a little place just off the Fulham Road – cheap and cheerful but adequate for homesick student appetites.' He folded the paper and handed it back, still without engaging her eyes. 'I'd certainly go if I were you.'

'Nicholas, would you consider coming with me? As my guest in case I need an interpreter – all expenses faithfully charged to the production budget, of course.'

Penhaligon shook his head theatrically and thrust both hands deep into the pockets of the zip-fronted blouson as though to emphasise the finality of his decision. 'Very kind of you to offer. But I think I'd better not. There are bound to be students there who'd know me. It would seem strange to them if I turned up. But report back by phone to me afterwards by all means.'

He turned and began pacing towards the Banqueting Room once more and Joceline fell into step beside him. 'My knowledge of Thai politics is nearly zero at present – but the question I'd most like to answer is: who would want to give me potentially dangerous information like this. Could it be Thai Communists for instance?'

Penhaligon again shook his head, pursing his lips dismissively. 'Highly doubtful. Ten years ago the Communists had perhaps fifteen thousand fighters under arms. Now they can only muster a squalid force of a few hundred . . .'

Joceline let out a stifled gasp and he turned to look at her in surprise. They were crossing the threshold of the Banqueting Room and she was gazing up at the great vault of dark blue sky that soared into the interior of the Pavilion's most dramatic dome. A gigantic cluster of tropical plantain leaves reached down voraciously from this symbolic heaven; astonishingly life-like, they were a vivid reminder of the luxuriant, threatening jungle foliage through which Joceline had travelled to the fortified house on the Doi Suthep mountain three days earlier – and she felt a renewed tremor of the apprehension induced by that visit.

In the heart of the fleshy leaves hovered a scaly, winged dragon. Its curved talons held brilliant-studded chandelier chains that supported a cascade of smaller, writhing dragonets; lotus flowers aglow with artificial light blossomed from their throats and Joceline noticed that the glass petals were uncannily accurate replicas of those she had seen growing in the ornamental lotus pool before the Doi Suthep house.

'What an extraordinary room!' She smiled quickly at Penhaligon, wondering if he had registered the echoes of her unease. 'It's strangely powerful, isn't it?'

'In the same way as a very bad hangover perhaps.' Penhaligon's face twisted with distaste. 'I can only imagine that the Prince Regent's designers must have got very drunk before they conceived all this . . .'

'I'm sorry, I interrupted you. You said you didn't think the Thai Communists could be behind this?'

'Virtually out of the question. Most of the Communist remnants are skulking in the jungles of the far south – definitely a spent force, I'd say. In any event they would never have been sophisticated enough to attempt something as subtle as this.'

'Who would be then?'

'Does it really matter?' Penhaligon turned away, his manner suddenly brusque, and peered at a giant silk tapestry that depicted a Chinese beauty being carried by bearers in a bridal procession. 'So long as they provide you with newsworthy material for your programme, does it matter what source it comes from?'

'This information is entirely unsolicited, Nicholas,' said Joceline firmly. 'The sources could easily be "tainted". There's no shortage of people wanting to exploit the media for their own ends today. My television film might well be shown around the world as well as in Britain. So it's important for me to try to establish a motive and the background of those supplying the raw material.'

'A very pretty speech – I congratulate you.' Penhaligon turned on an actorish smile and swung round to face her, his brusqueness giving way to studied charm. 'I didn't mean, Joceline, believe me, to doubt your integrity. But if you knew anything about the political scene in Bangkok, you'd realise how difficult it is to pin down something like this.'

'Please try me.'

'Okay . . .' Penhaligon's brow furrowed for a moment; then he began pacing slowly back towards the Long Gallery. 'Party politics in our sense scarcely exist in Thailand. A succession of army 'strongmen' have effectively run the country since 1932. There *are* political parties now but they merely represent different cliques and groups of cronies, not electoral platforms. Various personalities scramble for the levers of power – but again their main ambition too often is to get their hands on the financial rewards of office. According to one academic analyst who obviously enjoys digging in the dirt, Thailand today is the fifth most corrupt country in the world . . .'

'So intrigue is endemic in Bangkok, is that what you're saying?'

Penhaligon nodded vigorously. 'And how! Apologists will say that civilians have run the country successfully since 1980. All that means is we've seen no successful military takeover in that time. There were a couple of attempted coups by young officers in 1982 and 1985 – and there have been no less than fourteen coups in all. So the high hopes of 1932 when an absolute monarchy was replaced by a "constitutional" form of government have been disappointed. All that really altered was that the absolute power of the army replaced the absolute power of the king.'

'But if the military hasn't intervened for a long time, doesn't that suggest at least that times are changing?'

Penhaligon shook his head with equal vigour. 'Not at all. There hasn't been a successful military coup for the past nine years because the generals have been getting what they want anyway. Bangkok is booming. Rice exports are flowing out, sex tourists are flooding in – both on an ever-increasing scale. The old generals are pulling the political strings now from air-conditioned limousines and executive golf courses. But they'll dash back to their command bunkers at a moment's notice to call out the tanks if necessary – and everyone from the prime minister to the poorest monk knows it.'

'That brings me to a key question.' Joceline glanced sideways at her companion. 'Where do the king and the royal family fit into the picture?'

'King Bhoomipol to his everlasting credit is popular and widely revered,' said Penhaligon quietly. 'He's put the tragic circumstances in which he came to the throne firmly behind him. Most of Thailand's fifty millions live in the countryside and the king has shown a genuine personal interest in improving their conditions. He's also launched admirable projects to wean the northern hill tribes away from opium growing. He's been a model monarch, I suppose you could say. As a boy he was very high-spirited. But he didn't smile in public for more than a decade after his brother's death. He's been on the throne forty-three years – a reign of almost Victorian proportions.

It's certainly the longest of the two-hundred-year-old Chakri dynasty.'

'So why would anybody want to throw mud at such a popular and respected monarchy?'

Penhaligon lifted his shoulders in a mystified shrug. 'From what you've told me so far it's quite impossible to say. Perhaps we need to wait and see what comes out of your trip to the Fulham Road . . .'

'Has there ever been any sort of republican movement that wanted to end the monarchy altogether?'

'Not apart from the indigenous Communist Party, no. The king's near-divine status makes that unattractive for most of the highly superstitious people of Thailand.'

'And is everybody else happy with things just the way they are?' Joceline's brow crinkled. 'I seem to remember seeing stories about student protests in Bangkok on the foreign pages a few years back, don't I?'

Penhaligon drew a coloured handkerchief from a trouser pocket, keeping his eyes fixed firmly ahead. He blew and fussed his nose needlessly for a long time, then nodded. 'Yes, you're right. Radical students groups have caused the regime political headaches from time to time. But they're not very active right now. Haven't been for quite a while.'

'Why do you think that is?'

Penhaligon sucked in a long, slow breath. 'The students were brave enough to tackle the generals head-on in 1973. They mounted massive demonstrations demanding the sacking of the current strongman, Field-Marshal Thanom – and to their amazement pulled it off. Three years of real democracy followed – but Thanom suddenly returned in 1976 and the students mounted new demonstrations against him. In reply special anti-insurgency troops and security men attacked the unarmed students Tien An Men Square-style on their university campus in Bangkok . . .' Penhaligon paused and Joceline saw his features tighten. '. . . Right-wing groups also hanged quite a few and butchered others in a variety of ingenious ways. It was just a year after the fall of Saigon and Phnom Penh. Bangkok domino theorists were playing God. It was a deliberate and appalling act of terror in my view. More than a hundred students died all told. Afterwards a lot of frightened survivors fled into the jungles to shelter with the Communists . . .'

Although his voice had become brusque and matter-of-fact again, Joceline could see that a trace of tension had crept into his manner, which he was doing his best to conceal. 'And did those students all turn into full-blown Communists?'

'No. Virtually all of them are back home now. They were granted official "pardons" after a few years . . . And perhaps understandably most of 'em have been content to submerge themselves anonymously in the new prosperity.'

They had entered the Royal Pavilion's great kitchen, which gleamed with a vast array of highly burnished copper cauldrons and saucepans. Models of skinned oxen twisted slowly on spits, game birds and ducks lay ready for plucking and long scrubbed tables were heaped with platters of succulent-looking pies and pastries. The Pavilion's Oriental motif was echoed in the kitchen by four tall bamboo-clad pillars. They had been topped at ceiling level with curved sprays of tropical leaves to make it seem that the roof was supported by living palm trees and big hexagonal lanterns were suspended between them.

'The Bangkok generals would have been quite happy with George IV as their king, I think,' continued Penhaligon, gazing round mockingly at the lavish fare laid out in countless baskets, bowls and dishes. 'Prinny was just their kind of man. This is the sort of conspicuous consumption of which they'd approve unreservedly. If this feast could be laced with plenty of *tom yang gung* soup and served with rice, they'd probably feel quite at home here.'

His levity, Joceline could see, was forced, and the ironic smile on his face faded quickly. 'Did your time in Thailand cover the period of the student massacre?' she asked gently.

Penhaligon turned to look at her and gave a curt nod of his head. 'Yes it did, unfortunately.'

'How long were you there all told?'

'I spent five years at the embassy – 1971 to 1976.'

'So you left soon after the massacre.'

'Yes.' Penhaligon glanced openly at his watch. 'And never went back.'

'Did you know any of the Thais involved personally?'

'One or two, yes.' He peered unnecessarily at his watch again.

72

'Please forgive that personal question, Nicholas,' said Joceline gently. 'I sensed you might have done. It must have been absolutely awful.'

'It was.' He looked straight at her and in his unguarded expression she saw a fleeting hint of genuine pain. 'Look, Joceline, I'm sorry but this group of mine from London will be here any minute. I'd better get outside to meet them. Sorry it's all been such a rush. I hope we can talk longer next time.'

'Don't apologise. You've been more than kind. Just hurry on ahead.'

'Good luck in the Fulham Road.' Penhaligon summoned another stage smile as he pressed her hand briefly in parting. 'I'm looking forward very much to hearing from you again.'

He hurried away through the growing crowd in the direction of the nearest exit and Joceline followed more slowly, watching his willowy figure weaving in and out amongst the slower moving groups of tourists. Lost in her own thoughts, she wandered into two more salons, hardly seeing the rich silks and satinwood furnishings. After a few minutes she left by a different exit and walked through the gardens, gazing abstractedly at the giant Mughal cupolas and minarets inspired by the ancient temples of India. Approaching the North Gate she caught sight of Nicholas Penhaligon again, waiting outside among the streams of visitors flowing through the ornately carved stone archway.

As she watched, a group of half a dozen young Thais approached him, smiling cheerfully. Three diminutive girls in their late teens wearing trousers and neat blouses pressed their palms together and bowed in shy, half-playful *wais*. Two youths of a similar age and a taller, handsome Thai extended their hands in a Western-style greeting. Watching from the shadows of the turreted gate, Joceline saw that Penhaligon reserved his warmest welcome for the taller man, who appeared to be in his late twenties or early thirties. Smiling with genuine pleasure, Penhaligon gripped his arm affectionately during a long handshake.

As Joceline emerged from the gate and walked past the group, the taller Thai by chance looked in her direction. Their eyes met and for a second or two he stared hard at her. Penhaligon, noticing his distraction, swung round too. He looked back and forth from Joceline to the Thai, his expression momentarily startled. Then recovering, he lifted one hand smilingly in a theatrical gesture of farewell and hurried his guests away towards the exotic domes of the Royal Pavilion.

2

The words 'Top Secret' were the first thing that caught Joceline's eye. Typewritten in capitals and underlined, they formed a side-heading on a photocopied document fastened with several others inside the menu she had just opened. She glanced up at the Thai waitress who a moment before had placed the menu in her hands. Slenderly tall, dressed in a narrow black skirt and white blouse, she was walking quickly away across the dimly lit basement restaurant. Joceline watched her until she reached the swing-door that led to the kitchen. But she did not once turn her head and went into the kitchen without looking back.

Joceline's eye fell again on the security classification. The words seemed curiously melodramatic in the drab setting of the cheap restaurant. She had never seen an official communication bearing that precise term before and her first reaction was a suspicion that the document could not be genuine. Then a feeling of unease seized her and she looked quickly round at the other tables. A dozen couples and mixed groups were occupying alcoves decorated with shabby lacquer paintings of Siamese dancing girls. Because it was barely 8.30 the less popular tables in the middle of the restaurant were still empty. About half the diners were young Thais, the others English. A subdued buzz of conversation in both languages was rising from the tables but she felt faintly relieved to find that none of those present seemed to be paying her any attention.

Joceline had chosen a corner alcove and was seated facing the door. She had handed the Doi Suthep slip of paper to the waitress in an envelope while being escorted to her table, asking quietly for it to be passed to the manager. The waitress had smiled and agreed to do as she was asked, showing no surprise. Only two or three minutes elapsed before the same waitress had returned. She had made no reference to the enclosures, merely smiling again as though she were handing over nothing more than a menu and wine list.

Turning her attention to the top document, Joceline glanced at the foot of it. 'After this has been cyphered,' the writer announced, 'I am destroying the draft. Please burn after perusal.' Its heading showed that it had been telegraphed in code to London from the British Embassy in Bangkok. Dated 12 June 1946, three days after the death of King Ananda and evidently drafted by the ambassador, it described a dramatic late-night visit to the Bangkok Embassy by 'a leading member of the royal family'.

'His Royal Highness told me there was no doubt whatever that the late king had been murdered,' said the report, which had obviously been encoded in the embassy cypher room immediately after the Thai prince had departed. 'The prince himself has seen the remains and he could assure me that the bullet entered the back of the head and emerged in the front. The motive for the crime, he claimed, was to prove once and for all to the royal family that they must toe the line . . .'

Although the telegram had been drafted in the stilted language traditionally employed by British diplomats, it had a powerful immediacy. As she read it, Joceline could sense the fear and panic experienced by the anonymous Thai prince and the other numerous members of the royal family. Their first act of 'toeing the line', he had said, was signing the government communique announcing that the king's death had come about by accident while playing with a gun. During the 1932 *coup d'état*, the prince had added in desperation, the whole Siamese royal family would have been massacred but for fear of British intervention. Would British troops, now in Bangkok disarming the Japanese, protect them, he had pleaded, if a new massacre was threatened?

The British envoy, according to his own report, conveyed diplomatic regret that Britain could not take sides between Thai factions. Neither could he discuss 'the spate of sensational and even terrible rumours'. He therefore advised the royal family not to get carried away by their emotions and the prince had left around midnight in a calmer, more realistic mood. 'I can only hope my words sank in,' concluded the diplomat, 'for I don't doubt that the prince was sent here by elements who, under the impact of recent events, may be contemplating some wild initiative.'

Joceline came to the concluding instruction 'Burn after perusal' and turned thoughtfully to the second document. Headed 'Secret', it was handwritten and dated the day of the king's death.

'The king apparently shot himself through the centre of his forehead about 0900, carrying away the whole back of his skull,' said the report, which had been labelled in different handwriting 'Internal British Legation Memorandum'. It quoted 'general opinion' as believing that another member of his family was 'indirectly responsible' and added that the relative in question was believed to have bullied the king over several years. Just before his death, the report went on, efforts were made to force the young king to favour a political party he disliked for the sake of the royal family's finances. 'Should the dead king's younger brother accept the crown,' it concluded, 'it is felt he will not stand for such interference.'

Joceline read carefully through the rest of the unnamed diplomat's account, which he said had been compiled after he attended a social gathering at the home of a prominent Thai aristocrat. It outlined intimate details of palace and political intrigues which had preceded the king's death and she shook her head occasionally in wonderment at the sharp contrasts between the two reports, separated by only two days. Then, sensing a presence by her table, she closed the menu to cover the papers and looked up.

'Would you like to order now?'

With a start Joceline recognised the soft, cultivated voice of the man who called himself Surachai. But because he was wearing the white jacket of a waiter and peering expressionlessly at the pen he held poised over a small order-pad, she stared at him for several seconds before visual recognition followed.

'I hope you found something you liked in our menu.' Surachai's blank expression did not change and he still did not look at her directly. 'If you prefer I can recommend something.'

The Thai had spoken in a low voice and Joceline glanced quickly round the restaurant. Nothing had changed and nobody was looking in their direction. 'Is it necessary to be quite so mysterious?' asked Joceline quietly. 'We're in England now.'

'The *tom yang gung* is good – a hot spicy shrimp soup.'
Surachai's dark face was strangely tense and his unease immediately transferred itself to Joceline. 'You might also like to try *kai ho bai toei*, seasoned fried chicken wrapped in leaves. That is also very tasty. Would you take a glass of dry French wine too?'

'Very well.' A faint note of irritation crept into Joceline's voice. 'But I *was* expecting something from Chiang Mai. Do you remember?'

'We will give you a very nice dessert – *thong yot*,' said Surachai. He paused, glanced at the closed menu beside her elbow on the table, and dropped his voice lower. 'A motorcycle messenger will bring you "something from Chiang Mai" as you prepare to leave. Meantime, I hope all our offerings please you . . . *bon appetit*.'

Joceline watched the stocky figure hurry back to the kitchen. Her stomach was tight with tension and she doubted that she would be able to eat much. Again she glanced slowly round the restaurant, searching for some sign that might explain Surachai's guarded behaviour. Other groups of Asians were arriving, one or two accompanied by English friends. Some called greetings to one another and glanced casually towards her table. But still nobody appeared to be taking any special notice of her. One young Thai, dressed in leather jacket, jeans and training shoes, caught her eye momentarily across the room. He was sitting with two companions, similarly clad, who had their backs to her. His thick black hair was cut in a Beatle fringe which he flicked repeatedly from his narrow eyes as he talked. But although Joceline continued to watch his table from the corner of her eye, he did not appear to look her way again and she turned back to the next sheet of paper clipped inside the menu.

Unlike the previous document its title was bland and unsensational. Dated in late February 1948 and headed 'Office Memorandum – United States Government', its security classification was no higher than 'Confidential'. But as Joceline ran a professional journalist's eye quickly over the typed report, several sentences leapt dramatically off the page.

According to the most recent reports in Bangkok, it said, the Thai prime minister designate was preparing to announce that a member of the royal household had killed King Ananda accidentally and that because of this the new king would soon abdicate. The writer, a diplomat specialising in South-East Asian politics, outlined the background to these reports, then added dispassionately, 'It may be true that someone in the royal household killed the late king either intentionally or accidentally. Such a possibility was indicated in an earlier memorandum by me on this subject. Politically it does not matter much if the purpose behind the accusation is to put another prince on the throne . . .'

Joceline broke off from her reading and sat staring at the page before her, no longer seeing the words. That the violent death of a young king could remain an unsolved mystery for forty-three years was tragedy enough. Now in matter-of-fact diplomatic language the chilling suggestion was being made that some individual close to the throne might have been accidentally responsible. If there ever had been any truth in the suggestion, Joceline reflected, the sense of horror and unease within the Thai royal family would surely have endured for many years. Fear of exposure through political intrigue would also have been a constant factor in all their lives.

The enormity of this possible explanation suddenly made her see the mystery of King Ananda's death in a new light. If the manuscript she had begun to read in Chiang Mai contained genuinely new evidence, its effects could still be far-reaching. If the elephant mahout Jutulak had truly been an eyewitness, his testimony could possibly provide the final piece in a forty-year-old jigsaw of mystery and subterfuge. All rumour and speculation might finally be laid to rest.

Feeling a rising sense of excitement, Joceline flicked over the American diplomat's memorandum and scanned a last document that was also headed 'Top Secret'. It was an account by a celebrated British statesman of a conversation with a Thai prince in New Delhi in May 1948, nearly two years after King Ananda's death. The prince had come specially to Delhi to seek the British statesman's advice about Thailand's political future. The statesman, in his report, said he had expressed the view that the whole future of the Thai monarchy was in jeopardy because a number of thinking people in Thailand and Asia generally believed it possible that King Ananda, 'through sheer mischance and ill-fortune', had been killed by somebody related to him. It was well known, the British statesman added, that the late king and some of his relatives were inordinately fond of firearms and were constantly firing off their revolvers.

The statesman added: 'I said that if this theory was indeed true, I would urge that the individual or individuals concerned should fully and frankly confess, saying that they had been so overcome by grief at having accidentally killed King Ananda that they had allowed themselves to be persuaded not to make a statement at the time lest the shock might prove too great for the Thai people . . .'

Joceline read and reread the carefully drafted sentences, searching for hints that the suspicions expressed by the British statesman might be based on some greater, unstated certainty. But this second scrutiny revealed nothing further. The response of the Thai prince to the statesman's assertions amounted to an emphatic denial and Joceline subjected his words to a similar searching analysis – but again without being able to cast any doubt on their face value.

The prince was quoted as saying that if the 'accidental killing' theory were true, the statesman's advice would certainly have been followed. But the prince said certain enquiries which had been made had cleared the individual concerned completely. There had been a cast-iron alibi because that person was in another bedroom elsewhere in the Grand Palace when the shot was fired. The question of a relative's complicity therefore did not arise, the prince had concluded.

Asked why that particular relative's innocence had not previously been publicised to scotch the widespread rumours, the prince said he presumed it was to prevent people imagining there was any remote possibility that the late king could have been killed by a relation. The prince said he believed a young Thai naval officer had been the assassin. It was thought the king had suffered a similar fate to that of Thomas à Becket – his assassin committing the deed in the hope he would please his superior, the former prime minister and regent, Nai Pridi, who had become dissatisfied with the king.

The document said the prince had requested the meeting to seek an invitation to the United Kingdom for a particular member of the Thai royal family who wished to study British court life and the armed forces. In his concluding paragraphs the British statesman said he had agreed to help arrange an invitation to Britain if the prince could obtain absolute assurances that the alibi of the suspected individual was cast-iron. Steps should also then be taken, he said, to make this alibi widely known so that the whole matter could be cleared up 'satisfactorily and publicly'.

The prince, the account added, agreed to the conditions. He undertook to report back with his findings and the meeting appeared to end there. Nothing in the document indicated what the final outcome had been – but a freshly written minute in ink had been added at the bottom of the page. It said: 'Please note that nothing more was ever heard of this.'

Joceline sat back in her seat, pondering the implications of all she had read. The waitress brought the *tom yang gung* and she absently tasted a spoonful or two of the spicy, aromatic liquid without really registering its flavour. The photocopied documents, she reflected, appeared genuine enough. Most of them bore government date stamps and initials of bureaucrats or cypher clerks. Although classified 'secret' and 'top secret' when originated, they were now obviously old enough to have been obtained legitimately. Determined and astute researchers could have ferreted out the American document, using the United States Freedom of Information Act; the British papers might equally have been traced among those files opened up regularly under the 'thirty-year rule' at the Public Records Office in London.

She glanced at her watch, wondering impatiently how much longer she would have to wait for the motorcycle messenger to arrive. The waitress brought dishes of *kai ho bai toei*, spiced vegetables, rice and a glass of wine, setting them down and positioning them precisely on the table with an elaborate, smiling politeness. But although Joceline watched her closely, the gentle expression on her face remained bafflingly neutral and impenetrable; she neither spoke nor betrayed any sign that she was aware of the existence of the papers she had handed over clipped inside the menu. Her ever-present smile also acted as an invisible barrier which obviously made questions pointless.

When the waitress had gone Joceline toyed distractedly with the food and sipped her wine, still deep in thought. Then turning back to the papers again, intending to reread something, she noticed a small envelope had been fastened to the last page of the British statesman's report. Unclipping it, she found that the envelope bore her name. Inside was a single sheet of white paper on which an unsigned message had been typewritten.

It read: 'To Joceline Hampson. The king of Thailand was shot dead forty-three years ago – but the people of Thailand still do not know the truth about what happened! These secret documents contain information known to people in government in many foreign countries – but the people of Thailand still remain completely ignorant about them!

'The great Russian novelist Alexander Solzhenitsyn has said: "One word of truth outweighs the whole world." . . . But only lies and more lies have been told about the sad death of King Rama VIII. The most terrible event in Thailand's turbulent modern history still affects Thailand today. The play continues with some of the same leading actors or their understudies! Two palace attendants and the king's secretary were made scapegoats and executed. This issue of the king's death was ruthlessly used to eliminate opponents and establish new political ascendencies. Many people, including Nai Pridi, the former regent and prime minister, had to flee abroad. Some of them have sadly died in exile.

'The people of Thailand have been fooled for too long by false accounts of these events. These historical facts should at last be known to them. So isn't it time that a journalist in the West had enough courage to broadcast the facts widely to the world? Widely enough so that they cannot fail to reach the ears and eyes of the people of Thailand, too? By concealing what they know, haven't the Superpowers of the world colluded over the years with the ruling cliques in Thailand? Haven't they determined who should rule, rather than the people of Thailand who are the real owners of the country? Using these documents and other information we have promised you, we hope you will be the first journalist courageous enough to throw new light into four decades of deep darkness . . .'

Joceline started as something was placed on the table. She looked up to find Surachai standing expressionlessly beside her. He had positioned a small plate bearing the bill for the meal at her elbow and was waiting pointedly for her to pay. As she reached for the notecase in her handbag a motorcycle engine revved noisily in the street close to the top of the basement steps, then cut out.

Joceline took out some money and placed it on the plate. Surachai went immediately to the cash register and returned quickly with her change. At that moment a tall, narrow-hipped figure wearing black riding leathers, long boots and a large, visored crash helmet came into sight. With a messenger's canvas bag slung over one shoulder he was moving slowly down the stairs; in the restaurant doorway, he paused, looking round.

Because he did not lift his smoked visor, the rider's features remained concealed from view inside his metallic silver helmet. Eventually his gaze came to rest on Joceline. For a long moment he stared, then he began making his way clumsily through the tables towards her.

Watching him approach, Joceline was struck by his sinister anonymity. Like all London despatch riders, his cumbersome boots, helmet, leathers and waterproofs robbed him of all identifying features. Even his nationality was concealed by the protective clothing. In addition, the slowness of his movements and his featureless head gave him the menacing air of a robot or a creature from another world. When he finally stopped beside her table and reached a hand into the canvas bag, Joceline had to fight down an impulse to shrink from him.

But in the act of extracting a manuscript-sized package, he pushed up the helmet's visor with his other hand. To her astonishment Joceline recognised the dark, piercing eyes of the Thai she had seen greeting Nicholas Penhaligon outside the Royal Pavilion in Brighton. The eyes smiled faintly at her surprise; then as she held out her hand to take the package from him, the helmet dipped forward in a slight, formal bow.

At that instant the two Asians who had been sitting with their backs to her on the far side of the restaurant knocked over their chairs with a crash. Rising swiftly from the table they hurled themselves towards the messenger. The youth with the Beatle fringe leapt across the fallen chairs and followed them. With a loud yell the first assailant flung out his right leg in a high *muay-thai* boxing kick. His booted foot landed with sickening force on the side of the messenger's crash helmet and he staggered sideways, dropping the package before Joceline could take it from him.

The second Asian closed in quickly, yelling ritual chants and aiming a flurry of kicks and open-handed punches at the head and body of the off-balance messenger. He almost fell, knocking over an empty table and its chairs. But he recovered and, rising, lashed back at his attackers with his own feet. Stifled screams rose from some of the tables and Joceline edged away from the mêlée, her face pale with fright. The Thai with the Beatle fringe swooped to pick up the fallen package; then looking round quickly, he snatched up Joceline's menu and its sheaf of documents and rushed away with a shout towards the stairs.

A scything, roundhouse kick from the helmeted messenger sent one of his assailants sprawling across a table, blood flowing from a wound on his forehead. But before he could turn, the other closed in on him from behind. Chopping and cuffing at the messenger's upper body with his fists, he drove him to his knees. Then he sent him sprawling with a powerful downward kick delivered to the back of the neck. Grabbing his stunned companion, he hauled him upright. With a supporting arm around his shoulder, he hurried him across the restaurant and up the exit stairs.

Outside at street level, a car started up noisily. Doors banged in a rapid flurry of sound and the car immediately accelerated away. Hearing this, the messenger dragged himself to his feet and lunged up the steps. Seconds later Joceline and the other shocked diners heard a powerful motorcycle engine burst into life. Looking at one another white-faced, they listened as the machine roared away in pursuit of the car.

3

'It's a great pity that you honour Paris and myself so rarely with your presence.' The elegant, silver-haired Frenchman seated opposite Joceline saluted her gallantly with a newly poured glass of claret, smiling with undisguised affection. 'I'm not sure yet why you've decided to pay us both this brief, flying visit. But whatever the reason I raise my glass to it and to you, my dear.'

Joceline smiled as warmly and lifted her own glass in response. For a moment they both basked consciously in their awareness of a long, enduring intimacy, instantly renewed.

'There are at least two reasons, Philippe. One perhaps is not so important . . .' She hesitated and sipped her wine reflectively. 'The other is possibly very important – something on which I need your approval and support.'

The Frenchman raised one eyebrow and waited, his expression concerned. Around them the waiters of the *Deux Magots* moved briskly from table to table, dispensing efficient, respectful service without ever resorting to servility. Outside the window in the Boulevard St Michel, the early Saturday evening Left Bank traffic was already dense. Relaxed, slow-moving crowds of Parisians and visitors filled the pavements, milling around the fire-eaters, magicians and mimes who offered entertainment at the kerbside.

'I suppose I was a little shaken by the fight in the Thai restaurant last night,' continued Joceline thoughtfully. 'And there's nobody else in the world, Philippe, who's as good as you are at making me feel safe and secure. So jumping on a plane at Heathrow and coming here was the most obvious thing to do.'

The Frenchman reached across the snowy-white table-cloth and patted her hand briefly. 'Just "a little shaken" you say? I personally would have been absolutely terrified.'

He studied her without speaking. She was wearing a sleeveless couturier dress of pale green silk. Her hair, loose about her sunburned shoulders, shone like gold in the lamplight, lending her natural beauty an air of delicate, feminine vulnerability.

'You are as lovely as your mother ever was, Joceline,' he added softly. 'But you have even more courage. You never seem to stop travelling to remote, dangerous countries. Don't you ever get frightened when you are alone out there?'

'Yes, I'm frightened all the time.'

'Then how do you manage?'

She smiled and shrugged her slender shoulders. 'I suppose I follow my own simple, home-made rules . . . Never show fear. Never court trouble unnecessarily. Always act outwardly with confidence . . . If anybody mistakes that for "courage", it's fine by me. But it's hardly the truth.'

'And was wanting to feel "safe and secure" the very important reason for coming? Or the less important one?'

'The less important of the two,' said Joceline unhesitatingly. She smiled mischievously. 'I'm probably being indulgent. I knew you'd bring me to the *Deux Magots* – and I knew the waiters here would never allow vulgar brawling or the passing of secret documents.'

'I'm glad your sense of humour has survived intact, my dear Joceline.' Admiration showed clearly in his smile. 'But what, may I ask, was the more important reason?'

Joceline turned her glass slowly on the table-cloth, watching the soft light shimmer through the wine. 'Philippe, I left out two important facts this afternoon when I told you what happened in Chiang Mai.'

'You did?'

'Yes. And I haven't told anybody else yet, either.' She continued to twist her glass, holding it by the stem. Then she looked up at him with a faintly anxious expression. 'I left them out because in a way, they concern you . . .'

'How could they?'

'The manuscript they showed me is supposed to have been written by my father.'

The Frenchman's expression remained unchanged but a wariness that had not been apparent before entered his eyes. 'Do you think it really was?'

'Yes. It's no more than instinct – but I feel he wrote it.'

'I don't see, my dear,' he said gently, 'how that involves me.'

'A lot of it's probably in my mind.' Joceline smiled ruefully and reached across the table to touch one of his hands in a gesture of apology. 'Until I got to Chiang Mai, you see, I thought I was impervious to any emotional feelings about him. In every practical sense you've always been my father. Ever since that day you both told me the truth, the little girl inside me has thought of *him* as my stepfather and *you* as my real father. He'd never been remotely real to me . . . So I went purely out of curiosity because I had a couple of days leave to use up and I was passing through the area on my way home from Australia. At least that's what I told myself . . .'

'And what happened to change your feelings?'

Joceline pushed her hair back from her face with both hands, gazing pensively above his head. 'It was several things, I think . . . It was standing beside his grave, hearing a friend of his talk about him . . . It was reading his story, learning for myself that he had flesh and blood feelings . . .'

Her voice tailed off and the Frenchman waited, watching her closely. 'Is there something else? Knowing how level-headed you are, that doesn't seem quite enough, somehow.'

Her eyes came back to his face and she stared at him, letting her hair fall back into place. 'Yes, there is something more . . . It's just possible he might still be alive . . .'

'Still alive?' The Frenchman's eyebrows shot up in surprise. 'But he is buried. How can he possibly be alive?'

Joceline quickly described the suspicions of the Chiang Mai Foreign Cemetery secretary, then leaned earnestly across the table. 'Philippe, I suppose I want somebody to reassure me that I'm not being foolish – not letting silly emotions run away with me. I've stumbled across this information by chance, I know. But I feel the story of the king's death deserves to be pursued. Especially if the facts really have been hidden for forty-three years. It seems appalling that the people of Thailand still don't know what happened. Or the rest of the world for that matter. Nothing can be more important than the truth, can it?'

A waiter arrived with soup dishes, a silvered tureen and croutons, and they sat back while he busied himself serving them. Then the Frenchman gave his full attention to tasting the soup and breaking bread on to his plate. Although his face remained thoughtful throughout, he showed no sign of answering her question.

'So much television is superficial, Philippe. Dishonest even in subtle ways.' Joceline paused, her soup spoon halfway to her lips. 'There's a terrible obsession with images and pictures. The truth is much more than that. Too often words are manip-ulated to fit. Self-regarding editors, programme controllers and even presenters change and distort things in small ways to suit their own vanity. It gets difficult sometimes to sustain enthusiasm for a subject against those odds . . .' She drew a long breath, considering her words carefully. 'But this story, I know, is different. It justifies itself. It's got a deeper signifi-cance than almost anything I've done. I don't think I've ever wanted to do a film so much.'

'It sounds, then, as though your mind is already made up.'
The Frenchman raised his shoulders questioningly. 'Do you
really need any advice from me?'

'Perhaps I just need you to tell me I haven't lost my sense
of perspective. Because the ghost of my "real" father is looming
in the shadows.'

'My dear, there's no need to be so defensive about it – at
least not with me. It's quite natural after all.'

'I don't intend to tell my superiors at Metropolitan Television,' said Joceline quickly. 'It will cost a mint of money to
send a film crew and a producer to Thailand for six weeks,
say. It will also be a bit dangerous. We'll have to pretend to
the government in Bangkok that we're making a film about
tourism or something non-controversial. Otherwise we'll
never get in to shoot at all – and certainly not in places like
the Grand Palace and the northern jungles. If Metropolitan
thought I wanted to do all this as part of a private quest "to
find out about my long-lost father", they'd run a mile before
approving a penny of the budget.'

'Is *not* telling them entirely wise?'

'If the film turns up trumps, it won't really matter. If it
doesn't, it will be irrelevant.'

'They will see the name on the manuscript, won't they?'

'Yes – but I'll keep that to myself until it's too late to make
any difference.'

'Would you want to make the documentary film if Adam
Hampson hadn't been remotely involved?'

Joceline hesitated, returning her stepfather's gaze steadily.
'I think I would, yes.'

The Frenchman laid aside his soup spoon and pressed his
starched napkin briefly to his lips. Still he did not take his
eyes from her face. 'At the end of it all, do you have some
romantic idea of finding your father alive? And filming him
in a remote jungle hideout?'

'I'm sorry, Philippe,' said Joceline quietly, looking away. 'I
didn't realise it was that obvious.'

'There's absolutely no need to apologise for . . .'

'But there is,' she broke in gently. 'To you, I can't help
feeling, it must seem ungrateful. You've always been unfail-
ingly kind and affectionate – more than ever since my mother
died. When I was small you were an absolute paragon of

fatherly virtue. All the time I was away at school you never failed to turn up to take me out at half-term or weekends. You succeeded in making me feel it was unnecessary, disloyal even, to think about my natural father. And that's how it's been for as long as I can remember. You've always been positively noble . . .'

Joceline smiled fondly at him but she was surprised to see her stepfather's face become grave. 'Like you, my dear, I had my own "home-made rules". I never told anybody what they were or why. But, to misquote you, if anybody mistook them for "nobility" it wasn't necessarily the truth.'

'I don't understand, Philippe.' Joceline frowned. 'What do you mean?'

The Frenchman, looking uncomfortable, toyed with a piece of cutlery. 'Like all craven cowards, I've always avoided telling you anything that might spoil your good opinion of me. And I know your mother was never able to tell you these things herself. But to be absolutely fair to you, perhaps now is the time.' He fell silent while the waiter cleared their plates and brought the main dish. Then he sighed quietly. 'Your dear mother and I, you see, went through some turbulent times in our early days.'

'That's not necessarily unusual.'

'Yes, but our turbulence went to extremes. And I'm afraid I was largely to blame . . . We didn't, as you've been led to believe, meet for the first time after your father went back to the Far East. We knew one another long before he arrived home.' He smiled sadly. 'I came to London to open a new fine art gallery for my family early in 1954. Your mother was recommended to me to run it. We fell passionately in love from the start. Not long afterwards my father died and I inherited a considerable sum of money. Those were heady days – the beginning of the end of post-war austerity in Europe. Sad to say, the money went straight to my head . . .'

'Philippe, don't! It's not necessary.' Joceline gazed anxiously at him. 'I can see this is upsetting for you . . . There's no need to dig up the past on my account.'

His lips tightened in a resigned smile. 'You asked me just now if anything could be more important than the truth. I didn't answer. But you're right – you should know these things now, for better or worse . . . A beautiful but penniless Italian contessa "set her cap at me". Foolishly, I ran off round the world taking her with me. Your mother was hurt very badly indeed . . .'

Joceline shook her head silently in dismay. 'What did she do?'

The Frenchman's face tautened. 'Once she tried, quite seriously I think, to take her life with sleeping tablets. Luckily a friend arrived at her home unexpectedly. The door was unlocked and they were able to save her . . .'

Joceline closed her eyes for an instant, wincing at the thought.

'A month or two later Adam Hampson arrived home from the teak forests. They met at a cocktail party. He was a mysterious stranger in the cities of the world after spending years in the jungles. Your mother was still young and emotionally off-balance. There is an English expression for that situation but I have forgotten it . . . They married at Caxton Hall after just a few weeks.

His hand trembled slightly as he lifted his glass to sip some wine. They had both stopped eating and Joceline waited tensely for him to continue.

'It was a year before I got back to London – without the Italian contessa of course. She had helped me dispose of considerable sums of money. I was somewhat poorer but much wiser . . .'

'What brought you back together?'

'I'd realised some time before what my true feelings were. A terrible remorse seized me when I learned of how near your mother had been to death. As soon as I arrived home I rushed round to see her. It was a very emotional reunion. Our feelings flared up again, stronger than ever before. We both realised we had made a terrible mistake . . .'

'Did you ever meet my father face to face?'

'Only once – it was brief and very, very unpleasant. He seemed to be a fine man . . . good-looking, strong, straightforward in his manner. He was beside himself with anger. But he apparently decided to return at once to the Far East when we told him the truth . . .'

The Frenchman paused, looking at Joceline. She noticed that the effort of recollection had brought a faint pallor to his sunburned features. Momentarily, his vitality had drained away and he seemed to be making an invisible effort to straighten up under the burden of his regret.

'You weren't yet born. I vowed to myself to make amends – to you both. And, although he would never appreciate it, to your father too, I suppose. I brought us all here to Paris to live until the divorce came through. It took two years. It was then that I formulated my particular "home-made rules".'

Joceline felt compassion well up inside her. 'Philippe, I'm very glad you told me . . .'

He sighed deeply. 'I think I'm also glad now it's over . . . If I hadn't been so foolish and so cruel, you or somebody very like you would really have been my daughter. So I tried always to think that you were. After a while I didn't have to try any more, it seemed to be true.' He smiled and shrugged. 'We hoped to have other children . . . But it was not to be. And you know well enough we all had much happiness together in the years before she died.'

They sat in silence for a minute or two, enveloped in their individual thoughts. When the waiter approached, raising an eyebrow at their unfinished dishes, the Frenchman quietly elaborated a mock complaint about the 'gigantic portions' they had been served. Despite the delicious nature of the food, surely no civilised person could be expected to consume so much in a single evening? Did the management of the *Deux Magots* think all their clients had the indulgent eating habits of Roman emperors? The waiter smiled and played the game, making respectful references to 'the highly valued opinions of a regular patron' in his own mock apology. After the same waiter had served coffee and cognac and retreated, Joceline leaned across the table and rested her hand lightly on her stepfather's sleeve.

'Despite everything you've told me, I believe you acted nobly. Since realising your mistake, you've made handsome amends.'

'Perhaps . . . perhaps not. It's very kind of you to think so.'

'But surely you must be happy now? You have a lovely home in Paris, a charming second wife, enough money to live well and travel. You can do as much or as little work as you like in your business . . .'

'You're right, of course.' He patted the hand on his arm.

'The only abiding regret I have, my dear, is that I see so little of you.'

Joceline smiled apologetically and withdrew her hand. 'Somehow, Philippe, it just wouldn't feel right to come and stay with you here. I hope you understand. And you know how attached I am to my work.'

He nodded, looking at her speculatively. 'Have you become attached to anything or anybody outside of your work since we talked last?'

She shook her head firmly. 'No.'

'Nobody since the married documentary director at the BBC?'

'Nobody serious.'

'And that particular romance hasn't revived?'

'Not remotely – he's still very married. I left the BBC three years ago specifically to avoid any revival.' She picked up her balloon glass in both hands, making small, circular movements with it, and stared reflectively into the spinning disc of cognac. 'Unfortunately, there's been another mass exodus from the BBC to the independent companies this year. The "married documentary director" concerned moved to Metropolitan a year ago to become programme controller. Fortunately, I don't have to see much of him . . .'

'Will he need to approve the budget for your Thailand film?'

Joceline glanced up sharply from her glass; her thoughtful expression showed that she was considering the question for the first time. 'Yes, I suppose he's the last of several people who will have to consider it.'

The Frenchman warmed his own cognac between his palms, looking steadily at his stepdaughter. 'Do you still hope to obtain the rest of your father's manuscript?'

'Yes, of course.'

'How will you go about it?'

'I'll go back to the restaurant. I'll try to find Surachai.' She glanced at her watch. 'I'm also going to make a telephone call to Brighton tonight as soon as I get back to my hotel room. I want to find out what Nicholas Penhaligon makes of all this.'

'Please, my dear Joceline, be very careful. At the restaurant – and in Thailand.' He raised his glass an inch or two in her direction. 'I wish you *bonne chance* with your quest.'

'Thank you.' Joceline's voice softened as she raised her own glass in acknowledgement. 'Thank you especially, Philippe, for being so honest. It's made me more determined than ever to go on. And now that I've finally made up my mind, I won't give up, I promise you.'

4

When the telephone began ringing in the sitting room of his Brighton house, Nicholas Penhaligon was barefoot, wearing only a white towelling dressing-gown. He was kneading the naked shoulders of the youth with the Beatle fringe who had snatched up the fallen package at the Thai restaurant. The youth, stripped to the waist and wearing blue jeans, was inspecting his bruised face in a gilded French mirror that hung above an Adam fireplace. For a moment their eyes met in the mirror, then the Englishman frowned at the sound of the telephone and turned away.

'Excuse me, Narong,' he said quietly in Thai. 'I'll deal with this as quickly as I can.'

The old-fashioned white telephone was ringing on a table in the hall. As he went out Penhaligon closed the door after him. Through the coloured panels of glass in the top half of the door he could see into the room, which was furnished with a judicious blend of English antiques and Oriental art. The Thai youth was still standing before the mirror and for a second or two Penhaligon watched him bemusedly through the glass; then he turned away to pick up the telephone receiver.

'Hello?'

'Nicholas, it's Joceline. I'm sorry to bother you so late on Saturday night. But I'd appreciate your advice rather urgently, if you can spare a minute or two.'

'For you, Joceline, of course I can.' As he was speaking he turned and moved to a position from which he could see the young Thai through the coloured glass. 'Go ahead.'

'I'm in Paris because I had to see somebody urgently. But I wanted to tell you that I went to the restaurant last night . . .'

Penhaligon raised his eyebrows in an artificial expression of surprise. 'You did? How did it go off?'

'Rather violently, in the end, I'm afraid. There was a fight. Three unidentified Asians grabbed a package that a motorbike messenger tried to deliver to me – and they got away with it.'

'Good Lord!' Penhaligon injected an explosive note of feigned surprise into his voice. 'Were you hurt?'

'Luckily, no. But they also grabbed some photocopied documents marked "top secret" that I was given with the menu.'

'Heavens above, Joceline! That's awful. How on earth are you feeling?'

'I'm perfectly okay now. I was a little shaken, that's all.' Joceline's voice grew impatient. 'But more importantly, I'm keen to know your reaction to a couple of things.'

'Fire away.'

'The messenger, Nicholas, I'm almost certain, was the tall Thai I saw with you outside the Royal Pavilion last week. Could that be possible? Do you know more about this than you've let on so far?'

'Joceline, you amaze me! Are you absolutely sure?'

'As near as "damn it" is to swearing. He was wearing a motorcycle helmet and leathers but I'm fairly sure it was him.'

'How strange!'

'And another thing. Surachai, the right-hand man of my host at the fortified Chiang Mai house, was there. He appeared to be in charge . . .'

Penhaligon narrowed his eyes to focus on the Thai youth through a pane of roseate glass. He had moved away from the French mirror and was bending over a coffee table on which lay the photocopied documents and the opened manuscript package. As Penhaligon watched, the youth pulled the manuscript from its envelope, flicked it open and began to read.

'Will you go back to the start, Joceline, and give it to me chronologically, if you've got time,' he said smoothly. 'Then perhaps I can give you a considered view.'

He listened carefully, but continued peering through the door as Joceline quickly outlined the contents of the five documents. She also described briefly the sequence of events leading up to the flight of the messenger and his three assailants. When she had finished he let out a long, low theatrical whistle.

'Extraordinary! Quite extraordinary.'

'What do you make of the "secret" documents, Nicholas. Are their contents new to you?'

'Ye-es,' said Penhaligon, drawing the word out slowly. 'And then again no . . . I haven't actually seen those you describe myself. The sense of them is certainly known among South-East Asia historians who've taken a special interest in that particular period. And from the dates, I'd say they've been obtained astutely but quite legally from the public archives here and in Washington.'

'And the allegations concerning a member of the royal family? What about those?'

'Not entirely new, either. There was a very thorough book published in the mid-sixties by a South African writer. It reconstructed the trial and went through all the evidence available with a fine toothcomb. It rehearsed most of that stuff you've mentioned, quoting different sources. But the writer said there wasn't any really conclusive evidence as far as he could see to support the theory of accidental killing by anyone in the family.'

'What was the book's ultimate verdict?'

'Ahmm, if I recall correctly, I think the writer plumped for suicide on account of a ruined love affair. Apparently there had been a Swiss student girlfriend who had to be abandoned in Lausanne when King Ananda took the throne.'

'What's your own view on the possibilities, Nicholas? Which theory do you prefer?'

Penhaligon hesitated. 'I think if you were an opinion poll-ster, Joceline, I'd ask you to put me down with the world's five billion or so "don't knows" . . . There was another book by a London forensic pathologist that came out in the late 1970s. A Thai police major-general came quietly to London to consult him. Brought details of all the relevant evidence and the pathologist concluded it was definitely murder. The trajectory of the bullet found in the mattress proved he had been shot while lying down, I think he said. Nobody in his experience had ever shot himself through the front of the head while lying down. The Thais paid the pathologist for his trouble in crisp fivers one night under a street-light in the Cromwell Road – but never asked him to Bangkok to give evidence at the trial.'

'What do you think I should do next, Nicholas? My inclination is to go back to the restaurant to find Surachai.'

Penhaligon turned away from the glass door and lowered his voice. 'Were the police called, Joceline? Were you there when they came?'

'Surachai made a discreet signal for me to leave very quickly after it happened. So I did. I don't know whether it ever reached the ears of the police.'

'Hmmm . . . Might be safer to telephone before you go back again.'

'Nicholas, those three Asians were waiting there deliberately. Who might they have been?'

'I honestly can't imagine, Joceline. But if you want to hold your hand for a day or two I'll make some enquiries with Prem Somiboon, the tall Thai you described. We'll see if he knows anything. I'll get back to you by phone in London. When will you be there again?'

'I'm flying home tomorrow.' She paused, seemingly gathering her thoughts. 'Nicholas, you haven't offered any comment about the unsigned note attached to the documents. Doesn't that suggest something or someone fairly specific?'

'It certainly does.' Penhaligon turned and bent distractedly towards the glass door again. 'I've said nothing so far because I haven't really had the chance to formulate my thoughts. At present I'm standing in my draughty front hall in a towelling bathrobe. But the note begins to suggest that an underground political group of some kind might be behind all this. Whether it's a known organisation or a new one it's impossible to say as yet. I'd like to think about that note carefully before committing myself.'

'Of course . . . I'm sorry to spring all this on you so late. I've tried you a couple of times before today without any luck.'

'No need to apologise.' Penhaligon moved his face close to the coloured glass and peered through again. The slightly built Thai was in the act of stretching out full-length on one of the sitting room's two white sofas. Penhaligon watched him until he had settled, his brow furrowed in a frown of puzzlement and consternation. 'It's all very curious . . . But I'm glad you called.'

'If this film goes ahead, Nicholas, I'd like to shoot a comprehensive question-and-answer sequence with you. I could edit it into the story to give essential background. Would you consider doing that with me?'

'I'd certainly *consider* it, Joceline. Always provided a gigantic fee is offered by Metropolitan. You might think of filming it outside the Thai temple in SW19.'

'What's that?'

'It's a genuine Buddhist *wat* where a dozen Thai *bikkhus* live and chant, swathed in saffron robes. Very beautiful visually. You drive down a quiet road off the Common, passing lots of typical English suburban residences. Then suddenly in deepest Wimbledon you see soaring gold roofs glittering in the sun. Mythological *chofas* and *nagras* strain majestically towards heaven from every upswept eave. There are pools and streams with lotus flowers growing in the water. You suddenly think you're dreaming and you've been transported in an instant to the Grand Palace in Bangkok . . .'

'It sounds a marvellous background setting . . . I just hope I can still get my hands on the rest of my father's typescript. The film rather depends on that.'

'I hope so too.' Through the door Penhaligon watched the Thai youth lay the manuscript aside and kick off his shoes. 'I'll call you again as soon as I have something to tell you.'

'Thank you, Nicholas. Goodnight.'

Replacing the receiver carefully, Penhaligon took one final look through the coloured glass. The young Thai had turned on his side and was looking towards the door. His face thoughtful, Penhaligon opened it and stepped back into the sitting room. He walked slowly towards the sofa and stood looking down at the youth.

'That was Joceline Hampson,' he said in Thai. 'Luckily for you she was not interviewed by the British police.' He sat down on the sofa and reached out tentatively to touch the large bruise on the youth's cheek. 'It was very foolish indeed, Narong, to quarrel in public with Prem. And dangerous, too.'

'Why dangerous?' The young Thai stared back uneasily at Penhaligon, not reacting in any way to the touch of his fingers.

'Because I've heard through friends today that police from Bangkok are in London again, sniffing around.'

The youth's eyes widened. 'What for?'

'They've told their British counterparts they're trying to track down Thai heroin smugglers. But they could also be on the look-out for people trying to do exactly what you and Prem and your friends are doing.'

'Do you think they suspect us?'

'There's no indication at all of that.'

'But then why do they come to London?'

Penhaligon sighed in exasperation. 'Six years ago there were scarcely a hundred people from Thailand living in England. Now there are fifteen thousand. There are two hundred Thai restaurants – all good listening posts. Your policemen probably check out a lot of them when they come here as a matter of routine. If it had been your unlucky day they might have seen your crazy scuffle. You could have ruined everything with your rashness.'

The Thai frowned. 'Prem shouldn't be so secretive! The rest of us ought to know what's happening, too.'

'Prem is very experienced,' said Penhaligon firmly. 'He knows the value of secrecy. He dodged the machine-gun bullets when the soldiers attacked Thammasat campus in 1976. He saw his friends hanged from trees. He spent five years hiding in the jungle before his "pardon". He knows sensible secrecy often cuts down the risk of betrayal. You must trust him.'

'But he doesn't trust us,' said the youth hotly. 'And we want to right the injustices of the past just as much as he does!'

Penhaligon moved his hand, letting it rest for a moment on the youth's bare shoulder. 'Have you read the manuscript and the documents?'

'I've tried to.' The youth shook his head in frustration. 'But I don't really understand what's happening. Perhaps my English is not good enough . . .'

'Did you show any of your friends?'

'I tried to. But most of them were frightened when they heard what I had done . . . They said I'd been a fool and that I should bring the material to you immediately and beg for your help.'

'Who were the two men who attacked Prem?'

'They were refugees living here – from Vietnam and Cambodia. I went to the centre for Indo-China refugees in Islington to find two tough fighters. They didn't know or care what the manuscript was. I just paid them to help me.'

Penhaligon sat staring perplexedly at the fresh, naive features of the young Thai. Then a look of anguish showed suddenly in his eyes and he withdrew his hand. Standing up, he strode to the chair over which the youth had flung his shirt. Taking it in his hand, he returned to the sofa.

'Why are you looking at me so strangely?' asked the Thai anxiously.

'Because you remind me of somebody – somebody I knew thirteen years ago in Bangkok!' Penhaligon spoke fiercely through his teeth, his lined face suddenly stiff with tension. 'He was a Thammasat student – young and idealistic like you. I cultivated his friendship at first for the sake of my diplomatic reports. Our friendship quickly became something much stronger. But the night before the soldiers attacked the campus I betrayed him . . .'

Penhaligon broke off, swaying slightly on his feet. The Thai stared at him in alarm. 'How did you do that?'

'He fled to my apartment and begged me to hide him. But I was too afraid. Afraid of scandal, afraid of losing my good reputation, afraid of losing my job.' Penhaligon ran a hand through his thinning hair and squeezed his eyes tightly closed as though suffering physical pain. 'I shut my door in his face . . . A few hours later they caught and hanged him. The next day his friends brought me photographs of his twisted body, dangling from a wire . . . They spat on me . . . I resigned from the diplomatic service and came home at once – but in nightmares I still see him hanging from that tree.' Penhaligon opened his eyes and looked agonisedly at the youth on the sofa. 'Now you come to my door late at night. You beg me to help you. You strip off your shirt and offer to stay with me. Why have you done that?'

There was a long silence. 'Because some of my friends thought you would want it,' said the Thai at last.

'Well, they were wrong.' Penhaligon dropped the shirt abruptly in the Thai's lap and turned away, rubbing his eyes distractedly with one hand. 'If you say nothing of what I've told you and leave the manuscript and the documents here, I'll try to explain your foolishness to Prem.'

He stood silent for a moment in the middle of the room with his shoulders hunched; then he swung back again suddenly to face the youth, his expression incredulous.

'How could I have been so blind? Somebody must have put you up to this, Narong! Did you know already what I've just told you. Are you some kind of police informer?'

'No! I'm not!' The Thai stared back at him aghast. 'I swear I'm telling the truth.'

Penhaligon looked at him for a long time without speaking. 'I hope you are. If you're even suspected of having shown the papers to anybody else, especially the policemen from Bangkok, you could be in grave danger.'

'I've shown nothing to anybody,' gasped the Thai.

'Very well.' Penhaligon walked slowly across the room, opened the hall door and stood by it. 'You'd better get dressed now and go home. This time it would be wrong *not* to send you away.'

5

It was only a little after 11.30 on Tuesday morning but Joceline noticed that the ashtray on the big executive desk of the programme controller of Metropolitan Television was already overflowing with ash and crushed cigar butts. Robert Lancaster himself was at ease in his high-backed swivel chair of black leather. During the weekly planning conference that had just ended he had shifted it far enough to allow him to lift one expensive elastic-sided boot comfortably to the edge of the desk. With his dark mohair jacket off and his silk tie loosened, he was watching Joceline intently through the curling blue smoke of a freshly lit cigar.

'It seems ages, Joceline, since we had the chance to talk alone.' He smiled with evident pleasure at her. 'I asked you to look in because the editor of "Perspective" told me over a drink last night that you're working up a rather unusual story on Thailand. Am I right?'

'Yes.' She found herself readily returning his smile. 'But I've hardly had time to get it together yet. I'm still burning midnight oil in the editing suite with my producer on the Woomera aboriginees.'

'I know. I saw the rough cut yesterday. With a typically

poignant Joceline Hampson commentary, I think it will be very thought-provoking indeed.'

'Thank you.'

'And for my money, Joceline, you're looking more glamorous than ever on camera – even in a dusty safari shirt in the Aussie outback.'

Joceline looked away. The frank directness of his gaze in the otherwise empty office suite had brought back memories of the fierce physical intimacy they had once shared. Five years, she could see, had added a hint of weight to his face and body. Attainment of influence and prestige, however, had enhanced the air of determination and self-confidence which she had at first found so intensely attractive. In his early forties, his dark unruly hair still bore no trace of grey and his complexion was bright with health. He was obviously a gifted man at or near his prime. But something in his manner also suggested that too great an awareness of the fact might amount to a flaw and this realisation suddenly lessened the awe Joceline felt for their shared past.

'Glamour, or the lack of it, Robert, is irrelevant if you're making a film about the plight of Australia's aboriginees,' she said mildly. 'Or at least it should be.'

Lancaster stood up, stubbed out the half-finished cigar, brushed a shower of silver ash from his striped shirt-front and instructed his secretary via the intercom to allow no interruptions until further notice. Then he moved out from his desk. Joceline was already seated among a cluster of chairs surrounding a coffee table which allowed the programme controller to descend to the level of his visitors. He did not sit down immediately but stood beside her chair, still smiling easily at her, his hands thrust deep into his trouser pockets.

'It's not irrelevant in the minds of the punters, Joceline. A touch of glamour adds spice for them, whatever they're watching.'

'It's hardly necessary for serious subjects.'

'It's *especially* necessary for serious subjects.' Lancaster's smile broadened. 'Like the cinema or the theatre, successful television is a matter of "bums on seats". Except in our case the bums are sitting at home on seats in their own living rooms. And when your fair face and widely admired bosom appear on screen, you drive strong men wild and lesser women to despair. Metropolitan ratings go up, whatever the subject matter. We can reflect that fact on our rate-card and make advertisers pay us more to help sell their beans or their motor cars – it's as simple as that.'

'It's a point of view more common here on the top floor than down below in the engine room,' said Joceline shortly. 'Does any of this have a bearing on my proposed Thailand project?'

'Unfortunately, Joceline, in one sense, yes.' He moved to the window and looked out between the broad slats of a blind. From the higher floors of the Metropolitan glass tower which reared above West London, a glint of reflected autumn sunlight was turning a sickle-bow curve of the Thames into a glittering question mark. For a moment Lancaster stared at it, his expression pensive; then he spoke to her without turning round. 'The Chancellor's almost certainly going to put up interest rates again this afternoon. The inflation problem is going to get worse before it gets better. Which means belt-tightening measures all round. I've more or less decided to cut the foreign investigative unit's budget to the bone – that means there'll be little or no cash to spare for Thailand and the like.'

'No matter what the merits of the case?'

Lancaster shook his head and, turning from the window, came and sat down at the coffee table. He rested one arm on the back of her chair, looking directly at her. 'An exception might be made for something very special. Otherwise, I'm afraid, the answer will be "no".' They faced one another in silence for a few moments. 'How would you have structured the Thailand film? Your editor gave me a quick run-down of what you'd told him. To my mind it all sounded rather difficult to pull together.'

'I'd film it as a straight investigation. We'd have to go into Thailand pretending we were making a film about tourism or something similar to put them off the scent. But there's plenty of meat . . . a lot of obvious sequences to get our teeth into.'

'Such as?'

'I'd film the settings in Chiang Mai where I was first approached with the manuscript. I'd do the Foreign Cemetery. I'd interview people I talked to in Chiang Mai, where possible. I'd film the Grand Palace in Bangkok, do my statements to camera there when government busybodies were out of earshot. I'd ferret out all the old black-and-white newsreels of

1946 and the subsequent connected events. I'd film here in England at that shabby Thai restaurant in Fulham. I'd interview Penhaligon, the top British expert, probably in front of the spectacular Thai Buddhist temple in Wimbledon. Most importantly, I'd follow up every single clue in the full manuscript, which I'm still trying to obtain. I'd plan to go into the jungle in the Golden Triangle area to get footage of working elephants, typical spirit shrines and so on . . . The conclusion of the film would depend on whatever I find . . .'

'Hmmm . . . well, it's a pity.' Lancaster smiled sympathetically. 'You've obviously spent a lot of time thinking about it. But I don't imagine it will be a great loss to world television if it isn't done, will it?'

Joceline turned her face away to hide her disappointment. 'What fascinating programmes *are* you planning to spend Metropolitan's millions on at present? Or is that a state secret?'

Lancaster smiled wryly and raised his eyebrows. 'Safe women's subjects. Anything inexpensive and close to home will get a lot of votes right now. HRT – Hormone Replacement Therapy – for one. And PMT – Pre-Menstrual Tension – for another. You could do them both for "Perspective" standing on your head. Fronted by a beauty like you, they would certainly have an added edge. And that would raise the audience ratings several percentage points . . .'

Joceline looked at him, saying nothing. Her expression was faintly quizzical, as though some vague, underlying truth behind what he was saying eluded her. In the silence he reached out and gently took hold of one of her hands.

'You seem to be obsessed by foreign stories, Joceline. Watching your rough-cut camera pieces from the outback yesterday, I wondered if you were always running off to outlandish places to get away from something – or someone – here at home . . .'

She neither responded to his touch nor removed her hand from his. Sitting unmoving on her chair, she watched his face and listened with the same quizzical light in her eyes.

'Why don't you think about the domestic scene in Britain a bit more.' He moved closer, mistaking her silence for acquiescence, and his manner became more animated. 'I've got to go to the Tory Party Conference in Blackpool next week in my flag-waving capacity. Why don't you come along? You can work on the "Perspective" special we're doing, if you really insist. Or just come as my Metropolitan co-hostess. Ambitious MPs and even ministers will fall over themselves to be seen dining with you. It's high time anyway that Metropolitan started to give you greater star billing. It's in our own interests. I don't think you realise just how high your prestige is here. You never stay in the country long enough to find out.'

Joceline smiled slowly. 'And would you make sure we had rooms side by side in the best hotel – with a connecting door just like the last time.'

He laughed, and the tone of his laughter conveyed panto-mime shock at her request. 'If you absolutely insist, of course I will.'

She did not withdraw her hand at once but the speed with which her smile faded gave him the first warning that he had miscalculated. Their love affair had flared into life at the same season exactly five years before in Blackpool. He had directed her interview for a late-night BBC current affairs programme in which she had visibly rattled the Foreign Secretary. All the Fleet Street newspapers had carried front-page reports next day quoting her cool, persistent questions about the unnecessary crisis into which the British government had plunged the European Community over the common agricultural policy and monetary union.

Some political correspondents immediately predicted in print that a new television star had been born. After an uproari-ous midnight champagne celebration with all their colleagues, they had become ecstatic lovers in her bed during the rest of the night. A wave of passionate euphoria had borne them on its crest through the rest of the conference and into the following weeks in London. But the elation and excitement of their new romance had been gradually soured by furtive daytime meetings in anonymous West End hotel rooms. His reluctance to part at once from his rich, well-connected wife and their young son had incensed and humiliated Joceline. During a last stormy meeting at a hotel overlooking Hyde Park just before Christmas, they had both wept in one another's arms; but it had been Joceline who had insisted on making the final, irrevocable break there and then, although her mind was dark with despair.

Remembering again the emotional agony of that moment, she withdrew her hand quietly from his and stood up.

Lancaster looked at her uncertainly. She felt a strong impulse to hurry from the room but instead went to the window and stood gazing out in her turn at the sunlit question mark shining in the river.

'It wouldn't be for nothing this time.' He rose and moved slowly across the office to her side. 'I will make sure things happen for you.'

Joceline closed her eyes, blotting out the distant shimmer of sunshine. Her voice, when she spoke, was almost inaudible. 'Robert, you are what you've done. I wouldn't want you now under any circumstances. I did once – more than I believed I could want anything. But even if your degrading offer means you'd approve Thailand after I come to Blackpool, my answer is still no.'

She swung round angrily to look at him and he shook his head in a little gesture of denial. 'I'm not sure I *was* making you any such offer, Joceline.'

'Perhaps that's your trouble, Robert, "never being sure". About what you really mean . . . about what's really important in your life . . .' She sucked in her breath sharply. 'You talk disparagingly about "the punters" and putting "bums on seats", as though you despise the public we make programmes for. Once you had high ideals. But now you're in danger of sounding smug and vain. God only knows, we all risk falling into the tabloid trap – we all lust after strong images. We all tend to distort and trivialise the truth by glib editing and not bothering to explain carefully enough what lies behind our dramatic pictures. You could help change that – but no . . . You seem more concerned nowadays with injecting spurious "glamour" into serious documentary films. And the only kind of "truth" you're interested in has to be cut-price and easily affordable. Your dearest ambition when we first met was "to shed light in dark places". Now you just want to break new records with the advertising revenues . . . What's happened to you?'

Lancaster's face had turned pale and his lips had tightened into a thin line. 'I can only assume from this emotional tirade that you've had a serious offer from the BBC to go back – or to join one of the other independents . . . Have you?'

Joceline shook her head slowly from side to side, staring at him in total disbelief. 'You see money behind absolutely everything, Robert! I'm trying to tell you what I truly care about. And all you can assume is that I'm taking a gratuitous side-swipe at you before running away to the protection of a fatter salary cheque elsewhere . . .'

'I'm sorry, but that's how it seemed.'

'You asked me just now whether I was always fleeing abroad from "something or someone". Well, perhaps I am.' She glanced pointedly towards his desk. 'I suppose among other things I'm getting away from people who fill their ashtrays to overflowing with expensive Havana cigars before mid-morning every day. In the Third World, whole families can live for a month on what's just gone into your ashtray. But although they're poor, they retain something very important that we've lost – their humanity. The poorest people still respect their fellows as human beings. That's what makes them nicer to be with than most people in London . . .'

'You're wrong, Joceline, if you think others here at Metropolitan don't share your laudable concerns.'

'Then why does your axe fall first on the most deserving areas? I don't suppose you've ever considered that Metropolitan, by spending money on investigative stories in the Third World, might in fact be helping to alleviate some of the suffering there . . .' She paused significantly. 'Or in the case of Thailand, you might unravel a secret that's been kept from its people for over forty years. A secret which they have every right to know . . .'

She moved round him and walked quickly away across the office. He stood abstractedly clenching and unclenching his fists as he watched her go. But Joceline did not turn or look back and she went out, closing the door quietly behind her.

6

Standing beside a white Japanese grand piano on deep fleece-pile carpet of a similar shade, the burly Thai known to Joceline as Surachai peered warily out of a window overlooking the green expanse of London's Regents Park. From the penthouse apartment of a block close to the foot of Avenue Road, cars flowing alongside the Grand Union Canal twelve storeys below were toy-sized. Surachai, however, showed no interest in the moving traffic; his gaze was fixed on a stationary cream 350 SE Mercedes parked illegally outside the canopied entrance to the apartment block. A faint plume of smoke trickling from its exhaust indicated that its engine was running. Surachai could also see the jacketed elbow of a man protruding through the driver's window.

Beside him on the lowered lid of the grand piano lay two open briefcases of reddish leather. Both held four or five identical white packages roughly the size of a supermarket bag of flour or sugar. All were stamped with red labels indicating in Chinese characters and romanised English that they each contained a kilogram of high-grade heroin.

'Have they reached their car yet?'

The voice that rapped out the question in Thai from the far side of the room was curt and impatient. Surachai turned his head for an instant to glance towards the Chinese who had received Joceline in the fortified house above Chiang Mai. He was wearing the same dark glasses with broad, wrap-around side-pieces and his hair was again plastered sleekly against his head. Ostentatious gold cufflinks, an over-large gold tie-clip, a gold watch bracelet and several gold rings similar to those he had worn in Chiang Mai glimmered now in the slanting light of London's autumn sun. The Chinese, whose lean face was pitted with pock-marks, had been in the act of fitting thick, uniform bundles of British fifty-pound notes into another briefcase. When Surachai did not reply at once, he held his head cocked on one side, watching the Thai's face closely.

'They must be in the foyer by now,' replied Surachai at last, glancing at his watch. 'Perhaps they're stopping to admire the fountains and the golden carp. The foolish driver is risking police attention by parking unlawfully right outside the main door.'

'As soon as they're clear of the area, telephone and say there will be no further supplies for them in future,' said the Chinese angrily. 'They were given the strictest orders to park legally at least a quarter of a mile away and walk here.'

Surachai nodded and leaned towards the window again. Three men were emerging on to the pavement from beneath the entrance canopy. One, a tall West Indian wearing a smart business suit, carried a briefcase similar to the two that remained beside Surachai on the piano lid. He was smiling broadly and jigging a little as he talked to his two companions, a well-dressed Arab and a nondescript European. The briefcase he was carrying contained four one-kilo packages of No. 4 grade heroin from the Golden Triangle area of Thailand. A fluffy white powder more than eighty per cent pure, it had been refined from ten times that amount of raw opium. Easily soluble in water, it was ideal for the kind of syringe injection preferred by addicts in Europe or America.

The Chinese had bought the raw opium that produced the four packages from hill tribespeople who had grown the poppies and harvested their resin. He had paid the equivalent of £150. The West Indian had just handed the Chinese £300,000 for the heroin, which had been carefully refined at secret jungle locations in Laos. Later he and his collaborators would employ others to dilute it carefully with quinine or milk sugar. The resulting powder would be divided into minute quantities and packaged in two hundred thousand gelatin capsules. Each one would be sold in London for £10.

The gross proceeds, therefore, would be two million pounds sterling and in the act of getting into the car, the West Indian lifted his head and looked directly up at the window where Surachai stood. The Thai quickly stepped back out of sight but the West Indian, already savouring the illicit profits in his mind, waved the briefcase delightedly as he ducked into the car with the others.

Before the doors were properly closed, the Mercedes jerked away from the kerb and forced its way into the heavy afternoon traffic flowing eastward along Prince Albert Road. The following car had to brake and swerve violently to avoid a collision and Surachai muttered fiercely under his breath as he watched the Mercedes accelerate away, weaving dangerously in and out of the traffic stream. After waiting for a minute or two, he picked up a portable telephone from the piano and pressed out a number. As soon as the connection was made he curtly announced that no further supplies would be available to the group because of their lax attention to security. The West Indian began to protest in a high-pitched voice but Surachai casually broke the connection and turned back enquiringly to the Chinese.

'There are still five cars cruising in the district. Shall I call in the next group?'

The Chinese looked at his own watch and shook his head. 'What about the Triad team you hired for me? Have they picked up the traitor Narong Chumto yet?'

Surachai nodded. 'Yes, half an hour ago.'

'Where are they now?'

Surachai pressed out another number on his portable telephone. He spoke into it for a second or two then looked up. 'They are in their car about to enter the underground garage below us. They're awaiting instructions.'

'Tell them to bring him up at once. Tell them to be sure to use the high-speed lift which comes only to the penthouse. Then there will be no risk of anybody seeing that he is brought here by force.' The Chinese listened to the instructions which Surachai immediately murmured into the mouthpiece; then he glanced towards the two briefcases still lying open on the piano. 'Bring them over here.'

He rose and swung aside a modern abstract painting splashed with broad swathes of primary colour. Twirling a combination lock on a wall safe behind it, he opened its door and inserted the two cases. Then he closed the safe, straightened the painting and sat down again. For a moment he glanced round the room; furnished lavishly with white leather sofas and tables and chairs of tubular aluminium and glass, it was typical of the kind of luxury apartment available for lease to very wealthy visitors to London by the day, week or month, cash in advance, no questions asked. Its pristine surfaces typically contained no books, personal objects or anything else that could give a clue to its occupant's identity. The Chinese, as though acknowledging this, gave a little nod of satisfaction before checking his watch again.

'What time will Prem and the Englishman Penhaligon arrive?'

'They're walking here through the park.'

Surachai crossed to the window. In silence he scanned the great oasis of trees and grass beyond the canal. A strong wind was plucking flurries of dead leaves from the ground and sending them spinning about the heads of the people walking along the paths.

'Since you're only here for two days, I've issued Prem with

a telephone case. He's carrying it now.' Surachai inspected his watch. 'They should be here at 4.30 but I can call Prem and find out exactly where they are ...'

The persistent buzz of the doorbell interrupted Surachai and the Chinese motioned for him to answer it. The moment Surachai opened the door, three tough-looking Chinese dressed in jeans, sneakers and hooded bomber-jackets pushed Narong Chumto roughly into the hall. Two of them held him by the arms and a third had clamped a hand over his mouth from behind. At a signal from Surachai they frogmarched him quickly into the sitting room.

'Why did you steal the manuscript?' barked the Chinese in Thai, leaning forward angrily on the leather sofa.

Surachai motioned for the man clamping Narong's mouth to remove his hand. Trembling visibly in the grip of the two other men, Narong stared at the seated Chinese with an expression of terror on his face. 'I ... I ... wanted to know ... what was happening ... That's all ... Nobody else would ... tell me.'

'You're lying. You're a treacherous police spy for the *Santiban*! Admit it!'

Narong flinched at the mention of the Central Intelligence Division of Thailand's national police force. 'No! ... No! ... It's not true.'

'The manuscript has been chemically tested,' snapped the Chinese. 'You had it photocopied!'

Narong's face registered a new extreme of fear. His eyes seemed to glaze but he did not acknowledge or admit the new charge. Instead he continued to stare dumbly at his accuser.

'Fetch the "royal regalia",' ordered the Chinese curtly, nodding at Surachai. 'Perhaps that will refresh his memory.'

Surachai hesitated for an instant, then hurried from the room. He reappeared a moment later, his expression faintly uneasy, carrying a folded canvas sack in one hand and a long-handled baseball bat in the other.

'You once boasted to us that your father had distant links to the royal family, did you not?' asked the Chinese in an icy tone. 'We are not sure we believe you – but even so, being loyal Thai subjects, we don't wish to risk offending tradition. Therefore we shall observe the venerable rituals of Ayutthaya.

We have no wish to spill "royal blood" on these handsome carpets.'

The Chinese motioned with his head and Surachai handed the baseball bat to one of Narong's Triad abductors. He gave the canvas sack to another, then the Chinese snapped out orders in his own language to each of the two men holding the young Thai. Manhandling him without ceremony, the Triad men shook open the long sack, which had a draw-cord threaded through brass-ringed holes in its top. Lifting him bodily off the floor, they forced his feet into it and drew the canvas up around his body. Narong began to struggle and yell hysterically but the third Triad man immediately covered the Thai's mouth again.

'Tie his hands and gag him!'

The seated Chinese barked the command in a military fashion and one of the Triad men obediently pulled Narong's belt from its loops to bind his wrists behind his back. A companion tugged a scarf from his own neck and tied it tightly around Narong's mouth. The Thai's eyes rolled wildly as he struggled ineffectively against the iron grip of the two men but they worked on unemotionally, ignoring his distress.

Before they had finished, the door buzzer sounded again; three long bursts of sound separated by deliberate intervals. Surachai glanced anxiously towards his Chinese superior. 'That will be Prem and the Englishman.'

'Let them in!' The Chinese waved a hand towards the three Triad men and they waited watchfully while Surachai went to open the door.

As soon as Nicholas Penhaligon entered the room he halted in his tracks, staring with a startled expression at the group before him. Narong's captors had succeeded in dragging the sack up around his neck; only his terrified face remained visible and one of the Triad Chinese was pulling on the draw-cord so that the tightened top of the sack formed a sinister frill around Narong's throat. Behind Penhaligon, the tall young Thai whom he had greeted warmly outside the Royal Pavilion in Brighton stopped too. His eyes took in the scene at a glance but his expression did not change. Surachai, following close behind them, urged them forward into the room, looking expectantly towards the seated Chinese.

'What in heaven's name is happening here?' Penhaligon

spoke Thai in a tone of angry protest, looking back and forth from Surachai to the Chinese. 'What are you doing to Narong?'

'We are sorry we don't have the correct materials,' replied the Chinese, using a single index finger to adjust the dark glasses on the bridge of his nose. 'The sack, we know, should be made of silk. The bludgeon should be fashioned from scented sandalwood. But these are the nearest replacements we can obtain so far from home to deal with a "royal" traitor.'

'What has he done?' demanded Penhaligon.

'He photocopied the manuscript that he stole from Prem.' The Chinese nodded briefly towards the tall Thai at Penhaligon's side. 'I have had its pages chemically tested today. He refuses to disclose why he made the copy or what he did with it. So it is only right that a stubborn traitor should suffer this fate.'

The Chinese paused for a moment then spoke sharply to the Triad men. The individual holding the baseball bat immediately stepped away, flexing his wrists and drew back the club in readiness to strike. The eyes of the young Thai, which had been fixed beseechingly on Penhaligon, dilated suddenly and his features contracted into a grimace of terror.

'For God's sake, stop this!' Penhaligon took a pace forward, staring fixedly at Narong. His own features were working convulsively and he had turned very pale. 'Nothing can justify such cruelty!'

The Triad men glanced questioningly towards their paymaster. He nodded coolly, confirming that they should continue. Ignoring Penhaligon, they pushed the head of the young Thai out of sight. Tugging the draw-cord tight, they began tying a knot to secure the mouth of the sack.

With a choking cry Penhaligon lunged towards them. He grappled first with the man wielding the baseball bat; but in late middle age Penhaligon could not match his youthful strength and he was easily shaken off. The Triad man raised the club as if to strike Penhaligon and only a shout from the seated Chinese stopped him.

The Englishman turned and scrabbled frantically at the knotted cord securing the sack. He succeeded in untying it but on a further shouted order from the Chinese, one of the other Triad men stepped forward. Dropping into a bent-kneed crouch he joined his fists together and swung hard at Penhaligon's head. The two-handed blow drew an instant trickle of blood from the corner of Penhaligon's mouth and he staggered backwards across the room until the piano stopped him. His hand flew to his face and his fingers came away red. Grey-faced and paralysed with shock, he stared wordlessly at the half-dozen Asians watching him.

'I think Mr Penhaligon is right. We're perhaps being too hasty.' Prem, who had spoken out urgently in Thai, strode over to the sack. Inside it Narong had sunk to his knees and Prem stood pointedly beside him. 'Give him one last chance to explain himself.'

Silence at first greeted Prem's request; then the Chinese nodded reluctantly, his expression sour. The Triad men quickly unfastened the sack, hauled Narong clear and removed the scarf from his face. When they stepped away, he was left swaying unsteadily in the middle of the room.

'Who did you copy the manuscript for?' rasped the Chinese in an unforgiving tone.

Narong had difficulty summoning his voice and when he did it was little more than a croak. 'I copied it for myself . . . I've told you before . . . I wanted to try and understand . . .'

Prem reached inside the short coat he wore and produced a sheaf of manuscript. 'I went to Narong's room this morning to search. I found this identical copy there – fully intact.'

Behind the dark glasses the eyes of the Chinese switched suspiciously back and forth between Narong and Prem. 'This doesn't necessarily prove he's telling us the truth. Further copies could have been made and passed to the *Santiban*.'

Narong looked fearfully over his shoulder at the crumpled sack and the man holding the baseball bat. Then he hung his head and closed his eyes, waiting dumbly to hear what was decided about his fate.

'I propose we give Narong the benefit of the doubt,' said Prem quietly. 'Time is slipping away. It's more important that we contact the television journalist to pass on the manuscript. I will take a copy with me when I visit the Buddhapadipa Temple tomorrow morning at 10 am. She could come there to collect it.'

The Chinese turned to look in Surachai's direction and lifted his chin to indicate the Thai should arrange it. Surachai reached for his portable telephone and pressed out a number. When a switchboard girl at Metropolitan Television head-quarters answered, he handed the phone to Penhaligon.

'Joceline Hampson, please,' said the Englishman in a shaky voice. When she came on the line, he turned his back to the listening Asians. 'Joceline, this is Nick Penhaligon . . . Sorry it's taken me longer than I thought . . . But I think I've sorted out the confusion over the manuscript . . .'

'Nicholas, are you all right?' asked Joceline in a concerned voice. 'You sound very faint.'

'Yes, I'm all right. There was apparently a misunderstanding among friends. There's no need to go back to the restaurant. Prem will give you a full copy of the manuscript tomorrow morning. Meet him outside the Thai Buddhist temple in Wimbledon just after ten o'clock . . .'

He returned the telephone to Surachai and took a neatly folded cotton handkerchief from a trouser pocket. Dabbing at his face, he peered distractedly at the red stains. Prem, the terrified Narong, his three Triad captors, the seated Chinese and Surachai were all watching Penhaligon intently but to their surprise he did not speak further. Instead he turned his back on them and with his shoulders hunched in an attitude of defeat, he walked unsteadily from the room.

7

'I don't want you to think I'm disloyal to the king.' Prem's expressive face, framed by the exotic 'sky tassels' curving upwards from the golden gables of the Buddhapadipa Temple, became earnest and intense. 'And I'm not a Communist either. It's in my blood to revere our royal family. I grew up in a poor northern village. Buddhist monks like these men here gave me my first education in the dust of the village temple compound. Despite everything that's happened to me, deep inside I still have the simple instincts of a poor Thai peasant. And the peasants of my country adore their monarch.'

The light in Prem's eyes seemed to intensify as he looked hard at Joceline. She was instantly reminded of the moment when she had first caught sight of him outside the Royal Pavilion at Brighton. There had been a similar concentrated stillness in his gaze then, as if he was grappling with some striking thought triggered by the sight of her. He was standing now with his back to the Buddhist temple in the suburbs of West London, a faint breeze ruffling his glossy black hair. At close quarters the controlled fervour of his speech enhanced the handsome lines of his broad face. He spoke English with a deliberate correctness rare among Thais and Joceline immediately sensed the attractiveness of a strong, determined mind. Seeing him close up, she guessed he was roughly her own age and as before he wore neatly pressed jeans, suede boots and a short navy-blue coat. From one shoulder hung a small canvas bag, its buckle undone and jutting tantalisingly from beneath its flap, Joceline could see the corner of a typescript fastened between blue covers.

'Why do you choose to tell me about your loyalty to the king?'

'Because from what you've read so far you might have thought I was a republican, an anti-monarchist – and that's not true.'

'Did you write the covering note that was given to me with the secret documents?' asked Joceline.

Prem nodded quickly, still holding her gaze. 'Yes, I did.'

'And was it you that ferreted them out of government archives here and in Washington?'

'Yes.' He nodded again, his features relaxing into the hint of a smile. 'You see, I believe in the power of truth. Lies have their own terrible force – if we don't fight with all our strength, lies can destroy everything we value.' He paused for a second or two, still watching her closely. 'I sense you believe as strongly as I do in the truth. Am I right?'

They were walking along an avenue of tall pines that curved through the temple grounds. From each tree jutted a narrow signboard of pale wood into which quotations from the Buddhist scriptures had been burned in English. To conceal the faint disconcertment which she felt at Prem's question, Joceline stopped beside one tree to read its quotation and did not reply immediately.

She had driven into the temple compound just before ten o'clock to find it deserted. After parking her car beneath the pine trees, she had walked slowly towards the white-walled temple, listening to the gentle sound of chanting which came from inside. Built on a central grassy mound, the traditional Thai *wat* was crowned with multi-tiered roofs of crimson and gold that gave it the exaggerated charm of a make-believe palace. Golden finials shaped like the elongated necks of mythical birds curved gracefully towards the heavens from every ridge-end, and its balustrades were decorated with tiers of circular discs representing the ascending levels of Buddhist perfection.

After waiting for a few minutes without seeing anybody, Joceline had climbed one of the stone stairways to the main doors, which stood open. In the carpeted interior, a gilded Buddha image presided above a dazzling bank of flowers and at intervals during their chanting, several saffron-robed Thai monks and a handful of other Asians dressed in Western clothes leaned forward to prostrate themselves in the direction of the Buddha. Among them Joceline had easily picked out the tall, straight-backed figure of Prem. When the devotions ended, he had been the first to emerge through the temple doors, hitching the canvas bag on to his shoulder.

He had approached her immediately, introduced himself with a polite handshake and suggested that they take a stroll through the temple grounds. With his first words he had begun to assure her of his loyalty to the Thai monarchy. He neither made any mention of the purpose of their meeting, nor showed any sign of handing over the manuscript. These omissions had left Joceline feeling vaguely disconcerted and this showed in her face as she attempted to frame an answer to his question about whether she shared his devotion to the truth.

'As a television journalist I feel it's my duty to reveal any truth that the public has a right to know,' she said slowly, turning to face him. 'But in checking facts, it's essential to discover whether you're dealing with people you can trust. The last time we met, a fight broke out before you could hand me the manuscript. Don't you owe me some explanation about that?'

'I apologise sincerely for what happened at the restaurant,' said Prem hastily. 'I should have said so before.'

'What caused the fight? What was behind it?'

He stared at the ground, his brow furrowed in consternation.

'It's difficult to explain briefly. It has much to do with the character of the Thai people. We are individualists because our national religion, Buddhism, teaches every individual to strive for his own salvation. We don't believe as you do in the West that there is a god who helps us. We are encouraged to attain merit as individuals, not as part of a group. So we like to act alone – especially in political matters . . . That sometimes causes trouble . . .'

'I don't quite understand.'

'I'm sorry.' Prem smiled apologetically. 'Narong, who snatched the manuscript from me, is a friend, someone who feels as I do . . .'

'What sort of "friend" does something like that?'

'Like me, Narong wants to help Thailand live up to its name. "Thai-Land" means "the Land of the Free". But apart from the years between 1973 and 1976, my country has never known complete freedom.' He shook his head in a little gesture of frustration. 'We had an absolute monarchy until 1932. For centuries our kings had governed us through their powerful bureaucrats. Since 1932 the army has ruled Thailand most of the time with the help of those same bureaucrats . . . We want to help change that.'

'But you don't seem to be able to agree on how.'

Prem paused and drew a long, deep breath. 'I need to explain our different backgrounds. Army generals ended our brief spell of liberty by sending soldiers to massacre students in Bangkok in October 1976 – just as China's Communist leaders crushed the democracy movement in Peking four months ago by slaughtering Chinese students in Tien An Men Square . . .'

'And were you involved in Bangkok in '76?'

Prem nodded, his face becoming grave. 'I was a student leader at Thammasat University. I watched my friends die . . . some were burned to death, some were hanged from trees before my eyes. I had to flee to the jungle and hide with the Communists for four years – until a general amnesty was granted.'

Joceline saw that the memories still pained the Thai and they walked in silence for a while beneath the pine trees. 'But Narong looks too young to have taken part in all that,' she said at last.

'Exactly – he's only twenty now. And remembering lessons

I'd learned about security in Bangkok and in the jungle, I told him very little about your father's manuscript. Perhaps I was wrong. Perhaps I should have confided in him. Anyway, he lost his head and foolishly paid people to help him steal it. He said he only wanted to find out what was going on . . .'

'Are you and Narong part of an underground political organisation?' Joceline watched his face closely as she waited for him to reply. 'You lived with the Communists for four years. You could still be a Communist for all I know.'

The Thai laughed humourlessly and shook his head. 'While I was in the jungle at the end of the seventies, the Communist cause began to collapse like a house of cards. First Vietnam invaded Cambodia, then China launched military attacks against Vietnam. Pol Pot's Communists had already committed genocide against their own people . . . And if that wasn't enough to destroy Communism as a political religion in Asia, China's leaders showed the world their true face in Peking this summer. Now the Soviet Union is in turmoil, too. Hundreds of thousands of people are marching for freedom in East Germany, Poland has a non-Communist prime minister and Hungary has rejected Communism altogether . . .' Prem paused and turned his head to look calmly at Joceline. 'I've never been a Communist. And I would be swimming against a very strong tide if I were to become one now . . .'

'That makes sense.' Joceline looked at him thoughtfully. 'But are you involved with some other secret political organisation?'

'No, not any longer.' Prem snapped out his answer without any hesitation and his tone betrayed strong feelings of remorse. 'Before, far too many organisations sprang up. As a young student I took part in the big, organised street demonstrations that overthrew our military dictators in 1973. Their troops fired into the crowds at first. It was almost as bad as 1976. Many were killed – but the sacrifices were not in vain because two military dictators were driven into exile and we won our precious freedom for the first time . . .'

'Then why do you say there were "too many organisations"?'

'Because we were politically naive. Our three years of freedom were years of confusion and political hysteria. There were countless campaigns and protests by hundreds of different groups. And history, too, was against us.'

'What do you mean by that?'

'In 1975 Vietnam and Cambodia fell to the Communists. The monarchy in Laos was overthrown. So in Thailand the army was able to stir up right-wing opinion against radical students. After the 1973 massacre it was the king himself who ordered the military dictators into exile. But when heavily armed troops attacked the Thammasat campus in 1976 there was no general protest . . .'

'Why not?'

'Because many people were terrified that Thailand would go the way of Vietnam and Cambodia. They feared Communism would replace the monarchy. The Western world didn't care if military rule was restored so long as we helped "resist the Communist menace". That was much more important than any precious freedom that the people of Thailand might have lost . . . Since then it's been difficult. Our present political parties and our National Assembly are still little more than window dressing for a corrupt military autocracy. But there are others who think like Narong and me. We want to try and find a new way forward . . .'

'Presumably those people include Surachai – and the Chinese I met in Chiang Mai?'

Joceline thought she saw Prem's eyes cloud momentarily and he hesitated before speaking. 'Yes, Surachai shares our beliefs . . . Unfortunately, we also need the help of others. We have no money, nothing to finance our travel and research . . .'

Joceline considered his oblique answer in silence. 'How come you're playing a leading role in all this, Prem? Have you got some special interest of your own?'

The Thai dropped his hand for the first time on to the blue-covered typescript which was visible in the shoulder bag and motioned towards it with his head. 'I think you'll understand better when you have read these pages.'

Joceline looked at him in surprise. 'Do you mean you're connected in some way with what my father has written?'

Prem smiled faintly, looking at her again with the strangely intent expression in his eyes. 'Yes, I am.'

She waited for him to continue but he remained silent.

'Before we go any further, perhaps you should explain what you mean by that.'

They had stopped beneath another of the pine trees and

Prem turned away for a moment to read the Buddhist quotation burned into its signboard. Following his gaze Joceline read it too. It said: 'The common people know not that in this quarrel they will perish. But those who realise this truth have their quarrels calmed thereby.' Turning back to face Joceline, Prem smiled again.

'I think my father and your father would both have liked this quotation.'

'Why do you say that?'

'Because they were good friends.'

'Who was your father?'

'My father was once employed in the elephant stables at the Grand Palace . . . I'm the son of Jutulak.'

Joceline stared at him in astonishment.

'As you know, Adam Hampson saved my father's life. But for that, I wouldn't be standing here today.'

Suddenly Joceline felt she understood the still intensity of Prem's gaze. 'You know that I could say something similar – your father showed great bravery when they were breaking up the log-jam in the river.'

Prem nodded and smiled. 'We both owe a debt of gratitude to their courage.'

For several seconds they stood beneath the pine tree, looking at one another without speaking. The strangeness of the bond they shared had created a powerful feeling of intimacy between them and Joceline suddenly felt herself strongly drawn to the handsome young Thai. 'Did you ever meet my father, Prem?' she asked quietly.

'Yes, I did.'

'How did it happen?'

'I went to look for him in the north.'

'When was that?'

'About a year and a half ago.'

'Where did you see him?'

'In a remote hill-tribe village where he was living.'

Joceline reached out impulsively and touched Prem's sleeve. 'Do you think it's possible that he could still be alive?'

Instead of answering, the Thai slipped his hand into the canvas shoulder bag and drew out the blue-covered script. He glanced quickly around the temple grounds before looking at her again. 'I was told he had been trampled to death by an elephant and buried in the Chiang Mai Foreign Cemetery. How could he still be alive?'

She searched Prem's face, looking for some clue that he might be hiding something. But he continued to hold her gaze without flinching.

'Please don't ask any more questions now. Take this away and study it carefully.' Placing the manuscript in her hands, Prem bowed his head slightly towards her. 'I hope you'll excuse me. I must leave. I trust you won't be disappointed with what you find in there.'

8

Joceline kept glancing at the manuscript on the passenger seat as she drove slowly back from Wimbledon towards the West End. When she had covered half the distance she realised that she had been driving with exceptional, unnecessary care. Subconsciously she had been behaving as if she were transporting something unusually fragile that might instantly shatter in a thousand pieces if she were to bump the car in front. The return journey, she noticed, was taking twice as long as the outward trip and she pressed on the accelerator to speed up.

Once or twice she felt a strong urge to pull into the side of the road and begin reading at once. But she resisted the impulse, reasoning that it would be more sensible and safer to wait until she reached home. As she drove, she turned over in her mind Prem's dramatic claim that he was the son of Jutulak. Could he be telling the truth? And had he really visited Adam Hampson at a hill-tribe village in the mountainous jungles of the north? Prem's face had seemed open and honest, she reflected; but his evasive reaction to all questions about her father's death made her wonder about his ultimate truthfulness.

Remembering that he had urged her to study the manuscript rather than ask questions, she felt more impatient than usual with London's slow-moving traffic. As soon as she crossed the Thames she encountered the usual daytime jams and tailbacks that clogged the heart of the capital summer and winter alike.

This routine congestion ensured that the return journey took nearly an hour all told. When at last she found a vacant 'residents parking' bay close to her Cadogan Square maisonette, she breathed a long sigh of relief. Clutching the manuscript tightly under one arm, she hurried from the car.

Outside a local newsagent's shop a large billboard for a London evening newspaper caught Joceline's eye. It proclaimed in heavy type: 'San Francisco Earthquake – 270 feared dead.' Emerging from the shop doorway carrying an early edition, an elderly male neighbour stopped to greet her. He tapped the newspaper, shaking his head sorrowfully at the news of the disaster, and she listened politely while he described what he had just read. Glancing down at the newspaper, Joceline's eye was drawn to the likeness of a vaguely familiar face illustrating a separate story on the front page. Beneath a small subsidiary headline near the bottom of the column was a passport-style photograph of a young Asian. After a moment or two she realised with a start it was the youth who had snatched the manuscript from the motorcycle messenger at the Thai restaurant. The headline said: 'Heroin Crash Murder Hunt.'

Joceline controlled her impatience long enough to exchange parting pleasantries with the neighbour, then hurried into the shop to buy a newspaper for herself. On the way to her front door she read quickly through the brief report. Police had given chase to a car in north-west London the previous night when it had failed to stop for a routine check, the report said. The driver had escaped after crashing the vehicle. But the dead body of the Thai youth – identified from his passport as Narong Chumto, a twenty-year-old student – had been found in the boot of the car, bound, gagged and hidden inside a canvas sack. A briefcase containing heroin worth half a million pounds had also been found in the car. It was not immediately known how the youth had died, the report added, but police were treating the case as murder.

Outside her front door, Joceline stopped and reached into her shoulder bag for her key. She felt a faint chill of apprehension begin to grow in the pit of her stomach. In her mind she heard Nicholas Penhaligon speaking with a strangely weak voice: '. . . I think I've sorted out the confusion about the manuscript . . . There was apparently a misunderstanding among friends.'

She opened her door, stepped inside and stood looking indecisively at the large envelope containing the manuscript which she carried in her hand. Fleetingly she wondered whether it might not be wiser to destroy it unread and ignore all the ghosts of the past that it threatened to raise. Clearly there were different kinds of dangers to be faced, both personal and impersonal. But she entertained the idea of destroying the manuscript for no more than a minute. Having come this far, she knew it was not in her nature to turn her back on the mystery, no matter what difficulties might be involved. Her mind made up, she closed the door and, still standing in the hall, went carefully over the short news report in the evening newspaper. But she found no new hints or innuendoes that shed any further light on the circumstances of Narong's death and she carried the manuscript and the evening paper through the sitting room towards her study.

On the way she looked at her watch, wondering whether to try to telephone Nicholas Penhaligon at his home in Brighton – but before she reached the study she heard the telephone begin to ring. It stopped almost as soon as it began, indicating that the fax machine attached to it had been activated to receive messages. She found a space on her desk for the manuscript and watched the message emerge slowly from the machine. Even from a distance she could see that the memorandum bore the distinctive Metropolitan TV logo. When she picked it up she found it was headed 'From the Office of the Programme Controller'.

It read: 'Attention Joceline Hampson. From Robert Lancaster. After careful consideration of all aspects of our last conversation I've decided to approve special funds for your proposed Thailand documentary. At our last meeting you made a very convincing case for the continuance of investigative films of this kind – especially in the Third World. So full steam ahead. Good luck with the research and filming. You will have my full support whenever needed. I shall follow all your progress with close interest – R. L.'

Joceline read and reread the fax several times, absorbing one by one the possible implications behind the unemotional, formalised words of the message. Remembering both the unpleasantness of their last meeting and how close they had once been, she felt tears of remorse start to her eyes. Then with an effort she fought them back and pushed all personal considerations from her mind. At the top of the page she saw that a code indicated that the sheet she held in her hands was the first of two, and she set it aside as a second page dropped into the delivery tray. When she picked it up, her eyes widened in dismay.

It read: 'Attention Joceline Hampson. From Robert Lancaster (continued) P.S. Only one black spot. Have just caught our midday news bulletin. It seems you will have to manage without the services of Professor Nicholas Penhaligon. He has been found dead at his home in Brighton this morning. Hope you can find another reliable South-East Asia expert. Penhaligon's death suicide, apparently. R. L.'

Joceline walked slowly over to her desk. For a minute or more she stood looking down at the evening paper without seeing it. Then she picked up the buff envelope and drew out the manuscript. Opening it, she ran her eye quickly over the chapters she had seen in Chiang Mai. They appeared to be unchanged and she began to read from where she had left off, standing tense and unmoving beside the desk.

INTERLUDE

1955

It was the dark hour just before dawn. From the walled execution yard of Bangkok's central prison came the ominous clank of wrist and ankle chains. Awake unnaturally early, the prison's population of five thousand convicted criminals stirred uneasily in their cells. Straining their ears, they listened and waited tensely for the harsh sound of gunfire.

In the centre of the dimly lit execution yard a cross of wood had been erected. Close to the cross stood a rectangular frame over which a blue curtain was drawn. A white circular target was stamped on the curtain. A few yards away a machine-gun had been mounted on a tripod. Its muzzle already pointed towards the white target on the curtain.

At about 4 am the distinguished, middle-aged Thai who had once served the young King Ananda as private secretary was led stumbling from a small building towards the cross. He was blindfolded and shackled hand and foot. It was Thursday, 17 February 1955. Nearly nine years had passed since King Rama VIII had died of a bullet wound in the head. More than seven years had passed since the private secretary was arrested along with two adult pages of the royal bedchamber.

They had all been accused of plotting with or assisting 'unnamed accomplices' in the assassination of King Rama VIII. By implication the 'accomplices' were the former civilian prime minister Nai Pridi and aides who had fled abroad after being ousted in a coup in November 1947. The trial verdict, reached in September 1951 after five years of investigation and hearings, was that only one page was guilty. The other two men at that time were released. Defence and prosecution appeals, however, were lodged. More than two years passed before that appeal verdict was announced – and then the second page was convicted as well.

Final appeals to Thailand's highest court consumed nearly

another year. This time the judges surprisingly convicted the former private secretary too. All three condemned men, who had protested their innocence throughout, then made one last desperate petition to the military government for mercy. They had been compelled to wait four more agonising months in their condemned cells for the answer. The final, irrevocable refusal of their pleas had at last been announced the previous afternoon – 16 February 1955. All the inmates of Bang-Kwang prison a few miles north of Bangkok knew something unusual was coming because they had been ordered back to their cells from their work an hour early.

In the cells close to the execution yard many prisoners clearly heard the ex-secretary's chains rattling as he was dragged out. Some of his escorts pressed him face-forward against the wooden cross and bound his feet to its base. Others lashed his hands around the horizontal bar. Afterwards they inserted between his trapped fingers the kind of flower garlands and joss sticks which are traditionally placed before the spirit shrines which adorn every home in Thailand.

On the nearby frame the blue curtain was drawn carefully into place, concealing the victim from the eyes of his executioner. The white target on the curtain marked the precise position of the condemned man's heart. When the prison governor gave the signal with a red flag, the executioner crouched down behind the machine-gun tripod. After taking aim, he fired a lethal burst of bullets through the centre of the target. They smashed into the back of the former private secretary, convulsing his body against the wooden cross. A moment later he hung dead from his bindings.

Twice more, at further twenty-minute intervals, the listening prisoners heard chains rattle as the two pages of the royal bedchamber were led out and bound in identical fashion. Similar short bursts of machine-gun fire followed. By 5 am all three convicted men were dead. Soon afterwards their bodies were carried into a nearby Buddhist monastery where relatives could reclaim them. Thailand's official files on the 'King's Death Case' at that moment were effectively closed.

Police-General Phao, the most dreaded figure in Thailand during the decade following the Second World War, was the chief spectator at the executions. Dressed in a white lounge suit and a red beret, Phao watched closely as the prison doctor certified the death of each of the three prisoners. The unscrupulous commander of the nation's paramilitary police force, General Phao terrorised many political opponents of the military regime during the decade after 1947. Employing ruthless methods of imprisonment, torture and assassination, he stifled all opposition to Field Marshal Pibul, who was prime minister for fifteen years until overthrown by a *coup d'état* in 1957. Nicknamed 'the Butcher of Bangkok', Phao also enriched himself from his involvement in opium smuggling and Bangkok's brothels and gambling dens. In effect Phao turned Thailand into a brutal police state until the 1957 coup forced him into exile in Switzerland.

The popular Western image of exotic, little-known Thailand during those years could not have been more different. It was coloured entirely by the phenomenally successful 1950s Broadway stage musical and Hollywood film, *The King and I*. The quaint story sentimentalised the successful, real-life efforts of King Rama IV – great grandfather of King Ananda – to modernise his country by introducing advanced European ideas. Its frivolous focus was Rama IV's fictionalised relationship with the English governess he hired to educate his numerous children. A ban was imposed on the entertainments in Thailand from the outset. They were held to demean and insult the Chakri monarchy and both film and stage musical have remained banned by the Thais in their own country up to the present day.

But *The King and I*, for all its frivolity, portrayed an essential historical truth. It illuminated the shrewdness of King Mongkhut who was Rama IV. It was Mongkhut and his son King Chulanglonkorn who ensured that Siam, alone among South-East Asian nations, would be able to resist European colonisation. They took vital steps to invite British and other foreign advisers to Siam and saw to it that growing numbers of Siamese went abroad to study in Europe. Ironically it was this process that led eventually to the ending of absolute monarchy in Thailand in 1932.

Both Field Marshal Pibul and the civilian Nai Pridi were among those Siamese who went abroad to France in the twenties to study. They returned to lead the bloodless 1932 coup which was designed to break the political stranglehold of the country's numerous royal princes and their despotic bureaucrats. Pridi, who studied law at the Sorbonne, became the civilian champion of democratisation and social reform. But in the late 1930s Field Marshal Pibul who, like Napoleon, had been educated at the Fontainebleu Artillery School, became prime minister. It was his admiration for Hitler, Mussolini and ultimately Japan's military leaders that persuaded him to take Thailand into the Pacific War on the side of the Axis powers.

Pibul held the premiership for six years until Japan's waning fortunes brought about his fall in 1944. Pridi, who had led an underground 'Free Thai' movement during the war, then became prime minister. He presided over Thailand's first real National Assembly elections and for two years pushed the military leaders on to the political sidelines. But Pibul and his disgruntled generals quickly exploited post-war economic difficulties and the 'King's Death Case' to mount the *coup d'état* of November 1947. Nai Pridi, his reputation undermined by the dubious accusations of regicide, fled to exile in China and later France. It was the success of the 1947 coup against this champion of democracy and civilian rule that put the nation's military leaders firmly back in power in Thailand for the next twenty-five years.

PART THREE

THE GOLDEN TRIANGLE

เดอะ บางกอก ซีเคร็ท

THE
BANGKOK
SECRET

Chapter Five

The sheer exhilaration of being alive and full of vigour in the wild beauty of the northern Thai jungle was still with me next day. After the close brush with death on Poo Tongkam's back amongst the surge of unjammed logs in the river, I was still experiencing each throbbing colour and every forest scent as though for the first time. By dawn I was awake, swinging along a jungle path on foot beneath towering banyan trees. Sixty feet tall, they laced their branches into a solid canopy of foliage high overhead. Fine arrows of sunlight were being shot through this great, vaulted roof into the green shade all around me, turning the forest into an enchanted natural cathedral.

Inside my mind as I walked I offered a silent prayer of gratitude and thanks for my survival. As I had done many times before when striding free and empty-handed along an isolated jungle trail, I felt that I had been greatly blessed. Every two or three hundred yards I passed a splendid teak tree – *tectona grandis* in its full Latin dignity – soaring majestically upward into the gloom. These mighty trees were, to me, the monarchs of the inanimate forest. To be working them with the aid of the biggest and noblest beasts of the entire animal kingdom had seemed from my earliest days in the jungle to invest life with a unique grandeur. Now this feeling was more intense than ever; I looked around myself, I listened, I breathed in the fresh, tangy air with the febrile excitement of a man discovering himself new-born at the height of his physical strength. All the sights, sounds and smells of that morning imprinted themselves on my senses with a brilliant sharpness.

It felt then as though inside me they were being specially recorded for all eternity.

These recollections, I'm sure, were made permanent in my memory by the new, shocking events involving Jutulak that then lay only an hour or two ahead. Without the sudden, unexpected intrusion of armed violence into our camp, the clarity of that morning might eventually have faded. It was the awful contrasts that ultimately froze all images, good and evil, on the retina of my mind. First the unspoiled, paradisial beauty of the dawn hours; then the ugly crash of gunfire, sudden fear, the camp clearing filled with running, yelling men. The very air had seemed to change and become rank with murderous human emotions.

But striding briskly at first light along one of the many trails made by wild elephants, my eyes were drawn repeatedly upward to the lower limbs of the great trees. Minute, pinpoint orchid blossoms dusted the boughs, filling the glades with the sweetness of their fragrance. Bigger blooms the size of a man's hand glowed brilliantly red, gold and purple amongst the festoons of smaller flowers. There were giant lilies, violets, wild rhododendrons and many-hued butterflies flitting amongst them. The jungle became more dense and the trails, carpeted thickly with sound-deadening leaves, wound on between impenetrable clumps of fern, tangled bamboo, groves of wild bananas and slender saplings. Creeper vines laced all these dense green thickets together, creating within them a stark, sensual silence through which I walked on that special morning with a greater than usual sense of awe.

The tranquil stillness was relieved only by the faint sighing of the wind in the high forest roof. Occasionally an invisible dove gurgled or a large bird, perched unseen overhead, shrieked out at my approach. Sometimes a rustling beside the path indicated that a snake was slithering away on hearing human footsteps. Once, after passing out of the trees into a waving area of sea-green elephant grass which met in an arch six feet above my head I heard the snarling cough of a panther. I immediately stopped and held up my hand. Poo Tongkam's spearman who was following me with a spare harness slung around his shoulders, froze in his tracks. Together we held our breath and listened to the faint sounds of the panther's stealthy movements. When we recognised that the animal was shifting away from the trail, we breathed again, grinned thankfully at one another and moved on.

From time to time I knelt on the path to check the distinctive tracks made by Poo Tongkam's feet. Bigger than all of the wild elephants who had passed along the trail in the night, they were easy to distinguish in the soft ground. After the drama in the log-jammed river I decided that Poo Tongkam had redeemed himself and earned the reward of some free grazing. I had therefore released him, carefully hobbled, well before dusk along with the other dozen or so elephants, as was my usual practice during the working season.

It was the task of each elephant's young mahout to track down his charge wherever it happened to be grazing at dawn. But because nobody had yet volunteered to replace the Thai whom Poo Tongkam had killed, I had allowed myself the pleasure of tracking him and bringing him back to camp. On returning from Europe I had brought sporting guns with me to Thailand and at first had greatly enjoyed hunting the region's big game in off-duty periods. The gaur, the giant wild ox of Asia, was one of the most sought-after prizes. I was a moderately good shot in those days and had killed two or three fine bulls. But as my respect and fascination for the jungle and its creatures grew, their massive horns mounted on my bungalow walls became a silent reproach and I felt less and less inclined to kill needlessly.

All aspects of jungle lore, however, had continued to intrigue me. Tracking and understanding the habits of the animals, I realised, was the part of hunting that had given me the greatest pleasure and satisfaction. Consequently I always seized any opportunity I could in the course of my work to put my growing knowledge to the test. On that morning, to help me recover Poo Tongkam I had taken along with me the Thai spearman who had worked regularly with his now dead mahout. The spearman also knew Tongkam's footmarks at a glance and smilingly nodded his approval whenever I looked to him for confirmation. On passing a heap of Tongkam's droppings the spearman obligingly kicked at it with his bare foot as his mahout would have done and together we studied the proof of his earlier presence.

'Not yet cold,' grunted the spearman.

'And he's eaten more than his fair share of bamboo,' I said

reflectively. 'He'll want several mouthfuls of *kaing* after that. I think we'll very likely find him quite soon – in the next sea of *kaing* grass close to a creek.'

The spearman indicated his agreement with an admiring grin and we hurried on. A few minutes later from beyond a ridge I heard the dull but distinctive clank of a teak bell I had hollowed out specially myself. On an impulse I had decided to replace Tongkam's brass 'danger' bell with the standard *kalouk* worn by most elephants. No two *kalouks* ever had precisely the same note as each mahout carved his own to help identify his charge unseen at a distance. I had also wanted to see if Tongkam would respond to the subtle indication of trust implied in the removal of the noisier 'danger' signal from his neck. That would take time to prove but the moment I detected the sound of the first *kalouk* I had ever made with my own hands, I ran eagerly to the top of the ridge and looked over.

The faint breeze was sending rippling waves through the tall *kaing* covering the sides of a long, broad valley. But because the first dazzling rays of the rising sun were bursting through the eastern mountains at a low angle, I couldn't immediately locate Poo Tongkam. Instead my eye was drawn to unfamiliar movement deeper in the valley. Winding along a curving track, passing in and out of great patches of shadow, was the same long train of heavily laden mules that I had first seen from another ridge the previous afternoon.

The spearman spotted them at the same time and tugged at my sleeve. 'Who are those men, Master?' he asked in a mystified voice. 'They're carrying guns.'

'I'm not sure – but they're almost certainly opium smugglers of one kind or another . . . Kuomintang troops or Shan state soldiers from Burma.'

I screwed up my eyes, trying to discern detail. I hadn't brought my field glasses with me because I'd wanted to travel fast and light to find Poo Tongkam just as a native mahout would have done. I had buckled on my holstered pistol for self-protection before leaving camp but that was all. From the top of the ridge I tried to count the mules; then I lost track of the number among the shadows after picking out about ninety. I had occasionally seen distant caravans moving through the region in the past and had questioned my coolies about them.

I knew each animal could carry about fifty kilos. That meant that perhaps ten tons of raw opium was passing south down the valley that morning.

Later, when I saw the troops at close quarters, I was to discover that my first guess was right – they were Kuomintang irregulars forced out of China by Mao Tse-tung's Communists six years earlier. As usual they were using hill tribesmen as muleteers and guards. The number of Nationalist Chinese escort soldiers was not large, no more than a hundred. But they carried powerful weapons – 60 millimetre mortars, .50 calibre machine-guns, 75 millimetre recoilless rifles and semi-automatic carbines. These armaments, I guessed, were designed to deter attacks by Burmese army units or jealous Shan rebels in the dangerous border regions. In addition, at least two field radios were being carried, one at the front and one at the rear of the column. This meant that the opium caravan commander could seek instant reinforcement from other irregular garrisons guarding Kuomintang radio posts that had been set up throughout the Golden Triangle border regions of Burma, China, Thailand and Laos.

'Look, Master!' said the spearman, tugging again at my sleeve. 'Part of the group is breaking away.'

I shaded my eyes again, peering eastward towards the sun. I could just make out a smaller file of mules that was beginning to separate itself from the main column, turning sharply southward up the side of the valley. There appeared to be about thirty soldiers accompanying only six or seven mules. They were moving faster and with more determination than the main body of the column. In silhouette I could see they carried their rifles slung slantwise across their backs.

'If they maintain that route they will pass very close to our camp,' I said, feeling a vague sense of alarm grow inside me. 'We'd better find Poo Tongkam quickly and get back there.'

We cast around until we found the elephant's tracks in the flattened grass and pressed on westward with a greater sense of urgency. Again I heard the distant clank of the teak kalouk hung around Poo Tongkam's neck and changed direction towards a higher reach of the same river into which we had plunged together the previous day. Although my anxiety to return to camp was mounting, I had to remind myself to be patient. It was always dangerous, I knew, to startle any animal, tame or wild, in the jungle. Also, I knew that the abrupt emergence of myself and the spearman from the ten-foot-tall grass would remind Tongkam that a new day of strenuous log-dragging was about to begin. This could make him rebellious and delay us further. So as all native mahouts did in these circumstances, I began to sing quite loudly to make him aware of our presence gradually as we approached.

Poo Tongkam was grazing close to the river bank when at last we sighted him, partially visible above the *kaing*. He raised his head to stare in our direction as I sauntered slowly towards him, still singing. Usually Thai mahouts sang native folk songs to their charges but I had already found a more familiar refrain equally effective. If the massive bull elephant found anything odd in hearing a tuneless English voice crooning 'If You Were the Only Girl in the World' in his direction he gave no sign. He stood watching me and listening to the pre-World War Two popular song as attentively as other Thai elephants on whom I'd used it. But when I was about thirty yards from him he swung his great head away to look towards the river.

Seeing this I lowered myself gingerly into a sitting position on a riverside rock and lit a cheroot with studied casualness. In my mind's eye I could see the breakaway group of opium soldiers and mules nearing the top of the valley trail en route to our camp. I had no inkling what their intentions were but the urgent manner of their climbing had increased the vague sense of alarm I felt. If Poo Tongkam, out of mischief, decided to plunge into the river and swim across to the far bank I knew we could not retrieve him in time to reach the camp before the soldiers.

As I sat and smoked, watched anxiously by the spearman, I began to intermingle my singing with bouts of gentle chiding directed at Tongkam. In English I told him good-humouredly he had already led us a long dance, and wasn't it about time he allowed us to take him home? In between I began to call to him repeatedly in a low, gentle voice: 'Mah! Mah! – Come on! Come on!'

For some minutes he continued to graze, lowering his head from sight, ignoring me utterly. I found myself glancing more and more anxiously at my watch. When I was at the point of exasperation, the *kaing* grass suddenly parted and Poo

Tongkam appeared, moving slowly and majestically in my direction.

I watched him warily as he approached, trying to gauge his mood. He came quietly without tension or anxiety and when he was twenty yards away I rapped out a crisp command for him to stop and go down on all fours.

'Hmit!'

Without hesitation Tongkam obediently lowered his haunches to the ground. Then he settled into a fully recumbent position with legs extended front and rear. In this posture the elephant was clearly signalling his approval of my wish to approach. Rising from the rock, I carefully put out my cheroot. Once at his side I gave him the firm command to stand up.

'Tah!'

Showing the same kind of obedience again, Poo Tongkam stood up. The spearman moved forward unobtrusively to his guard position and I bent down to disconnect the chain fetters which I'd fastened tightly in place the previous day. Remembering how rapidly he had moved when charging me in the darkness, I had left virtually no slack in the chains this time. Even so, although he could only shuffle over flat tracks or climb in a series of hops, he had roamed more than four miles from the camp.

As soon as I removed his hobbles I took the pack harness from the spearman and secured it. Then I ordered the elephant to sit again while I climbed up into my saddle position at the back of his head. As soon as the spearman was squatting securely behind me, we set off towards the camp. Poo Tongkam, at my urging, lunged along the track at a fast trot and we covered four miles in about twenty minutes, retracing the entire route along which he had grazed and fed. I began to feel confident that we would arrive at the camp before the opium soldiers. But I was wrong – we were still two hundred yards away when the first shocking volley of shots from their semi-automatic carbines broke the dawn stillness.

Poo Tongkam trumpeted loudly, as though both alarmed and angered at the sound of the firing. Some of my other unseen elephants that were being prepared for work around the camp began roaring fearfully too. Further shots rang out beyond the trees screening the camp from my view and I had to work hard to keep Tongkam going forward. Although I could see nothing, I heard hoarse yells and shouted replies in Chinese. Amongst them I thought I identified the frightened voices of my Thai coolies.

Some instinct made me slow Tongkam to a walk as he carried us towards the last bend in the track approaching the camp. I didn't know what to expect but on rounding the curve, I was appalled to see the great grey bulk of a fallen elephant sprawled in the mud outside my tent. Even at a distance I could see a large pool of blood was oozing from its head. In the same instant that I realised that the animal must be dead, I recognised Jutulak's coloured harness stretched across its withers.

A man's body was spreadeagled in the mud at the edge of the clearing, and fleetingly I was aware that four or five soldiers dressed in khaki battledress were dashing across the track leading eastward out of the camp. They carried rifles at the ready in their hands and moved with practised speed in a fighting crouch. Two of my coolies were flinging themselves headlong towards me, their faces contorted with fear. The sight of them increased Poo Tongkam's alarm so I turned him quickly into the trees, ordered him to kneel and dismounted. The spearman leapt down to stand guard while I fastened his tethering chain securely to a sturdy cotton tree; then we dashed back to the track to waylay the terrified coolies.

I grabbed the first man by the arm and the spearman stopped his companion. 'What's happened?' I demanded, pulling them into the protection of the underbrush. 'What's going on?'

'Soldiers, Master! Many soldiers have come to kill us all!' The first near-hysterical coolie turned to point wildly towards the body lying at the side of the clearing. 'They already kill Prapoth, Master! We must get away! Please let us go!'

'Try to be brave. I think the soldiers have gone.' I shook the man gently, attempting to calm him. 'Have they killed Jutulak?'

'No, Master, I don't think so.' The coolie opened and closed his mouth like a fish out of water, his eyes still rolling wildly from fear.

'What happened to him?'

'He was riding his elephant, Master. The soldiers grabbed us and held guns at our heads. They asked over and over again: "Who is Prapoth? Who is Jutulak?" We had to tell them or they would have killed us. All the other coolies and mahouts ran away before they came.'

'What did they do when you told them?'

'Prapoth tried to run away too, but they shot him down . . . Jutulak was already mounted. He tried to charge the soldiers to save Prapoth. Three of them shot his elephant . . . That's when we escaped. If it hadn't been for Jutulak we'd be dead too!'

I glanced out through the trees towards the camp. There was no longer any sign of the opium soldiers and an eerie silence had fallen over the scene.

'What did they do to Jutulak?'

'They seized him, Master. They tied up his mouth and bound his arms behind him.' The coolie struggled to control himself, looking fearfully over his shoulder towards the motionless bodies of Prapoth and the dead elephant. 'They brought their mule caravan near the camp, Master. They threw Jutulak across a mule's back and took him away.'

'Stay here out of sight with the spearman,' I commanded them and drew my revolver from its holster.

Keeping to the shelter of the trees I skirted the clearing, looking for signs of the armed attackers. I remained hidden for several minutes but still nothing broke the terrible hush which had descended on the camp. When I considered it safe I walked over to where Prapoth lay and saw that he had been shot many times in the back.

Flies attracted by the blood were already buzzing around the corpse of the man and the dead elephant. Brass cartridges scattered from the soldiers' guns glinted on the muddy ground. Without thinking I began scouring the clearing, peering intently at every visible mark in the soft earth. Inside a minute I had located the hoof-prints of several mules. I followed them for a few paces, finding that they led eastward out of the camp. As I stared down at them I felt anger well up inside me. It was in that moment that I made up my mind what I must do.

ป ช

เดอะ บางกอก ซีเคร็ท

THE
BANGKOK
SECRET

Chapter Six

แมแมง คอมมก ฉยง

At the edge of a high ridge above a narrow rice plain I reined in my sturdy-legged pony and removed my solar topee. Drenched with perspiration, I flapped at my face with the helmet. The slow-moving sweat-bees that had attached themselves to my neck and face as I rode, swung ponderously away into the late afternoon shade.

My eyes were stinging, my legs ached from the long ride, but despite the growing heat of early March I felt an elusive shiver crawl up my spine. Such shivering in any season, I knew well enough, could be an early warning of fever. But in my determination not to lose the trail of the opium caravan I deliberately ignored it.

Hauling my field glasses from a leather saddle pannier, I lifted them to my eyes to begin a careful inspection of the cultivated plain below. As I did so I fancied I could feel half a dozen leeches that had fallen into my collar from overhead trees gorging themselves inside my sweat-soaked shirt. I suspected I'd find blood in my boots too. I'd dismounted many times to search for clues among leech-infested leaves and I knew from long experience that these loathsome worms were able to wriggle through the lace-holes of a boot in the time it takes to wink an eye. Restoring order at my forest camp had taken several hours and I'd been riding in pursuit of the caravan without any real break since before noon. Despite my impatience I knew I would have to rest soon and clean myself up. My pony, too, was tiring rapidly and if I went much further my baggage and camp coolies would not catch me up before dark.

I swung the binoculars very slowly across the rice paddies that were dotted with tranquil thatched villages. Dykes gleamed silver in the afternoon sun, punctuated here and there by the dark shadows of wading and wallowing water buffaloes. But I could find no trace of the opium caravan, although I was sure I had not misread the tracks of the mules and the foot-soldiers.

They were obviously moving faster than I had anticipated and I wondered if the troops had hired mule drivers and animals from Yunnan, China's most southerly province. The tall, strong Yunnanese, who smoked small opium pipes themselves as they marched, had always been famous for their speed. They were reputed to cover up to fifteen miles a day, carrying heavy loads for anybody who would pay them well enough. This was more than twice the distance traditional bullock or elephant caravans of the region could achieve. Despite the advent of Communism in China these peasant drivers still somehow managed to find their way over the closed borders to work regularly through Burma into Thailand and back again.

Beyond the narrow rice plain I could see a range of low hills clad in dense, evergreen jungle. It was obvious that the train of opium mules had already disappeared from view among the trees. The sun was dipping towards the western mountains and I knew it could not be long before the caravan made camp. But if I waited at the top of the ridge for my coolies and spent the night there, I risked losing the trail on the plain next day, especially if rain fell before dawn. Yet if I rode on heedless in its wake I faced the prospect of spending a dangerous night in unknown jungle sleeping rough without tent, food or protection. Again I shivered and this time I noticed that my head had begun to ache slightly. If these signs were warnings of an imminent bout of fever, I knew the ordinary dangers of the jungle would be multiplied many times.

I pondered the dilemma for a minute or more, still seated on the lathered pony. I imagined the frightened Jutulak, bound and gagged, jolting through the dark, evergreen jungle somewhere up ahead, lashed to a mule's back and surrounded by armed guards. It seemed likely that the caravan's ultimate destination might be Chiang Mai. The mules had been bearing steadily south-west at every junction along the narrow forest trails, convincing me that they were not heading for the more northerly centre of Chiangrai.

The illicit opium itself, I knew from teak company gossip, would be shipped south to Bangkok after transactions in or around Chiang Mai. The irregular Kuomintang generals would use the revenue from the opium sales to buy arms. This would enable them to continue their sporadic raids across the south-western borders of Communist China and help keep alive Chiang Kai-shek's dwindling hopes of reconquering the mainland from Taiwan. At least part of the opium, according to other rumours drifting up the company grapevine from Bangkok, would find its way into the hands of Police-General Phao, who lined his pockets well from many criminal activities.

I felt almost certain that Jutulak, too, would be delivered south into the hands of the notorious Phao or one of his corrupt henchmen. Phao, according to the same rumours, was being encouraged by the American Central Intelligence Agency to support the anti-Communist raids of the Kuomintang from their bases along Thailand's northern borders. It seemed logical that the Chinese troops in return would willingly carry out a kidnapping for Phao if asked.

Thoughts of this kind had been whirling through my mind repeatedly during my ride in pursuit of the opium caravan. Every time I pondered why my headman, Prapoth, should have been shot dead, a vivid image from the night of Poo Tongkam's lethal rampage returned. In my mind's eye I saw again the moment when Prapoth and Jutulak stood staring open-mouthed at one another in my tent. The headman had clearly overheard something of what Jutulak had told me about the death of King Ananda and his role at the palace. Only Prapoth himself could have passed on information to some higher Thai authority about Jutulak's previously unsuspected presence among my mahouts. The Chinese irregular troops carried field radios, so orders or requests could easily have been relayed for them to divert to our forest camp. There appeared to be no other logical explanation for the attack which had led to the cold-blooded murder of Prapoth and the seizure of Jutulak. So if the caravan reached its destination in Chiang Mai and Jutulak was handed over to local police or army commanders, it seemed certain that he would be transported rapidly south to one of Police-General Phao's many dungeons in Bangkok.

The thought that Jutulak might never see the light of day again if he entered a Bangkok jail cell helped me make up my mind. I took a jungle knife from my saddle pannier and quickly cut large twin blazes in a giant cotton tree beside the track. This prearranged sign would serve as an order to my baggage coolies to wait and make camp nearby when they reached the spot.

I estimated that they were three or four miles behind me and I had been marking trees regularly along my route with a single blaze to guide them. There were half a dozen coolies, a cook and a senior mahout in the party, marching with a spare pony and two elephants. One of the elephants was Poo Tongkam. At the last minute as they were preparing to load howdahs on two young 'travellers', I had on impulse ordered them to prepare Tongkam to take the place of one of them.

The best trained Asiatic elephants in my experience were like massive, jungle sheepdogs. They displayed natural wisdom as well as strength. They could be unusually sensitive for such gigantic animals, sometimes strangely nervous. But they never acted out their trained roles dully or mechanically. They were constantly alert like sheepdogs, always thinking intelligently, and the events of those past few days had made me feel that Poo Tongkam had become a close ally in the mystery surrounding Jutulak. Seated astride his neck in the river amidst the disintegrating log-jam, I had sensed the beginning of the best kind of intuitive understanding that can sometimes occur between a man and an animal. In a time of crisis in the jungle, I knew instinctively that such an understanding could be a priceless asset.

Although the clammy, shivering feelings that threatened to become a fever were increasing in frequency as I re-sheathed the jungle knife, I felt vastly reassured by the thought that Poo Tongkam was plodding along not far behind with my cook and coolies. The tents, sleeping cots and other necessary equipment he carried on his back would provide the vital protection I needed against the night hazards of the jungle. Even if the threatened fever worsened, I could try to fight it off in the rough comfort of the camp.

Moving out to the centre of the track, I checked to make sure the blazes on the giant cotton tree were clearly visible. Then after a last sweep of the distant evergreen forest with my binoculars, I mounted and urged my pony forward over the ridge, heading at a fast trot down into the small rice plain, still following the tracks of the mules.

ป ช

เดอะ บางกอก ซีเคร๊ท

THE
BANGKOK
SECRET

Chapter Seven

A white European spurring his pony at speed through the remote northern villages and rice fields caused the usual stir. Dressed in pith helmet, khaki bush shirt, shorts, puttees and jungle boots, I cut a curiously colonial figure in a country which alone in South-East Asia had never been colonised. What's more, even as I hurried across the plain, I was treated with the exaggerated respect that subjugated nationals of other countries in the region had once shown to their foreign over-lords.

'Good day, Master,' intoned almost every peasant I passed, speaking the Lao dialect which is heard everywhere in the north. Often from the side of the path they salaamed in my direction, bowing their heads over their joined palms as they would have done for any jungle wallah they encountered from a foreign teak company. This habitual public veneration slowed me up, heightening my impatience and increasing my sense of frustration at not being able to sight my quarry. Whenever I stopped and dismounted to hunt frantically for traces of the opium caravan's passage, humble, deferential offers of help were immediately forthcoming.

'May I be of service to the Master?' murmured peasant boys and local elders alike when small crowds gathered in the dusty village streets or between the paddy fields. 'What is the Master searching for so earnestly? We can surely assist.' They took in my lathered pony and my perspiring face but still smiled the simple, joyful smiles which have become Thailand's enduring trademark.

'I am seeking the trail of the mules that passed earlier,' I told them, speaking carefully in Lao. 'I must deliver a message urgently to someone travelling with the caravan.'

They continued smiling, although it was clear from their eyes that they were greatly puzzled. Why should a lordly white representative from one of the highly respected teak companies be pursuing hard-bitten outlaw bands of Chinese soldiers? Hadn't the teak companies for decades sent white masters marching proudly across the jungle-covered mountains accompanied, like royalty, by trains of baggage elephants, local bearers, cooks, mahouts and coolies? Hadn't the European jungle wallahs always been polite, almost regal, in their manner, speaking fractured Lao and respecting local customs? And weren't the Chinese soldiers, on the other hand, little more than foreign bandits, to be avoided like the plague? Didn't they carry ugly war weapons wherever they travelled? And didn't they constantly smuggle and barter opium in order to survive and carry on a strange and brutal war across the northern borders into China? All these questions obviously tingled in their minds – but they continued smiling nevertheless and all of them waved their arms helpfully towards the south.

'The mules headed that way, Master,' they said cheerfully. 'Towards the *pa dum* – the black forest. You must go very carefully in that region, Master. It will be dark soon.'

'I shall mark the trail where it enters the *pa dum*, then return to my camp until dawn,' I told them, motioning with my head towards the ridge from which I had descended. 'I think that is the wisest course.'

'Yes, Master, that is the wisest course, indeed,' they responded, watching with further puzzlement as I shivered involuntarily. 'Good luck, Master.'

In those early March days of 1955 the mock-colonial, jungle-wallah era in northern Thailand was already drawing to a close. It had seen its heyday between the two world wars when a number of foreign companies were licensed to harvest teak from the wild mountainsides. In 1960 Thailand's forests were to be nationalised and then the last white forest managers would disappear for ever from the tangled teak trails. For me change was to come sooner and more dramatically – precipitated by my impulsive decision to try to rescue Jutulak.

But I didn't know this as I remounted my pony and rode on anxiously across the plain that afternoon. My thoughts were fixed obsessively on the mountain and jungle landscape that lay ahead and the angle of the sun which was sinking fast into the western uplands.

I had some knowledge of the area from a 'girdling' visit made several years before. Teak trees had to be killed two or three years prior to felling because they didn't float when green. So a girdle of the outer sapwood, three or four feet above the ground, was always cut away in advance. This exposed the red-brown heart of the tree and the wood became dry and buoyant by the time it was cut. Working with my coolie teams I had girdled several hundred trees on the mountainsides above that plain where the jungle ranged from scrub to dense giant bamboo. But I knew that unusually large patches of *pa dum* – 'black forest' – had also interlaced themselves into the surrounding valleys and hillsides.

In those dense evergreen jungles, I remembered, vast trees festooned with dark, fleshy leaves screened out almost all daylight. Mosquitoes swarmed amidst thorn bushes and creepers bristling with their own natural spikes; a foul odour of rotting vegetation had also invaded my nostrils at every step. Large tracts of *pa dum* are more frequently encountered in central and southern Thailand. In the north it is usually found in smaller belts. But the strange twilight of the 'black forest' around that rice plain had been particularly unnerving, I recalled as I rode on towards it, because it stretched a long way south, unbroken often for many miles.

Helped by the deferential peasants of the plain, I tracked the caravan without too much difficulty to the fringes of the jungle's strange twilight zone. The mules had entered by means of a narrow, little-used trail and my pony baulked at first from following them into the fetid gloom. But I urged him on and rode in among the trees for two or three hundred yards, checking the ground and stopping occasionally to cut a blaze in a tree with my jungle knife.

In the heat of the day it was sometimes refreshing to escape the burning rays of the sun and enter the cool shade of the 'black forest'. But with darkness approaching rapidly the silent shadows beneath the close-packed evergreens were more ominous than usual. Mosquitoes rose in clouds around my head and gradually my shivering, which had previously been intermittent, became continuous. I decided I needed to turn and spur back to camp as quickly as possible but at the moment of wheeling my pony, it reared abruptly on its hind legs, whinnying and neighing loudly with fright.

I fought to control the terrified animal as it bucked and plunged. From the corner of my eye I could see a sinuous shadow swaying in the middle of the track along which we needed to pass to return to the rice plain. I knew then that my efforts to control the horse were futile. We were in the threatening presence of a hamadryad, the most fearsome poisonous snake in northern Thailand. Almost all other snakes, I knew from a decade of experience in the jungle, slithered away from contact with humans. Only the hamadryad invariably stood its ground – but what was worse, if its eggs were near, it could be relied on to strike aggressively and with great speed.

Within seconds the pony had become hopelessly crazed with fear and I grabbed desperately at the butt of my Springfield rifle, jerking it from its carrying holster as I fell backwards out of the saddle. The pony, freed of my weight, lunged sideways and crashed through the dense undergrowth, still whinnying piteously. It managed to regain the track twenty yards beyond the snake, then fled headlong towards the plain. My fall knocked the wind from me and for a moment or two I couldn't move. When I did scramble to my knees I found myself staring at the swaying snake from a distance of only two or three yards.

There was enough light for me to see the outline of its long, black body streaked faintly with white. Its coils curved away into the undergrowth but the oblate, hooded head that had led us to call the snake 'king cobra' was raised, ready to strike. Without moving the rest of my body I groped behind me with my right hand for the rifle which had fallen from my grasp as I hit the ground. All the time, by instinct, I kept my eyes fixed intently on the snake, hoping that somehow this posture might discourage it from attacking.

At all costs I knew I had to avoid sudden movements. The hamadryad, according to jungle lore, could move as swiftly as a galloping horse over short distances and its venom was known to be particularly deadly. Escape on foot in either direction was therefore out of the question. There was no option left but to try to kill the snake and the moment my searching hand made contact with the stock of the double-barrelled Springfield, I began drawing it slowly into a position where I could lift it to my shoulder.

In those fateful moments, a peculiar calm descended on me. Only a matter of feet away, the head of the hamadryad was swaying very slowly from side to side, as if it too was gathering its strength, waiting for the right moment. Its evil mouth was open but no sound came from between the narrow jaws. Silence gripped that entire sector of jungle as if every creature within earshot was holding its breath. Even my feverish shivering had suddenly ceased. This strange clarity of mind, perhaps induced by the adrenalin of fear, seemed to slow down the passage of time as well as the movements of myself and the snake.

In the act of lifting the rifle from the ground I had ample time to reflect on all the consequences that might flow from my actions. Would any shot I fired be heard across the silent jungle by the Chinese troops camped with the opium caravan? If they heard gunfire, would they dash to the scene? If I failed in my attempt to kill the hamadryad, would Jutulak's fate as well as my own be decided by that failure? In the end would the king cobra's lethal venom set an ironic seal on the secret of the 'King's Death Case'?

I was still kneeling and adjusting my grip on the Springfield behind my right hip when I saw the hamadryad ready itself to strike. Its head stopped swaying and for an instant became utterly still. I knew then I would not have the chance to get the rifle to my shoulder. My right hand had already found the trigger-guard and I had curled the fingers of my left hand around the barrel. From this position I thrust the Springfield suddenly towards the snake. At the selfsame instant it made its lunge, striking directly at the muzzle.

I squeezed the trigger in desperation, trying to struggle upright and away from the snake in the same moment. The Springfield recoiled sharply in my outstretched hands and this momentum helped send me staggering backwards, off balance. The snake, wounded but not disabled by the blast, threshed and writhed as it pursued me. Coiling and uncoiling by turns, it still seemed to be advancing in hideous slow motion. To prevent myself falling I clutched wildly at an overhanging creeper and after regaining my balance pressed the butt of the rifle into my right shoulder. Then from point-blank range I emptied the second barrel between the eyes of the hideous creature.

I knew that if I failed to kill the snake this time I would not have a chance to reload. But to my overwhelming relief I saw my second shot had blown off its head. The snake's long body, after jerking spasmodically on the track, came to rest twitching slightly, then finally lay still.

For some moments my shots continued to echo eerily through the silent jungle, the sound bouncing back and forth amongst the close-packed trees. Looking down at the motion-less coils of the snake, which stretched to all of fifteen feet, the tension drained out of me in a rush. My stomach heaved and I leaned against a tree, retching uncontrollably; almost immediately I began shuddering convulsively again.

By now there was little or no light filtering through the evergreen foliage from the darkening sky. Night was falling with customary sub-tropical suddenness, bringing with it new, unseen threats. I began to worry I might collapse before I could get out of that belt of ominous black forest. If I did I knew nobody would come looking for me before dawn next day. Stepping warily over the remains of the dead hamadryad, I began to head back towards the open plain, moving as fast as I could in an unsteady, lurching run.

ນ ໝ

เดอะ บางกอก ซีเคร็ท

THE
BANGKOK
SECRET

Chapter Eight

My body burned like fire and my head ached as though it would burst. But as always during the onset of malarial fever my skin remained agonisingly hot and dry. The palsied shuddering of my limbs was continuing relentlessly too, despite the weight pressing down on them. Lying prostrate on my back I heard the night sounds of the jungle as though at a great distance: a tiger roared faintly, an isolated bird screeched a strangled warning. After a further long period of silence a large body crashed and turned somewhere in a faraway bamboo thicket.

Then an elephant trumpeted softly nearer at hand. The sound had a gentle, reflective quality and I opened my eyes. Perhaps I had fallen into an uneasy sleep for a few seconds because I had difficulty at first in focusing. Eventually through a gap in the tent flaps I saw the glow of fire. Beyond the circle of light the dim outline of Poo Tongkam's great head and tusks became gradually visible. Tethered to a tree, he was stripping leaves from its lowest branches with his trunk.

Watching the leisured, rhythmic movements of the elephant as it fed helped calm me. I was stretched out helplessly on my camp-bed under a heavy mountain of blankets, my mind as feverish as my shivering body. Desperate to induce the great sweat that could lead to recovery, I had already swallowed fifteen grains of quinine and a similar amount of aspirin.

Malaria in its many guises had always been a common occupational hazard for white jungle wallahs. At the very worst the fever it induced could be fatal; at best it disabled a man for an unpredictable number of hours, days or weeks. I was no exception to the rule, having suffered half a dozen attacks of varying severity over the previous ten years. For me the onset of sweating had always been preceded by a painful, long-drawn-out period of uncertainty. This time my urgent need to resume pursuit of the opium caravan heightened the physical and mental agony of waiting.

To my inexpressible relief, on staggering out of the 'black forest' at dusk I had met a group of Lao peasants who were patiently holding my frightened pony. They had recaptured it in a rice paddy only half a mile from the edge of the *pa dum*. I was able to summon enough energy to reward them with a handful of coins before slumping into the saddle and the pony had found his own way back up the ridge.

My relief turned to joy on seeing that my coolies had already pitched my tent. They had also constructed leaf shelters for themselves and lit a fire. As soon as I slid from the pony's back I called feebly for my 'boy'. Within seconds he came running with a medicine chest, my thickest clothes and all the blankets that had been brought on the elephants. After struggling into flannel shirts, two pairs of English pyjamas and a tennis sweater I had collapsed shuddering on to the camp-bed. The 'boy' had heaped the blankets high around me, lit an oil lamp and hovered silently nearby with a concerned expression on his dark face.

In an attempt to hasten the sweat I ordered him to bring me several mugs of near-scalding filtered drinking water. I gulped down one after the other, burning my throat in the process. This had helped raise my temperature still higher – but the surface of my whole body remained as dry as tinder. In my mind the battle to survive the fever was becoming synonymous with the race against time to save Jutulak. I knew if I was to stand any chance of overhauling the caravan and attempting a rescue, I had to throw off the sickness before morning.

I took a further fifteen grains of quinine and ordered the waiting boy to add the fibre rugs from the tent floor to the pile of blankets covering me. My body temperature seemed to rise again, threatening to stifle me. But still not one drop of sweat oozed from my pores.

I began to feel panic rising inside me. I wanted desperately to throw off my covers, to escape at all costs from the unbearable, suffocating heat. As I lay there in agony I began to wonder fearfully whether this intense bout of fever might prove fatal. Over the years white jungle wallahs from the teak companies had frequently died from malaria. Some succumbed in England years after leaving the forests. Usually the illness flared up after a chill or some sudden burst of debilitating exercise.

I knew my own rashness in riding non-stop through the heat of the day, forcing myself to the limits of exhaustion after a punishing morning, had helped bring on the attack. After rounding up my frightened mahouts and setting them to work, I had ridden hard for an hour through the forest back to my residential compound. I had originally taken over the work at that remote forest camp myself because one of my English forest assistants had fallen ill with dysentery. As I'd hoped, he was well enough to take charge again and I roused him from his comfortable bungalow to order him back into action. Then I had ridden into the village to report the attack by the Chinese troops to the local Thai gendarmes.

Their simple, peasant faces had betrayed their uneasiness as they listened to my report. The Chinese irregular troops were obviously beyond the law; simple village gendarmes could take no effective action against bands of tough, well-armed foreign soldiers. This confirmed what I already instinctively knew: Jutulak in his new plight could expect no help from anybody except me.

Taking a fresh pony I had ridden hard back to the camp ahead of the forest assistant. I gave immediate orders to the deputy headman to load baggage animals and select coolies to form a small camp party to follow in my wake. After the exhilarating eight-mile dawn journey to retrieve Poo Tongkam, the shock of the attack and the trips to and from the compound, I was already tired. But I had gulped down a hasty tiffin of cold chicken and rice prepared by my cook and set out to track the opium caravan through the noonday heat without taking any rest.

There had been no time to seek approval for the decision from my immediate superior, the district manager for the company's north-west region based at Nakon Lampang. Sending a telegraph message from my office and awaiting a reply would have delayed me several more hours. Besides which, explaining my motives to him in a convincing way would have been impossible.

But work in all other parts of my forest was virtually complete and that had helped me reach my hasty decision. With the onset of the hot season which lasts from February to May, all elephants were customarily moved to rest camps for three months. So taking Poo Tongkam away from the camp would not interfere unduly with its remaining work. All felled teak had to be dragged to the safety of the nearest creek to avoid the risk of destruction in hot season fires and I knew that my forest assistant could complete that task easily in forty-eight hours. In any event, I had reasoned, if I were to overtake the opium caravan, it had to be done quickly; and if successful I'd be back at the company compound within days.

As I continued to shudder beneath my covers I tried to reassure myself that my thinking and my actions had been logical and rational. There had never seemed to be any choice but to do what I had done. Yet with my body racked alternately by fierce sensations of burning and freezing, I realised suddenly that I was jeopardising my entire livelihood and even putting my life at risk in the hazardous venture I had so impulsively undertaken. While I wrestled mentally with this fear, the intermittent buzzing in my ears which had accompanied the fever grew suddenly louder; then abruptly it ceased altogether and a frightening cloak of total silence enveloped the tent and the jungle outside.

I knew that over-large doses of quinine could sometimes induce temporary deafness. But even this knowledge could not entirely dispel the sense of panic which was threatening to engulf me. I felt a surge of irrational fear that all the things which had been a familiar part of my life for more than ten years were on the point of disintegrating and dissolving into nothing. In a foolish effort to prevent this fear becoming reality I gripped the wooden sides of the camp-bed tightly with both hands. At the same time I yelled frantically at the top of my voice for my 'boy'. But I heard absolutely nothing of my own shout; the new, terrifying silence surrounding me remained complete.

When the 'boy' entered the tent I could tell from the expression on his dark face that he was frightened by my appearance. Although I could not hear my own voice, I ordered him to bring me more boiled drinking water. When he reappeared a minute later I sat up and gulped down the steaming liquid as fast as I could. But still it had no effect. With my fingertips I touched my brow. It seemed to burn like a tin roof at noon; there was still not the faintest sign of sweat breaking out and as soon as I'd finished drinking I shouted again for the 'boy' to bring more hot water.

Beyond the orange firelight outside the tent at that moment I again caught sight of Poo Tongkam's massive outline. He had stopped feeding and possibly in response to my wild shout, he turned his head slowly to stare towards the tent. The firelight gleamed on the ivory of his long, curved tusks, just as light from the spirit medium's smoking torches had done on that fatal night by the jungle shrines to the Crystal Prince and the Lord of the White Hat.

Perhaps it was this awe-inspiring sight of a huge elephant outlined starkly against the darkened forest that suddenly awakened imagined, primeval powers of perception inside me. Whatever the cause, it was from that instant that my fevered brain began to register and relay intangible messages about powerful, unseen spirit forces. Ancient, evil and malign, swirling massively around the vortex of a tormented, possibly royal soul, these demonic energies appeared to be closing inexorably around the tent and its jungle clearing.

บ ช

THE
BANGKOK
SECRET

Chapter Nine

With the suddenness of a dam breaking, all the ordinary things around me seemed to take on new and sinister significance. The folding table and chair at which I normally took my meals beneath the front fly; the long chair on which I rested and smoked in the cool of the evening; the tin bath and metal washbasin set up for ablutions in the space between the inner and outer canvas walls – to each of these objects in turn my eyes were drawn, slowly and deliberately, as though acting under compulsion from some irresistible, unseen force. The metal and wood alike seemed to glow with their own individual inner fire as though revealing for the first time that they too, like everything else in and on the earth, was possessed of living, throbbing spiritual energy.

The emptied elephant howdahs propped outside against one canvas wall, the coolies' carrying baskets still containing tinned and bottled foods, the scuffed trunk in which I kept spare clothing close to the bed – as my gaze ranged over them, these objects, too, seemed to vibrate with their own ominous vitality. Even the canvas walls of the tent appeared to be expanding and contracting gently, pulsing with a mysterious, disembodied life of their own.

In part of my fevered brain I tried desperately to rationalise these alarming sensations. I must be suffering hallucinations, I told myself, brought on by my persistent high temperature and temporary loss of hearing. Or I must be dreaming. To test these theories I pinched the flesh of my left forearm hard with my right hand. To my relief I felt it clearly.

More likely then, I conjectured, prolonged high temperature had triggered in my brain an exaggerated level of sensory perception. In which case I needed to adjust calmly to this new intensity. I was probably making the experience more frightening, I told myself, by imagining connections with the all-pervasive spirit world of Thai culture which struck terror into the hearts of many of the country's people.

I made up my mind to concentrate hard on something mundane to restore a sane perspective. Leaning over the side of my camp-bed I peered at one of the four shallow tins of kerosene in which each of its legs were planted. The kerosene was there to prevent stinging ants from climbing the bedframe. Usually one or two ants were to be seen squirming in their death throes in the yellow liquid. But again my senses were invaded by the same strange feelings of intensity and significance. Slowly my gaze was drawn to each leg of the bed in succession as though my head were being turned forcibly by a giant hand. Instead of seeing one or two long-tentacled ants dying in the kerosene I saw that each tin was encrusted to a depth of several inches with dead insects. Live ants were still crawling into the tins in large numbers and shifting laboriously across the rafts of corpses to mount the legs of the bed.

I cried out involuntarily at the sight – but because of my deafness I heard nothing of my own cry. Instead, inside my head the long-drawn howling of a dog began. My unease deepened at once because I knew that according to northern Thai folklore, dogs howled when tormented spirits were passing. I raised my hands to block my ears, frantic to stifle the sound. But in my head the howling of the dog continued as loudly as before.

Watching the stinging ants climb across the kerosene and hearing the dog howl caused a stark, primal fear to stir within me. That part of my brain athrob with heightened perception interpreted what I was seeing. Symbolised before my eyes, it said, was the cosmic struggle between life and death, goodness and evil, light and darkness – and the battle was ending in defeat for the sane, rational forces of goodness and light.

Looking up I saw that the fire in the centre of the clearing was guttering. The dome of blackness beyond the front flaps was becoming ever more dense and it seemed suddenly to move closer. My growing fear turned with jolting suddenness to a profound, unutterable terror. The dark abyss, man's first and deepest dread, seemed to be reaching into my feebly lit canvas sanctuary, threatening to bring with it unknown spirit forces of enormous power.

My terror bore an invisible part of me effortlessly upward to the low ridge of the tent. From there, close beside the flickering oil lamp, I looked down. I found I could see myself distantly, as though from a great height. Still prostrate and shuddering beneath the camp-bed covers, I was a small, vulnerable figure staring wild-eyed towards the front opening.

Deeply shocked, my watching self seemed to explode. Expanding rapidly, I became first the dim, smoking oil lamp, then the rustling green canvas of the tent walls and ceiling. I felt as the lamp and the walls felt, could see as they saw from every side and angle. In quick succession my energy and essence merged further with that of the table and chairs, the battered trunk of clothes, the washbasin, the pungent kerosene, even the ants, living, dead and dying. For an immeasurable span of time I became every object in the tent, both separately and jointly.

Simultaneously I saw and felt all things from all points of view: the searing heat of the oil flame licking at the lamp's glass funnel, the agony of the ants choking horribly in the kerosene, the emptiness of the long chair, the strain of the camp-bed bearing the shaking human body. I was the coolness of the tin bath, the hardness of the wood and metal howdahs, the suppleness of the woven bamboo in the coolies' baskets as well as the anguished flesh and blood of the man trembling in ignorance at the centre of it all. I was all of these things, all these things were me, and we were all connected, without separate definition, indivisibly one.

Like swift-spreading ripples on a pond, my watching, intangible self continued to expand outwards. I could still see my physical body lying far below on the camp-bed – but within moments, I knew, my separate identity would come to an end. My true essence would flow out beyond the confines of the tent to merge into the wide blackness of the night; I would become an indistinguishable part of the jungle, its trees, its wild creatures. But worst of all I suddenly knew with great certainty I would also be swallowed irretrievably into that vast dimension of malevolent forces which invisibly enshrouded

Thailand – the spirit hordes of forest, field and river, the *phra phum chao thi* that haunted every village and city home, the legion of tormented, wandering souls who had died sudden, violent deaths through the ages.

Suddenly the howling of the solitary dog that had never ceased was augmented by the awful wailing and shrieking of a million other disembodied voices. The pandemonium of noise grew louder as if a door into another world had been abruptly opened. Among them, at the heart of the maelstrom, there seemed to be one especially anguished spirit. There was a suggestion too of familiarity; Jutulak, Poo Tongkam and the forest medium flickered briefly in my consciousness. Could Jutulak, flying in the face of all rationality, have been right? Could a tormented royal spirit have taken possession of a rogue elephant in the heart of the northern jungles? Could that be what I was sensing? A feeling of all-knowingness had grown in me as my essence continued flowing out to merge with my surroundings. I knew instinctively I was about to find out beyond any remaining shred of doubt. The alien realm I was about to enter quite certainly held the answers to all enigmas.

There was one last, terrible moment of trembling at the brink. Until then, all that had happened had appeared ineluctable; I had seemed to be caught fast in an inevitable, irresistible progress. But in the act of contemplating the unthinkable horrors that lay ahead, a small spark of resistance was ignited. Without knowing how, I fanned it desperately.

It glowed into life in the instant that my watching self flowed beyond the confines of the tent into the black night outside. The clamouring, wailing forces tore at me, trying to drag me into their midst, pulling me down towards the hostile jungle. But the new determination to resist somehow catapulted me free and the banshee shrieking gave way at once to a different kind of uproar. Equally loud but comfortingly hoarse and familiar, it was rising from British throats.

My feelings of terror and dread evaporated in an instant. Smiles of pleasure wreathed my face as I galloped hard across a broad stretch of greensward on Minto, my favourite pony. I was twirling a polo mallet in my right hand and all around me galloped a gaggle of yelling, pith-helmeted, British jungle wallahs. They were all forest assistants and managers for the handful of European teak companies that had permanent quarters and office compounds in Nakon Lampang. Urged on by a small vociferous crowd of other white Europeans, we were pursuing the fast-rolling ball towards a set of white goal-posts as though our lives depended on it.

Swerving Minto expertly, I swung my mallet and cracked the ball accurately between the posts. This stimulated the male spectators to a wild bout of cheering. All this I watched simultaneously from above and from amongst them, first through the eyes of one, then another, then my own. Some men jubilantly swigged champagne, others puffed grandly on cigars and pipes. All were ostentatiously in high good humour, enjoying the traditional 'Christmas meeting' at Lampang for which all Europeans trooped gladly out of the jungle once a year at the height of the cool season.

The polo match gave way first to rowdy evening games of bridge, then wild drinking parties. Large quantities of alcohol were consumed. I joined uproariously in the laughter, I relished the cigar smoke, the ale, the wines. I enjoyed the hearty company of other English jungle wallahs – Oxbridge sporting 'blues', young ex-army and ex-navy officers, public school men – all of them liberally imbued with a sense of adventure.

Events swirled through and into one another. With surprise I recognised the laughing faces of men long since dead or retired. One, a good friend, had died of malaria in the jungle years before. Suddenly at midnight on New Year's Eve he appeared amongst the dinner-jacketed crowd on the compound lawn. Dapper and smiling, he wore a silk hat tipped rakishly over one eye and when another whipped it from his head, he merely grinned good-naturedly. Circling my shoulder with one arm he formed up a rowdy rugger scrum. A fast and furious game ensued. The silk hat was deliberately and hilariously ruined. Each man in turn sprawled to the ground, helpless with laughter, until I too fell to the grass, gasping for breath, clutching the torn and crumpled hat to my chest.

From out of the crowd the same friend appeared again, perspiring, jacketless, his tie and collar awry. His face was suddenly that of a cadaver and for a moment he stood looking grimly down at me. Then from behind his back he produced a frosted bottle of champagne. Shaking it furiously, he drew the cork with his teeth and drenched me with a fierce stream of chilled foam. Only when I gasped in protest and tried to roll aside did he let out a delighted whoop of laughter.

His laughter was still pealing in my tent when the first sweat leapt to my brow. Within moments my face was streaming; beneath the blankets my body quickly became drenched with perspiration. My watching self, hovering beside the smoking oil lamp, saw the 'boy' run into the tent a few minutes later. The 'boy' exclaimed with delight, then helped me off the bed and into the long chair. After a minute or two he returned bearing a large towel and hot tea. With quiet efficiency he emptied and refilled the four kerosene tins then remade the bed while I dried myself. Still sweating slightly but dressed in clean clothes, I climbed back into the small bed. Sinking slowly downward, my watching self rejoined me and gently surrendered its separate identity.

From the comfort of the bed I glanced out between the tent flaps. The fire in the centre of the clearing had been built up again and was blazing brightly. Poo Tongkam was motionless in the shadows, seemingly asleep. I heard sticks in the fire crack and splutter as they burned and I realised with relief that my hearing was restored.

Inside the tent there was no longer any sign of stinging ants. All around me the everyday objects seemed mundane and ordinary once more. Feeling bewildered and weak I finished the tea, put down the mug and fell back against the pillows into an exhausted sleep.

บ ช

เดอะ บางกอก ซีเคร็ท

THE
BANGKOK
SECRET

Chapter Ten

I caught sight of the rear mules of the opium caravan for the first time late the following afternoon. They were moving southward at an unhurried pace along the crest of a treeless escarpment that curved around the rim of a deep, jungle-choked valley. Silhouetted against the brightness of the sky, they were perhaps six miles ahead of us, heading in the direction of a stark limestone crag shaped like a human skull which dominated the far horizon. We had just emerged from an arduous trek through dense bamboo jungle and I was seated behind Poo Tongkam's head, still feeling dazed and weak from the after-effects of the fever.

Because of my condition I had decided not to risk riding ahead of the camp party on a pony. Although travelling with the baggage elephants and coolies was slower, it seemed a safer and wiser course in my enfeebled state. The senior mahout whom I had made responsible for Poo Tongkam had acted as chief tracker in my place throughout the day, hurrying on in front to call back questions or confirm each change of direction made by the caravan.

Once or twice, because my concentration lapsed easily, we had taken the wrong route and become lost along narrow paths which had become overgrown and impassable. Often the baggage coolies and my camp boy had been forced to hack through the fast-growing bamboo thickets with their long jungle knives to help us find our way back quickly to the main trail. Because my strength had not fully returned I could only sit and watch them helplessly from my place astride Poo

Tongkam's head. But I had been greatly relieved as the day progressed to find that the fever showed no sign of returning.

During the easier stages of the march my thoughts had returned again and again to the eerie traumas I had suffered in the night. Turning the haunting memories over in my mind as I jolted hazily along on Poo Tongkam, I knew with a terrible certainty that I had come very close to dying. Although I had endured numerous bouts of fever in the past, never before had I been struck in that fashion. Hallucinations were not uncommon with bad attacks of malaria; but the vivid intensity of what I had experienced as life drained from me lingered throughout the day in every cell and membrane of my aching body.

All the rules of logic and rationality around which my English education had been built cautioned me to dismiss the experiences as nothing more than fantastical, delirious dreams – but still some part of my mind stubbornly refused to follow its training. I could not free myself from the conviction that for fleeting moments I had hovered above an unimaginable brink. What lay beyond would remain for ever indefinable in the clear light of day. But after that long, shuddering night in the jungle I knew I would never again easily dismiss ancient belief in the existence of a primeval spirit world. Neither did Jutulak's fears about the anguished spectre of a dead king any longer seem quite so wild and outlandish. These new feelings also heightened the urgency of our pursuit of the opium mules and although still feeling light-headed I was glad that I had regained enough energy to remain shakily upright on the elephant.

The tail of the opium caravan was first spotted by the senior mahout, Satharn, whom I had entrusted with the tracking. He had run ahead and climbed to the top of a rise to make a survey as we emerged from the dense bamboo thickets. Turning almost at once, he sprinted back in my direction, grinning delightedly and waving an arm towards the distant ridge.

'Master, the mules are not far ahead now,' he panted. 'I can see some of them.'

'Well done, Satharn!' I felt new strength flood back at the news. 'You've followed the trail with great skill.'

Applying pressure with my shoeless feet I urged Tongkam to accelerate. He moved smoothly forward at once, responding as much to the new vigour in our voices as to the foot signals. He clambered rapidly to the crest of the rise and after ordering him to halt, I pulled my binoculars from their case and focused them on the distant ridge.

The unmistakable sight of half a dozen heavily laden pack mules winding towards the summit of a trail along which the others had already passed sent an intense thrill of satisfaction through me. My self-imposed mission to attempt the rescue of Jutulak had for more than forty-eight hours erased all other topics from my mind. For reasons I would have found impossible to explain to another Englishman, pursuit of the opium caravan had taken on the nature of a life-and-death obsession. I had given no thought to how the remaining work might be going at the camp we had deserted so abruptly. Or what other matters might have needed attention elsewhere in my stretch of forest. Neither had I spent a moment worrying how my superiors in Nakon Lampang and even Bangkok might be reacting to my rash decision.

They would, I knew, disapprove strongly of my turning my back on all my other work and responsibilities. They would have viewed the attack on the camp and the killing of the headman as a very serious matter, to be handled with diplomacy and tact; but they would probably have been astonished to learn that my decision to 'desert my post' and take the law into my own hands had been prompted by nothing more than the apparent abduction of a single native mahout.

If I had attempted to explain the background and the reasons for my actions, I imagined they would have raised their eyebrows very sharply indeed and begun to wonder whether too many years in the tropical forests weren't having an adverse effect on the soundness of my mind. I suspect that, if they could, they would have ordered me to undergo an immediate medical examination, instructing the company doctor to probe carefully for signs of strain and possible mental breakdown. Whatever the outcome of the venture, I knew that before very long I would have to face searching enquiries into my conduct. A teak forest manager's prime duty was to ensure the profitability and good order of operations in his region. After that, he should do everything possible to preserve the company's good name and reputation. My actions, I was fully aware, served neither of those aims directly.

With the caravan of marauding mules in sight for the first time, I realised I was about to pass the point of no return. Yet still I gave no real thought to abandoning the chase, which was clearly dangerous and not a little foolhardy. Through my field glasses I could see that, as they neared the top of the ridge, a dozen or more armed Nationalist Chinese troops were marching as a rearguard behind the last pack animals. How I might find and free a prisoner being held by such a tough, well-armed military force I had absolutely no idea. There had been no time to make any plan. My greatest anxiety had been not to lose track of Jutulak and his captors. If the opium smugglers succeeded in carrying him out of the jungles, I knew that all would be lost. Jutulak would disappear rapidly into Police-General Phao's dreaded jail network, taking whatever secret knowledge he had of King Ananda's death with him. The next step, to the grave, would not be far distant.

Whenever I had put my mind to the problem of the rescue, I was only too painfully aware of the fact that I had no great military experience to call on. During my comparatively brief wartime service with the XIVth Army's elephant companies in Burma I had been involved in nothing more than minor skirmishes with Japanese patrols which had always been anxious to disengage quickly and move on. Most importantly perhaps from that period as a junior officer, I had learned to make up my mind quickly and give decisive orders. At Cambridge I had gained my rugby blue as a wing-three-quarter when the University XV was happy to employ a bludgeon rather than a rapier in my position. Although possessed of a reasonable turn of speed I had not been cast by nature in the mould of a high-stepping lightweight. I was accustomed to charging on full-bloodedly, full steam ahead, once I had fixed on my course, trusting more in the power of my own physical momentum than subtleties of footwork or swerve.

As I sat on Poo Tongkam's head at the edge of the escarpment that afternoon, I was still close enough to those exuberant, youthful days to be applying the same rough and ready principles of physical self-confidence. It was true that I had applied them effectively often enough in the hard, practical work of the teak forests. Indeed the more humorous wags among my fellow jungle wallahs liked to say that I had just the right excess of brawn over brains to make me the ideal candidate for my job. But brawn alone, I knew, would not be sufficient against well-armed troops. And as far as weapons were concerned, I was carrying only two pistols and a pair of Springfield shotguns. So I had little else in which to trust except the surprise and momentum of my headlong dash in the caravan's wake.

What role Satharn, the other mahout and the baggage coolies would play in the next stage, was unknown to them – and me. They had asked no direct questions about my ultimate purpose; on the journey they had continued to carry out their daily tasks dutifully and with the same quiet loyalty that they showed in the teak forests. I was acutely aware that I could not ask them to endanger their lives in order to assist in a risky venture well outside the scope of their normal work – unless they volunteered to do so. When all was said and done, I had no alternative but to wait and improvise when the moment of decision arrived.

While these thoughts were surfacing one after another in my mind I used my binoculars to inspect the region spread out before me, scrutinising it slowly, section by section. The mule caravan, on emerging from the belt of bamboo jungle, had obviously turned eastward in a wide detour so as to follow the broad trail along the rim of the open escarpment. Soon its commanders would have to decide whether to pass east or west of the great limestone crag lying directly ahead; for us, I realised with a stab of alarm, this decision would be crucial. It raised a new possibility that, just as we were congratulating ourselves on catching a first glimpse of our quarry, we might be about to lose its trail again in the darkness.

I calculated that if we followed the same easy route it would take us more than an hour and a half to reach the point where the mules were disappearing. By then the light would be fading fast. Fighting down a feeling of desperation I peered anxiously through the glasses again, concentrating on the densely forested valley that separated us from the rear of the caravan. After a long search I identified a narrow track which descended steeply below us to disappear among the trees. On the far edge of the valley I thought I detected traces of another narrow path winding up out of the tangled jungle towards the ridge over which the tail-end mules were plodding. Would it be wise to assume that the two tenuous trails joined to make one, I wondered?

If they did, and we could find our way rapidly across the valley, I felt it might be possible to reach the far ridge in half the time. If we got there before sunset, we could hope to discover where the caravan was camping for the night. But if we got lost or delayed in the steep-sided valley, if there was no single trail through its jungle, it seemed highly likely that we would lose contact with Jutulak and his captors, perhaps for the last time.

As I agonised over my decision I felt Satharn's eyes on me. A bachelor in his late twenties, he had handled elephants for the company for ten years or more. He was a hard-working, respectful Lao whose father before him had been a mahout for the company and I had chosen him for the journey because of his reputation for quiet reliability. While waiting for my orders he stood patiently beside Poo Tongkam, his expression as usual calm and trusting.

'Can you see a narrow track, Satharn – rising out of the jungle on the far side of the valley?' I asked at last in quiet desperation, handing down the binoculars to him.

Satharn looked long and carefully through the glasses, then returned them, his expression regretful. 'I can't be sure, Master.'

'Do you think there might be a single track that leads across to the other side? . . . There's a way down, from here, look!'

Satharn peered round again conscientiously, then shook his head. 'It's hard to say, Master.'

'Do you think our elephants could climb down into the valley and up the other side in less than an hour – if we can find a path?'

'The elephants are tired, Master,' he replied after a pause. 'They have already come a long way today with very good loads. It would be best for them to follow the easier ridge track.'

I looked round at the second elephant, a female, who was standing silently behind us. At rest under her laden howdahs she was swaying slightly on her feet and her whole appearance suggested weariness. I had insisted that we start out soon after dawn, although I had felt very shaky then. I had kept halts for food and water to a minimum throughout the day and had often urged the elephants along at rates well above the three miles per hour which they found comfortable. I guessed that we had covered twenty miles all told through difficult country and the strain was clearly showing.

The coolies leading the two ponies had stopped a hundred yards to the rear. Ponies and elephants habitually caused unreasoning panic in one another and I always kept them well apart, in camp and on the move; but even at a distance I could see that men and horses alike were also tired. Beneath me Poo Tongkam himself was standing quiet and at ease; because of his exceptional size and strength he displayed no obvious ill-effects from the day's hard march and something in his calm, untroubled demeanour acted as a sudden spur of encouragement to me.

'Satharn, I think Poo Tongkam could do it! We could lighten his load a little. Transfer some of his baggage to the female, perhaps. Do you think it would work?'

The face of the mahout continued to register doubt. Looking towards the ridge I saw that the last of the mules had already disappeared from sight and I felt my sense of desperation grow. 'If we don't get over there before dusk, we could lose the caravan in the darkness. Will you at least give it a try – and come down through the valley with me?'

Satharn looked at me steadily for a moment; then he smiled politely. 'You may easily lose your way if you go down into the valley alone, Master – so it will be best if I come with you.'

Without fuss he called up several coolies and quickly supervised the transfer of as much baggage as possible from Poo Tongkam to the female elephant. A rendezvous point was agreed and within minutes the coolies, the second mahout and my camp boy were setting out again along the broad ridge trail. Relieved of a good part of his load, Poo Tongkam moved off with a new eagerness almost before I had given the signal, and Satharn followed behind.

The track leading into the valley proved to be very steep and narrow. But Poo Tongkam picked his way down the precipitous incline with the same remarkable nimbleness that he had displayed when negotiating the slippery river bank beside the log-jam. On the steepest sections he slowed up, lifted his head and fanned his ears as he had done at the river, seemingly sensing that in my weakened state I needed help to continue clinging to my precarious perch. When we reached the level ground of the valley bottom, he trumpeted once quietly. Then he lowered his tusks and trunk and sped towards the thick jungle without any urging at all from me.

บ ฌ

เดอะ บางกอก ซีเคร็ท

THE
BANGKOK
SECRET

Chapter Eleven

แอนโธนี เกรย์

แปลโดย

กุลวดี กฤษฎาภา

นุชนาฏ นอกนา ?อยา

My hands shook violently as I raised the binoculars to focus on a circle of firelit Chinese faces. My heart was thudding fast inside my chest, my palms were sweating and my mouth was dry. Although I was sprawled full-length on the ground amongst clumps of *kaing* grass, my legs suddenly felt as though they had turned to jelly.

I had been crawling through the darkness towards the fires for perhaps twenty minutes. Somewhere behind me Satharn and the junior mahout were standing by, restraining Poo Tong-kam and the female pack elephant by special leading ropes attached to their ears. I had ordered them to follow me and wait in concealment beyond the outer circle of sentries that had been deployed at fifty-yard intervals around the camp.

While slithering through the *kaing* grass and underbrush, taking every precaution to avoid detection, I had been utterly absorbed. Every nerve had been stretched taut in the effort to remain silent and unobserved. Near enough at last to see the dirt and sweat on the faces of the soldiers and their hill-tribe muleteers, all those nerves seemed to go into spasm at the same moment. My hands in particular trembled so violently that I dropped the binoculars. In an effort to regain my self-control I turned over and lay still on my back, breathing deeply and letting the night dew fall gently on my face from the leaves of overhanging trees. In the distance bullfrogs croaked; fireflies darted like wind-borne sparks among the tree-trunks and from a nearby thicket unseen cicadas were generating their mesmerising, high-pitched trill. After listening to these soothing night sounds for a minute or two, calm returned and I turned over again.

The troops, bivouacked at the foot of the limestone crag beside a fast-flowing creek, were seated around crackling fires only fifty yards away. They were smoking, talking in bursts, occasionally laughing. In the quietness of the night the harsh, staccato cadences of their language echoed back strangely from the rocky wall that reared up abruptly on the creek's far bank.

One or two of the soldiers had strung sheets of canvas between saplings to form rough shelters but most had simply laid out their bedrolls in the open. Pots were simmering over some fires and hill tribesmen squatted in groups around them, scooping boiled rice into their mouths with their hands. Others appeared to be quietly smoking opium in crude bamboo pipes.

Many of the soldiers still carried carbines slung across their backs but heavier weapons like 60 millimetre mortars and .50 calibre machine-guns had been stacked tidily beneath a tarpaulin. A few soldiers were stripping and cleaning their rifles, working methodically and silently away from the others. A handful had already wrapped themselves in their blankets and were stretched out on the ground close to the flames, snoring loudly.

Beyond the circle of light cast by the fires I could see a tent pitched against a jagged outcrop of rock. The caravan had broken up into half a dozen such bivouacs and it was the only tent of any kind to be seen. I had concluded that it must house the caravan commander; I had further deduced that any important prisoner would almost certainly be held under guard not far away. By this time I had crawled near enough to see the white sun shoulder-flashes of the nearest Kuomintang soldiers without binoculars – but nowhere in the clearing was there the faintest sign of a manacled prisoner.

Around the bivouac, ammunition boxes, sacks of raw opium and other bales and stores which had been unloaded had been dumped on the ground to form a rough, horseshoe-shaped rampart. Close by, twenty or thirty pack mules were tethered in lines, just as they were beside the other bivouacs that stretched along the bank of the creek. At either end of the horseshoe I could see that armed men had been posted as extra guards. The firelight glinted ominously on the steel bayonets fixed to their rifles but their bearing was sloppy; they were

170

smoking cigarettes, they yawned frequently and lolled in a slovenly manner against the stacks of stores they were guarding.

On noticing this, my spirits rose a little. Having crept into the midst of the heavily armed troops and their contraband opium, I had become acutely aware of just how insane my ambition was. Even if I could eventually locate Jutulak, my chances of freeing him seemed more remote than ever. The difficult crawl through the grass had itself wearied me again; finding no sign of a prisoner heightened the feeling of exhaustion and I wondered whether the wisest course might not be to try to creep silently away and retreat. As a counterweight to these negative thoughts, two visibly careless sentries was not much – but they encouraged a belief that my task might be easier once the soldiers and muleteers had fallen asleep.

As I lay there I reminded myself that the earlier risk I had taken in plunging across the bowl-shaped valley had paid handsome dividends. We had found that a number of well-trodden animal trails, invisible from the ridge above, had been bulldozed through the dense jungle by wild elephant herds. They all led to a creek which opened out into a placid pool in the heart of the valley. We had halted at the pool long enough for Poo Tongkam to drink and hose himself down with the cool, clear water. Greatly refreshed, he had lumbered onward with renewed energy, following the wild elephant tracks easily to the far side of the valley without needing much guidance from me. He had climbed steadily up the steep incline and we had crested the escarpment well before sunset. Hurrying over another similar watershed a mile further on, we had sighted the mule caravan again half an hour before darkness descended. It had already halted and through the field glasses I had watched the troops cutting down bushes and gathering dead wood, preparing to camp close to the foot of the forested crag of skull-shaped limestone.

Limp with exhaustion, I had called an immediate halt. After choosing a sheltered site below the watershed that would conceal our fires from the Chinese soldiers, I had collapsed on to a camp cot which Satharn unloaded from the elephant. With Poo Tongkam tethered securely to a giant teak, Satharn went forward on my orders to identify and mark a trail which after dark had led us indirectly to the camp. I had slept soundly for nearly two hours and felt much stronger when I awoke. By then Satharn had returned and the coolies with the second elephant had arrived and set up camp around me. After gulping down a hot meal of fried chicken I had called a hurried conference, then set off with the two elephants and the mahouts, using electric torches to find the way.

Both Satharn and the second mahout – a Lao boy of nineteen nicknamed Kit – had insisted that they must support me with the elephants, whatever I did. They said they liked and admired Jutulak as a mahout and a friend and therefore felt it was their duty to try to help. But in pledging their assistance they had admitted they would be very frightened – not of the troops or the wild animals but of the evil spirits they might encounter in the jungle after dark. Although, like the rest of the mahouts and camp coolies, they had never voiced their thoughts in my presence, I had been able to see that memories of the *kon song's* death and the destruction of the spirit shrines were still vivid in their minds.

The coolies and the camp boy, although similarly afraid, had volunteered to follow and remain beside the track at a safe distance from the caravan camp. There they would be available to help us if the rescue attempt was successful. I had thanked all of them with great sincerity and said that if anything happened to me, they should disperse and try to avoid the troops at all costs. When it got light they should make their way back to the company compound with the elephants and mahouts as best they could.

On coming in sight of the distant camp fires I had moved very cautiously ahead of the elephants. Fortunately the night was still and moonless; only faint starlight came from the sky, which provided enough deep shadow to make concealment easy. Also, because the soldiers had chosen to camp in the bend of the creek, the noise of the rushing water was loud enough to cover any faint sounds I made. I had located the outer ring of sentries by chance when one of the soldiers on duty coughed and spat loudly. Moving sideways with as much stealth as I could muster, I had circled the entire camp at a distance, reconnoitring each of the bivouacs in turn.

Later I had led Satharn and Kit to a hiding place near the bivouac surrounding the tent. Stationing the elephants and mahouts within earshot, I had carefully finalised a series of signals with them. Then I had set out on the long, exhausting crawl through the ring of sentries that had ended when I reached my place of concealment fifty yards from the camp fires, trembling like an aspen leaf.

The moment my nerves stopped jangling, I picked up the fallen binoculars again to double-check, one by one, the identity of each man visible in the firelight. I lingered carefully on every individual face, Chinese and hill tribesman alike, without finding one that bore the faintest resemblance to Jutulak. I swept the whole camp once more, very slowly, with the glasses but still could not detect any sign at all of a prisoner.

Feeling at a loss I turned my attention to the tent which had attracted me to that bivouac in the first instance. Because it had been pitched beyond the glow of the fires close to the creek, it was only partly visible in the shadow of the jagged outcrop of rock that rose above it to a height of fifteen feet. In the gloom beside the tent I could dimly see a radio operator bent over equipment set up on a folding table. Intermittent bursts of static reached my ears above the rushing of the stream, suggesting that messages were being transmitted and received. Although the flaps of the tent itself were closed, an oil lamp flickered faintly within its khaki canvas walls and I held the binoculars steady on it for fifteen minutes or more. But nobody entered, nobody approached, nobody emerged — and all the time the front flaps remained tantalisingly impenetrable.

I lowered the glasses, cursing softly to myself, and lay staring helplessly towards the fires. More of the troops and tribesmen were rolling themselves in blankets and settling themselves for the night, placing their rifles carefully on the ground within reach. Soon most of them were sleeping but as I watched, I saw a fully dressed soldier carrying a rifle step suddenly into the firelight from the deep shadows behind the tent.

He walked yawning towards a camp fire, then knelt and shook awake one of the men who had been snoring loudly when I arrived. With a mounting sense of excitement I watched the wakened man struggle to his feet. He grumbled and stretched, then jammed his peaked uniform cap on his tousled head. Taking the rifle from the other soldier, he muttered a few words, then set off towards the tent and the limestone outcrop. Snatching up the binoculars, I watched him go, hardly daring to breathe. He did not slacken his pace as he approached the shadowy rocks but walked on and disappeared abruptly from view.

I raised myself higher on my elbows, straining to discern some detail in the distant blackness but without any success. My heart began to thud wildly again because there could only be one explanation for the soldier's disappearance – a cleft or a cave in the rocks! Something or someone was surely under special guard there and there seemed to be a very good chance it was Jutulak. I felt exultant and must have made careless noise in raising my head because suddenly I sensed a presence in the dark above me. In the same instant a sharp Chinese shout of challenge rang out and I felt the point of a bayonet press against my back between the shoulder blades.

I recoiled in horror and rolled over sideways. The torch in my right hand came on and some instinct prompted me to direct its beam upward in an effort to blind my attacker. In response he opened fire. The explosion of the rifle so close to my head deafened me momentarily, making my head ring like a steeple full of bells. Shocked and stunned I jack-knifed to my feet, swinging a wild blow in the vague direction of his head with my heavy torch. By the greatest good fortune it struck home and the sentry staggered and fell backward with a cry, dropping his rifle in the grass.

Out of the corner of my eye I saw that many of the men around the fires were scrambling anxiously out of their blankets. Snatching up the fallen rifle, I ran bent double through the darkness towards the creek. Pointing the weapon upward as I ran, I fired two deliberately spaced shots into the air before slinging it across my back and scrambling down the bank of the creek into the rushing water. Wading knee-deep downstream I pulled my pistol from its holster and carefully fired off two more shots at similar intervals.

In the silence that followed, echoes of the shots bounced eerily off the high limestone rockface. A moment later the darkness was rent by perhaps the most blood-chilling sound of the wild – the long, trumpeting roar of a mature bull elephant that mingles anger and furious aggression. It was the same sound that I'd heard Poo Tongkam unleash many times deep in the forest when straining at his chains to shift a three-ton teak log. Led now by Satharn on his aggravating ear-rope, Tongkam had obviously begun moving rapidly towards the camp as arranged, bellowing in protest as he ran. The female elephant being led in similar discomfort at Tongkam's heels quickly began to shriek and rant too.

The combined trumpeting of the two animals sent shivers down my own spine; Poo Tongkam, I was sure, understood with some part of his instinct what he had to do and the female was blindly following his lead. Their fearful clamour instantly convinced the sleep-befuddled troops that a wild elephant herd was rampaging through the trees to charge down their camp. Seconds earlier they had been struggling to gather their wits after being woken by a confusion of shots and noise in the darkness. But as I watched they panicked and began to flee for their lives.

Crouching below the level of the bank, I rushed on down the shallow creek, stumbling and slithering over the slippery rocks in my haste. Most of the troops and muleteers as far as I could see were running helter-skelter in the opposite direction, afraid of being trapped against the rockface that effectively blockaded the far bank. When I reached the rock outcrop beside which the tent was pitched, I scrambled out of the creek and pulled myself up hand over hand on to its ridge. Switching on my torch, I crept forward, shading the light with my free hand, searching frantically for a hiding place suitable for a prisoner.

Glancing for an instant towards the fires I saw an awe-inspiring sight: Poo Tongkam, a massive, grey-black shape, was thundering out of the trees closely followed by the female elephant. Both animals were still trumpeting fiercely as they swerved towards the bivouac. At their approach pandemonium broke out in the nearby mule lines; braying in abject terror, the pack animals reared and plunged wildly, lashing out with their hooves in a desperate effort to free themselves. Some had fallen and become hopelessly tangled among the tethering ropes; those that broke loose galloped dementedly in circles, knocking down fleeing troops and muleteers in their frenzy.

Because the mahouts were no longer sprinting beside the elephants, I assumed they'd had the good sense to pull back and conceal themselves among the trees. I had ordered them to ensure that the animals bore down noisily on the camp — but to release their hold on the ear-ropes when they judged it was necessary for their own safety. In deciding not to hobble either elephant, I knew we faced the danger of losing them both in the jungle. In fact there had been little choice; hobbling would have inhibited the momentum of their charge and greatly increased the danger of their being shot. What happened afterwards, I decided, had to be left to providence.

I watched Poo Tongkam scatter opium sacks and other stores like chaff with one sweep of his tusks when he reached the bivouac; then he trampled on through a tarpaulin-covered arms dump without pausing in his stride. One or two stray shots rang out from the trees but the bullets sang harmlessly overhead and I began to feel confident that none of the panic-stricken troops had sufficient nerve to stand their ground and kill the two elephants.

Then a sudden movement below me caught my eye. Looking down, I saw that a figure had emerged from the closed tent. In the firelight I saw I had guessed right – on his crumpled shirt the Chinese wore officer's insignia. Taking aim swiftly he raised a pistol at arm's length and loosed off two quick shots in Poo Tongkam's direction. The elephant had been in the act of turning away but he roared suddenly as though in pain and swerved back towards the tent. The officer, thunderstruck by the sight of the elephant bearing down on him like an express train, turned and plunged headlong into the shadows, making for the creek.

I dashed forward along the top of the rock, shining my torch frantically into every niche and crevice as Poo Tongkam charged. I had seen blood high on his left shoulder where a bullet had struck home and knew that his rage had become genuine. Ripping the tent from its moorings, he trampled its contents underfoot; then still bellowing, he turned towards the rock where I crouched, rearing up to his full, terrifying height with the fabric and ropes of the tent still dangling from his tusks.

I knew I was in as much danger then as the caravan troops. Clearly in some pain, Poo Tongkam was swaying dangerously on his hind legs only twenty yards from me. My torch was switched on and I knew that if I moved and attracted his wrath, a single, scything blow of his trunk could sweep me from the rock and break every bone in my body. While I crouched there gripped by indecision, the searching beam of my torch shone into a wedge-shaped fissure. The light showed that it opened into a cave and kneeling before it was the guard I had seen disappear so abruptly into the shadows; squinting through his rifle sights at the nightmarish image of Poo Tong-kam towering above him, he was preparing to fire.

I rose, took two quick steps and flung myself down on to him in a clumsy dive. We collided heavily and the rifle exploded as it fell from his hands. I heard the bullet chip fragments from the rock a few yards away, then ricochet into the darkness. Scrambling to my feet, I seized the fallen weapon by the barrel and swung the butt with all my force at the guard's head. It connected with sickening force and he rolled on to his face and lay still. I became aware then that Poo Tongkam's bellowing had ceased and I turned to see him running fast in the direction of the jungle again.

When I shone my torch into the back of the cave, the first thing I saw were Jutulak's haunted eyes. His arms and ankles were bound with thick rope, a gag had been tied tightly round his mouth and he lay huddled on the earth floor, staring fixedly at me without showing any sign of recognition. I dropped to one knee and quickly worked the gag free; then I removed the bayonet from the guard's rifle to begin sawing through his bonds.

'Don't worry, this isn't a dream, Jutulak,' I said quietly in Thai, leaning close to his ear. 'That really *was* Poo Tongkam – we've come to get you out of here.'

บ ๒

เดอะ บางกอก ซีเค๊ท

THE
BANGKOK
SECRET

Chapter Twelve

แนแจ๊ แอนเท ?อ๊ท

Jutulak could not stand unaided. Bound tightly for so long, his arms and legs had become badly swollen and numb. After cutting him free I chafed his wrists and ankles in an effort to restore circulation. But when I tried to help him to his feet he crumpled and went limp in my arms like a stringless marionette.

Although he moaned a little in pain, he made no effort to speak. By the light of the torch I could see he was still gazing at me with that strange, blank fixity of expression. I thought then that the cruelly tied gag had numbed his facial muscles or that he was too shocked to summon words. Only later did I find how wrong I was.

From the cleft in the rocks I could hear that the sounds made by Poo Tongkam and the female elephant were growing fainter as they moved away into the jungle. Fearing the Chinese troops would return any second, I hoisted Jutulak hurriedly on to my shoulders, scrambled up the limestone outcrop and crawled along its ridge towards the creek.

With difficulty I slithered down into the rushing water and began wading upstream. I knew I wouldn't be able to move very far or very fast carrying such a weight and I searched the banks with my shaded torch as I went. On spotting a narrow ledge choked with bushes winding away round the gnarled base of the limestone cliff, I clambered out of the water.

My only thought was to find a hiding place quickly where we could rest and gather our strength. But after skirting a scree of loose shale, the crumbling path turned steeply upward across a bare rockface. I hesitated, peering up the cliff in the darkness, wondering whether I should risk returning to the creek. Then from the direction of the bivouac I heard shouts. Gritting my teeth, I shifted Jutulak to a more comfortable position on my shoulder and struggled on, hoping either to hide higher up the mountain or find another track leading down away from the bivouac.

I felt vaguely comforted by the thought that any pursuers would have to advance in single file; at times I had to face the cliff and edge sideways along the crumbling path, clinging with one hand to the grass and bushes that sprouted from cracks and crevices. I climbed in this fashion for nearly half an hour before lowering Jutulak to the ground beneath a shelf of overhanging rock close to the summit.

My chest was heaving, my lungs seemed close to bursting and the muscles in my legs burned with a fiery ache. I cut a few scrawny bushes from a shallow rain gully nearby to cover the hard ground, listened carefully for a moment for signs of pursuit, then sank down exhausted opposite Jutulak. His wrists and ankles still looked swollen and painful but when I asked quietly whether he felt he would be able to walk soon, he ignored the question.

Pulling a small metal flask of brandy from my shirt pocket I swallowed a mouthful, then grinned and held the flask questioningly towards him. But Jutulak ignored this too; by the light of my shaded torch I could see he was sitting against the rocky wall, his back strangely rigid, staring unwaveringly into the void of darkness. He had not uttered a single word nor made any sign of recognition since my arrival at the bivouac; his manner and bearing had an unsettling quality and I became conscious for the first time that an eerie blanket of silence enveloped us and the summit of the limestone mountain.

I estimated we had climbed round to the north-west face, well away from the caravan camp and its noise. No sounds of cicadas or bullfrogs reached up to those weirdly weathered heights. I strained my ears from time to time, hoping to catch a sound of Poo Tongkam's presence in the jungle far below, but I heard nothing; even the noise of the rushing creek at the foot of the cliff had become inaudible.

'Are you all right, Jutulak?' I asked uneasily in Thai. 'Is anything worrying you?'

For a long time he neither replied nor looked in my direction. Then very slowly he turned to face me. His eyes were still fixed and staring and I recognised in his expression an acute, paralysing fear.

'You should not have come, Master,' he croaked. 'You should leave me to my fate!'

I stared back at him aghast. 'Jutulak, what are you saying?'

He remained unmoving, gazing mutely into the black night. When at last he spoke again, it was in a despairing whisper, as though he were speaking aloud to himself. 'It's just as the shaman foretold. As soon as we made camp in this terrible place, I knew it would happen here . . . I knew you would come . . . Now other disastrous things will happen!'

My clothes, damp from the creek and the perspiration of the climb, felt suddenly cold and clammy against my body. Taking out the flask again, I swallowed another mouthful of the warming cognac. 'Perhaps you've misunderstood something that a spirit medium told you, Jutulak,' I said gently, trying to calm him. 'They're not all to be trusted.'

'These things were foretold by the renowned shaman of the Akha tribal village north of our camp. It was only three days after Tongkam demolished the shrines to the Lord of the White Hat and the Crystal Prince . . .'

'Why did you go to the Akha village?' I asked, mystified.

'I had sometimes seen a beautiful Akha girl watching us from among the trees as we worked. I talked to her . . . We became friendly.' Jutulak dropped his eyes, looking shame-faced. 'She came every day. Her name is Ladhya. Her uncle is the shaman of the village. Foolishly I fell a little in love with her. She is very beautiful. I told her some small things of my life at the Grand Palace, perhaps to impress her. Later I realised she really loved only the elephants – that's what she came to watch . . . But she spoke to her uncle of what I'd said. And one day she came running through the jungle calling out excitedly for me to hurry to her village.'

'What for?'

Jutulak swung round to face me, his eyes dilating. 'I was rushed to the shaman's hut. When I arrived he was already in a deep trance. He had become possessed by the powerful spirit of a famous Siamese king from the ancient past! Ladhya heard everything. She was there too. In a loud, angry voice he foretold my abduction exactly as it happened – "by a band of armed warriors". He said also that a "white bird" would try to snatch me to safety by the "Dark Region of Wandering Souls" . . . and that worse calamities would follow if he succeeded!'

'White birds', I knew, was a term used in Thai and Lao classical mythology to identify human beings born beyond Thailand's borders. Whatever the Akha spirit medium had said, the allusion to a 'white bird' would have been correct as far as I was concerned. Moved by Jutulak's obvious distress, I dropped a friendly arm on his shoulder. 'Try not to worry – it could all be coincidence . . . Such things often are . . .'

Jutulak's chest heaved suddenly and new lines of anxiety creased his face. 'Master, it is much more than coincidence! This mountain is called "The Black World of Lost Spirits" by local hill tribes. I heard the muleteers muttering – they were very afraid. No human being ever comes up here because the tormented spirits wail all night long . . . Listen! Can't you hear? . . . They're beginning again!'

He broke off, raising his hands to press them desperately over his ears. For several minutes he rocked from side to side with his eyes squeezed shut, making little whimpering noises. I could hear nothing in the strange, deep silence but Jutulak was behaving as though enduring a fierce, inner agony. I recalled suddenly the terrible pandemonium of banshee shrieking which had seemed to fill my head on the night of the fever and watched him with a growing sense of alarm.

'I can't hear anything, Jutulak,' I said, leaning close. 'But you're in a lot of pain and utterly exhausted. You've been through a terrible ordeal. Try to be calm.'

He opened his eyes, staring frantically at me, but after a while the clenched expression on his face relaxed a little. 'It is impossible for me to be calm, Master!'

'Why?'

'Because the ancient spirit said other things that must also be true. It said the white bird would be attacked in its flight by a great black serpent. It said the serpent would threaten the very life of the white bird . . .' He paused and looked hard at me. 'Did a big snake attack you on your journey here?'

I let my arm drop from his shoulder. The image of the king

cobra swaying before me in the 'black forest' swam into my memory again with the sickening force of a remembered nightmare. Jutulak was watching me closely and I nodded reluctantly. 'Yes, I met a giant hamadryad on the trail.'

'And was it black?'

Again, with reluctance, I nodded. 'It was largely black – with a white streak.'

'And what happened?'

'I was fortunate. It attacked my pony and unseated me – but I managed to kill the snake with my rifle.'

Jutulak sucked in his breath sharply. 'You see, the shaman was absolutely correct. Through him the spirit of the ancient king said the white bird would cut off the head of the great black snake. Now you must believe that all his predictions are coming true!'

Before replying I took a long, deep breath. 'There are spirit mediums in other countries, Jutulak, as well as Thailand. They are often very skilled. They perhaps tell many things when they speak. Sometimes you remember only those things that seem to come true.'

'No, the spirit of the ancient king said very little!' Jutulak shook his head violently. 'Only what I have told you . . .' He paused for a moment. 'And one other thing.'

'What was that?'

'Through the shaman the king's spirit said that the white bird would suffer a terrible illness on its journey, a fever . . . Did you suffer a bad attack of fever on the journey?'

I sat in silence for a long time looking at Jutulak, pondering carefully all that he had said. Then I nodded once. 'Yes, I did – the worst I've ever had in my life.'

'The king's spirit said the white bird would come very close to death for a second time on the journey,' continued Jutulak in the same strained whisper. 'The spirit said that the soul of the white bird would spring free and look briefly beyond – into unknown worlds. The experience, he said, would change the white bird for ever although at first he wouldn't realise . . .'

The beam of the torch which had been growing dimmer as we spoke began to flicker, indicating that its batteries were running low. I swore quietly and explained to Jutulak that I would have to switch it off in an effort to conserve what energy was left for emergency use. His pale features registered a new wave of apprehension in the moment before I extinguished the torch and in the darkness I could sense the heightened tension in him, although we sat several feet apart.

Without the torch the blackness of the night beyond our ledge seemed to become more dense and flow in all around us. The faint starlight which had helped me earlier had been snuffed out, seemingly by heavy cloud. As we sat side by side without speaking, the vibrant silence surrounding the crag seemed to thicken, too, and draw closer.

Gradually it came to feel as though we were floating weightless in a void high above the darkened jungle. Against my will, my mind filled itself with the most vivid image of the supernatural terror which had gripped me two nights earlier: the unknown black abyss at the heart of all human dread. In the deep, natural darkness on the mountain I again seemed to be teetering before a similar chasm – but now in hard, physical reality.

As I sat there I had a strong sense of life being suspended; all movement in time and space appeared to have ceased. It was like staring blankly at the awful stillness and immobility of eternity. And if we had risen and stepped forward two paces, we would have tumbled downward, head over heels, to become a part of the mystery. A feeling swelled in me that the moment would always be of the profoundest importance, although precisely why would remain elusive. This feeling lingered subliminally, pierced the heart, then was gone. The next moment I was aware only of Jutulak's anxious breathing beside me and the need to calm him.

'I came to try and save your life, Jutulak,' I said softly. 'If you had reached Chiang Mai, you'd have been sent to Bangkok in chains. Phao's men would almost certainly have murdered you because of what you know – because of whatever you saw at the Grand Palace . . .' I paused to see if he was listening and heard his breathing again, ragged and uneven as before. 'Surely, Jutulak, it wasn't wrong of me to try to prevent that happening.'

'The spirit of the ancient king said greater disasters would follow!' Jutulak repeated himself automatically in the same fearful voice, as though he had no thoughts or opinions of his own. 'I deserved my fate! I took the gift of a pistol to the Grand Palace. The king died of a shot from such a pistol . . . If I hadn't taken the weapon to the palace, the king might be alive today. So I deserve to die!'

'That isn't true, Jutulak,' I insisted gently. 'You haven't told me everything yet. But it seems to me you presented your gift in good faith, as a token of respect and devotion. The king enjoyed such things. You had no control over what was done with the pistol. And it may not have been the weapon which killed the king. So you were not personally the cause of the king's death . . .'

'The ancient royal spirit said I must expiate my thoughtless action at once!' Jutulak's breathing quickened in agitation. 'We must all answer for what we do! It may take many lifetimes to atone for the impulsive act of a moment . . . Can't you understand? I was glad when the soldiers stormed our camp. I was glad when they captured me. But you have interfered where you had no right!'

I reached out to rest my hand consolingly on his shoulder. 'I can see the shaman frightened you badly, Jutulak. But I understand the teachings of the Buddha, too. I've studied them . . . "Neither in a cleft in the mountains, nor in the depths of the sea, can any man escape the consequences of his deeds." That's what the *Dhamma* says, isn't it?'

'Yes! And the soldiers were taking me to my fate! It was in accordance with the law of karma.'

'But the law of karma is a living law, Jutulak.' I continued gently: 'It decrees that a man who breaks the harmony should set out to restore it himself, no matter what sacrifice is required . . . If a man smashes a plate he is responsible for replacing it, isn't he? And isn't it better if he replaces the plate and restores harmony to the table quickly – in *this* life. Rather than carry the painful burden into the next?'

'I am meant to die,' gasped Jutulak. 'That is my punishment.'

'But wouldn't it be better to stay alive and help make the truth known among your people? Wouldn't that restore greater harmony?'

'No! I took a vow of silence in the temple where I served as a novice. I can't break that.'

'Which temple was that?'

'In Bangkok – near my home on the *klong*, *Wat Kwan Kittima*. The *acharn* hid me from the troops for a week. On his advice I swore a solemn oath . . .'

Jutulak's voice faded to nothing and he seemed to be lost in thought. I waited in silence for a minute or more, wondering what was running through his mind. When he spoke again his tone was subdued and reverent.

'. . . I promised the spirit of the dead king that I would never speak of what I saw. I held a personal gift from him in my hands before the image of the Buddha while I made the vow . . . His Majesty had given me the special present with an engraved inscription after I told him of something beautiful I admired in a wall painting in the temple. It had been in his family a very long time, he said . . . The gift was just as beautiful as in the ancient painting. So I left it by the altar.'

'Did you tell the *acharn* what you saw at the Grand Palace?'

'I can't answer you because of my vow,' said Jutulak quickly. 'You must know that.'

'All right, I accept that – but remember that the Chinese soldiers who captured you are not on the side of harmony and truth. They are opium smugglers, armed bands who live beyond the law. They must have been acting on orders from highly placed men in Bangkok – perhaps the same men who presided over the execution of the three royal courtiers. You told me yourself that people do not believe the courtiers were guilty . . . So dying now would be a vain sacrifice . . .'

I paused, listening in the darkness, trying to gauge his reaction to my argument. His breathing had grown quieter as though he were concentrating intently on what I was saying, so I hurried on.

'Your country's leaders in Bangkok used the "King's Death Case" to drive the former prime minister into exile. They overthrew him by exploiting the mystery for their own ends. They've clung to power for the past nine years by hiding the truth. Because you know what really happened you're a serious danger to them. And they want to kill you to make sure the truth remains hidden for ever. Don't you see, dying at their hands wouldn't be an atonement? The deaths of the courtiers perhaps helped give credence to their lies. Your own death would serve the same end – and it would only add to the cloud of black karma which already surrounds these events.'

I heard Jutulak breathe in noisily as though experiencing a sharp stab of pain. 'The men who govern us now are leaders of the national army. The people of Thailand believe the generals must have built up much merit in earlier lives. Otherwise they would not be able to lead our country today.'

'That fits your people's beliefs, Jutulak, and the generals encourage that view – but such ideas are very difficult for a *farang* to accept.'

'But why did a *farang* like you decide to try and help me, Master?' asked Jutulak in a barely audible voice. 'What made you risk your own life so many times to save mine? Thailand isn't your country. Your own home is far away across the world . . . Why do you care so much?'

The queries immediately triggered uneasy feelings in me. Whenever similar questions had surfaced in my own mind during the past two weeks, I'd consciously brushed them aside and I knew I would find it no easier to answer Jutulak.

'In England people of my background, I suppose, are brought up to hate injustice of any kind,' I began haltingly, 'and to fight against it wherever possible . . . Our religion teaches us to love God and our fellow men equally. Those are the simple rules at the core of everything Christians believe . . . In practice they're the hardest of all to live up to, day in day out. But still a lot of us go on trying . . .'

I broke off, feeling faintly foolish. Trying to give logical reasons for what had been rash, impulsive actions sounded naive, even in my own ears. Also I knew there were other instincts at work, which I'd never consciously formed into coherent thoughts. Squatting beside that precipice in the middle of an ominously black night seemed a bizarre moment to try to define complex feelings. By nature I had always felt gauche in such situations. But the earnestness of the question compelled me to make the effort.

'Over the past few years, Jutulak, I've become deeply attached to your country. Among graceful, smiling people it's not difficult to feel at ease . . . Perhaps I've become more attached to Thailand than I've ever admitted to myself. Sometimes while tracking the mules I asked myself, "Why?" I'd acted almost without thinking. Physically I enjoy the challenge of the jungle . . . tracking animals, climbing this crag – things like that are meat and drink to me. You'd been taken prisoner unjustly because by chance you saw what happened at the Grand Palace in 1946. But I could still do something to help you – and suddenly it seemed like a duty. Instinctively I feel that the truth about what happened to King Ananda is important for your country . . .'

I paused; in the darkness beside me I could hear movement. For the first time it sounded as though Jutulak had begun to chafe at his own wrists and ankles. He didn't reply but I was glad his mind seemed to be focusing at last on practical matters. We appeared to have reached an important turning point and I laughed awkwardly in the darkness.

'I think I'd feel like a fish out of water anywhere else now, Jutulak. Perhaps I might take a Thai wife one day, give up the jungle, the giant teak trees and settle down . . . I think my future lies in this country. That's why I care what happens to Thailand – and you. Does knowing all that make it easier for you to understand why I've acted the way I have?'

I waited but Jutulak made no response. Suddenly I noticed a new quality in the silence which filled me with foreboding. I reached out to pat his shoulder again by way of reassurance – but my hand encountered nothing except hard rock. I grabbed for the torch and switched it on. By its feeble light I saw that Jutulak's place on the bed of underbrush was empty.

I leapt to my feet and took a pace forward, pointing the fading torch-beam into the blackness. I could see nothing at all. Holding my breath I turned my head to listen, first in one direction, then the other. No sound of footsteps climbing or descending the crag path was audible. Silence, absolute and unbroken, prevailed in all directions.

My first instinct was to give chase but I hesitated in an agony of indecision: there was no indication whether he had gone up or down the mountain. I took a breath, preparing to yell his name with all the force of my lungs – then caught myself, fearing that I might alert any Chinese troops who were within earshot. I stood staring helplessly into darkness that was now more ominous than ever. In an unguarded moment the malevolent 'Black World of Lost Spirits' seemed to have swallowed Jutulak from off the face of the earth.

บ ช

เดอะ บางกอก ซีเคร็ท

THE
BANGKOK
SECRET

Chapter Thirteen

แบนจบ เลขกา ้วยา

It took me two days to struggle back to the company compound. There, footsore and drained by my experiences, I walked into the centre of a very different storm. A deluge of angry messages from Nakon Lampang and Bangkok, provoked by my five days of absence without leave, littered my desk. My immediate superior, the senior manager from Lampang who had just arrived to investigate the crisis, took one look at my dishevelled appearance and asked brusquely if I had entirely taken leave of my senses.

Then he ordered me to prepare to depart at once for Bangkok. The head offices of the company were in an unholy uproar, he said. Senior managers had been deeply shocked by unpleasant visits from armed men of General Phao's security police. Some explanation of my extraordinary conduct, he added in an ominous tone, was urgently required.

When I admitted that I had nothing to show for my long absence and that I had lost two elephants and two ponies in the jungle – one elephant, our biggest and strongest, shot and injured by Chinese troops – he was reduced to speechless incredulity. But I gave him no more than the briefest of outlines as to what had happened. I was too weary and still a little unnerved by the mysterious disappearance of Jutulak on the limestone mountain.

Through the remaining hours of darkness after he vanished, I had waited impatiently for dawn to break; then I'd searched the nearby area of the summit thoroughly without finding any sign of him or any kind of tracks at all in the hard, stony ground. After satisfying myself that the opium caravan had moved on, I descended from the crag and set out despondently on the return trek.

I had caught up with the two mahouts and the coolies on the second day after passing the night in a village temple. They had been unable to track down either Poo Tongkam or the female elephant in the dense jungle below the mountain when daylight came. The ponies, terrified by the elephants' trumpeting, had also broken free and disappeared. So carrying what equipment we could on our backs, we walked every step of the way back to the compound.

I had not expected a warm welcome there; but the severity of the Lampang manager's manner took me by surprise. While I was throwing clothes into a battered suitcase in my bungalow, readying myself for departure to Bangkok, full realisation struck. The long journey by river-raft and train to the capital was almost certainly going to be one-way only. Dismissal in disgrace from the company and another one-way ticket – this time back to England – seemed to be the minimum punishment that awaited me.

Desolated by the thought, I stopped packing, showered, threw on fresh clothes and slipped outside to the stables. I saddled a pony without being noticed and galloped from the compound before anybody could stop me. A few minutes later I was riding hard northwards, heading for the high forested ridges bordering Burma where a group of the Akha hill tribe had built a settlement a year earlier.

Among the many inexplicable experiences of that period, Jutulak's account of his meeting with Ladhya and the Akha shaman had remained most hauntingly in my memory. The uncanny accuracy of the shaman's predictions about my journey seemed, in the wake of Jutulak's disappearance, to provide the only point of reference in a baffling void. As I rode the pony hard along the rising jungle trails I reminded myself that by my actions I was giving in, at least in part, to the kind of ancient native superstition which accepted the existence of an invisible spirit world. That I did so was perhaps a good measure of my bemusement at having lost Jutulak so soon after freeing him.

I knew that giving the slightest credence to such beliefs would make me suspect in the eyes of all rational fellow

Englishmen; but at the same time, because of the circumstances and the whole background to Jutulak's story, I felt
there was an inescapable logic in what I was doing. In any
event, I knew that I could not leave those northern jungles so
abruptly without making one last effort at the Akha village to
achieve some understanding of the complex events I had lived
through.

The Akha are the most primitive of half a dozen hill tribes
who still roam the northern fringes of Thailand. They alone
like to build their small, temporary settlements on the highest
mountain ridges so that they are not disturbed by other
peoples. Descended from ancient nomads of Chinese-Tibetan
blood, they, like the Thais and other hill tribes, fear and
worship a legion of unseen spirits; but their rituals and prac-
tices are distinctive. Because over nine years I had often
worked close to the Akha in remote parts of the forest, I had
taken the trouble to learn something of their language. During
visits to their semi-nomadic settlements I came to admire
their cheerful, placid simplicity. The lives of the Akha were
spartan; they grew cotton and sometimes rice on family-sized
plots and hunted small animals in the jungle with catapults
and bows and arrows. They chewed betel and some grew and
smoked opium; but in my experience the tribespeople seemed
carefree, visibly content, and were normally hospitable to the
few strangers they encountered.

Due to the steepness of the ridge on which the village of
Ladhya and the shaman stood, I had to dismount and lead my
pony the last two miles through the late afternoon heat. As I
drew near to the village's spirit gates made of arched bamboo,
I found myself wondering about Ladhya. Akha women were
often stocky and heavy-boned, yet Jutulak, used to the
sophistication of service in the Grand Palace, had found
her beautiful. Her interest in elephants, too, I reflected, was
a rare trait among the hill tribes who in my experience
usually feared and avoided the giants of the forest. But as
soon as I caught sight of Ladhya I understood the reasons
for Jutulak's infatuation.

Naked to the hips and shoeless, she stood pounding rice on
the platform of the first palm-thatch hut I came to after passing
through a protective passage of arrow-shaped poles. Her bearing was proudly erect and her small, bare breasts quivered

rhythmically as she pounded and twisted the handle of the long, pivoted rice-pestle inside a narrow wooden tub. An unconscious half-smile softened her features as she worked, suggesting a seraphic inner calm; I remember thinking it was the kind of expression you would perhaps expect to find on the face of an angel. Thirty years later I can still recall that first glimpse of her as if it were yesterday.

She was taller and more slender than the rest of the Akha village women; this alone made her an arresting figure. A skirt of dyed cotton, decorated with embroidery and coloured beads, hung low around her hips. In the steady rhythms of her work, silver-tasselled ornaments suspended from a waist-belt of red cotton brushed her uncovered belly and the tops of her thighs. Around her neck she wore a silver necklace from which was suspended a large, circular, silver disc.

A throng of curious Akha children and dogs had gathered at my heels as I entered the village and, hearing us draw near, Ladhya raised her head for the first time to look in my direction. Holding my gaze unself-consciously, she continued to sway from side to side, still clutching the rough haft of the rice-pestle in both her small fists. It was in that moment that I realised how extraordinarily beautiful she was.

Her lips and cheeks had a lustrous bloom, her eyes were large and round, and her teeth, unstained by the betel juice which disfigured so many hill-tribe women of the region, were a gleaming white. Her skin mingled the smoky tints and the pale gold of north and south and I guessed that, unusually, she had mixed Siamese and hill-tribe blood. Her hair, thick and glossy, was tucked inside a traditional bonnet which Akha females never remove in the presence of men. Made of cone-shaped bamboo adorned with silver coins, feathers, polished pearls of grain and small tusks of the wild boar, it added a primitive glamour to her quiet, natural beauty.

'Tsak-tsak hanh mattya – the head-dress has many beautiful ornaments,' I said in the Akha language, pausing before the hut. 'But the beauty of the bonnet does not match the beauty of its wearer.'

Ladhya continued to pound the rice but made no reply.

'I have come to see the famous shaman of the village,' I continued slowly. 'And his niece Ladhya – have I already found her?'

She nodded once, still without pausing in her work. 'Yes – you have found Ladhya.'

'I am Adam Hampson . . .' I said hesitantly.

'I know – the master of Jutulak.'

Taken aback, I smiled. 'How can Ladhya possibly know that?'

'Ladhya watches,' she replied. 'On many days she sees the master of Jutulak work with his elephants. He does not see Ladhya hidden among the trees. Ladhya notices that the master of Jutulak has deep affection for the elephants – especially the biggest one of all.'

Continuing to give her full attention to pounding the rice, she spoke casually without looking for any reaction to what she said. Studying her at close quarters, I guessed she was perhaps seventeen or eighteen. But the innocence of her expression seemed paradoxically mingled with a deep and natural knowingness.

'The biggest of all elephants has been shot in the shoulder,' I said quietly. 'Today he is lost in the jungle . . . near "The Black World of Lost Spirits". Jutulak was taken captive by Chinese soldiers. The master of Jutulak followed and managed to rescue him. But Jutulak disappeared again – that is why his master comes here. He seeks the honour of speaking to your uncle, the shaman – very urgently.'

Ladhya stopped working the rice-pestle and frowned. 'To-night is the full moon . . . The shaman must lead the village ritual. He has already begun to prepare himself.'

'After the rescue, Jutulak talked about this village,' I said in some desperation. 'And about Ladhya . . .' I hesitated, feeling myself on unfamiliar ground. 'He said Ladhya had heard the mighty spirit of an ancient king speak. He said the spirit prophesied many important things . . .'

'Jutulak spoke the truth.'

'Some prophecy has already come true . . . Jutulak's master was attacked by a big snake. He also suffered a terrible fever just as the spirit said he would. But worst of all, Jutulak disappeared from his master's side again on the mountain in a single moment. Afterwards there was no trace of Jutulak at all . . . What has happened to him? Where is he? The uncle of Ladhya is the only man who can help now . . .'

Ladhya put aside her rice-pestle and came silently down

from the platform of the hut. In front of me she stopped. For a moment she looked directly at me in silence; then the gentle half-smile returned to her face again.

'It is good that the master of Jutulak has come here at last,' she said softly.

Uncertain of her meaning, I said nothing.

'If the master of Jutulak has a horse, it should be given water now,' she added in the same quiet tone. 'Ladhya will go to her uncle, the shaman, to ask permission for Jutulak's master to watch the ritual. Perhaps he will agree . . . The full moon is a good time for the ancient spirit to come a third time . . . The master of Jutulak should wait for Ladhya before the gates of the village at dusk.'

She called to one of the boys among the crowd of children and ordered him to fetch a gourd bowl and a bamboo pipe of water for my pony. Then without speaking further she hurried away along the dusty track between the palm-thatch houses.

ひ 乃

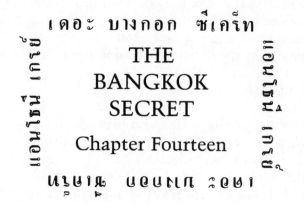

เดอะ บางกอก ซีเคร็ท

THE
BANGKOK
SECRET

Chapter Fourteen

The curious Akha children followed me out of the village, chattering like a tree full of birds. They watched closely while my thirsty pony drank. But after a time the novelty of gazing at a fair-haired 'white bird' and his mount wore off; growing bored, they drifted away in search of new distractions.

The sun was falling towards the jungle on the western horizon but the light had not yet begun to fade. Stretching myself wearily on the ground to rest, I watched a group of Akha youths and girls giggling and dancing boisterously in a clearing on the edge of the village. Vibrant music was flowing from a *naw*, an instrument made of flattened bamboo, and from time to time I saw couples break away to run laughing into the trees. Others were emerging intermittently from the forest to rejoin the group, looking flushed and excited.

The Akha, I knew, encouraged the young from puberty onwards to follow their natural physical instincts. The forest remained their playground during this adolescent period of discovery, as it had been in childhood. On the fringes of the village I could see several thatched huts that stood higher than other houses, some rising to a height of twenty feet or more. In all the Akha settlements that I'd visited, such elevated huts were built for the use of young, newly wed Akha who had not yet set up their own family homes; the only known taboos the tribe placed on erotic love-play seemed to concern the locations where it took place. Yet despite this uninhibited, primitive morality, after marriage the Akha people appeared to be unique among the hill tribes in practising unswerving fidelity to their partners.

As the sun dipped lower, I saw that the boisterous group of youngsters was thinning and breaking up. Girls and youths alike began to hurry purposefully towards the heart of the village. Soon, from the direction of the ritual long-house, I began to hear the urgent throb of drums: then gourd-flutes and bamboo pipes wailed into life in accompaniment.

Rising to my feet I watched the silver rim of the full moon appear above the distant treetops. Night had arrived with its usual tropical abruptness and pale, ghostly light was spilling across the dark ocean of foliage below the ridge like cream on black velvet. An unbroken hush had fallen over the entire forest, as though everything living was awaiting the ascent of the full moon; watching and listening, I shivered without understanding why.

Steadily the distant music became more insistent. The rhythm deepened, augmented by the throb of many stamping feet. Feeling my nerves tighten, I walked to the spirit gates and waited impatiently beside the twisted arches of bamboo, straining my eyes in the thickening darkness. With every passing minute I became more anxious that the shaman might have refused the request of his niece.

The gates were adorned at the foot of each pillar with wood carvings. Male and female fertility figures grappled in primitive acts of copulation and higher up I could see wooden images of birds and small animals jumbled among other symbols woven of straw. With a shock I saw that the carcasses and skins of freshly slaughtered rats and dogs had been stretched across the highest arches, presumably as part of the ritual that was just beginning. Standing there in the luminous moonlight, I suddenly sensed something of the spirit gates' primeval force; in those moments the hairs on the back of my neck gradually stiffened and stood upright.

'Evil spirits fear the ugliness of the gates. That is why they are made this way. Good spirits see only the beauty.'

Ladhya's voice, no more than a whisper from the darkness close by, startled me. The next moment she touched my arm and began to guide me down the sloping track between the pointed bamboos.

'The shaman did not wish to grant the request at first. But Ladhya pleaded for the master of Jutulak.'

In the glow of the moon, now enormous and fully visible above the jungle, I could see that the half-smile had given way to a serious expression. We walked in silence for a while, then she turned her head to look at me.

'In the long-house sit against the back wall – do not move. Ladhya cannot stay with the master of Jutulak . . . If the mighty spirit of the ancient king comes, be very still and say nothing.'

Fires were glowing in earthen hearths inside each empty hut that we passed. I could see that they were so rudimentary that they contained only mats and blankets rolled up against the walls. Each hut had its own ramshackle spirit shrine outside, a miniature dwelling before which bedraggled offerings of rice and flowers had been placed. Pigs and goats snorted and snuffled in the rubbish beneath some of the huts and occasional chickens fled from our path as we approached. But no other humans were visible; every single inhabitant had joined the ritual dance, leaving the rest of the village eerily deserted under the giant moon.

The music and the frenzied drumming of feet grew rapidly louder as we neared the long-house. Constructed on stilts against a steep hillside of red loam, it was perhaps a hundred feet in length. Its walls were matting and bamboo slats and its roof was thatched with palm leaves. Even before we mounted the stepped log to its doors, I could see that the whole building was swaying and shaking on its stilts with the force of the dance.

Inside, my eyes encountered a mass of bodies glistening with perspiration as they jerked and writhed round several central fires. Moving parallel to the walls of the hut in a slow, deliberate procession, bare-chested men and women spaced alternately were clutching the waist of the dancer in front. The men wore only dark cotton trousers and the women black skirts. At their head was a small, gaunt man of indeterminate age wearing a red blindfold around his eyes. He was dancing and chanting, moving a few simple paces forwards and sideways each time, stretching his arms high above his head. In his hands he flourished whisks of foliage and metal rattles and all those behind him chanted energetic responses in unison as they followed at his heels.

I could see other adults and children squatting in the shadows around the walls. At one end of the hut, a row of young women were seated, pounding a teak log with hollow bamboo rods of varying lengths. After indicating the empty space against a wall where I should take my place, Ladhya hurried away to kneel behind the same log and picked up a piece of bamboo. The other females seated alongside her were bare-breasted too and wore similar decorated bonnets. They all struck the log in strict rotation, creating a strange variety of plangent notes. Men clashing cymbals, banging drums or playing gourd-flutes were ranged on both sides of the women; with eyes closed, all were absorbed in the slow, driving rhythms of the dance.

The firelight flickered and flashed on the quivering bodies of dancers and musicians alike. The women in the circle retained a curiously erect posture, their heads thrown back, their arms hanging loose and unused at their sides. They swayed and twisted their torsoes in strange, serpentine movements and I saw that tears were running down the cheeks of some of them; whether they were tears of joy or sadness was impossible to tell. The silver necklaces, bangles and bonnets they wore shimmered in the glow of the flames and the half-darkness enhanced the physical allure of their golden-brown bodies.

With these slow, tantalising movements and ritualised chants the dancers seemed to be miming the timeless, unchanging elements of their daily lives; planting, harvesting, birth, death, heat, rain, the ineluctable passage of the seasons. Through repetition the actions became increasingly mesmeric for both dancers and watchers. The small, gaunt man leading them, I could see, was the shaman. From time to time as his chanting rose higher, his whole body shook in a convulsive seizure. The rattles and whisks trembled in his hands each time and this seemed to be a signal for the tempo of the dance to be stepped up.

I had often heard rumours about the ritual dances of the hill tribes. But at that time few, if any, foreigners had ever seen them performed. I knew they could last for hours, beginning very slowly to relax body and mind. Old jungle wallahs had told me they believed the rituals progressed in spirals of intensity towards a wild climax of elation and exhaustion. At such mystical moments of mass frenzy, shamans and witch-doctors traditionally attempted feats of exorcism, healing or the raising of spirits.

What unknown depths of the human psyche were plumbed by the dance on that night of the full moon, I can't say, but I felt myself succumb rapidly to its hypnotic force. Although I remained crouched in the shadows by the wall, part of me seemed to be drawn into the gyrating mass of stamping, swirling, semi-naked bodies. Although my fascination was laced with some apprehension at what might lie ahead, I was unable to take my eyes from the scene before me. Several times I looked in Ladhya's direction; but in the smoky gloom I was uncertain whether she was able to see me. Like all those around her, she seemed to have been transported to another realm by the throb of the music.

Whether an hour or two passed, I wasn't sure. From the ponderous plodding and stamping of the early stages the dancers gradually accelerated their steps; the shaman's movements became more erratic and jerky and his chanting rose to a higher pitch than before. Breaking ranks, the younger men, who looked like the hunters of the tribe, started to whirl, jerk their arms and kick out their legs, the powerful thrust of their limbs conveying joy and triumph, anger and sorrow, fear and aggression. The girls and women too began to twist and fling their bodies into wilder contortions; they spun in frantic circles among the shouting men, staring wide-eyed, grimacing, crying out incoherently.

Beneath their flying feet the floor of the hut shook much more violently. The dancing became wilder, more abandoned; heads lolled, eyes rolled, limbs jerked strangely as though no longer controlled by the dancers. A stocky Akha girl whirling crazily in front of me suddenly collapsed at my feet. Trembling in every limb, her naked breasts heaving, she rolled dementedly from side to side, fighting to regain her breath.

In all parts of the hut, other dancers began to cry out and fall semi-conscious to the matting-covered floor. They lay writhing and twitching in heaps, men and women alike, moaning loudly as though undergoing terrible pain. I expected the savage music to cease but just the reverse occurred.

The tempo became harsher, more urgent and discordant than ever; those dancers still on their feet whirled faster in response. The blindfolded shaman, I noticed suddenly, was staggering unsteadily in the centre of the hut. Something in his manner fixed my attention on him and as I watched he spun round slowly several times, then came to a halt close to one of the fires. Holding his rattles and whisks aloft, he remained motionless, swaying very slightly at the heart of the churning maelstrom.

The remaining dancers, mostly young men and girls, were whirling dizzily around him, leaping and spinning close to the flames. Some stumbled against one another and fell; others continued to move blindly like automatons. Suddenly I saw that the shaman had turned and, although still blindfolded, was moving towards me.

When he was a few feet away he stopped. Facing me he whirled his arms wildly, like a windmill, flourishing his whisks and rattles. I felt my blood run cold; unmistakably I had become the focus of what was happening. The shaman was grunting unintelligibly, his head twisting strangely on his neck; then he sprang into the air, emitting an ear-splitting shriek and fell lifeless in a heap on the floor in front of me.

Simultaneously the drums and all the other instruments ceased their clamour. One by one the other dancers sank to the floor. For a moment or two only the crackle of the flames and the quiet moaning of the stricken dancers broke the stillness. Then two young Akha men ran forward from the shadows and helped the shaman to his feet. They took off his blindfold and stood one at either side, supporting him.

In the guttering light of the fires, his wrinkled face with its jutting, mongoloid cheekbones seemed to become more primitive than before. His narrow eyes, sunk deep in their sockets, were glazed and staring; although they were fixed on my face, they seemed not to see me. When he spoke, his deep voice reverberated through the long-house with a strange sonority, as though he were speaking through water.

'Sinister spirits are gathering about the dark trees! ... The black sun rises to overshadow the red ...'

The shaman fell silent again and from around the walls of the hut I heard uneasy whispering break out among the watchers.

'The black forests of the Lost World seize new prey ... The forsaken spirit will wander for many years ... Worse darkness will spread across the face of the land ...'

All moaning had ceased and everybody in the hut seemed to be listening fearfully. I felt too that all Akha eyes were on me. Like a rabbit transfixed by the gaze of a stoat, I crouched on the floor as though paralysed, staring back at the shaman.

'Black winds will blow ... black rain will fall ... Great calamities lie ahead for the peoples of Siam ...'

The apprehensive whispering grew louder; suddenly the flames of the fires were stirred by a blast of cold wind, gusting through the open doors at one end of the hut. New gasps of fear greeted the wind and some of the watchers began rising to their feet.

'The life of the white bird is now in great danger,' proclaimed the shaman in a loud voice. 'The white bird must flee swiftly to a land far away ... This is not the time to fight.' He paused, summoning fresh effort, and his voice finally rose to a hoarse shout. 'Go out at once, white bird! Go from the lands of the Akha people! ... Go out from Siam!'

The shaman's head fell forward suddenly on his chest and his body sagged in the arms of his supporters. Nodding to one another, they carried him to a place beside one of the fires where after a few seconds he opened his eyes, blinking quickly, as if awakening from a light sleep. Within half a minute he was entirely himself again, the apparent possession of his body ended. Without speaking he rose to his feet and made a perfunctory sign with his raised whisk. Immediately the Akha girls resumed their rhythmic beating of the teak log; the crude cymbals clashed, drumbeats followed and the gourd-flutes began to wail as before.

Rising from the floor, the men and women of the tribe formed themselves into a new ritual circle behind the shaman. Taking my chance, I slipped outside into the moonlit darkness. On the platform before the door I hesitated, looking back. But my departure appeared to have been little noticed; the Akha had again become oblivious to their surroundings. The hut began to shake and shudder to the throb of the new dance and as I turned away I heard scores of bare feet begin stamping again in slow, ponderous unison.

ህ ໜ

เดอะ บางกอก ซีเค๊ท

THE
BANGKOK
SECRET

Chapter Fifteen

I felt dazed and light-headed as I moved through the silent, deserted village towards the spirit gates. The shouted warning of the shaman was still ringing alarmingly in my ears, my eyes were smarting from the smoke and my throat was parched. The fierce passions aroused by the ritual dance and its aftermath seemed to have sucked every remaining ounce of energy from me; as I walked I knew that I was swaying like a drunken man.

The moon, smaller now, was riding high in the sky. Its light was sharply bright, more radiant than before, and I stopped, staring up at it. The rising wind played refreshingly on my face and I closed my eyes, standing perfectly still, trying to gather my reeling senses and assess what had taken place.

Had an ancient spirit truly taken possession of the shaman or was it cunning trumpery? Would it be unwise to ignore the dire warnings about my life being in danger? Should I flee the country at once, put in a request to be sent home to England, no matter what awaited me in Bangkok? Most importantly, could the 'forsaken spirit' mentioned by the shaman be a reference to Jutulak? Had he been recaptured? Or did it mean he had already died on the mountain?

My brain, in the event, proved itself too numbed and sluggish to answer any of the questions. I opened my eyes wearily and walked on, catching a glimpse as I did so of an indistinct figure dashing swiftly between two stilted huts just ahead of me. Then in quick succession I spotted two other dark shapes hugging the shadows on the opposite side of the village street.

I strained my eyes without success, trying to see if they carried crossbows and jungle knives.

Deep shadows cast by overhanging trees fell across the street just ahead of me and I slowed down. Then, realising I was unarmed and helpless in a village of two hundred tribespeople, I shrugged and walked on. In the deepest part of the darkness, unseen hands clutched at my arm. They made me turn aside between the huts and I offered no resistance.

'The master of Jutulak must not leave yet,' murmured Ladhya close at my side. 'It is very dangerous to ride through the forest at this hour. Also the master is too weary. He has eaten nothing and taken no drink at all for hours.'

She was guiding me along a narrow path between the trees but I could not see where I was stepping and I stumbled frequently over roots and other obstructions. 'The shaman ordered the master of Jutulak to leave the lands of the Akha people at once,' I protested. 'If he is found in the village, surely there will be trouble for Ladhya . . .'

'The ritual dances will continue until daybreak,' replied Ladhya calmly. 'Just before dawn the master of Jutulak will wake and leave . . .'

'But there were others following the master of Jutulak. Who are they?'

'Do not worry. They are friends of Ladhya . . . They come to fetch a pipe of water for you to drink. And sticks to kindle a fire.'

'Where are you taking me?' I asked.

'To one of the high-houses. On the very edge of the village. Nobody will think to look for you there . . .'

She led the way to the most remote high-house which stood swaying in the wind some twenty feet above the ground. I followed her up the steep ladder and crawled behind her into the tiny thatched hut. The floor inside was strewn with sweet-smelling dried grasses but the hut was otherwise empty.

Almost at once two other Akha girls appeared; like Ladhya they wore ornate tribal bonnets and were naked to the waist. They smiled shyly without looking directly at me but didn't speak. After the turmoil of the long-house, their quiet presence along with Ladhya was gentle and soothing. One carried a bamboo tube of water and drinking gourds, the other held dry sticks and a pan containing lighted brands from another fire.

After kindling flames in a central clay hearth and pouring water for me, they departed quietly without speaking.

Ladhya knelt by the fire, watching me as I gulped down two bowls of the cool mountain water. 'The master of Jutulak must rest now,' she said softly. 'I will go to prepare some food . . .'

'Please, let Ladhya wait a moment,' I said quickly. 'Tell the master of Jutulak about the spirit who spoke through the shaman tonight – was it the ancient king who came before?'

Ladhya nodded. 'Yes, he has come twice before.'

'Twice?'

She nodded again. 'The ancient king's spirit came the second time three days ago.'

'Tonight the king said nothing of Jutulak – what did he say then?'

'Three days ago he said: "The white bird has set Jutulak free from the warriors . . ."'

I sat upright, staring hard at her. 'Was that all?'

'No. The spirit also said: "The white bird has become confused. But Jutulak is free and safe . . . The warriors are unable to find him . . ."'

She sat looking steadily at me in the firelight and again I was struck by the strange knowingness of her expression. In the silence I began to feel irrationally that she was capable of seeing secret and hidden things in me – things of which I was not myself aware.

'So after all, the master of Jutulak succeeded,' added Ladhya quietly. 'He defied the spirits. That takes much courage . . . Jutulak has been set free.'

I stared hard at her. 'But why did the ancient king not speak of Jutulak tonight?'

'The ancient king spoke of Jutulak when he said: "The forsaken spirit will wander for many years . . ."'

I shook my head uncomprehendingly. A deep weariness was beginning to steal over me and I sank back into the soft bed of scented grasses. My mind suddenly felt incapable of grappling any longer with the complexities of the shaman's words. Outside I could hear the wind sighing. In response the whole hut was swaying pleasantly like a well-built ship riding a modest swell at sea. All my senses dimmed suddenly and I was unable to prevent my eyes falling closed.

'The wind rocks the high-house like a cradle,' I heard Ladhya say with a smile in her voice. 'The Akha people believe, "The higher the house, the happier its users will be."'

'The master of Jutulak is sorry . . . He is very tired,' I said apologetically.

'That is good . . . The master of Jutulak can rest while Ladhya goes to prepare food.'

I heard her rise and the grass strewn on the floor rustled under her feet as she moved to the door.

'This hut is the highest of all in the village,' I heard her say; then she was gone and I was left alone in the firelit gloom.

I had thought I would sleep but my eyes opened again. I lay peacefully on my back for a long time, watching the light cast by the orange flames flickering on the thatched roof and walls. When Ladhya returned she made no sound, but I was surprised to see that she came empty-handed. Inside the door she knelt down, stretching out her fingers towards the fire; then very slowly she turned her head in my direction and I saw a smile of quiet joy on her face.

She rose and came soundlessly near. Kneeling again, at my side, she placed the palms of both her hands gently against my chest and I seemed to feel the warmth from her soul flood into me. Bending near, she whispered something, smiling even more joyously than before.

Dappled by the shimmering firelight, her youthful beauty seemed absolute, perfect. Now it was as though her soul was shining from her. In that moment my own soul was roused from me in response and suddenly I was able to see myself with her eyes: I was looking down at my own face, seeing my fair hair falling across my forehead. But not only was my sight, her sight, I could also feel what her hands felt: the roughness of my shirt, the hard bone and muscle of my chest.

I knew too with great certainty that she was at that moment in *my* eyes, seeing herself as I saw her. Seeing with a man's understanding the perfection of her own beauty, the curve of her cheek, the delicate slenderness of her wrists, her arms, her shoulders, the thrilling swell of her young breasts. I *knew* that she could feel my shuddering desire welling up suddenly, just as I felt the exquisite glow of pain deep within her, as if it were my own. To the depths of our being, I was she, she was me – and we were one.

I remembered the thought that my first glimpse of Ladhya had inspired and suddenly I knew instinctively that it had been a glimpse of the truth; the half-smile *was* the expression of an angel. In that towering palm-thatch house, illuminated by fire, swaying wildly beneath the full moon, Ladhya, niece of the Akha shaman, was both a living woman *and* a divine spirit! She was an angel, a *thewada*, mediating between heaven and earth, those baffling, contradictory but complementary worlds of the flesh and the spirit. In that moment, too, I felt with great certainty that we had always been joined from the birth of time: twin souls, twin spirits, the paired wings of one soul. Meeting her in that ancient mountain village was not our first encounter; it was, I was sure, a glorious reunion.

Stretching languorously, Ladhya pressed herself against the length of my body. I felt the delicious softness of her breasts and all her flesh moving against my own nakedness; in the next instant I shivered with the piercing joy she knew in surrendering sweetly to my masculine strength. I entered deeply, strongly: she cried out in welcome, a golden beach yielding joyously to the crash of a single, surging wave. We shook and shivered with the shock of being in turn giver, then receiver, then giver again. I was she, she was me, then to ourselves we returned. Being male, female, then male again unendingly, moment by moment, storming and being dizzyingly stormed, we were both seized at last by the fiercest and sweetest of physical frenzies. Like giant hands they swept us up to new zeniths of sensation, love and fulfilment.

The tall stilt-house continued to sway for a long time, but less wildly. The fire in the clay hearth flickered lower, the guttering flames still dancing to the wind's untamed rhythms. With passion diminishing, we clung more closely to one another. By melting, merging and possessing both our clamouring bodies, our souls had fused anew. As we became slowly aware of our separate selves, we knew with greater certainty than before that we were one and undivided.

A long, exhilarating silence ensued; then a sound at the door made me turn my head. Ladhya was stepping carefully from the ladder; moving bent low through the open doorway, her face intent on her task, she was carrying a steaming pot in both her hands. She didn't look my way or stop. When she reached the fire she busied herself with the food. Trembling from the vividness of my dream, I found I was lying quite alone on the bed of fragrant grasses.

บช

เดอะ บางกอก ซีเคร็ท

THE
BANGKOK
SECRET

Chapter Sixteen

I watched Ladhya settle the cooking pot carefully on the fire. She was totally absorbed in what she was doing and quite unaware of my feeling of confusion. With a blackened ladle she scooped steaming rice, chillies, salt and some meat into a gourd bowl. As she turned and moved towards me, holding the gourd, she smiled.

'Has Ladhya just returned?' I asked uncertainly. 'While resting, the master of Jutulak dreamed . . . But it was so vivid, he thought Ladhya was really here all the time . . .'

'The master of Jutulak must eat, not talk.'

She bent and placed the food before me on the floor of the hut, her manner bordering on reverence. Then she settled into a kneeling attitude on the dried grass a few feet away, watching me expectantly. She made no attempt to speak, intent, it seemed, on doing nothing to distract me from my eating. As I could see no chopsticks or other eating utensils, I used my fingers to scoop up the rice and meat, which proved to be delicious and tasted like the flesh of a small barking deer.

'While she cooked the rice, Ladhya's spirit was restless within her,' she said softly as I finished eating. 'All the time it tugged fiercely to return here to the high-house . . .'

In the softness of the firelight her face and body looked as they had done in my dream. Natural and unself-conscious, with the ethereal half-smile softening her features, she radiated gentle, youthful perfection.

'Why?' I asked, my eyes fixed obsessively upon her.

She busied herself pouring water into a drinking gourd and

handed it to me, holding it out like a sacred offering with both hands. Again she watched and waited until I had drained the last drop before making any attempt to reply. Then she lowered her eyes, suddenly shy under my scrutiny.

'Ladhya's spirit knows many things – things the heart of Ladhya cannot always understand or say,' she whispered. 'But her heart knows Ladhya has one big wish.'

'What is that?'

'To tell the master of Jutulak about her own dream.'

'Which one?' I asked gently.

'A dream Ladhya had many weeks ago . . . Like that of the master of Jutulak tonight, it was bright and clear. It seemed as real as life . . .'

'Who was in it?'

She looked up at me, the kind of joyful smile I'd seen in my own sleeping vision of her beginning to light her face. '. . . The big elephant you call Poo Tongkam . . . Ladhya . . . and . . .' She broke off, seemingly overcome with shyness again.

'And who?' I prompted.

She hesitated. '. . . And the master of Jutulak.'

'And what happened in Ladhya's dream?'

'Almost nothing.'

'Then why did Ladhya wish to tell the master of Jutulak about it?'

She took a deep breath. 'The master of Jutulak was riding Poo Tongkam through the forest. He was sitting on Tongkam's head . . . Ladhya walked below, beside the elephant. She carried a gourd pitcher filled with clear water from a mountain stream. The sun was bright. The trees were green and fresh . . .'

'Is that all?'

She shook her head. 'No. Ladhya has not said how things felt.'

'How did things feel?'

'Ladhya was very happy. Poo Tongkam was very happy. The master of Jutulak was smiling. Happiness was all around.' She stopped and folded her arms, unconsciously hugging herself. 'After Ladhya woke she was still very happy. The happiness lasted all that day. And all the next night. Whenever Ladhya thinks of the dream, it still makes her feel very happy.'

Infected by her smile, I smiled too. 'How did Ladhya come to love elephants so much?'

To my surprise her face clouded for the first time with sadness. 'When Ladhya was very small her mother was killed in the forest – by a wild elephant. Ladhya was very unhappy ... As Ladhya grew up she wondered why. So every day for many years Ladhya goes into the forests. To watch the wild elephants. To learn about them ...' She smiled wistfully. 'Perhaps that is why the spirits of the forest made the elephants kill Ladhya's mother – to make Ladhya watch and learn about them ...'

Moved by the poignancy of her words I fell silent. Ladhya too seemed content to say nothing further. For a while we sat in a companionable silence, feeling growing pleasure in our closeness.

'Ladhya must know a lot about elephants,' I said at last.

'Yes ... And the elephants know Ladhya. The herds do not run away when she comes – or try to hurt her.'

As always she spoke simply and modestly without seeking reaction to what she said. Rising, she went to the fire to add some dry sticks to the flames. Then for several seconds she sat gazing into the crackling glow.

'Ladhya understands the spirits of the elephants, too. That is also important ...'

Another silence fell between us and from outside I heard again the faint, wind-borne throb of drums, bamboo flutes and pounding feet coming from the long-house.

'Has Ladhya brothers and sisters?' I asked.

She shook her head, still looking into the fire. 'Ladhya's father was not of the Akha people. After Ladhya's mother was killed, he went away and never came back ... The shaman, the brother of Ladhya's mother, took care of Ladhya. The shaman has children ... But the real brothers and sisters of Ladhya are the forests and the animals in them.'

'Does Ladhya help the shaman in his work?'

She nodded. 'Yes, sometimes.'

'Won't the shaman be angry if he knows Ladhya has left the full-moon ceremonies?'

'Yes. The shaman warned Ladhya. He said, "Have nothing to do with the outsider."'

'Why did he say that?'

'The shaman fears the master of Jutulak will bring evil spirits to our village.'

'Then why did Ladhya not obey the shaman?'

She turned from the fire to look in my direction. 'Watching in the forests, Ladhya has learned many things . . . It is not always good to fear the spirits. It is not right always to obey them . . .'

She moved back from the fire and knelt again in the dried grass a few feet away. The rekindled fire shone softly on her curved cheeks, her bare shoulders, her arms, her dark-tipped breasts and the silver ornaments she wore on her forehead and around her neck. Looking steadily at me, she smiled again.

'The shaman does not know the master of Jutulak. The shaman has not seen him working in the forests. Ladhya knows what the elephants know. The master's spirit is always in harmony with the spirits of his elephants. Such a man can bring no evil to our village . . .'

'Did the shaman prophesy against the master of Jutulak tonight because he is afraid?'

She shook her head. 'The shaman spoke truly with the voice of the ancient king's spirit.'

'And does Ladhya believe too that there is great danger for the master of Jutulak?'

'Yes.' She nodded without hesitation.

'And that he should leave the lands of the Akha people at once and go far away?'

She thought for a long time before replying, her face serious. 'It takes courage to defy the spirits. The master of Jutulak has shown such courage. But it is wrong to act always against them . . . The ancient king said: "Now it is *not* the time to fight . . ." Ladhya believes it is wise to obey the ancient spirit.'

I considered her words in silence, going over in my mind all that the shaman had said in his apparent trance. As I did so, the gusting wind brought louder sounds from the ritual long-house. A new dance was accelerating towards its climax and hearing the unrelenting rhythms added a new sense of urgency to my thoughts.

'Perhaps the master of Jutulak will have to leave – but Ladhya must remember this: one day he will return.' I looked directly at her. 'Does Ladhya understand that?'

She gazed back at me steadily for a long time; then she nodded gravely. 'Ladhya understands.'

I paused. 'When the master of Jutulak first arrived in the

village, Ladhya said, "It is good he has come here at last." Why did she say that?'

'Because she wished to speak to him of her dream.' Her glowing smile returned. 'It was very important for the master of Jutulak to know about that.'

I sat and stared, transfixed by the sight of her.

'Before . . . he . . . leaves . . .' I said groping for words, 'the master of Jutulak . . . must say something of his own dream in this high-house . . . But it is difficult, because he does not really understand what he is going to say . . .'

She waited expectantly, her eyes fixed on mine.

'In the dream, the spirits of Ladhya and the master of Jutulak seemed . . . to change bodies . . . This happened many times . . . It seemed as if they became one another in turn. And could see themselves through the eyes of the other . . . And could feel what the other felt . . . very strongly . . . and in every way . . .'

I broke off. Recalling and relating the details of the dream required more effort than I'd imagined. To my surprise, putting into words for the first time what had previously been vaguely sensed intuitions brought the damp of perspiration to my brow.

'. . . But it also felt as if the spirits, the very souls of Ladhya and the master of Jutulak, were one . . . Or perhaps twin spirits who had been joined through many past ages and many lives . . . No words were said . . . It was very mysterious . . . The master of Jutulak had never thought of such things being possible . . .'

Ladhya made no move to speak. She sat watching and listening as she must have learned to do in the forests over the years, waiting patiently until she was sure I had finished.

'There was also one other thing,' I went on, then hesitated.

What I was about to say seemed more outlandish even than the rest. Then I looked again at the beauty of her face and body. Kneeling close to me in the twilit hut with the knowing half-smile on her face, it seemed as if she was already aware of what I would say.

'Like the other things it was impossible . . . In the dream Ladhya seemed to be an angel, a divine spirit, a messenger between heaven and earth . . . But she was a living woman, too – both angel and woman in one body . . . And as in Ladhya's dream, there were feelings of great happiness . . . It was more beautiful than anything I could have imagined . . .'

In the silence that followed the sound of the ritual from the long-house again became audible. It was rising to a rapturous frenzy of drumming, stamping and chanting. Then abruptly it ceased and only the sighing of the wind could be heard.

'Ladhya thanks the master of Jutulak for telling her his dream,' she said softly. 'It is most beautiful – and it is all true.'

'How?' I exclaimed. 'How can it be true?'

'Although Ladhya was awake, she had the same dream while she prepared the food . . . Her spirit truly came to the master of Jutulak . . . Now the master of Jutulak knows what Ladhya has known for a long time . . .'

I shifted closer and kneeled in the dried grass facing her. Taking both her hands in mine, I held them against my chest. 'In the dream,' I said in a whisper, 'Ladhya and the master of Jutulak embraced in passion. At her first touch he seemed to feel the warmth of her soul flow into him . . .'

She smiled and pressed gently against me with both her hands. 'Can the master of Jutulak feel that now?'

'Yes.'

We looked at one another for a long time; then I put my arms around her slender shoulders. Her skin was as smooth as brushed silk and with an involuntary groan, I drew her fiercely against myself. Beneath my knees I could feel the grass and hard bamboo rods of the hut floor; if I had reached out I could have brushed a hand through the flickering flames of the fire and experienced the pain of burning; I could feel the whole hut swaying and hear its timbers creaking in the wind. This time without any doubt I was awake, fully alive, not slumbering and dreaming.

I smelled the food in the cooking pot. I inhaled the living scents of Ladhya's hair and body mixed with rank fragrances from the forest, the earth and the trees. I bent my head until our mouths met. Our breath mingled and quickened as our bodies moved urgently together in the fierce, instinctive reflexes of love. What had happened in the dream happened again in reality. While the high-house continued swaying in the wind and the ritual chanting grew loud once more in the village long-house, our physical senses shuddered and trembled towards a redoubled ecstasy.

ข ข

เดอะ บางกอก ซีเคร็ท

THE
BANGKOK
SECRET

Chapter Seventeen

แบนช บอนชกั ะอน่

My heart sank when the train carrying me from Nakon Lampang to Bangkok at last rolled down out of the jungle-covered
hills on to Thailand's flat, central plain. Staring through my
carriage window at the unending paddy fields and empty
swamps, I experienced a keen sense of loss. While the train
was toiling southward over the tree-shrouded gradients and
foaming ravines north of Phitsanulok, I had not been able to
convince myself I was leaving the wondrous teak forests behind. But the featureless flatlands through which the train
rattled for hour after hour on its way to the capital finally
convinced me of the reality of my situation.

At Hualampong Station I half expected to find a reception
committee of grim-faced senior managers from the company's
head office. In the event a former jungle wallah of my own age
whom I knew and liked had brought a horse-drawn gharry for
me and my luggage. Impeccably dressed in a white linen suit
and a solar topee helmet that befitted a rising young executive
of the Anglo-Siamese Teak Trading Company, Jack Purling
greeted me with a guarded smile.

'I must say you appear remarkably sane, Adam,' he said after
looking me up and down and taking a suitcase from my hand.
'We'd been led to believe down here you'd had too much jungle
and gone completely off your head.'

I had made up my mind to try to say as little as possible
about the events of recent days. So I merely grinned as we
loaded up the gharry and climbed aboard. It was late afternoon
and Purling explained that he had a couple of urgent business

calls to make which would take us on a roundabout route to the company's residential compound. The calls were connected with the crisis I'd caused, he said heavily, and being tired from the long train journey, I settled back against the leather seat, gratefully inhaling the fresh air.

The streets of 1950s Bangkok into which we jogged were still largely free of motor cars; electric trams rumbled along its near-empty boulevards and apart from the gharries which were driven by Chinese *sais*, rickshaws were the principal form of transport. The modern Bangkok of the 1980s, choking with exhaust fumes and traffic jams, still lay a long way in the future.

As our open four-wheeler ran smoothly along New Road towards the Chao Phraya river, I found myself scanning the pavement crowds of the business quarter. The sheer multitude of people made me realise how long I'd lived isolated in the jungle. Many nationalities were visible in the swarm: Chinese who dominated the commerce of Bangkok, a sprinkling of white Europeans, Malays, Burmese, Indians, Vietnamese, Cambodians. Many Thais, who today prefer Western clothes, then still wore their distinctive, brightly coloured *panung* wrapped around the lower parts of their bodies; Bhuddhist monks with shaven heads were also strikingly garbed in robes of saffron. But scanning the throng from the moving gharry reminded me suddenly that my time in Thailand was fast running out; then in that same instant I realised I was closely scrutinising the face of every Thai male under forty whom we passed. Even in Bangkok, part of my mind was still unconsciously searching for Jutulak!

'Why do you think I've been called down here?' I asked Jack Purling, still watching the crowds on both sides of the street. 'What do you think the company moguls have in mind for me?'

Purling subjected me to a searching appraisal. 'Obviously, Adam, you're not yet aware of how much flak has been flying our way as a result of your mysterious escapades in the north. We've had at least half a dozen very ugly visits from the Butcher of Bangkok's men . . . They come to our offices with the flaps of their pistol holsters ostentatiously unbuttoned. They say strange, threatening things – but they never become specific. We don't know what you've done or why they're so miffed with us.' He paused significantly. 'There's even been a veiled threat about confiscating the major teak-extraction licences we hold in the area you've been working. If they do that, the company could be ruined.'

I stared at him, appalled by the seriousness of what he had said. 'Would they really go that far?'

Purling shrugged and a frown settled on his brow. 'There's no telling . . . It all depends on what they really want and why.'

He stopped the gharry to drop off the first of two packages he carried; then we rode on side by side in silence. During the long train journey my mind had refused to anticipate the likely effect of my actions in Bangkok. My head was still seething with thoughts of Jutulak and the mystery surrounding him. The events of the night I had spent in the Akha village still loomed large, too, among my reflections. On arrival back at my northern headquarters the following morning I had refused to give any explanation for my absence. I had packed my bags and thanked as many of my staff as I could personally before taking formal leave of my furious superior. Perhaps this refusal to look facts squarely in the face had been a sign of exhaustion – but in the bustle of Bangkok's busy streets, my mind for the first time began trying to come to terms with what I needed to do.

'If you'll pardon my frankness, Adam,' Purling was saying in a serious voice, 'you seem to have got yourself in a hell of a mess. Between you and me, the directors are probably in two minds – whether to allow the authorities to arrest you, interrogate you, put you on trial, do whatever they like with you – or to ship you home fast to save your skin.'

'Which course do you think they favour right now?' I asked, still looking hard at the passing throngs of people.

'Well, since you didn't seem overly sensitive to the company's interests up north, I don't think there's a great deal of sympathy for your lily-white neck down here. Quite the reverse. There's a definite feeling, I know, among certain directors that they'd like to "hand that blighter Hampson over to the Butcher and let him take his chances".'

'I haven't actually committed any crime, Jack, you know . . .' I began mildly, then broke off in mid-sentence on catching sight of a familiar face.

'What do you mean "you haven't committed any crime"?' asked Purling.

I didn't reply; the face I had seen was neither from the distant past nor from the northern forests. It wasn't among the cosmopolitan flow of peoples on the crowded pavements either. It belonged in fact to the passenger in another horse-drawn gharry following close behind us. A young Thai in the crowd moving in the opposite direction had caused me to turn suddenly in my seat. I saw at once I was guilty of wishful thinking since the boy was really nothing like Jutulak. But in that same instant my eyes locked with those of a scowling, beetle-browed Thai who had travelled in another compartment of my carriage all the way from Nakon Lampang.

He immediately lifted a newspaper in front of him and just as quickly I turned to face forwards. I told myself that it could be a coincidence: that particular passenger might merely have been taking the same route away from the station. Then our gharry swung into a narrower street and I looked round to find that the other carriage had turned too. This time I also saw another face from the train. Riding in a canvas-hooded rick-shaw was a thin, dark-faced southerner who had stared into my compartment whenever he passed along the corridor. I waited and watched while our gharry made two further changes of direction, then looked quickly behind once more. At a glance I saw that both the carriage and the rickshaw were still moving steadily behind us at a distance.

'What do you mean, "you didn't commit any crime"?' asked Purling impatiently, a second time.

'My camp was attacked by Chinese bandits. They killed my headman and kidnapped one of my best mahouts. I gave chase and tried to rescue him . . .'

'Why on earth did you try to do it yourself?' demanded Purling in an incredulous voice.

'Because the provincial Thai gendarmes wouldn't have dared go near an armed caravan of Kuomintang smugglers escorting ten tons of opium on a hundred mules,' I said exasperatedly.

Purling turned in his seat to face me, his eyebrows raised in disbelief. 'Do I understand you to say, you did "dare to go near" this armed caravan of Chinese opium smugglers?'

'Yes, that's right.'

'May I ask why?'

'Because the mahout had done nothing to deserve being kidnapped.'

Purling stared hard at me again, as though having great difficulty giving any credence at all to my story. 'And with what success, Adam, in the end, did you "dare to go near" the armed caravan?'

'I was lucky – in the dark I managed to free the mahout. I used two elephants to create a diversion.'

'You did?' Purling's eyebrows shot up even higher. 'My dear Adam, didn't you know that Police-General Phao and his cronies are all up to their necks in the opium smuggling racket – and every other racket for that matter?'

I smiled ruefully. 'I suppose I didn't stop to think too deeply.'

'Correct, you didn't. And where is this precious mahout now, may I enquire?'

'I don't know. He disappeared again . . .'

I let my voice trail off and stared ahead. We had come suddenly in sight of the white, crenellated walls of the Grand Palace. Above the high battlements the gold and azure roofs of the royal pavilions reflected the sinking sun; tapering, needle-like spires, exotically ornamented *chedis* and *prangs* soared above the dazzling ramparts, stamping a fairy-tale image of a king's dwelling on the bright sky. My first sight of the Grand Palace on arrival in Bangkok nearly a decade earlier had left a deep impression on my mind. Ever since, those flamboyant palaces and shrines had symbolised for me the mystical heart of the nation. But on catching sight of them this time, they also served as a powerful reminder of the harrowing drama in which I had become embroiled in recent weeks: this was the fabled setting in which King Ananda had met his mysterious and violent death.

Just outside the Grand Palace, close to the north-east corner occupied by the fabled Temple of the Emerald Buddha, stood the Lak Muang, another pavilion sacred to the Siamese. It housed a gilded pillar erected nearly two centuries earlier by King Rama I as the foundation stone of both Bangkok and the Chakri dynasty. The shrine is believed to be the home of the capital's guardian spirit and is always aswarm with Bangkok people making offerings in the hope of securing good fortune. As our gharry rolled by, I remembered that I had released two miniature sparrows from a tiny cage at the shrine during my first visit. This symbolic act of 'merit-making' was a Buddhist custom and the tiny birds had winged joyfully away into the sunset over the spires of the Emerald Buddha Temple. With the sun again beginning to dip towards those same spires, I found myself doubting very much whether any symbolic merit I might have acquired then, or since, would help ward off the various disasters threatening me.

Thinking these thoughts, I glanced round casually. My two fellow passengers from the train were still following us in the shadow of the Grand Palace walls. They appeared to be taking pains not to narrow the gap; both the rickshaw and the gharry were continuing to move at a steady pace, matching our speed exactly.

'This mahout of yours "disappeared" again, you say?' asked Purling thoughtfully, as if he had woken suddenly from digesting what I'd said. 'How exactly did he disappear?'

'I don't know,' I said slowly. 'We were resting on a mountain in the dark. The next thing I knew, he'd gone. He said he didn't want to be rescued . . .'

Purling let out a muffled exclamation. 'Why, for heaven's sake?'

I shook my head helplessly. 'I don't know – if I told you he said it was something to do with evil spirits and karmic retribution, would you be any the wiser?'

'Aaaah . . . evil spirits, old chap . . . I see!' Purling relaxed back into his seat with an exaggerated show of relief. 'Yes, of course, evil spirits! The explanation for all the inexplicable things that happen in modern Thailand!' He stared up at the blue sky and tipped his solar topee to the back of his head. 'And in the meantime you lost two very valuable elephants in the jungle as well as two ponies. You also left important work unfinished and completely disrupted the smooth running of the entire northern region by throwing Nakon Lampang into a panic.'

'I took a calculated risk, Jack, I admit. But you've worked the northern forests yourself . . . You know well enough that in the jungle you're often forced to take tough decisions quickly . . .'

'Forgive me again, Adam,' said Purling, a note of sarcasm creeping into his voice, 'but may I remind you that you were sent to the northern forests to fell and extract teak trees.

Girdle them, fell them, drag them into creeks and rivers with elephants. Then float them down to the sawmills here in Bangkok. So they can be used in the humdrum, domestic process of building houses and so on. Do you remember that now? You were never authorised to use our elephants to create brilliant military diversions at night. Or to attack armed opium smugglers. Or to use mahouts and camp coolies as your own private expeditionary force for ill-advised rescue operations of your own design.' He cleared his throat portentously. 'You should never have left the army, Adam, if you wanted to do that sort of thing . . .'

'This begins to sound like my meeting with the Old Man,' I remarked gloomily. 'Until now I'd always thought of you as a friend.'

'I'm sorry, old chap.' Purling adopted a more conciliatory tone. 'I didn't mean to preachify . . . But that's certainly something of what the General Manager will say to you.'

'I've always done my work conscientiously, Jack. For nearly ten years I've enjoyed every minute of it and never given any grounds for complaint.'

'That's what makes it all the more incredible. You're not only one of the best jungle wallahs the company has, you're one of the very best it's *ever* had. That's why everybody's so staggered now this has happened.'

'There were exceptional reasons, Jack, for what I did,' I said quietly. 'But I don't want to talk any more now.'

Purling leaned forward and touched the Chinese *sais* lightly on the shoulder. Pulling on the reins, he drew the gharry into the kerb in front of a nondescript office building in a business area close to the river. Picking up a large manila envelope from behind the seats, Purling prepared to climb out.

'These are papers for the company's Thai lawyers,' he said, gesturing with the package to the upper storeys of the building. 'They're working day and night trying to puzzle out how we can hang on to those forest licences and leases.' He leaned towards me, lowering his voice. 'Lawyers won't be much use if the crooked generals decide they're going to take them from us anyway. But we have to try everything we can.' He straightened up. 'I'll be one minute only. Wait right here.'

Purling made to turn away but I reached out and touched

his arm to halt him. 'Jack, what are your instructions regarding me?'

'I've been given responsibility for escorting you back to the Chumsheds,' he said, using the humorous nickname generations of jungle wallahs had given to the drab, monastic living quarters reserved for bachelors that adjoined the company's head offices. 'I'm to see you're settled into your room there. Then make sure you get some dinner, before escorting you to the home of the General Manager at 9.30 sharp this evening for the showdown . . . There just happens to be a liner leaving for England at midnight. If you're lucky, you'll be on it. A berth has been provisionally booked in your name.'

As he strode purposefully away, I looked round again. The other gharry had halted at the kerb fifty yards away and its occupant was again concealed behind his newspaper. The rickshaw had stopped on the opposite side of the street; but the dark-faced southerner had not climbed out.

Moving unhurriedly so as not to arouse their suspicions, I got down from the gharry and began to pace slowly back and forth beside it, as though stretching cramped legs. From the carriage, I had seen the glint of water at the end of an alley leading alongside the office building. Without raising my head I checked again as I wandered aimlessly up and down. When I was sure the two watching men were convinced I was merely killing time, I turned suddenly and dived into the mouth of the alley. Sprinting as hard as I could, I headed towards a small landing stage that I could see jutting out into the Chao Phraya river.

ບ ຫ

เดอะ บางกอก ซีเคริท

THE
BANGKOK
SECRET

Chapter Eighteen

In the sunset, the mighty spires of the Temple of the Dawn had suddenly become dramatic, black silhouettes. Behind them the western sky blazed the colour of molten gold. In their shadow the empty lighterman's boat I had hired rocked and rolled alarmingly as it butted downstream through choppy water with its rusty, antiquated engine roaring at full throttle.

The Chao Phraya, effectively Bangkok's central boulevard, was teeming as usual with sampans, rice barges, ferries, freighters, lighters and single-oared skiffs all plying busily up and down and across the broad river. Narrowing my eyes in the glare of the sun, I peered upstream, trying to see if the men from the gharry and the rickshaw had succeeded in chartering any kind of boat. But among the swarm of craft speckling the river I could not be certain.

I had put about a hundred yards between myself and the landing stage at the foot of the alley before my two shadows from Nakon Lampang emerged breathless and dishevelled on the waterfront. They had spotted me, I was sure, but no other boat appeared to be immediately available for them to give chase. By good fortune I had found a Chinese lighterman curled up asleep in the stern of the only craft which was moored close to the alley. Jumping from the wharf, I had shaken him firmly and flourished a large enough wad of *tical* under his nose to shock him into instant wakefulness. I shouted, '*Wat Kwan Kittima! Wat Kwan Kittima!*' several times, while gesturing for him to start the engine and head for Thonburi, the once separate city criss-crossed by *klongs* that comprises the western bank of the Chao Phraya.

To the Chinese boatman's credit, the lighter was started up and under way within seconds, although the rickety engine belched smoke unceasingly and occasionally faltered. I immediately thrust a hundred *tical* into his hand, promising him more if he got me to *Wat Kwan Kittima* quickly. Bemused by the magnitude of the sum and the speed of events, he clung to his tiller, weaving riskily between ships and skiffs, looking back and forth from my face to the banknotes in his hand as though he suspected he might still be dreaming.

While veering sharply across the river, the engine gave an almighty cough and lost power altogether. We spun to a halt directly in the path of a large international freighter and wallowed at rest, watching helplessly as it bore down on us. For a tense minute or more the oncoming freighter loomed ever larger above us, but in the nick of time the Chinese succeeded in restarting the engine. With a deafening roar, we shot across to the far bank and the Chinese giggled in relief as we swung westward into *Klong Bangkok Yai* without further mishap.

Soon we were careering past the verandas of open-fronted wooden-pile houses that projected over the canal. Naked children splashed in and out of the *klong* from their doorsteps, mothers laundered clothes in the water, girls stood waist-deep washing their long black hair; peasant women plied boats laden with vegetables from door to door and the smell of spices and cooking floated from charcoal stoves wedged on the boats of itinerant food vendors. We passed clusters of moored sampans that served as waterborne homes and from time to time my hopes rose as the gilded, ornamented eaves of a Buddhist *wat* came in sight, glowing in the light of the sinking sun. Each time I turned questioningly to my boatman asking '*Wat Kwan Kittima?*' But each time he shook his head and replied, 'Not yet.'

In seeking out the Buddhist temple in Thonburi where Jutulak had taken his vow of silence, I was forcing the lighter and its stuttering engine along waterways where life had changed little in centuries. Because of its unique *klongs* dotted with temples and teak houses, Bangkok had long ago been dubbed the 'Venice of Asia'. Today, many of those canals that once veined the city have been filled with tarmacadam and concrete; but most remain in Thonburi, which, until the royal palaces were built across the river, was itself the original Siamese capital. The Emerald Buddha for a time had resided in Thonburi's pyramidal Temple of the Dawn – *Wat Arun* – and as the lighter's bows parted floating islands of water-hyacinth and duckweed on the surface of the *klongs*, I found myself wondering whether Jutulak had passed along these ancient water routes each day going to and from the Emerald Buddha's present home, the battlemented Grand Palace compound.

As we neared the temple where Jutulak had worshipped, we turned more frequently, entering ever-narrowing canals. Each time, I twisted in my seat and looked behind, checking for signs of pursuit. I saw no fast-moving craft among the multitude of skiffs and market boats that thronged the waterways but I guessed that our erratic crossing of the river and our entry into the large *Klong Bangkok Yai* would have been easily noticed. If my pursuers were astute enough, I knew they would question families dwelling in the pile houses at the canal junctions; heads had invariably been raised as we sped by at a rate of knots which attracted natural curiosity. But dusk was closing in, flickering oil lamps were being lit on boats and in the houses, and there seemed to be good reason to hope that we had eluded them.

Wat Kwan Kittima, when we came in sight of it in the deepening gloom, possessed the fragile, ethereal beauty common to many of Thailand's ancient Buddhist temples. Its multi-tiered roofs, tiled in orange and green, were crested with gilded serpents; a central golden *stupa*, slender as a needle at its tip, glimmered in the fading light. The white-walled *bot* faced the canal, flanked by smaller chapels, and the courtyard was surrounded by cloisters in which rows of placid Buddha figures were visible. Climbing out on to the bank, I told the Chinese to conceal his boat nearby and wait for me; then I entered the front gate and walked briskly across the deserted courtyard.

The gilded doors of the *bot*, carved with writhing Chinese dragons, were firmly closed so I stepped quietly into the *viharn* where I could see a young, shaven-headed monk wearing the robes of a novice. I placed my palms together politely in a *wai* and asked the youth if I could speak urgently with the *acharn* of the temple – the abbot. The novice listened to me with an expressionless face, then indicated I should wait and walked slowly away as if unable to comprehend the worldly concept of urgency.

Left alone in the silent *viharn* I found myself glancing anxiously towards the *klong* every few seconds: the darkness was deepening but the longer I had to wait, the more likely it seemed that my pursuers would track me down. My anxiety mounted and I began to pace agitatedly back and forth across the stone floor. Then faintly at first, but growing louder, I heard the melodious, repetitive sounds of monks chanting prayers in Pali, the sacred language of Buddhism. Their voices were coming from behind the closed doors of the *bot* and I stopped to listen. It was suddenly obvious that the *acharn* was leading the evening prayers and I would have to await their conclusion. Soon, to my surprise, the sounds began to soothe away some of my anxiety and I gave up my pacing. The walls bore mural paintings that were dimly visible in the altar candlelight and I began to examine them casually as I waited.

While travelling in the north I had spent many nights in village temples and I quickly recognised the faded paintings as scenes from the *Jataka*, Buddhist nativity tales which dealt with the ten previous lives of the Buddha. In sequences running round the whole chapel he was shown in various guises, eventually overcoming temptation in his tenth life and descending to teach amidst symbols of earth, heaven and hell. All the paintings were at the same time, I noticed, meticulous representations of Siamese life; ornate jewellery and betel boxes, vaunted symbols of rank and wealth among the elite of the nation, were frequently depicted in the panels. Registering these details jogged an elusive memory of something Jutulak had said during our last conversation and I was cudgelling my brain, trying to recall exactly what it was, when I heard a soft footfall behind me. Turning, I saw the novice monk had returned and was beckoning to me.

He led the way through the doors of the dimly lit main shrine and I followed to find the *acharn* seated close to the altar, dwarfed by a huge, golden Buddha statue. Beneath the idol an altar was decked with bright-coloured flowers, heaps of fruits and a seven-branched candelabra. Flickering light from the candles illuminated a shimmering array of incense burners, statuettes and ornaments which had been set about the foot of the altar. Finely wrought in silver and gold, the objects added a glow of material opulence to the silent shrine.

In the mysterious half-light, I could see that the *acharn* was a small, wrinkled southern Thai with deep-set eyes. Illogically, something in his immobile, high-cheekboned face reminded me at once of the Akha shaman. Seated in the lotus position with his hands spread palm upwards on his knees, he wore a simple saffron-coloured robe which left one gnarled shoulder bare. He neither moved nor spoke as the novice motioned for me to kneel before him. Scarcely blinking in his absolute stillness, he waited patiently for me to speak, watching intently without seeming to look directly into my eyes.

'I've come here, Venerable *Acharn*, to seek your advice about Jutulak Somiboon,' I murmured in Thai, joining my hands in another respectful *wai*. 'Jutulak served as a novice in your temple. Later, he told me, you hid him here when he was in grave danger. He saw something very important at the Grand Palace . . . Do you remember Jutulak?'

The *acharn* did not speak or move a muscle. He continued to sit perfectly still, giving me his full attention, signalling his affirmation, I assumed, by his lack of protest. A deep hush had fallen over the temple and, looking round, I saw that the novice had retreated, leaving the doors to the courtyard open.

'In the northern forests Jutulak worked with elephants as he had done at the Grand Palace. Recently troops came to capture him. I followed them and rescued him – but he disappeared again. Before he went he told me about this temple and the generous help you gave him. I am in some danger myself now because I helped him. I may have to leave Thailand tonight . . .' I paused, looking uncertainly at the impassive, unreadable features of the abbot. 'Can you give me any information that might help me find Jutulak again? Are his parents still alive? . . . Are they here in Bangkok? . . . Where do you think he might go to hide?'

The aged monk shifted his gaze slightly until his eyes held mine. He stared at me with great intensity for a minute or more, as though minutely inspecting my inner soul. Eventually, still without speaking, he motioned with his chin for me to draw nearer to him.

When I complied, he picked up a taper, dipped it into a pitcher of lustral water at his side and with quick, deft movements sprinkled a few drops on my face and upper body. His lips moved silently in time with his actions. Then he motioned me to bend forward while he placed around my neck a brass Buddha amulet suspended from twisted threads of saffron cotton. Taking my right hand, he tied a shorter bracelet of the same coloured cotton around my wrist, then resumed his impassive, unblinking posture.

This ritual blessing and unrequested bestowal of protective symbols served greatly to increase my unease; it seemed to me as if the ageing monk had divined some urgent need for help from my manner and, despite myself, I turned and peered nervously into the darkness that was fast enveloping the *klong*. But as far as I could tell there was no interruption of the normal rhythms of canal life; the night appeared to be still and peaceful.

'Venerable *Acharn*,' I said quietly, 'I believe Jutulak told you all he knew about the terrible events of 1946 at the Grand Palace . . . Perhaps you and he are the only two people outside the palace who know the real truth. I tried to help Jutulak because I believe it is very important. I hope the truth will not be allowed to wither and die behind a temple vow of silence.'

'I have not seen Jutulak Somiboon for many years,' said the abbot in an undertone, still gazing fixedly at me. 'If ever he comes to *Wat Kwan Kittima* again I will give instructions for him to be told of your visit . . . Leave details of your name and the whereabouts of your home . . .' He drew in his breath slowly and I detected a sudden wariness in his eyes. 'You should be careful – do not linger too long here at *Wat Kwan Kittima* . . .'

'Thank you, Venerable *Acharn*, for your concern – but there's one more thing,' I said urgently. 'Jutulak told me he left something here. Something precious . . . something that he perhaps received from the king . . .'

The *acharn* nodded without hesitation towards the foot of the altar. Following his eye I found myself looking at a gold betel box inlaid with precious stones that, because of its beauty and craftsmanship, stood out among the other ornaments arrayed around the altar.

'The betel box?' I asked in surprise and the abbot nodded.

I stared at the little four-legged casket which was similar to those depicted in the murals over which I had browsed minutes earlier. It was then that I remembered that the king's gift to Jutulak had been inspired by something he had described in the temple paintings of *Wat Kwan Kittima*. Even without rising I could see that the betel box was embossed with the Thai royal insignia and a sudden wild thought struck me: perhaps the casket had contained some vital piece of evidence.

'Venerable *Acharn*, was anything found inside the betel box?' I asked in a low voice.

'We do not know. It has remained locked ever since Jutulak Somiboon brought it here . . .'

I rose to my feet and took an impulsive step towards the altar. 'Couldn't it be opened?'

'It is already too late!'

The unmistakable warning note in the voice of the monk stopped me in mid-stride. His face had taken on a neutral blankness and his gaze was flickering uneasily back and forth from me to the door. When I turned in that direction I saw twenty or more stockily built Thai troops in steel helmets and jungle-green battledress running fast across the courtyard.

Moving silently and warily in rubber-soled boots, the soldiers entered the *bot* and fanned out quickly in a semicircle on both sides of the door. They clutched ugly black sub-machine guns in front of them and the muzzles of the weapons were pointing directly at me. In response to a crisp order, half a dozen of the soldiers dashed forward to pinion my arms at my sides. Without speaking, they tied a blindfold around my eyes, snapped manacles on my wrists and dragged me bodily from the temple.

บ ช

เดอะ บางกอก ซีเคร็ท

THE
BANGKOK
SECRET

Chapter Nineteen

แปดเก้า แปดเก้า ยอยา

'I had you brought here, Hampson, to answer one or two questions,' rasped a disembodied voice speaking Thai close in front of my face. 'And it will be best for you – and for the Anglo-Siamese Teak Trading Company – if you are completely honest in your answers ... Do you understand what I'm saying?'

The blindfold remained over my eyes, my hands were still chained together behind my back and I could feel two guards standing at either side of the wooden stool on which I had been seated. I considered remaining silent, saying absolutely nothing in protest at my treatment, but my curiosity about the questions got the better of me and I nodded truculently. 'Yes, I understand very well what you're saying.'

'The mahout Jutulak Somiboon – where is he now?'

Despite my discomfort and apprehension I felt my spirits lift. By asking such a question my interrogator seemed to confirm what the Akha shaman had claimed – that Jutulak had not been recaptured. The revelation encouraged me to answer calmly and I made up my mind to give away as little as possible.

'I know absolutely nothing of Jutulak's whereabouts.'

'But you seized him from men authorised by the security forces to supervise his safety and protection.' The voice spoke harshly, its owner close enough for me to feel his breath on my face. 'You must know something!'

'After I rescued him, Jutulak ran away from me,' I replied evenly. 'He became lost in the jungle in the darkness. He was very frightened. He said it had been his fate to be captured. He wanted to die. He told me I shouldn't have interfered.'

From the nature of the silence that followed I guessed that the answer had surprised my listeners. My interrogator straightened up and I got the impression that he felt a slight sense of bafflement. Then he came close again, hunching over me, either to intimidate or better evaluate my answers.

'These are dangerous times in Thailand, Hampson,' he said in a threatening tone, speaking directly into my right ear. 'If we don't know where Jutulak Somiboon is, how can we protect him? He's in greater danger now than before . . . There are many bitter rivals in Bangkok – in the army, politics and in business. Different groups and individuals are contending over the smallest things – and the biggest! There is much distrust . . . The action we took, you should have known, was to ensure Jutulak Somiboon's safety and well-being . . . And our action in bringing you here tonight also springs from a similar concern for *your* security.'

'And these handcuffs are specially designed for the same purpose, I suppose,' I said sarcastically.

'There was no time for discussion about bringing you here,' replied the voice smoothly. 'We could not allow that. Your progress from Nakong Lampang was carefully monitored. After you arrived in Bangkok we formed the impression you might be exposing yourself to some new danger. We believed that you needed our assistance. We are very concerned, you see, to be hospitable to *farang* in our country – but there are many different ways of showing that concern . . .'

'Would removing this blindfold be another?' I asked.

'My apologies for the blindfold. But as you will appreciate, it does effectively free you from a burden – the unnecessary knowledge of our identities.' The voice broke off and laughed mirthlessly. 'You should be grateful to us, Hampson.'

I moved my head surreptitiously, flexing the muscles in my face in an effort to further loosen the blindfold which had begun to slacken a little during the journey from the temple. Up to that moment I had no idea where my nightmare interrogation was taking place. Having dragged me from the *bot*, the troops had bundled me roughly in and out of first a motor boat, then a wheeled vehicle – probably a canvas-covered pick-up truck or a jeep. After a short drive at high speed in a convoy of three or four other vehicles, I had been marched briskly along echoing corridors of what I guessed was a military or police barracks.

The room into which I had been led seemed to be small and bare; from faint shuffling noises that I'd heard on entry, I sensed there were several silent watchers positioned around its walls. After I was seated under guard on the stool, several minutes passed uneventfully; then the door flew open and my interrogator entered to the sound of men saluting and snapping to attention. He wore hard-heeled shoes or boots and paced around noisily for some time, inspecting me thoroughly before starting to bark out his questions. Robbed of sight, my other senses gave me an instinctive impression of an uneasy but powerful Thai military man: peremptory, impatient and arrogant, he was obviously accustomed to being obeyed at all times, promptly and without question.

'But whether you're grateful to be relieved of that burden or not, Hampson,' he continued, 'I should remind you of one thing: the future of the Anglo-Siamese Teak Trading Company will be very bleak indeed if you ever make any public reference to this privileged meeting.' He paused and laughed humourlessly again. 'I take it that's clear enough.'

I nodded. 'That's clear above all else.'

'Good – then perhaps you will answer one other important question. It concerns what Jutulak Somiboon may have seen at the Grand Palace on 9 June 1946. He spoke with you about that, we know, from informants. But did he tell you everything that he saw?'

An unnatural hush descended on the silent observers in the room. They ceased to fidget and stood perfectly still. Although I was unable to see them, I could sense they were keyed up waiting for my answer ...

'Jutulak told me nothing at all of what he saw. He had taken a vow of silence long ago – because of his affection and loyalty to the memory of the late King Ananda ...'

I felt my interrogator bend close over me again; this time he spoke very softly. 'Despite the warnings I've given you, Hampson, I believe you're lying!'

'No! I'm not! I'm telling the truth.'

Having felt the blindfold loosen, I let my voice rise in excitement. At the same time I shook my head violently from side to side as though in a desperate protest and succeeded in dislodging the cloth an inch or two at one side. It slipped down on to my cheek and I caught a clear glimpse of my interrogator's face before he cursed and turned away.

Wearing a red military beret with battledress tunic and colonel's shoulder brevets, he had a broad, cruelly handsome face. In that fleeting glance I saw that he was powerfully built, a burly, broad-shouldered man with the pale complexion of a northerner. Several years later, with the help of newspaper library photographs and the assistance of sympathetic friends in the diplomatic service, I was able to identify him as Colonel Kasem Petcharat, later to become a major-general.

Official military records showed that during those months Kasem Petcharat had been colonel-in-charge of police operations in the region around Chiang Rai; so it seemed almost certain he had been responsible for overseeing Jutulak's kidnapping, using Kuomintang irregulars who had been operating as unofficial border guards during those years. My successful rescue mission had obviously caused him great personal embarrassment and the eventual confirmation of his identity helped explain belatedly the mood of deep antagonism in which he conducted the interrogation.

His immediate reaction to my slipping off the blindfold was one of fury. Keeping his back turned, he yelled loudly at the guards to secure it again. They tied it so tightly this time that it cut painfully into the flesh of my face. Meanwhile Kasem Petcharat allowed several minutes to pass while he paced back and forth, seemingly settling his temper. When he stopped in front of me again, I heard him breathe deeply before he spoke.

'Whether or not you were lying just now, Hampson, I want you to answer me one other thing . . . Why did you go to *Wat Kwan Kittima*? What did you hope to learn there?'

Remembering the impassive *acharn* who had hidden Jutulak at great risk and the locked betel box he had left amongst the ornaments before the altar, I hesitated for some time before answering. 'I hoped the monks might help me find Jutulak's parents . . . in case they had news of him . . .'

'The mother and father of Jutulak Somiboon are both dead,' said Petcharat flatly. 'What did the monks tell you?'

'They were unable to help me. They said they had not seen

or heard of Jutulak for years . . . Then your troops interrupted our conversation.'

This answer was absorbed in silence and I wondered whether the old abbot was also being interrogated somewhere at that moment.

'We find one thing particularly difficult to understand, Hampson,' said Kasem Petcharat suddenly, his voice becoming friendly and confiding. 'Why exactly have you become so attached to the mahout? He seems to have become something of an obsession. Perhaps you would like to tell us the whole story, starting from the time you first met him . . .'

Omitting all detail that might compromise Jutulak or my own role, I quickly summarised the events of the past few weeks, beginning with my discovery of the mahout's fear that he was being haunted by the dead king's spirit. Again a deep hush fell over the room and I felt everybody present was listening intently. Knowing that high-ranking Thais were almost as likely as the peasantry to revere the spirit world, I wondered how those present were reacting to the parts of the story that seemed to defy rational explanation; but being unable to see their faces, I could gauge nothing. After I had finished speaking there was a long silence. Then Kasem Petcharat spoke again, this time in a neutral voice.

'And what finally was your chief motive, Hampson, in trying to help this unfortunate mahout?'

'To my way of thinking, Jutulak was the victim of gross injustice,' I said quietly. 'As his direct superior I felt personally responsible for his safety while he worked with me.'

There was yet another long silence; then Kasem Petcharat approached once more and stood in front of me. 'I have never really understood English sentimentality, Hampson. Your story is unlikely and illogical in many ways. But perhaps that's why I'm inclined to believe there might be some truth in it . . .'

He paused, appearing to consider his words very carefully. When at last he spoke again, his voice had taken on a hard, dangerous tone.

'If you remain at liberty in Thailand, Hampson, your safety can no longer be guaranteed. And if you were charged and brought before a court in Bangkok, you could be imprisoned for a very long time for interfering with the work of those commissioned to assist the security forces . . . That, of course, would be one way of ensuring your safety . . . But a better solution might be for you to leave Thailand and never return.' He paused for further reflection. 'So if you undertake to leave the country at once and say absolutely nothing of this meeting, no formal charges will be brought against you. Do you agree to give such undertakings?'

'I fully expect my company to order me home immediately,' I said resignedly. 'A berth has been booked for me on a liner that leaves for England at midnight.'

'Very well. My men will now escort you back to the compound of the Anglo-Siamese Teak Trading Company. You will be kept under discreet surveillance until you embark on that boat at midnight. I hope that's clear.'

He didn't wait for my response and his heels beat a rapid rhythm on the floor tiles as he walked across the room. Then there was a pause as he opened the door. 'You should count yourself very fortunate, you know, Hampson,' he said in a low voice. 'Things could have turned out much worse for you. Don't forget that.'

I made no reply and didn't bother to turn my head in his direction.

'Take him away,' he snapped to my guards. Then the door banged shut behind him and his footsteps retreated swiftly and confidently along the corridor.

บ ช

THE BANGKOK SECRET

Chapter Twenty

Three months later to the day, I was standing on Westminster Bridge in London in a chilling rainstorm. It was three o'clock in the morning, unseasonably cold for early June, and the bridge was deserted. Drenched to the skin, with my wet hair plastered across my face, I was staring down into the dark, swirling waters of the Thames, engulfed by a sense of desolation.

During the latter part of those three months I had wandered aimlessly like a stranger in my own country, feeling lost and out of place in its drab, grey streets. I had fallen in love, or so I thought then, and married in ecstatic haste. Although I did not know it at that moment, I had also apparently fathered a baby girl. Furthermore, within days of my wedding, I had lost my beautiful young wife to another man and was well on my way to a divorce.

I had no job, no means of earning my livelihood, and saw no immediate prospect of any suitable job arising. I had been interviewed for a post managing a country estate but there had been little enthusiasm on either side. The money I had saved in Thailand had run out, spent lavishly and unthinkingly during what, for a week or two, had seemed like a romance that would last a lifetime. All that was left of several years of careful savings was a few small coins that jingled forlornly in my damp trouser pockets as I walked.

Among London's teeming millions, as far as I could tell, there was not one living soul who knew me as a friend. During nine years in Thailand I had lost track of all companions from my army days and Cambridge. I had kept up a laggardly correspondence with one or two friends from my schooldays at Marlborough College but none of them was then living permanently in London. In the entire metropolis that night there seemed to be nobody who would want to extend me a social invitation – or even exchange a few warm words.

I had visited my only living relative, my uncle, at the dilapidated manor house left to him by my father in Cheshire. I dumped my tropical kit and trunks there but felt restless and ill at ease. Ailing and cared for by a sullen housekeeper, my uncle, who was a widower, assured me the house would be left to me on his death. But it was large, rambling and run-down and there was insufficient money for its proper upkeep. After two dismal days there I had fled back to London, preferring anonymity and the company of strangers to the oppressive intimacy of my uncle's mournful hearth.

I took a cheap hotel room behind Baker Street – but it was so cramped and unwelcoming that I couldn't remain in it for more than a few minutes unless I was sleeping. Because insomnia had added itself to my list of ills, I'd gone out walking well after midnight despite the wet and the cold. On the streets I scarcely felt any better; in all my years in the remote jungles of Thailand I had never felt as lonely as I did that rain-drenched night in the heart of my own capital city.

As I stood gazing down into the river, Big Ben struck the hour. I turned to look up at the illuminated clockface that crowns the Mother of Parliaments. Through the lashing rain and darkness I could just see its hands: symmetrically vertical and horizontal, they formed a perfect ninety-degree angle, pointing precisely to three o'clock.

I don't know how long I stood there, staring up into the night. It may have been a minute, possibly five, or even ten. I wasn't thinking about what I was seeing, as the rain drove down, stinging my face. I was thinking of the green Siamese forests and their giant teak trees; of the brilliant, fleshy orchids glowing like fire amid the dark branches; of heady morning scents of earth, flowers and trees; of the pungent odours of elephant dung around the grazing sites where the great animals had been put out in hobbles for the night.

I was recalling the magnificent strength and courage of Poo Tongkam. I was hearing the furious roar of aggression which so often marked his willing response to another super-Herculean task. I was listening inside my head to the crack and boom of teak logs breaking from a river jam and hurtling onward downstream . . .

I thought of Jutulak working on the head of his elephant – and of his paralysing fears of the unseen spirit world. I was wondering, too, where he was, and if he was still alive. I was thinking of my own imagined entry into the world of spirits during my terrible fever, and of those elusive moments of deep, indefinable insight on the mountain called 'the Black World of Lost Spirits'. I was thinking of the bamboo and thatch houses of the mystical Akha village strung along the top of a spectacular mountain ridge adjoining Burma; of the shaman and the ritual dances he led to mark the ascent of the full moon. I was thinking too of Ladhya, and of my dream of her in which our twin souls merged as one . . . and I was thinking of her real physical presence beside me, unself-conscious and gloriously naked in the firelight of the swaying high-house.

But as I thought of them, all those people and places and things seemed less and less real. With the passage of time they were all becoming the stuff of dreams. In a cold downpour of English summer rain, they seemed insubstantial, transient, creations of my own feverish imagination. That I was now banned from entering the country where those people lived also served to heighten their aura of unreality; and this deepened my feelings of loneliness and desolation.

While I was leaning against the parapet of the bridge, I began to shiver. Whether it was from the unfamiliar cold of England or from a possible bout of malaria, I couldn't tell. I realised then I was attracting attention because a police constable wearing a glistening rain cape about his shoulders stepped up beside me.

'Is there anything I can help you with, sir?' he said in a quiet, respectful voice. 'You're getting rather wet standing here.'

In those days there was a little, all-night tea stall wedged into the nook of the bridge at its northern end. The constable suggested we shelter from the rain beneath its raised front. He bought two strong, sweetened cups of tea and for a time we stood side by side in silence sipping them and watching the rain beat down.

236

'You've got an educated voice, sir, if I may say so,' said the policeman amiably. 'Very different to the type of person we normally meet on the streets at this time of night. May I ask what line of business you're in?'

I told him what line of business I had *been* in until recently and where. I explained how I couldn't go back to it because of certain mishaps that had befallen me and how I was finding it difficult to settle to anything in England, which seemed drab and austere by comparison. He nodded companionably, making no comment, while I talked. Then when I'd finished he grinned and shook some of the rain from his cape.

'Sounds like you've been leading what some would call "an adventurous existence" out in Siam, sir ... It's hardly surprising you're having trouble settling in back here.' The policeman nodded across the road in the direction of the Houses of Parliament. 'Now Sir Winston's resigned, heaven knows where the country's heading. Life's no bed of roses at present. And we don't know what sort of hash Mr Eden is going to make of things, do we?'

I nodded absently, unable to feel much concern about politics in Britain. The hot tea had stopped my shivering and I began to feel more at ease. But I sensed the policeman was making some appraisal of my appearance, looking me up and down.

'Perhaps the best thing an able-bodied young man like you could do, sir, would be to find yourself a pretty wife here in England and settle down. Raise some nippers, perhaps. Give yourself some roots and responsibilities ... They're the best incentives ...'

'I did get married two months ago, constable,' I said quietly. 'To a lovely English girl who's more than pretty. It was a whirlwind romance, I suppose you'd say. I proposed after ten days and we skipped to Rome and Athens for a carefree honeymoon ... Or so I thought ... I showered her with clothes and jewellery I couldn't really afford ... She had money of her own and said we didn't need to worry immediately about the future ...'

Conflicting emotions aroused by recalling those painful events caused me to break off and gulp down some more tea. The constable waited patiently, sipping from his own cup and watching the rain bounce fiercely off the paving stones at our feet.

'Then ten days ago something rather unexpected happened . . . A rich Frenchman she'd fallen in love with before we met turned up out of the blue from abroad . . . They both discovered they'd made a terrible mistake . . . They're together in Paris now. A couple of days ago I instructed solicitors to begin divorce proceedings . . .'

For a moment the policeman looked at me expressionlessly. 'I think I understand now, sir.'

'Understand what, constable?'

'Why you're taking long walks at unusual hours. And sometimes gazing down over bridges . . . Perhaps we'd better have another cup of tea.'

The policeman turned to give the order to the stallholder while I battled anew with the mixture of anger, regret and injured pride that was suddenly boiling inside me again. I had met my wife – I'll call her Caroline here although that wasn't her name – at an evening reception in a Bond Street art gallery. At the Travellers Club in Pall Mall two days after getting off the boat, I had run into an Old Marlburian of my year who'd become an international art dealer. He was on his way to the party being held to celebrate the opening of the new gallery. I was dragged along and the very first person I met was a lovely, fair-haired mannequin figure in her late twenties who was running the gallery for the distinguished French family who had just bought it.

I probably drank too much champagne and talked louder and more volubly than is usual for me. Vivacious and knowledgeable about every aspect of the world of art, Caroline seemed particularly fascinated by the earthy contrasts of my jungle wallah world which I described very light-heartedly. She accepted my invitation to lunch next day and suddenly we found ourselves laughing a great deal and smiling warmly at one another. I was captivated by her vitality and sophistication; flattered, I suppose, too by her interest in a shy, jungle recluse who had been so long away from civilisation.

Foolishly perhaps, I didn't stop to consider how genuine her attraction to me might be. That lunch was the first of a heady succession of restaurant and theatre visits in a London freeing itself at last from a long struggle with post-war shortages and austerity. I took a costly hotel room close to her flat in Jermyn Street; we immediately became lovers in both places, by day and by night. To propose with flowers and an expensive ring seemed to be the obvious next step. We followed that with an uncomplicated wedding at Caxton Hall and the extravagant honeymoon dash to Rome and Athens.

Intuitively I had felt it was right to hide my innermost feelings – at least at first. Consequently I never spoke to her of my troubles in Thailand. Perhaps because of my own evasion I also failed to recognise that her gaiety, like my own, was somewhat forced and brittle most of the time. Both of us failed to acknowledge the obvious – that our passion had arisen more from desperation and loneliness than anything else. In our different ways we both concealed painful internal wounds that blinded us to our real emotions.

On the last terrible day I returned unexpectedly to the flat in Jermyn Street and was thunderstruck to find her standing pale and trembling beside a dark-haired Frenchman who had his arm around her waist. His name I think was Philippe and he was the heir of the family that owned the Bond Street gallery. Both of them, to their credit, seemed overcome with remorse. By way of explanation, my wife of eight weeks admitted shakily that she had even tried to take her life with sleeping pills six months earlier, so great had been her despair at their parting. She apologised abjectly to me, as did the Frenchman. We were all very deeply shocked by what had happened but there was nothing words could do to bridge the gulf that had opened between us. Realising there was little to salvage from the wreckage, I turned my back on them both and marched numbly out into Jermyn Street.

Several years passed before my Marlborough chum wrote to me via the Travellers Club. He had been a witness of the wedding at Caxton Hall. In his letter he said Caroline had given birth to a baby girl, seven months or so after our wedding. He knew only that she was living happily in Paris with a French husband who treated the little girl as his own. For a long time I carried the letter around with me everywhere. Then I decided reluctantly that my original decision on that grim day in Jermyn Street had been correct and I burned it . . .

'They say time is a great healer, sir, don't they?' said the policeman in a matter-of-fact voice, passing me another steaming mug of tea. 'It may all seem pretty bleak now. But often in this life, you know, things happen for a reason. Although you can't always see it at the time . . .'

He peered through the rain at the lights of several empty coal barges passing beneath the bridge, heading downstream towards the London docks to take on new cargo. The heavy chug of their engines was solid and purposeful: in the cold, wet night it was a strangely reassuring sound.

'It's very possible, you know, sir, that there's something better in store for you . . . Something you haven't thought of yet. You'll no doubt be off somewhere else before long.' He sipped his tea reflectively for a minute or two. 'If you could choose to go anywhere in the world right now, where do you think you'd head for?'

I smiled for the first time in days at the fanciful question. Considering my answer I watched the moving navigation lights on the river fade behind the curtains of rain. 'I think I might jump on the next string of barges that we see going downstream. That's the right direction at least – for the first leg of a sea journey back to the Far East . . .'

The policeman nodded, silently reviewing my choice. 'Well, sir, to my certain knowledge, men still frequently work their passage in and out of the Port of London. I had a case involving just such a man only the other day . . . So for a strong young fellow like you, that's not an impossible dream . . .'

Looking downstream I could see the tarmacadam footpath gleaming wetly beneath the glow of the embankment street lamps. Lying alongside the Thames like a pale ribbon, it shimmered invitingly against the shadow of the river's retaining wall. Walking along it, I knew in an instant, would restore for me the essential sense of purpose enjoyed by the men working the night coal barges: it was my way ahead. Once I set foot on it, the path would lead me back towards the mystery that still intrigued my senses night and day – the events surrounding Jutulak and the 'King's Death Case'.

I reached into my trouser pockets and pulled out every last coin I possessed. Spreading them in the palm of my hand under the lights of the tea stall I saw I had a shilling in pennies and threepenny pieces – the exact price of four cups of tea. Smiling broadly at the policeman, I bunched them in my fist and held them out to him.

'Please take this,' I said. 'I'm very grateful. England doesn't seem such a bad place as it did half an hour ago – and I've made up my mind what I'm going to do.'

'What is that, sir?' asked the constable mildly.

'I'll take a working passage back to the Far East on the first ship that will have me.'

'Well, you'd better keep that money for your bus fares then, sir. You'll need to pick up your things from the hotel.'

'I'm not going back to my hotel.' I took one of his hands and placed the coins in his palm. 'I don't need anything now. I'll walk to the docks from here just as I am.'

I pulled up the collar of my gaberdine raincoat and tightened its belt. The rain was still pouring down as solidly as before but I hardly noticed it. Turning around the side of the tea stall, I stepped off the bridge and descended towards the gleam of the embankment footpath that led eastward past Charing Cross Station, the Savoy Hotel, Blackfriars Bridge and on to the Port of London and South-East Asia.

ย ย

INTERLUDE

1973–76

Dense clouds of black smoke swirled around the golden spires of the Temple of the Emerald Buddha, blotting them from sight. In debris-littered streets a few hundred yards away, Thai army tanks charged through the smoke, shuddering the very foundations of the Grand Palace. Crouched in the tanks, steel-helmeted troops directed withering bursts of machine-gun fire into massed groups of yelling students who brandished nothing more lethal than sticks in their hands.

It was Sunday, 14 October 1973 and the students were falling dead and wounded in their hundreds. Soon desperate hospital staffs in the city were running into the streets calling on the public to give blood. King Bhoomipol made an emergency televised address appealing for an end to the bloodshed; he said many Thais were dying on what was 'one of the saddest days in the nation's entire history'.

As the carnage continued, some of the survivors, in a symbolic act of heroism, bound the bloodied corpse of a fallen student in the red, white and blue flag of Thailand. Risking their lives in the climb, they hoisted his body to the pinnacles of the capital's Monument to Democracy which had been raised above Ratchadamnoen Boulevard to celebrate the end of the absolute monarchy in 1932. The body remained there for many hours, a bloodstained inspiration for the tens of thousands of young Thais who continued to give battle against the police and army units sent to quell their demonstrations calling for an end to military rule.

Binding mattresses and cardboard around commandeered buses and cars, they rammed some of the tanks to a standstill. Using similarly makeshift armour-cladding on trucks, fire engines and coaches, they smashed their way into police stations and government buildings in the heart of Bangkok. Hurling home-made petrol bombs, they set afire the government's main public relations office, a tax building, the national lottery premises and the headquarters of an official anti-corruption agency. The fires caused damage amounting to millions of dollars and the thick, black pall of smoke from the burning buildings could be seen for miles across the flatlands surrounding the capital.

Troops ringed Thammasat University, the seat of the protests close to the Grand Palace, and shot students who tried to escape. Helicopters and spotter planes flew back and forth through the smoke and some students claim they were also machine-gunned from the air. Estimates of the final casualty toll varied greatly: most sources eventually agreed that at the end of two days of conflict more than a thousand students had been wounded, killed or were missing. An official figure of seventy-two dead was eventually published but the total of fatalities in reality may have been higher.

The violence of what came to be known as 'Bloody Sunday' followed the biggest political demonstration in Thailand's history the previous day. Some two hundred thousand university and high school students had marched through Bangkok chanting demands that thirteen of their fellow activists be released from jail. The thirteen had been imprisoned several days previously on charges of treason. In fact they had merely been distributing leaflets calling on the country's military dictators to draw up and implement a new democratic constitution. The massive turnout clearly unnerved Bangkok's army rulers and they hastily agreed on Saturday night to release the thirteen activists without conditions. They also promised that a new constitution would be introduced within a year.

Many students, dissatisfied by the year's projected delay, refused to disperse. Bloodshed and destruction ensued when police opened fire at dawn on Sunday and chaos reigned for forty-eight hours. At its height the students stormed Bangkok's metropolitan police headquarters and set the buildings ablaze; the rioting ceased when, to the students' astonishment, an announcement was made that the country's two military dictators, Field Marshals Thanom and Praphat, had relinquished power and gone into exile abroad.

Their departure opened the way to genuine, civilian democratic rule in Thailand for the first time since the ending of the absolute monarchy in 1932. This heady period was destined to last only three short years but the achievements of the demonstrators were historic because at that time the student body in Thailand was the least politicised and the most conservative in Asia. The young, mainly middle-class students had never dreamed of achieving so much so quickly. In the event they had the support of a vital ally in their struggle – King Bhoomipol himself.

In their early demonstrations they had carried portraits of the nation's widely revered monarch with their banners. By then it was clear that the shy, unsure young man who had succeeded to the throne at the age of nineteen upon the violent death of his brother had developed shrewd and mature political instincts. The king had made it his business to present seven thousand university degrees annually in person and had already discreetly expressed sympathy with the students' aims. Appalled by the advent of Thais killing Thais in the centre of Bangkok, he is believed to have moved behind the scenes to secure vital support in the armed services for the ousting of the two unpopular and corrupt army leaders who had suspended the constitution two years earlier.

These bloody events provided a dramatic climax to the 'American era' of Thailand's modern history which brought great change to the country. The era had begun in 1947 when the wartime leader Field Marshal Pibul used the 'King's Death Case' as an excuse to restore himself to power. Pibul's second spell as premier lasted ten years until the corrupt tyranny of his chief henchman, Police-General Phao, prompted the army commander General Sarit to overthrow them both in the *coup d'état* of 1957.

In his turn, however, General Sarit tore up the 1932 constitution and became an absolute dictator. He imposed rigid censorship and imprisoned, exiled and occasionally executed progressive politicians. During a period dubbed by some Thais as *'Yuk Thamin'* – the Dark Ages – Generals Thanom and Praphat became his two closest supporters. When Sarit died of cirrhosis of the liver in 1963, they seized the reins of power and clung on to them until 1973.

In succession Pibul, Phao, Sarit, Thanom and Praphat all flourished because the United States showered financial and military aid on them following the 1949 victory of Communism in neighbouring China. The aim was to preserve Thailand as a 'bulwark of the Free World'. Then as United States forces moved into direct military conflict with the Communists in nearby Vietnam, Laos and Cambodia, Bangkok's military dictators shrewdly exploited their links with Washington to consolidate their rule.

By 1968 eight major American military installations and many minor bases had been set up across Thailand. They supported three hundred war-planes and nearly fifty thousand troops that Washington was able to deploy in its various Indo-China conflicts. To strengthen Thailand against Communism, its leadership was encouraged to tighten control of the country's civilian population. At the same time capitalist development was strenuously promoted, especially in the countryside; police forces and the army were expanded rapidly, anti-Communist repression increased and Thai mercenaries were sent to fight in Vietnam and other parts of Indo-China.

The massive injections of aid, investment and money spent supporting the US bases sparked a ten-year economic boom across Thailand. The American presence also produced a new surge of prostitution and drug addiction and a rash of fatherless Amerasian babies. In addition, Hollywood films and television programmes began to undermine traditional Thai culture. The intensive commercialisation of agriculture also deprived poorer peasants of their land and sent them flooding into city slums in search of a living. On the credit side, many new roads were built, electrification of rural areas became widespread and the uprush of prosperity created for the first time a new Thai middle class. Educational facilities consequently had to be expanded. More importantly, large numbers of Thai students left home in a new wave to study abroad in America and other countries.

It was this educational exodus of the 1960s that eventually led to the bloody but triumphant cataclysm of October 1973. Ironically it also produced a result that mirrored a similar previous exodus in the 1920s. Thai students sent abroad with royal approval after the First World War had returned home fired by Western ideas and quickly abolished Thailand's absolute monarchy. The students who went away to America in the sixties shook off the restraints of military censorship and discovered the truth about the Indo-China wars being waged by the Americans, in part from Thai soil. They saw French students come close to toppling President de Gaulle in Paris; they watched American students and intellectuals march publicly to victory over Presidents Johnson and Nixon, forcing the withdrawal of American troops from Vietnam.

So on their return home the Thai students began to emulate their American and French counterparts. Success beyond their wildest dreams resulted from the massive Bangkok marches of 1973. But unfortunately for them, history had not finished repeating itself. The combined effects of world events – the looming Second World War – and the Thai generals' lust for power had crushed student hopes of transferring sovereignty from the monarchy to the people in the 1930s. In the same way, in the autumn of 1976 the new generation of student idealists saw their briefly realised dreams of democracy founder yet again on similar reefs.

During three years of open politics which followed the events of October 1973, elections produced a succession of weak, unstable coalition governments. Little progress was made in solving key problems of inflation and corruption or counteracting the small but growing Communist insurgency in the north-east. Strikes and demonstrations became commonplace and hundreds of pressure groups sprang into being to heighten the political confusion. Among students some polarisation of political loyalties took place, although young Thais generally remained indifferent to extreme ideologies. Those termed 'Leftists' were more often middle-class radicals and liberals rather than Communists; in a country with no history of a right-wing student movement, 'Rightists', while anti-Communist, did not appear to hold the views of genuine right-wing extremists. Unfortunately, the country's civilian politicians were neither able to contain these political conflicts nor establish harmonious working relations with army leaders. Increasingly restive, the military men almost certainly began plotting behind the scenes for a return to power.

Even so, Thailand's fledgling democracy might have survived in a tranquil world. But by 1975 rampant Communist armies had triumphed all around Thailand's northern borders in Vietnam, Cambodia and Laos; the United States, a secondary target of the 1973 Bangkok protests, had shut down its bases and withdrawn its troops. In these circumstances the threat from peasant-led Communist guerrillas in the north-east suddenly loomed larger. Between 1970 and 1976 their forces were believed to have doubled in strength to a total of eight thousand and support and sanctuary were newly available in the Communist states beyond the northern borders. Rightly or wrongly, it was feared that Communists were infiltrating the student unions and Vietnam was also suspected of sending subversive agents into Bangkok. Against this background of growing anxiety, 'the City of Archangels' was abruptly plunged into another terrible bout of bloodshed in October 1976. Students were publicly massacred in scenes of far greater horror and brutality than those of 1973 – but this time survivors and relations of the dead did not have the compensation of victory to comfort them.

As before, the tragedy seemed to fall unexpectedly on the city from out of a clear, blue sky. The former dictator Field Marshal Thanom returned suddenly from exile with a shaven head and wearing the saffron robes of a monk. He entered a Buddhist monastery, ostensibly to 'earn merit' in the Thai tradition for his dying father, then aged ninety-one. But a steady stream of military visitors reportedly interrupted his meditations and it seems certain that there were secret political motives behind his provocative return. Students who had triumphantly driven him from the country three years earlier mounted demonstrations once more, along with relatives of those who had died in the 1973 violence. They demanded Thanom's deportation but in the changed atmosphere no concessions were offered and police openly harassed the demonstrators. In a defensive move, thousands of Thammasat University undergraduates of both sexes went on strike and retreated inside their barricaded campus close to the Chao Phraya river.

At dawn on Tuesday, 6 October a highly trained force of one thousand special warfare police stormed the campus and opened fire with automatic rifles, machine-guns and heavy weapons. For more than four hours the troops of airborne, border patrol, marine and riot units poured a barrage of fire at the university, shattering windows and punching holes in the walls of buildings where the students were hiding. Airborne units fired armour-piercing shells from eight-foot-long recoilless rifles normally employed against tanks; other troops used

M-79 grenade launchers to hurl explosives into the lecture rooms.

Throughout the barrage, wounded youths and girls staggered from the buildings to collapse on the ground. When the firing ceased hundreds had been injured and an unknown number killed. More than a thousand of the survivors were treated like prisoners of war: males and females alike were made to strip off their shirts and blouses, remove their shoes and crawl on to a football pitch in the centre of the campus. Some were bleeding profusely from their injuries but all were ordered to remain lying face-down with their hands locked behind their heads until buses carried them away to police detention centres.

Other students who managed to stumble out of the campus were lynched and clubbed to death by hysterical rightist mobs. Foreign journalists saw at least four Thammasat undergraduates hanged from trees in sight of the Grand Palace. While still alive their bodies were beaten savagely with bottles and wooden clubs. Then watching crowds, which swelled to twenty thousand, set upon the corpses with sticks, gouging out their eyes and cutting their throats. Some students who survived the police barrage were drenched with petrol by the mob and burned alive; half a dozen corpses were heaped upon a grisly human bonfire and set alight outside the portals of the Ministry of Justice.

These acts of barbarism took place in the wake of inflammatory military radio broadcasts that called on all Thai patriots to 'kill the Communists!'. They said the students inside the university were heavily armed and, with the help of Vietnamese Communist agents, intended to overthrow the monarchy. In particular the radio stations appealed to armed vigilantes and the general public to take revenge against the students for insulting the nation's beloved monarchy. It was claimed they had deliberately committed 'lese-majesty' while staging a dramatised re-enactment of the hanging of two student activists by police. Press photographs had shown that one of the actor-victims bore some resemblance to the crown prince, although the demonstrators insisted the likeness was purely coincidental. The students quickly apologised for any accidental offence, saying no insult had been intended, but the apology had little effect: the broadcasts had already played a vital role in whipping anti-leftist feelings to a fever pitch and turned popular sentiment against the students.

Following the broadcasts, thousands of armed peasants from the distant countryside appeared suddenly in Bangkok in the vicinity of the university. Members of anti-Communist self-defence forces organised to defend rural villages, these strangers to the capital joined with local right-wing groups and the elite units of warfare police to break on to the campus. In effect the Thammasat students, who had been protesting against nothing more than the return of an already disgraced dictator, were attacked by crack anti-insurgency troops and rural militias trained for jungle combat against hardened Communist guerrilla forces.

During the barrage some shooting had come from the left-wing students and the police reported a number of casualties. But radio claims that the students were heavily armed proved to be greatly exaggerated. Only a handful of weapons and explosives were found afterwards in the university buildings and more than six hundred girls were among the three thousand undergraduates arrested.

While the police troops shelled and machine-gunned the university, an admiral made a broadcast announcing that the armed forces had seized back political power. A military National Reform Council abolished the democratic constitution adopted in 1974 and took the civilian prime minister into 'protective custody'. All political parties and gatherings were immediately banned. The admiral said the armed forces had intervened 'to uphold the monarchy and the royal family and prevent Thailand falling prey to Communist imperialism'.

The speed with which this *coup d'état* was executed suggested that many of the participants in the tragedy had been victims of calculated intrigue. Immediately after the broadcast, tanks moved into defensive positions around Chitralada Palace, the modern, moated residence of King Bhoomipol that lies to the north of the city's race-course. This time, unlike 1973, the king and members of his family remained silent. Leftist student leaders who escaped the police troops had little alternative but to flee the capital and take temporary sanctuary with Communist insurgents in the jungles of the north. They were to remain there for several years. The official death toll was eventually given as forty-one; but again the real figure was almost certainly higher.

Ironically, a nation famed worldwide for its Buddhist pacifism and its graceful, smiling people had been traumatised for the second time in three years by public acts of appalling brutality and bloodshed in the centre of its capital city. Democracy, which had flowered from the first bout of violence, withered and died again as a result of the second. When the dust settled, many ordinary Thais, who understood little of what happened from their censored newspapers, appeared to be relieved that the troublesome students had been brought under control. But among educated families the grief of those who suffered in the tragedies of 1976 was added to that of the victims of the 1973 blood-letting. The politically aware sections of society who had resented the rule of non-intellectual military men and police for four decades became more embittered than before and they have never forgotten the students who died and the reasons why.

Over the intervening years Thailand has gradually stabilised; a new constitution was eventually promulgated in 1979 and since then elections have been held regularly. But the democratic principles enshrined in the constitution have never been properly implemented. Vote-buying for cash during elections remains endemic and corruption scandals continue to break at regular intervals. Most significantly, the Thai military remains poised in the wings to intervene and the invisible influence of senior officers continues to be a major factor in the nation's political life. Twice in the 1980s younger officers dissatisfied with the ways of senior generals launched coups in Bangkok. Neither was successful but these actions were a blunt reminder of the ever-present threat of armed military intervention in civilian politics. For these reasons the Thailand of the early 1990s remains a political enigma – and beneath the surface of everyday activity, echoes of the violent deaths of 1976 still haunt the life of the nation.

PART FOUR

BANGKOK

1

A faint tremor of excitement ran through Joceline as she lifted her head to gaze up at the rounded, finger-like spires of *Wat Arun*. Encrusted with millions of tiny fragments of porcelain and glass, they were sparkling like crystal in the early dawn sky. Mirror images shivered and danced below in the breeze-ruffled waters of the Chao Phraya river and as the sleek *hang yao* carrying her northward drew nearer to Bangkok's most famous landmark, Joceline recalled suddenly her father's tense description of the evening dash downstream past the temple, pursued by his two shadows from the Chiang Mai train.

That thought in its turn revived memories of the alarm she herself had felt on the day she had been given the full manuscript in London. The twin deaths of Nicholas Penhaligon and the young Thai, Narong Chumto, had raised anxieties which had robbed her of sleep on several nights; she had never seriously considered abandoning the project because of what had happened but recalling the manner in which she had received the news still triggered feelings of unease.

Despite the early hour, it was already warm and the river was alive with traffic just as it had been on that evening in 1955; ferries and water-buses laden with people, and barges wallowing beneath heavy loads of sand and rice, were passing and criss-crossing all around her. Along the Thonburi bank she could see the palm-fringed mouths of *klongs* opening into the river, and floating clumps of water-hyacinth, she noticed, still clustered on the river surface as they had in the manuscript account.

All these sights she found curiously reassuring. Often during the past four months her father's narrative, read and pored over time and time again, had come to resemble a fantasy or a dream – not least because she had become embroiled in some of the most dramatic news developments of her life which had also sometimes taken on a dream-like air of unreality. Like virtually every international journalist in the Western world, Joceline had been drawn irresistibly into the maelstrom of events which had convulsed Eastern Europe throughout the autumn and early winter of 1989. Only a day or so after receiving her father's manuscript from Prem in mid-October, she had been forced to fly to East Germany at a moment's notice to begin filming the massive street demonstrations in Leipzig. In quick succession she became involved in 'Perspective' specials mounted on the breaching of the Berlin Wall, the peaceful revolution of Wenceslas Square and the violent Christmas overthrow of Nicolae Ceausescu in Romania.

Torn between her fascination with these tumultuous events and her strong desire to continue investigating the background to 'The Bangkok Secret', she had always carried a copy of the manuscript with her whenever she left London, whether for Berlin, Prague or Bucharest. Although often exhausted and emotionally drained by the day-and-night dramas she was filming in the snowy Central European streets, she had read and reread the manuscript in a succession of bare hotel rooms in the small hours of the morning. More than once she had wept over the description of her father's misfortunes in London. In particular the terse references to his ill-fated romance with her mother and her own birth held a shocking poignancy for her.

By the end of January she could probably have recited long passages of the typescript by heart and it was perhaps for this reason that the narrative had begun to take on the quality of legend and myth in her mind. Also, the unbroken spell of intense work, constant travel and the risks she had faced amongst the tanks and flying bullets in Bucharest had eventually blunted her senses, leaving her weary and listless. She had taken a ten-day break at home before making preparations to depart for Bangkok but her former vitality had not immediately returned. She had continued to feel jaded during the journey from London but now, suddenly, in sight of the Temple of the Dawn, a flurry of real images resembling those in her father's narrative seemed for the first time to give flesh-and-blood proof of what had previously been only typewritten words on a page. At long last, to her great relief, the story was coming to life vividly before her eyes.

In the stern of the long-tailed boat, she noticed that her producer was giving quiet steering instructions to the boat driver, working through a young Thai interpreter who had been hired for the duration of filming. Beside them the cameraman, determined not to waste a single second of the extraordinary light, was bracing his legs against the swell to focus constantly on the shimmering riverside image of the ancient Khmer-style temple. Previously he had filmed Joceline and the *hang yao* from a larger, canopied boat that was following close behind carrying the rest of the film unit; then he had clambered across to shoot from behind her shoulder as they moved on slowly upstream.

Although not yet thirty, the cameraman was a very experienced documentary campaigner and without any instructions from the producer or Joceline he recorded a rapid sequence of scenes, including the temple, the rising sun and the shadow-dappled river that would edit easily and smoothly together back in London. Darting energetically from one position to another, he framed Joceline's profile artistically against a succession of 'mute' backgrounds of striking natural beauty; and while squinting through his lens he predicted loudly in a broad Scots accent that the footage would provide wonderful pictures for the opening titles or the closing credits of the finished 'Perspective' documentary.

The other film crew members smiled at his enthusiasm, watching from the second boat, and Joceline noticed that as usual on the first morning of filming, spirits were high. Crouching in the bows with his tape machine on his shoulder, the sound recordist was grinning happily and holding out a fleece-covered boom microphone to take 'wild' sound and 'atmosphere' of the river and its traffic; amidships a keen-eyed young assistant cameraman with a shock of blond hair was standing by ready to provide needed equipment from the jumble of cases and bags that contained lights, batteries, tripods, lenses and spare film stock.

At the recordist's side stood Metropolitan Television's most experienced female production assistant, Angela Gladstone, who had travelled to Thailand two weeks ahead of the unit to make all the logistical arrangements. She had obtained the necessary government permissions to film by submitting a very brief outline script indicating that the documentary would cover 'various aspects of modern Thailand, its colourful history and its continuing tourist boom in the 1990s'. Clutching a stopwatch and clipboard, she was watching everything that happened with the fixed intensity of a hovering hawk, at the same time keeping a meticulous running log of each and every shot taken by the cameraman.

The two boats were heading upstream towards the area of the Grand Palace where permission had been granted to film the royal temples and throne rooms. The producer and Joceline had decided to approach the heart of the old city along the ancient river highway in order to capture something of the historic flavour of Bangkok. They had taken the decision soon after their arrival by direct flight from London late the previous evening. Driven in taxis along a modern expressway to their city-centre hotel, they had passed through garishly lit, gridded streets flanked by high-rise buildings and pedestrian bridges that could have existed anywhere in the United States. Filled with clouds of acrid exhaust fumes and dense jams of Japanese-built cars, these thoroughfares of modern Bangkok seemed to have little in common with the picturesque *klongs* which had once caused the city to be dubbed 'the Venice of Asia'. After a brief discussion at the hotel, arrangements had been made to rent two river craft for the atmospheric dawn shooting.

The whole unit had driven in a hired crew bus to the embarkation point beside the celebrated, colonial-style Oriental Hotel, haunt of famous travellers in bygone days. As soon as she saw the majestic river reflecting the sun's first rays in front of the hotel, Joceline felt some of her tiredness leave her and her spirits lift. The grandeur and colourful bustle of the great waterway made it a natural backdrop against which to recount details of dramatic events. Unmistakably Asian and exotic to foreign eyes, the Chao Phraya was clearly the core and essence of Bangkok; over the striking dawn pictures she decided she would record an opening commentary explaining why she felt it was important to try to track down the truth behind the mysterious manuscript.

In her shoulder bag which lay in the bows of the *hang yao*, Joceline was carrying her own well-thumbed copy. This was partly because she believed it was unsafe to leave it in her hotel room and partly because, for reasons she could not quite pin down, she felt she ought, in any event, to carry it with her at all times while in Thailand. It seemed important just to have it at her side, even if she didn't consult it, and every few minutes as they continued to head upstream, she reached out in a near-reflex action to touch the bag and reassure herself that it was still safe.

Tucked deliberately inside the cover of the manuscript was a long, typewritten letter from Nicholas Penhaligon. To her dismay it had arrived at her home in London two days after his death. Written candidly and with some anguish on the day he died, it contained revelations about Penhaligon's own role in the affair which had greatly surprised her; it also threw important new light on the Thais who had contacted her and their links with political events in Thailand.

She had read the letter several times, although by no means as frequently as the manuscript. What it revealed had enabled her to make a more informed final decision to go ahead with the film. But its contents still left many questions tantalisingly unanswered and as she sat staring back at the receding outline of *Wat Arun*, she felt a sudden need to review its contents now that she had arrived in the heart of Bangkok. After checking that she was no longer actively needed for the continuing 'mute' filming of the river, she drew the letter from the bag and settled herself against the gunwale to reread it.

'My dear Joceline,' the letter began, 'First of all I owe you a sincere apology – for not revealing how deeply involved I've been to date in the fraught business of your father's manuscript. I ought to have been more forthcoming with you from the start. I feel somewhat ashamed of my behaviour. This letter is a belated attempt to make amends to you.

'My original intentions were, I believe, wholly honourable. But I have been deceitful with you in a way that has plagued my conscience considerably. There are also other matters quite unconnected with you which are troubling me more deeply. I hope that you, at least, will eventually feel able to forgive my lack of forthrightness. Perhaps what follows will aid that process. That is certainly my sincerest wish. This letter in any event will enable you to proceed with your eyes wide open. You already know, I think, that you could be moving into some dangerous and difficult territory – if you finally decide to go ahead and take the risks involved in filming in Thailand, that is . . .'

Joceline glanced up from the letter towards the stern of the boat; the Scottish cameraman was utterly absorbed, pointing his lens eagerly in the direction of the spectacular filials of *Wat Po* – the Temple of the Reclining Buddha – that were just beginning to show against the skyline on the near bank. Beside him the producer was also surveying the river and its shorelines with an enthusiastic eye, identifying other temples and landmarks for him from a map. Both men, Joceline could see, were responding strongly to Bangkok's potent visual charm; whatever they turned out to be, she reflected, the 'risks involved in filming in Thailand' were already being taken wholeheartedly.

'I didn't anticipate, Joceline, that you and I would ever meet personally,' the letter continued. 'But academics specialising in South-East Asia politics and history *are* fairly thin on the ground in England these days. So I shouldn't have been so surprised when you eventually beat a path to my door. Anyway, the important thing to tell you is that about two months before you telephoned, the man you know as Surachai had contacted me. He's a former Bangkok university lecturer who's been in prison a couple of times and wrongly branded a 'Communist' by the generals. I met him when I was first secretary at our embassy in Bangkok. Like a lot of other Thai radicals he wants sound, fully fledged democratic rule in his country instead of a behind-the-scenes military oligarchy that might spring a *coup d'état* any time. Prem had taken your father's manuscript to him, wondering how they could make the most political capital out of it. Surachai decided to come and consult me.

'Prem, I would guess, has by now told you that he's the son of Jutulak. He tracked down your father in the north about two years ago. Your father, because of his affection for Jutulak, apparently wrote the manuscript at Prem's request, having verbally related the whole extraordinary story of his friendship with Jutulak. Prem seemingly had no previous inkling of his father's involvement at the Grand Palace. The impact on him, as you can imagine, was enormous. Prem, you see, was deeply involved in the student movements of 1973 and 1976. He was a leading organiser and I met him once or twice in that role.

He had to flee for his life to the northern jungles after the second Thammasat massacre. He's one of many who suffered and still have strong motives for wanting to see an end once and for all to military rule – open or behind the scenes.

'What underground opposition groups there are in Bangkok at present are fairly erratic and unreliable. So Prem and Surachai made up their minds to try to achieve a sophisticated international impact with the Hampson manuscript. Their hope, I would think, is that, if they're successful, the results might feed back naturally into Thailand and spark a new, popular pro-democracy movement of some kind . . .'

Joceline stopped reading and let her gaze roam idly along the riverside. She had not seen or heard from the tall, quietly spoken Thai since the day he had handed her the manuscript outside the Buddhist temple in West London. But among a large pile of unopened mail awaiting her when she returned from Bucharest in January there had been a brief note bearing the signature 'Surachai'. Sent from what turned out to be an accommodation address, the letter asked merely if Metropolitan Television was still intending to proceed with the Thailand documentary. She had dictated an equally brief reply via her office secretary, saying that plans were being made to begin filming in mid-February. As an afterthought she had added a line asking Surachai or Prem to contact her if they wished to discuss the contents of the manuscript. But up until the day of her departure, there had been no response from either of them.

'Prem and Surachai if left to their own devices would have distributed copies of the manuscript to specialist press correspondents and academics in Britain and America,' the letter went on. 'It was me, I'm afraid, who persuaded them to offer it to you first on an exclusive basis. Somebody in Chiang Mai whom you'd written to about your intention to visit the Foreign Cemetery, by the sheerest chance made the connection for us. When I heard, it seemed like a gift from heaven. I felt the coincidence of your high profile in the media was too good an opportunity to miss. It seemed to me that an exclusive television documentary film with a strong personal flavour might achieve greater international impact than anything else. I thought, and still think, it might create front-page headlines if you decide to go ahead and get some good material. You, of course, will need to consider your final decision very carefully. I should perhaps say that Prem, who had seen several of your programmes, was particularly enthusiastic about the idea. I suggested he come to study in London for a spell to make contacting you easier.

'At the outset, I should also say, all of this seemed a comparatively straightforward exercise in political propaganda. Foolishly, I never imagined unpleasantness would creep in. I think I told you at Brighton I'd been personally close to several young Thai students victimised by the terrible trauma of 1976. For that reason alone I had no hesitation in agreeing to help. But unfortunately I've now become convinced that there are more sinister forces at work. And I feel it's my duty to give you some warning. Because he and Prem badly needed some financial support to bring the manuscript abroad and make contacts, Surachai involved a rich Chinese who I imagine might have been the anonymous "shadow figure" you talked of meeting in Chiang Mai. Surachai says the Chinese has financed their travel, their stay in England and much else besides because he fell foul of the Thai generals himself for unspecified reasons in the past. Surachai says the Chinese was sentenced to a long spell in a Bangkok jail in the fifties and sixties and that's why he eventually supported the radical student movements with funds.

'To be honest, Surachai wouldn't say too much more about this mysterious patron. I suspect he knows much more than Prem about him. Tread carefully on that. Surachai is a "fixer" as well as an idealist. He's prepared to do what's necessary without asking too many questions. Prem isn't like that at all. But having said that, I met the Chinese briefly in London recently and he proved himself to be more than a little unsavoury. He obviously has a lot of legitimate international business interests – but I think he's also involved in serious criminal activity of some kind. I'm guessing, but because of his Chiang Mai connections he could be one of the original Kuomintang opium smugglers. If that's true, by now he might easily have become an international drug trafficker on a grand scale. You must tackle Surachai head on about this at the first chance you get. At any rate I begin to suspect the Chinese is a "malignant presence". He might well have some personal axe to grind in all this. Worst of all I've had proof that he will resort to violence without any visible compunction . . .'

Joceline broke off with a frown as a sudden thought struck her. She had read the letter initially on a brief, snatched home visit during her hectic pre-Christmas coverage of events in Czechoslovakia and Germany. Then and during other readings, the fact that Penhaligon had written so poignantly of his feelings on the day of his death had always been uppermost in her mind. The fact that his communication came effectively from beyond the grave, she realised, had prevented her from viewing its contents with her normal objectivity. Now with the breezes of the Chao Phraya bringing a greater clarity to her thoughts, she wondered why on earth the possible connection between events had escaped her before. Remembering that she had learned of the death of Penhaligon and Narong Chumto on the same day, she carefully reread the paragraph about the mysterious Chinese a second time.

Before leaving London she had contacted Scotland Yard officially to check if any progress had been made with the investigation into the Thai youth's death. A police spokesman had given a laconic reply, saying only that there had been 'no significant leads'. A detective contact of a Metropolitan crime reporter had admitted that it was assumed the murder was directly connected with the murky *demi-monde* of international drug smuggling. But, unusually, he said, no information whatsoever about the killing had ever surfaced from police underworld contacts. From the known sequence of events, Joceline reflected, Penhaligon may have known nothing at all of Narong Chumto's death. Yet his cryptic reference to the Chinese being ready to 'resort to violence without any visible compunction' seemed deeply ominous in retrospect. Clearly no proof would ever be forthcoming and precise reasons would remain unknown – but suddenly Joceline felt intuitively certain that the mystery Chinese must have played a central role in the Thai youth's death.

'All in all, your decision on whether to jump into these very murky waters with Metropolitan's film cameras at your back will be a difficult one,' said the letter in drawing towards its conclusion. 'If you do go ahead, you might produce an admirable piece of journalism. If it helped to clear the air in Bangkok and produced some new momentum for the people to move towards a really stable democracy at long last, it would be a very worthwhile film indeed. Uncovering secrets is the life-blood of the journalist's craft, after all. But secrecy in high places is an endemic fault of human nature – and you must be ready in the end to run up against unclimbable walls. I sometimes tell my students not to worry too much about what we don't know. There will always be gaps. History would be vastly different at all levels if no state secrets existed. On this score we in Britain can't adopt any superior moral posture – towards Thailand or any other secrecy-obsessed nation. Those who govern and reign over us love their state secrets as much as anybody in the world. If we historians could penetrate, say, the closed royal archives at Windsor Castle, and all the secret government material never made public under the thirty-year rule, we might see many important things affecting all our lives very differently.

'In attempting to get the story surrounding "The Bangkok Secret" straight I recommend that you try to understand Prem better. He's a fierce idealist and he's desperate to help bring real political freedom to his country *and* to right the injustices done to his father. The two things go together in his mind. Jutulak's past finally caught up with him in a very unpleasant way, apparently. There's more to say about that – but Prem must tell you himself, I think. Talk to him at length if you can. As far as your father's manuscript is concerned, don't rule out the possibility that it might have been tampered with. At least one passage doesn't quite ring true, somehow – I'm talking about your father's interrogation in Bangkok. Also it appears to be unfinished, doesn't it? Perhaps a part is missing or has been withheld. In general, of course, the manuscript tells a very strange story – but then Thailand is a strange and alluring country in many different ways. It is often deceptive too. And the people can be deceptive without necessarily meaning to be. It's simply in their nature. Despite this, or perhaps because it makes them seem enigmatic, Westerners fall under Thailand's spell very easily. You may discover that for yourself. But be on your guard constantly. Failure to be on my guard at all times was one of the gravest mistakes I made in Bangkok. And I've come now to feel an unbearable regret about it . . .

'Finally, Joceline, I'm sorry but I can't under all the circumstances keep my promise to give you an interview for the film.

I couldn't have said any of this on the record, anyway. And you can easily get others like me to provide purely historical interpretation. Unfortunately, recent events have brought back extremely painful memories that I thought were buried for ever. Ghosts from those terrible days in Bangkok in 1976 have suddenly returned to haunt me with great ferocity. Eventually, I believe, sins from our past catch up with all of us. In my case it's entirely my own fault. You're certainly not to blame in any way, please don't think that. I'd gone in well over my head long before you appeared. I was rather heedless of the dangers still lurking inside myself and I can't bear some of the repercussions, I'm afraid.

'But let me finish this rather rambling letter by saying I sense you will decide in the end to go ahead with the film, mainly because of your strong personal connections to the subject. In my humble opinion, despite all my chicanery, I think that decision will be the right one – for you and every-body else concerned. And from the bottom of what passes for my heart I want to wish you all possible good fortune, every success and a safe return home.

'Very sincerely yours, Nicholas Penhaligon.'

With a distracted expression creasing her brow Joceline tucked the letter back into its envelope and put it away. Not for the first time she felt deeply moved by Penhaligon's wounded references to the nameless Bangkok ghosts that had returned to haunt him 'with great ferocity'. She had herself spent a morning in the library of the Royal Institute of International Affairs in St James's Square, scrutinising newspaper clippings of the twin bouts of violence in Bangkok in 1973 and 1976. Afterwards she had been quite unable to face eating lunch. Large, detailed photographs in several international newspapers showed leftist students being lynched, beaten to death with clubs and burned under the eyes of watching crowds. More than a decade after the events, the photographs were still horrifying in their brutal depravity. After looking at them and reading detailed accounts and comments in all the major British and foreign newspapers, Joceline felt she understood how deeply the terrible events must have affected those directly involved.

She had recently seen enough death and grief in the streets and cemeteries of Bucharest to know how sickening the impact of political violence could be on surviving family and friends. Those experiences, still fresh in her mind, had made her sympathy for the enduring agonies of Nicholas Penhaligon and Prem more acute than might otherwise have been the case. Musing on this, she sat staring out across the Chao Phraya, wondering inwardly at the bottomless capacity that peoples of all races seemed to have for inflicting death and mayhem on themselves. In little more than a year, in countries as diverse as China, Burma and Romania, army and security forces had turned their machine-guns ruthlessly on their own people with appalling effect. In each country tens of thousands of people were no doubt nursing dark hatreds and an understandable thirst for revenge. Equally in the Thailand which most Westerners knew as a friendly tourist paradise, similar animosities must still be smouldering in many minds, she thought, and shook her head involuntarily in a little gesture of dismay.

'You don't look too happy, Joceline – is anything wrong?'

She looked up to find the producer, Michael Ewington, standing beside her, smiling quizzically. A Cambridge graduate four or five years younger than Joceline, he had made his reputation filming social documentaries in northern England before joining Metropolitan six months earlier. Comparatively inexperienced in international reporting, he had undergone a baptism of fire working with Joceline for the first time through the long winter in Eastern Europe. His respect for her experience and reputation was evident in the deference he showed her and this had been a major reason behind her request that he be assigned to produce the Thailand film.

'I've just been rereading the Penhaligon letter, Michael – it's a very sobering document.' Joceline sighed and drew out the envelope again. 'Perhaps it would be a good idea if you found a few minutes to look over it, now we've actually arrived and got started.'

Ewington took the letter and stood tapping it against the thumb of his other hand, smiling pleasantly. 'Any special reason why? You've already given me the essentials, haven't you?'

Glancing towards the Thai interpreter who was talking to the cameraman in the stern, Joceline lowered her voice. 'Yes – but the letter contains some timely reminders about how dangerous our manuscript is. I thought it might help for you to see it all spelled out. We *are* sailing under false colours here, remember.'

'Okay,' said Ewington lightly. 'I'll go over the letter during our next break at the Grand Palace. But whatever the dangers are, they can't be any worse than Bucharest and Timisoara, can they? And we came through there all right – so don't worry.'

Grinning, he thrust the envelope into the back pocket of the baggy linen trousers he wore with a bush shirt, floppy sun hat and soft white-leather boots. The *hang yao* was pulling into the landing stage beside the Temple of the Reclining Buddha and he seized the mooring rope and jumped ashore to secure it. As soon as the second boat arrived, he began helping other members of the unit unload the equipment into the waiting crew bus.

Watching Ewington and the others, Joceline felt vaguely comforted by their display of youthful enthusiasm and energy. In London she had bided her time carefully before confiding the identity of the manuscript's author first to Ewington, then to Robert Lancaster. Ewington had grinned and welcomed the information as adding a final dash of spice to an already fascinating story. He had told the rest of the unit after their flight had taken off from Heathrow for Bangkok; he had also warned them to guard their tongues very carefully in public throughout the entire trip so as not to compromise the real purpose of the film. Perhaps influenced by his unconcealed enthusiasm, all of the crew without exception appeared to relish the extra dimension of drama the revelations gave to the film.

Joceline had deliberately not offered to show the manuscript to her editor or Robert Lancaster at any stage before their departure; and only at the last moment had she finally divulged the author's identity to Lancaster. He had invited her for a pre-departure glass of champagne in the programme controller's office minutes before she left to join the rest of the unit at the airport. His eyebrows had shot up in surprise when she made the revelation in a casual-sounding aside; then with a shrug he had acknowledged that it added a new dimension of drama to the very good case she had already made for going ahead with the film.

Before she left, he had raised his glass in a toast to the success of the film – but also, he made it very clear, equally to her. In his restrained, unsmiling expression Joceline thought she saw something indefinably sad; both of them felt uncomfortable, without knowing why, and all conversation between them quickly died away. Unable suddenly to look at him, Joceline had excused herself on a pretext and hurried out to her waiting taxi without finishing her champagne.

Climbing from the boat on to the *Wat Po* wharf, Joceline remembered the moment again. To her surprise she experienced a rare but real pang of regret about their parting four Christmases ago. It was the first feeling of its kind she'd had in a very long time and she could find no answer to what might have caused it. When she reached the crew vehicle she found everybody else had already boarded with the equipment. At the foot of the entry steps Michael Ewington was waiting for her, holding the door open and smiling as he watched her approach.

'All aboard for the Grand Palace,' he said jovially, taking her arm to help her up the steps. 'We're all set to film you now, Joceline – in the world's most fabulous setting for a murder.'

2

Joceline walked with measured steps past glaring, round-eyed demon statues two storeys high. They held swords that glittered with inlaid coloured ceramic and from their gaping mouths curled short, deadly looking tusks. A few yards in front of her, the Scottish cameraman was walking backwards, holding his camera on his shoulder and squinting through the lens as he filmed. The young second cameraman was grasping him by the waist from behind, guiding his progress while Angela Gladstone moved swiftly along their intended path, clearing a passage through the early crowds of tourists.

As she passed on her way, Joceline looked left and right at other mythological stone sentinels, half human and half bird, that stood guard over the royal shrines and throne pavilions. She brushed her hand over squirming dragons and seven-headed serpents of porcelain that flanked steps and balustrades; she glanced up at the gilded, bell-shaped towers and multi-tiered roofs of blue and orange on which curved finials glittered dazzlingly in the hot sunlight.

From time to time she paused so that the cameraman could film in close-up the striking decorative detail of statues, cornices and fretted stonework. In particular, outside the former elephant stables close to the Gate of Glorious and Precious Victory, she halted for a minute or more, as she had previously agreed with Michael Ewington. This allowed time for recording long-lens images of the elephant houses and yards over which Jutulak's role as a royal mahout could be explained in later commentary. When the cameraman grunted to indicate he had enough material, she walked on slowly towards the old Forbidden Quarter, the area surrounded by sparkling fountains and quiet gardens into which no man except the king had ever been allowed because it had housed the royal wives and their attendants.

'This square mile of fabled palaces, temples and throne halls was once the living core of "the Royal, Invincible and Beautiful City of Archangels",' said Joceline, addressing the camera through a tiny battery microphone clipped inside her shirtfront. 'Many of the buildings are like a dream come to life. The novelist Somerset Maugham once said: "It makes you laugh with delight to think that anything so fantastic could exist on this sombre earth." Here great elephants used to parade in rich, ceremonial trappings. And this was surely an appropriate home for the rare and scared white elephants much prized by Siamese kings of the past . . . Here, too, the real-life King Mongkhut – immortalised and misrepresented in our Western musical *The King and I* – dwelled with his eighty-two children and his thirty-five wives . . . But by inviting a governess to the Grand Palace from Victorian England, that same king ironically began the process of importing European and Western ideas which, in the end, led to the end of absolute rule by the Siamese monarchy in 1932 . . . Now, most of the ministries that were once housed inside the Grand Palace compound have been moved. And only occasional royal audiences and ceremonies are held here. Today, Thailand's highly revered royal family lives in a different, modern palace that's more in keeping with the twentieth century . . .'

Joceline stopped speaking and slowed her pace on seeing that other members of the unit ahead of her were having difficulties clearing people from their path. Over the years in many parts of the globe she had become accustomed to crowds gathering in streets and public places at the sight of television or film cameras. In her experience it was more often a problem in the Third World and she usually succeeded in ignoring the onlookers to concentrate wholly on her camera statements. But from the moment they began filming in the Grand Palace she had felt vaguely uneasy without knowing why.

To capture authentic atmosphere, they had deliberately chosen to film on one of the public days when large numbers of Thai people thronged the exquisite Temple of the Emerald Buddha to prostrate themselves in front of the nation's most sacred image. Large crowds had already begun to gather before they had finished their detailed reconnaissance of the compound and the moment Joceline stepped in front of the camera, she and the whole unit had become a focus of keen curiosity. Because of the heat they would encounter in Thailand she'd had her blonde hair cropped modishly short before leaving London; wearing a blue shirt, tailored white trousers and light sandals with small heels, she cut a striking figure – tall, pale-skinned and slender among the shorter, dark-haired, stocky Thai men and women all around her. They stared at her in the way similar crowds had often done in the past but as the unit moved from place to place she continued to feel ill at ease without knowing why.

Several times she found herself scanning the rows of faces that assembled and reassembled constantly in an arc all around the moving camera. They were always a mixture of male and female, Thai and European, young and old, but although she kept careful watch, she could not immediately see anybody or anything to justify her sense of unease. Michael Ewington was moving alongside the cameraman, watching and listening carefully to her every word. As usual his unlined face was relaxed and at ease and he was concentrating hard on his work, showing no sign whatsoever of apprehension.

Their Thai interpreter, Joceline noticed, was also staying within earshot; they had agreed that she should confine her comments to innocent historical references until they reached the Barompiman Hall, the European-style, two-storeyed mansion where King Ananda had died from his mysterious gunshot wound. Then, in accordance with Ewington's instructions, Angela Gladstone was to send the interpreter away on a fictitious errand while Joceline recorded a surreptitious camera statement about the scene of the king's death against the background of the mansion itself.

As they neared the Barompiman Hall, Joceline took another slow, careful look at the people pressing around her. At one point she thought she noticed a tall, swarthy Thai watching her intently from the back of the crowd; but he immediately turned away, avoiding her gaze when she looked in his direction. Otherwise she saw nothing suspicious and she began to wonder if she was becoming hypersensitive because of the subterfuge demanded by the project.

Some of the people in the crowds, she saw, were smiling; the few European tourist faces she could see appeared to radiate goodwill, and by their friendly expressions one or two British individuals indicated that they recognised her. Cheered a little by this, she pushed her misgivings to the back of her mind. In London she had spent several days in the British Library reading up Thailand's history and roughing out ideas for script statements which she carried with her in the shoulder bag. While filming was proceeding, the bag was being looked after by Angela Gladstone and Joceline made a signal to the production assistant so that she could refer briefly to her notes. Then, having gathered her thoughts, she nodded at Ewington to indicate she was ready and turned towards the magnificent gilded *chedis* and *prangs* of the Temple of the Emerald Buddha.

'This is the holiest and most deeply revered Buddhist shrine in all Thailand,' said Joceline in an even, respectful tone. 'Inside, amidst swirling clouds of incense, sits a tiny, delicate figure carved from a kind of apple-green jade. It seems to glow with a light of its own on a golden altar eleven metres high. Three times each year, at the start of the hot, rainy and cool seasons, the present king of Thailand comes here as all his ancestors have done before him. His Majesty takes part in a ceremony of the utmost solemnity, during which he drapes new robes fashioned from gold and diamonds on the Emerald Buddha ... The beauty and serenity of this Royal Temple in many ways symbolise this country and its peaceable, graceful people. But Thailand's history, unfortunately, also contains its share of violence and bloodshed . . .'

Joceline broke off despite herself and glanced round at the watching crowd; at once her eye fell on the same swarthy Thai she had noticed before, although this time he was half concealed in the crowd. He appeared to be making a discreet signal of some kind with one hand and turning quickly, Joceline thought she saw another poker-faced male nod his head slightly several yards away. She realised then that it must have been the movement of the first man's hand which had distracted her and she looked back towards the camera and Ewington. But the producer had apparently seen nothing; the camera was still running and Ewington made a little gesture indicating that they would be able to edit around the pause and she should carry on without breaking her flow.

'The Grand Palace was built here beside the river at Bangkok nearly two hundred years ago,' continued Joceline, enunciating her words with slow deliberation, 'because Siam's medieval capital, Ayutthaya, which lies further north, was razed to the ground at the climax of three centuries of war with neighbouring Burma. The war is said to have begun because Siam's king refused the Burmese monarch's request to give him one of seven splendid white elephants then in Siam's possession. Seven was believed to be a particularly auspicious number of white elephants – but during three hundred years of rule in Ayutthaya, a third of all Siam's medieval monarchs were either assassinated or murdered their opponents . . .

'For most of the past two centuries, the nine kings of the current Chakri dynasty have dwelt in these palaces in comparative peace. But as recently as 1946 there was a terrible reminder of those violent times. On 9 June in that year, the present king's predecessor died violently with a Colt .45 bullet wound in his brain, only a stone's throw from where I'm standing. For a time Thailand's ancient monarchy tottered. But King Bhoomipol ascended to the throne at the age of nineteen and over the years that have followed, he has demonstrated great resolution of character in weathering many violent political storms. Today, as Rama IX, he has become the longest-reigning monarch of the entire dynasty. And he enjoys a respect and reverence among his people that is possibly unmatched by any other reigning monarch in the world . . .'

The cameraman halted and Joceline walked on past him and out of shot. Ewington shouted 'End board, please!' and the assistant cameraman snapped the black-and-white clapper-frame loudly in front of the lens. Ewington exchanged hurried words with the sound recordist to check that he had got everything clearly, then hurried over to Joceline, smiling broadly.

'That was just great, Joceline. Word perfect and not even the hint of a fluff. All very clear and succinct. Thanks.'

Joceline nodded abstractedly, peering over his shoulder into the crowd. 'I'm worried, Michael,' she said in a tense under-tone. 'We're being watched.'

'Yes, by half the population of Bangkok, I'd say.' Ewington laughed amiably. 'But I should've thought you'd have got used to that sort of thing by now. That's the trouble with having star quality. It happens wherever you go, doesn't it?'

'I don't mean *casually*,' she said, still searching the faces of the crowd for the two men. 'I think we're being spied on . . . I'm sure I saw one man make a sign to another in the middle of my piece to camera.'

Noticing the seriousness of her tone, Ewington looked care-fully round too. Two hundred and more people were milling about them, watching the men handling the equipment for a clue as to what was to follow. But they were quiet and orderly and there was no sign of threat or any intrusion that might disrupt their work.

'I know you're feeling a bit on edge,' said Ewington, speaking softly and leaning close to her ear. 'It's understandable in view of the background to all this. But isn't it just possible you may be imagining things?'

Joceline shook her head, but without real conviction. 'I don't think so . . .'

Ewington studied her face, his own expression becoming concerned. 'This next camera statement of yours is likely to be one of the trickiest pieces of the trip – so if you can manage to keep on now, I think we should get it over and done with as quickly as possible.' He smiled encouragingly. 'What do you say?'

She summoned a half-smile in reply and nodded. 'All right, perhaps I'm just being oversensitive.'

'That's the style! We can shoot the close-ups of the Emerald

Buddha, the interiors and whatever else we need today without you . . . You can just leave us to it. Get your breath back, perhaps, by the pool at the hotel . . . How will that be?'

'Fine.' Joceline nodded and beckoned to Angela Gladstone to bring over her shoulder bag so that she could consult the notes on her clipboard one last time.

'I'm going to shoot your spiel about the king's death on the long lens and keep you on that battery mike,' murmured Ewington. 'Angela has already sent our Thai interpreter friend away on a long errand. And the crowd will have to keep behind us – so they'll be at least fifty yards away from you. If you speak in a nice, quiet, modulated tone nobody will hear a word you say except me – I'll be listening on the recordist's headphones. Okay?' He turned and pointed to a spot in front of the Barompiman Hall that would allow the cameraman to frame Joceline against the whole façade of the building in a wide shot. 'If you go and stand there by that dwarf tree, we shall be able to see very clearly the windows of the royal apartments where King Ananda was lying when the shot was fired . . .'

Joceline nodded again and smiled her thanks to the production assistant as she handed over the clipboard. She moved out of the hot sun into the shade of a giant statue to refresh her memory for a minute or two, then handed the notes back. After the sound recordist had readjusted the tiny microphone clipped inside her shirt-front, she walked slowly to her position and turned to face the camera, which had been mounted on a sturdy tripod. While she was waiting for Ewington's signal to begin, she noticed that the crowd pressing behind the unit had grown even larger. In a reflex action she searched without success for the faces of the two suspicious men; then Ewington raised and dropped his arm to indicate the camera was running.

'Nearly forty-four years have passed since a bullet killed King Rama VIII,' said Joceline quietly, looking steadily towards the distant camera. 'But still the people of Thailand – and most people in the rest of the world for that matter – don't know whose finger was on the trigger. The tragic event happened inside those rooms of the East Wing behind me where the king's bedroom, study and dressing room were located. Accident? Suicide? Assassination? All remain possibilities – but if there are politicians, courtiers or members of Thailand's large royal family and aristocracy who know the truth, they've made sure it has never leaked out . . .

'Ordinary people in Thailand, if they discuss this sensitive issue at all, talk about it in whispers, even today. Journalists here must also tread very carefully because the country's lese-majesty laws, which protect the large royal family from the slightest insult, are rigorously applied. In the presence of Thai royalty, commoners must still prostrate themselves and crawl on their knees as a mark of respect. As an institution, therefore, and a focus of national identity, the Thai monarchy continues to play a vital role – so if the truth can be established about what happened to their last king even at this late stage, the impact on the political life of the nation could be considerable . . .'

Joceline paused and took a long breath to indicate that she had reached the most significant part of her statement. 'Recently a mysterious manuscript that was found in northern Thailand has come into my hands. In claiming to throw important new light on the topic, it has dragged the issue out of history's shadows again. In this special edition of "Perspective", we will chronicle our efforts to uncover the truth behind the manuscript – and to establish, if possible, what really happened up in the royal apartments of the Barompiman Hall on that hot June morning four decades ago . . .'

A loud, high-pitched female shriek broke the serene stillness of the Grand Palace courtyards and Joceline's voice abruptly died away. A sudden commotion in the crowd had interrupted filming and Joceline heard the Scottish cameraman's distinctive voice raised in fury. She saw Ewington and the sound recordist struggling with several Thai men who seemed to be attacking Angela Gladstone. It was then that Joceline realised that it was the production assistant who had screamed; the next second she broke into a run.

The crowd, frightened by the violence, was scattering and breaking up by the time Joceline reached the other members of the unit. The attackers, whoever they had been, seemed to have escaped in the mêlée; the camera tripod was tipped on its side and she could see the lens was cracked. Ewington and some of the other men were helping the production assistant back to her feet and Joceline noticed that she still clutched the shoulder bag containing her father's manuscript.

'What happened?' gasped Joceline. 'Are you all right?'

'Somebody tried to steal both bags,' sobbed Angela. 'They grabbed mine – then tried to wrench yours from my other shoulder.'

'They've bust my sodding lens!' breathed the Scot, gazing round angrily. 'If I ever get my hands on those bastards . . .'

'There were two or three of them,' said Ewington shakily, wiping a trickle of blood away from his mouth with the back of his hand. 'I thought at first somebody had stumbled into me by accident. Then I felt two hands go round my neck from behind . . .'

'Did they get anything at all, Angela?' asked Joceline anxiously.

'Yes, they got clean away with my bag – all the shot lists were in it . . .'

'Well, I suppose we can just about survive that.' Joceline let out a sigh of relief on satisfying herself that her father's manuscript was still safe in her shoulder bag. 'You'll probably be able to remember most of what we've done so far . . .'

'The letter! Penhaligon's letter!' said Ewington suddenly in a strangled voice. 'I put it in my back pocket, Joceline, remember – it's gone.'

The producer's face was already pale with shock and Joceline stared at him in disbelief. Remembering all the confidential information that the letter contained, her spirits plummeted. She looked round in desperation at the silent faces of people in the crowd, who were now watching them with mystified expressions. But nowhere among them could Joceline see any sign of their attackers. They had disappeared without trace among the fabulous palaces and throne pavilions.

3

'I'm sorry, Joceline! God in heaven, I'm sorry. I feel so damned ashamed of my carelessness . . .'

Ewington ran a hand distractedly through his hair and raised agonised eyes from a photocopy of Nicholas Penhaligon's letter that he had just finished reading.

'If the authorities have seen this and circulated details to all departments, we're finished – we're all washed up!' He scraped his fingers through his long mop of brown hair again. 'We'd better head for the airport pretty damned quick, hadn't we? Get ourselves and the whole crew on the first available flight to London.'

'No!' Joceline's voice was uncompromisingly firm. 'Under no circumstances. We haven't got any proof at all that it was the authorities who sandbagged you and Angela this morning. To my mind it smacked of crude gangsterism rather than police methods. Remember what Penhaligon's letter said about the Chinese – he saw him as a "malignant presence". Possibly with his own axe to grind . . . Those men could have been sent by him. Penhaligon said he had little compunction about committing public violence . . .'

Ewington looked at her with an expression that was both surprised and impressed. 'That's possible . . . I hadn't thought of that.'

'He might be trying to check up on what we're doing, what we've found out, what line we're taking . . . To my mind that scuffle at the Grand Palace looked more like clumsy, spur-of-the-moment improvisation rather than careful planning.' She shook her head in a little gesture of frustration. 'My impression was that there were several men in the crowd watching our every move. I can't claim any intimate knowledge of Thai police methods – but they didn't feel like government snoopers to me.'

Ewington frowned in puzzlement. 'Why not?'

'The police and the security services would normally turn over our rooms here at the hotel first. And they'd do it rather more subtly, while we were out – unless they're very different to their counterparts that I've met in other parts of the world. "Perspective" has often trodden in sensitive areas abroad in the past.' She glanced round her room where they were seated in bamboo-cane chairs sipping malt whisky bought duty-free at Heathrow. 'It wouldn't be the first time. But there's no sign of breaking and entering – and we've been out all day.'

Although shaken by the attack on Angela Gladstone and Ewington, the unit had managed to complete the filming they had scheduled in the Grand Palace just before sunset. The uniformed Bangkok police who arrived several minutes after

the affray took statements from them politely, without showing any sign of hostility or suspicion. In response to a suggestion by Joceline, all the members of the unit had understated
the seriousness of the incidents. They said they imagined they
had been victims of simple, clumsy sneak-thieves who had
smashed the camera lens by chance. The police interviews
had lasted half an hour or so and afterwards everybody felt
sufficiently recovered from the shock to film inside the
Temple of the Emerald Buddha and record other necessary
exteriors. When the crowds had thinned in the late afternoon,
Joceline re-voiced her camera statement discreetly outside the
Barompiman Hall without further incident. By the time they
arrived back at the hotel it was dark and everybody had escaped
gratefully from the heat to shower and refresh themselves in
the air-conditioned coolness of their rooms. After talking by
telephone to all the crew members Joceline invited Ewington
to her room to look through a copy of Penhaligon's letter and
discuss what should be done.

'If those thugs at the Grand Palace were acting for the
anonymous Chinese,' mused the producer as he sipped his
whisky, 'what was it they were after? What would their motives be?'

'I don't pretend to know. Reading between the lines of
Penhaligon's letter, there could be tensions between him on
the one hand and Prem and Surachai on the other. If the
Chinese is the paymaster, he may quite understandably want
to reassure himself independently what he's paying
for . . .'

'So what do you think we should do?'

'We should just carry on as before,' replied Joceline calmly.

'But if we've been hit once, we could be hit again any time?
And whoever got Penhaligon's letter now knows what we're
really doing here. They're not likely just to melt away.' He
hesitated, his expression troubled. 'And we've got to think of
the crew's safety as well as ourselves.'

'The crew are all experienced and well travelled, Michael,'
said Joceline quietly. 'I've worked with all of them several
times before. I've had a quiet word with each of them individu-
ally – they're all prepared to go on. They're very loyal to
"Perspective", to you, and the film. They felt it was significant
that the Thai police this morning were sympathetic and

considerate. None of them wants to give up – they're not going to be intimidated that easily by a few hooligans.'

Ewington absorbed her information in silence. Then his expression clouded again. 'But what are our next moves going to be, Joceline? I saw how impressively you went into action during those difficult days in Romania. I've got the greatest respect for your experience. And I've been very happy to go along with your concept for this film without questioning you too closely. But this is very different to Romania. We ought to have a clear framework mapped out for our investigation. We've got to *make* the story this time. And we don't have that much to go on here in Bangkok, so far, do we?'

Joceline sipped her drink reflectively and avoided his eyes. 'No, you're quite right. On paper we don't have a great deal – yet.'

'What does that mean?'

'I've made enough documentaries – and I'm sure you have too in different fields – to know that sometimes you have to fly blind for a time. During that period you have to use your intuition. And when all else fails, the obvious presence of a camera team can often spark things off . . .'

'As we found today to our cost,' said Ewington heavily.

'Agreed – we don't want to spark anything like that again. But perhaps the strongarm stuff was meant to intimidate us. Getting the letter may have been an unexpected bonus. Their main purpose may have been to frighten us off the story . . .'

'It's just possible,' Ewington conceded quietly.

'But whatever the purpose was, that sneak attack proves my point. We'd only been in town a few hours – and already somebody's uneasy. Our presence is having a noticeable effect. Other lines of enquiry will open up, I feel certain . . . The most important thing for us to do is to keep our nerve and just carry on . . .'

'But filming what – and who?' asked Ewington with a note of exasperation in his voice.

'We must do the Buddhist temple on the *klong* where the monks hid Jutulak after the king's death. And the stilt-houses beside the canal like the one Jutulak would have lived in. Those settings should provide marvellous atmosphere. The old *acharn* has probably died or moved on. But we'll talk to the present monks at the temple. If we can locate the jewelled betel box given to Jutulak by the king, we must include that to illustrate the vow of silence story . . .'

'The temple will certainly be good scenically – but in the end it seems unlikely to produce any hard, dramatic revelations . . .'

'Why don't we wait and see,' said Joceline quickly. 'We also need contemporary shots of the army – soldiers guarding government buildings and so on. Any other military images we can pick up around the city on the run will help me explain the dominant role of the Thai military over the past sixty years. We'll also need current footage of the royal family to provide a modern point of reference . . . The king is taking part in a special river parade of the royal barges on the Chao Phraya next week. It will be very spectacular . . .'

'Yes, but who in the end, Joceline, is going to provide us with significant new information?' asked Ewington pointedly. 'That surely has to be the investigative nub of our story.'

Before replying Joceline pulled a sheaf of papers from her shoulder bag, leafed through them and handed over two type-written sheets. 'None of the British or American newspapers stations major correspondents here. But before we arrived, Angela contrived to chat to two or three of the best informed foreign freelances who write for the international dailies and weeklies from here. She managed to inject oblique questions into her conversations about King Ananda's death without saying that was to be one of the main topics of our film. The responses she got are summarised there.'

Ewington scanned the papers quickly, then raised an eyebrow in Joceline's direction. 'How significant do you think these answers are?'

'Not very significant at all, really. They rehash the familiar crop of rumours about the king's death – from "accident" to "suicide" to "assassination". You'll find the whole range is covered. Everybody seems to have their own favourite story.' She drained her glass, stood up and began pacing restlessly back and forth across the room; then she stopped and looked directly at Ewington. 'But I don't sense somehow, Michael, that we're going to find what we're looking for here in Bangkok.'

'Really?' Ewington frowned again. 'Then where the hell *are* we going to find it?'

'I think in the north. Chiang Mai – or thereabouts.'

'Why do you think that?'

'It's where the whole business of the manuscript originates from. So I think that's where we should do our best digging. It will be difficult there too, of course. Remember Penhaligon warned we may come up against "unclimbable walls" in the end. So we've got to follow up every clue that offers itself.'

'What do you think our plan should be?'

'Get our background filming here in Bangkok over and done with as soon as we can – in two or three days, say. Then head north on the train as quickly as possible.'

Ewington picked up Joceline's bottle of Chivas Regal from a bedside table and raised an eyebrow in the direction of her glass. She shook her head quickly but gestured that he should help himself. While she continued to pace back and forth, he refilled his own glass, his expression pensive. Then he swung round in his chair and looked straight at her.

'Joceline, may I bring up the delicate question of the manuscript and your late father?'

She stopped pacing and turned to face the producer. 'Yes, of course.'

'If you had to be specific, what would you say fascinates you most?' Ewington hesitated and took a sip of whisky. 'The true story of what really happened to King Ananda? Or the mysterious life – and death – of Adam Hampson?'

Joceline sat down on the side of the bed and looked at him levelly. 'I suppose I knew you'd ask me that question sooner or later. I've asked myself many times – often in the middle of the night.'

'And what did you tell yourself?'

She dropped her gaze. 'What do you think?'

He smiled sympathetically. 'I should imagine you find it quite impossible to disentangle the two.'

A little, embarrassed smile appeared on her face. 'I can see intuition is no longer an exclusively female preserve.'

'In your mind does solving one mystery go hand in hand with solving the other?'

'Perhaps it does – I'm not really sure.'

'Could that be why you feel it's so important to go north to Chiang Mai?'

She did not reply but her silence seemed to indicate that she found no fault with his deduction.

'There's one other thing that bothers me, Joceline – the story of your father's death. Doesn't that all sound a little too pat and melodramatic? Do you believe that's what really happened?'

'No, I don't!' Joceline stood up, her face becoming tense. 'You've got a perfect right to question me about what's in my mind – but after all that's happened today, Michael, I need to move. I just need to do something . . . Let's go out and walk, eat, anything . . .'

She plucked up her bag from a table and rushed from the room. Ewington, after gulping down the remainder of his whisky, rose and hurried out after her.

4

'From the moment in Chiang Mai that I began reading about the rogue elephant going on the rampage I felt instinctively that this was a challenge I shouldn't turn down. And although I still find it difficult to articulate the reasons why, that feeling has never left me . . .'

Joceline tightened her grip on a side-rail of a gaudily painted, three-wheeled *tuk-tuk* which was being driven with helter-skelter recklessness along Sukhumvit Road towards Siam Square.

'And I've never once wavered in my determination to get to the bottom of it all,' continued Joceline, raising her voice above the angry, high-pitched buzz of the *tuk-tuk*'s two-stroke engine. 'If I hadn't been able to persuade Metropolitan to make the film, I think I would have resigned and come back to research the story on my own . . .'

Beside her on the back seat Ewington listened intently. He had his feet and legs braced against the flimsy partition separating them from the driver. Keeping a wary eye on the dense traffic all around them, he was flexing his body against the erratic jolting and swaying of the tiny, open-sided vehicle as it dodged dangerously back and forth between streams of

cars being raced westward by their Thai drivers with a ferocious, Grand Prix intensity.

'I didn't understand that you felt that strongly from the
outset,' said Ewington, nodding. 'How would you have handled
it on your own?'

Joceline shrugged. 'A book perhaps, a series of newspaper or
magazine articles, possibly even a freelance film if I could have
found the finance – luckily I didn't have to think that far
because Metropolitan decided to back me . . .'

The *tuk-tuk* swerved violently to avoid a slow-moving
motorcycle and Joceline, alarmed, called loudly to the driver
in English to slow down. He grinned and nodded vigorously but
their speed did not noticeably slacken. Joceline had climbed
impulsively into the first of a row of tiny auxiliary taxis drawn
up in the street outside their hotel, ignoring the line of more
comfortable taxi saloons nearby. As soon as Ewington
scrambled into the *tuk-tuk*, she asked to be taken to 'the
centre of Bangkok'. Within seconds its driver had catapulted
the little vehicle expertly into the fast-flowing traffic. Unnoticed by them, a conventional Toyota taxi that had been
parked in the shadow of roadside trees had shot out in their
wake. Moving quickly, it had taken up station in the same
lane fifty yards behind them. Inside the Toyota the eyes of its
four male occupants were fixed intently on Joceline's *tuk-tuk*
and whenever it accelerated, slowed down or changed direction, the taxi followed suit.

'My mind was firmly made up long before I got the bulk of
the manuscript in London,' said Joceline, leaning towards
Ewington to make herself better heard above the traffic noise.
'Then reading it in its entirety was a very strange experience.
The story, as you know, is fascinating in itself. Before I went
to Chiang Mai I'd always truly believed I didn't care a fig for
my father because I'd never known him – but in the end every
clue to his character revealed in the story became a nugget of
the purest gold to me . . .'

'Why do you think that was?' asked Ewington.

'The manuscript turned him into a figure of flesh and blood
for me for the very first time . . . I felt the story he had written
contained important new insights about myself. I analysed it
all minutely, trying to decide what parts of my own character
might have been inherited from my father . . .'

'And did you reach any startling conclusions on that score?'

'For one thing, it made me look with new eyes at my restlessness and my constant desire to travel. Overall, the manuscript became something of an obsession, I suppose. Although I was exhausted, I stayed awake in Berlin and Bucharest night after night rereading it endlessly . . . We were reporting and analysing world-shaking events, I know. But all the time I was impatient to come out to Bangkok and get my teeth into this film . . .'

Their *tuk-tuk* accelerated again suddenly, racing in a solid wedge of cars, motorbikes and other *tuk-tuks* to beat a red light at a major intersection. But at the last moment the newly released stream of traffic began pouring at right angles across the junction into their path. Several vehicles ahead of them skidded squealing to a halt and their *tuk-tuk* driver braked wildly too. Only by clutching frantically at the little taxi's canopy did Ewington and Joceline manage to prevent themselves being pitched forward into the tiny front compartment.

'We may have survived the tanks and snipers of Bucharest,' said Ewington sarcastically, straightening himself on the back seat. 'But I'm not so sure we'll survive the devilish *tuk-tuks* of Bangkok.'

In the stationary vehicle they were robbed suddenly of the breeze created by its rapid movement. As they waited, the city's hot season blanket of damp heat and acrid exhaust fumes stifled them again. On the pavements on both sides of the broad street and on pedestrian bridges above it, they could see groups of male foreigners moving in slow throngs; many were heading into the narrow *soi* where bright neon signs were visible, advertising massage parlours, go-go joints, 'exclusive gay male bars' and 'exciting all-girl cabaret shows'. High-rise hotel and office blocks towered into the darkness and in the shadows at the pavement side Joceline from time to time saw grimy figures lying in the dust holding out tin begging bowls towards the passing tourists.

Only the ubiquitous spirit shrines and altars which Joceline saw everywhere distinguished Bangkok's urban vistas from any other modern capital; in the courtyards of all the hotels, office blocks, restaurants and clubs they passed she noticed miniature, carved temples had been set up on tables and plinths. Most of them were brightly painted and freshly decked with garlands of jasmine, joss sticks and offerings of food. Close to the traffic lights Joceline saw a group of Thai men and women lighting incense and bending to pray before one of the altars. Watching them, her thoughts turned to the spirit shrines of the northern Thai jungles described so vividly by her father at the very beginning of his story. She remembered the strange ritual and the ill-fated *kon song* who attempted vainly to exorcise the raging elephant with her fragile tray of straw effigies. Somehow the real spirit shrine that she could see on the pavement seemed to fuse with the images of the other shrines described by her father in the manuscript; she felt she sensed the strange kinship and continuity that existed between the one and the other and she fell into a reflective reverie.

Then at the end of a long, tantalising delay the lights changed without warning; the *tuk-tuk* leapt forward again, buzzing like an angry hornet and Joceline's attention was jerked rudely back to the present. All around them, vehicles of every size sprang to life again too; the frantic mass-start quickly developed into another furious speed battle to beat the lights at the next junction and after glancing enquiringly at Ewington, Joceline tapped their driver sharply on the shoulder. When he glanced round, she motioned for him to pull over as soon as safety allowed. Once they had alighted on to the pavement, she paid him off, thanking him politely, and added a generous tip.

Fifty yards behind them, the Toyota taxi swerved sharply into the nearside lane and pulled up at the kerb. Three of its occupants, wearing dark glasses, short-sleeved shirts and grey slacks climbed out. After a moment's conversation they began sauntering with a mock casualness in the same direction as Joceline and Ewington.

Further back a gleaming 1000 cc Japanese Suzuki that had been cruising at a discreet distance behind the Toyota slowed to a crawl and stopped. It was being ridden by two Thais wearing jeans, black leather jackets and white crash helmets. Their eyes grew narrow as they watched the three strolling Thai men; then the pillion rider, who was taller, climbed off the machine. After closing the darkened visor of his helmet, he began making his way purposefully along the crowded pavement, keeping the English couple and the group of three men following them carefully in sight.

'I just had to unburden myself of some of those emotional feelings before we got too far into the film,' said Joceline as they walked quickly along the crowded pavement on the south side of Phloenjhit Road. 'But I think there are two other things we need to talk over urgently . . .'

'Okay,' said Ewington amicably. 'I'm listening.'

'First, do you remember Penhaligon warned me in his letter that the manuscript might have been tampered with?'

'Yes, of course.'

'Well, I think we should keep that right in the front of our minds. I wanted you to know that I'm not taking it all as the gospel truth.'

'That's very wise, I think.'

'For a start, the name of the colonel who conducted my father's interrogation here in Bangkok sticks out like a sore thumb. The manuscript is notably free of that kind of detail otherwise.'

'So you think we ought to begin by finding out who he is?'

'Yes. In fact I've already asked Angela to try and check out the name with her local freelance contacts this evening.'

'Well done.' Ewington nodded his approval. 'I'll read over the whole manuscript again to see if anything else strikes me.'

They walked in silence for a minute or two, then Ewington turned to her again, his expression quizzical. 'You said just now there were "two other things", Joceline. What's the second?'

'It's a kind of confession . . .' Joceline hesitated and glanced sideways at him, as though apprehensive about how he might react. 'Ever since my visit to Chiang Mai in October one small thing has gnawed away at the journalist inside me . . . Whether it's big enough to call a doubt, I'm not sure . . .'

Another silence ensued until Ewington broke it with a smile. 'Well, I can't really be much help unless you tell me what it is you're confessing.'

Joceline frowned, staring down at the pavement. 'I've always felt strongly it was right to go on, but I suppose it worries me a little that I was hooked rather too cleverly in the first place.'

'What made you feel that?'

'Penhaligon's letter . . . That's why I wanted you to read it, chapter and verse . . . All that careful calculation that led up to my taking the bait of the manuscript – it made me aware I was being manipulated to some extent . . .'

Ewington looked thoughtful. 'So you're concerned that you've allowed your emotional interest in your father to distort your journalistic judgement? You feel you might be justifiably accused of serving the interests of the Thai radicals who are obviously behind all this?'

Joceline nodded. 'Do you think I'm right to worry about that?'

Ewington pondered his answer carefully. 'It's a healthy sign that you're aware of the danger. But how many news leaks or revelations are ever made public without there being a strong ulterior motive in the mind of the individual – or the public relations firm – responsible? Governments, the media, companies, individuals, aren't they all trying to manipulate one another most of the time?'

Joceline smiled in relief. 'I was hoping you'd say something like that.'

Ewington shrugged. 'Even in my limited experience it's the way of the world. So long as we don't take things at face value or give uncritical credence to something that doesn't deserve it, no source is irredeemably tainted. It's axiomatic in my book to test to the limit the background of any "leaked" information so as to give it the right perspective – if it's worthy of attention at all. And this story is obviously very worthy of attention, whichever way you look at it.'

'Michael, thank you.' She touched his arm briefly in a gesture of gratitude. 'That helps a lot. You've just spelled out the best possible reasons for trying to find out all we can about my father's role in this. We certainly need to test *that* to the limit.'

Ewington nodded his agreement.

'He alone knows the whole truth about the manuscript – he'll certainly know if anything's missing. He'll know better than anyone whether it's been tampered with. And only he can tell us if the story is genuine and reliable in its entirety or in parts. What's more, he has no personal axe to grind . . .'

'"He alone *knows* the whole truth"?' echoed Ewington, cutting in on her suddenly. '"He *has* no personal axe to grind" . . . You're obviously using the present tense very deliberately, Joceline.' He turned and stared at her as they continued walking. 'Does this mean you know something I don't? Isn't your father really dead after all?'

'You know everything I know now, Michael,' said Joceline quietly. 'But no, I don't feel my father is dead. The secretary at the Chiang Mai Foreign Cemetery to my amazement was dubious about the circumstances of his reported death and burial. And the more I've thought about it since finishing the manuscript, the less likely it seems that he would have been trampled to death by a wild elephant . . .'

Because the crowds around them on the pavement were thickening, they had to slow their pace. The fragrance of burning incense wafted to them on the heavy night air and they heard strains of traditional Thai music being played. They had reached the junction where Phloenjhit met Ratchadamri Road and suddenly they saw before them the reason for the congestion: at the street corner a dense crowd was milling around an ornate, pillared shrine enclosing a golden image of a four-headed Hindu god. Countless brilliantly coloured garlands of flowers were draped around it and hundreds of candles lit by worshippers glimmered at its base in the darkness. Troupes of sinuous Thai dancing girls in ornate golden costumes and spired head-dresses were weaving graceful movements among the crowd, accompanied by costumed musicians. With traffic roaring across one of Bangkok's busiest intersections only yards away, the shrine was a strange, unexpected oasis of peace and beauty and Joceline, on an impulse, turned into the compound. At her heels, Ewington hesitated, then followed, touching her arm gently to regain her attention.

'Where, Joceline,' he asked quietly, 'do you think your father might be, if he really *is* still alive?'

She turned to face him and shook her head in a little gesture of helplessness. 'Anywhere – but perhaps the logical place would be somewhere in the jungles north of Chiang Mai. He frequently disappeared into the forests for long periods in recent years . . .'

Ewington raised his eyebrows suddenly. 'And am I right in thinking that it's crossed your mind to go and look for him?'

Joceline continued to look steadily at him, her expression composed and serious. 'Yes, I think now that's absolutely essential.'

6

The three Thai men in dark glasses who had alighted from the Toyota taxi slowed their pace and stopped by the low, spiked railings that surrounded the compound of the Erawan Shrine. Because it was believed to be Bangkok's supreme source of good fortune, the shrine was thronged by many Thais and other Asian supplicants as well as languid groups of American and European tourists. As they surveyed the scene, the three Thai men hesitated, talking urgently together in low voices; then one detached himself from the others and began pushing his way through the crush towards Joceline and Ewington. His two companions remained outside the gate, keeping the two English television journalists discreetly under surveillance as they moved deeper into the crowd.

Fifty yards further away the pillion rider from the Suzuki stopped and lifted the visor of his crash helmet so as to give himself better vision under the street lighting. His companion, who had kept the motorbike moving slowly along the kerb, pulled up at his side and leaned towards him. He gestured briefly towards the gate of the Erawan Shrine, then ran his machine across the pavement to park and lock it. Without removing his helmet, he fell into step beside his taller companion and together they continued walking warily towards the shrine.

Other sharp-eyed Thai men were hovering on the fringes of the large crowd. Whenever a chance presented itself they were sidling up to solo male foreigners. Some placed their hands together in a respectful *wai* before pulling back their shirt sleeves to reveal rows of realistic-looking fake Rolex and Piaget wristwatches which they offered to sell for a few dollars. Others made the same ancient gesture before offering for inspection little, menu-like cards which bore handwritten details of obscene sex shows available at bars and cabarets in nearby streets. Accomplice groups of *tuk-tuk* drivers were also waiting nearby, ready to provide rapid transport for any takers of these discreetly advertised services.

Inside the compound railings close to a stall selling incense, flowers and other offerings, Ewington was standing silently at Joceline's side. Inside his mind he was testing camera angles for the ornate shrine, its seated god, the dancers, musicians and the praying crowds, wondering whether to add the brilliant night-time scene to the schedule of locations that they would film in Bangkok. A few feet away, Joceline was deep in conversation with an Indian woman who had just knelt reverently to place a small wooden replica of an elephant at the feet of the god. All around them dark-haired Asians were bowing their heads and praying as they lit candles or draped sweet-smelling jasmine on railings around the sacred statue or on four guardian elephants sculpted in stone.

'The shrine apparently is named after an elephant, "Erawan", who was the mythical mount of Brahma,' said Joceline, after thanking and bidding goodbye to the Indian woman. 'That's a statue of Brahma in the central pavilion. And this is the reason why some people are leaving little wooden elephants at his feet ...'

'It's certainly a striking scene,' mused Ewington, watching the exquisitely curved hands of the Thai dancers weave mysterious patterns in the incense-laden air. 'Perhaps we'll get a night-time shot or two of it.'

'Brahma seems to be a charmingly multi-purpose deity,' said Joceline, still speaking quietly. 'Hindus, Buddhists of every stripe, spirit worshippers – they all come here. They pay for the dancers and musicians to perform as an act of thanksgiving for wishes already granted. Or to ward off bad luck and seek help with anything from passing exams to winning the national lottery ...'

'What about investigative documentary film-making?' asked Ewington with a grim smile. 'Does the deity offer any help with that sort of activity? Metropolitan Television could maybe do worse than invest a few *baht* in a performance by the dancing troupe and the odd bunch of jasmine ...'

Joceline started to smile; then her expression changed and grew serious. She reached into the small handbag which she carried on a thin strap over her shoulder and took out some

Thai banknotes. 'Perhaps you've had a better idea than you realise, Michael . . . There's no reason I can think of why a lapsed Catholic shouldn't be allowed to make an offering too . . .'

She turned away and went over to the stall selling the votive offerings. He watched her hand over some notes, then make her way through the crowd towards the statue of Brahma, carrying candles, necklets of magenta flowers and a small wooden effigy of an elephant. She lit the candles from the flames of others already in place and added the flowers to the great banks of colour with which the shrine was already festooned. When she knelt to place the little carved elephant on the steps below the plinth, Ewington noticed that she did not rise immediately. As he continued to watch she became very still and he saw her bow her head slightly.

At that moment he felt somebody tap lightly on his right shoulder. He turned round sharply to find that a middle-aged, unshaven Thai had moved quietly up to the railings at his back and leaned over to touch him. Ewington watched warily as the man joined his palms in a *wai*, then held out a folded card towards him.

'What is that?' asked Ewington guardedly.

'You look, you look – very good!' urged the man, grinning craftily. 'You look.'

Ewington took the card and opened it. Inside, beneath the name of a bar, a numbered list had been written with a ballpoint pen in an uneven, uneducated hand. 'Smoke cigarette pussy,' 'Shoot balloon pussy,' 'Open Coca Cola bottle pussy' and 'Hide razor-blade pussy' were the first four entries and Ewington looked searchingly at the donor of the card, wondering if he was all he seemed to be. The Thai, misreading his expression, made a quick gesture with one hand towards the lower part of his own body and said: 'Girls – in show!', grinning lasciviously as he spoke.

Ewington handed the card back wordlessly and shook his head.

'No like Thai girls,' persisted the man in a fierce whisper, pulling another card from the pocket of his shirt and holding it towards Ewington. 'You like Thai boy?'

'Go away,' said Ewington firmly and turned his back on the man in time to see Joceline making her way towards him through the crowd. Her expression was subdued and she walked slowly as though she were deep in thought. When she reached him, she smiled but did not speak.

'Why don't we go and find somewhere pleasant to eat?' said Ewington quietly, touching her elbow to guide her in the direction of the gate. 'You must be very hungry by now.'

She nodded and they began making their way out of the compound. As they passed through the gate on to the crowded pavement, the same unshaven Thai who had accosted him minutes before reappeared suddenly in front of them in the crush. After joining his hands quickly and bowing his head in Joceline's direction, he produced a folded paper from his shirt pocket and held it towards her.

'Here message for lady,' he said, grinning at Joceline. 'Message special for you.'

Ewington reached out and knocked the man's arm angrily aside. 'Get out of our way!' he said harshly. 'The lady doesn't want your messages.'

The Thai shouted something unintelligible and tried to hold out the paper again. Joceline flinched as Ewington moved in front of her to push the man aside and people around them in the crowd began to draw back in alarm.

'Why don't you let him hand it over, Michael?' called Joceline anxiously. 'It won't do any harm.'

'He's touting for lurid sex shows,' said Ewington grimly over his shoulder as he grabbed the man and began to push him aside. 'He's already given me one of his unsavoury cards . . . There's no reason why you should . . .'

'No! Extra special message – special message for lady,' shouted the unshaven Thai, struggling in Ewington's grip and trying doggedly to hold out the paper towards Joceline. 'Man tell me give it to lady . . . He pay me much money . . .'

'Let him go, Michael!'

Joceline reached out and snatched the folded paper quickly from the man's hand. Without opening it, she slipped it into her handbag. Glancing around, she tried to see who might have given the note to the sex-show tout; but all heads were turning in their direction and curiosity was causing the crowd to close in around them.

'Come on, Michael, leave him!'

She began to push her way out of the crowd and Ewington

followed. They hurried away from the shrine and turned off Phloenjhit into the first quiet *soi* they came to. Neither of them spoke until they were seated facing one another in a small, inexpensive restaurant. Then Joceline took the folded paper from her handbag and opened it. She read it over several times without making any comment. When she raised her head to look at Ewington, he saw that her face was pale and tense.

'What does it say?' he asked in a tight voice.

Instead of replying she handed him the note. At the same time she frowned a silent warning to him not to make any comment aloud. After glancing round to make sure he was not overlooked, Ewington spread the paper flat between his hands on the table and bent over it.

Headed simply 'Joceline Hampson', the note was typewritten and brief. It said: 'If you wish to know the real truth about the "King's Death Case" and your father, come to the address below at midnight. Do not bring your cameras – or any companions.'

The address in Bangkok that followed gave them no immediate clue as to its precise location.

7

Joceline lifted her left wrist impatiently close to her face. Straining her eyes, she tried to read the hands of her small gold wristwatch but it was difficult in the smoky half-darkness of the run down go-go bar. She felt almost sure she could see the minute hand of the watch nearing the bottom of its downward sweep; if that was true, it was coming up to half past midnight.

Nearly thirty minutes had passed since she arrived and during that time nobody in the crowded bar had attempted to approach her – with the exception of a young, harassed male waiter from whom she had ordered a local Singha beer. On a tiny, raised stage lit from above in the middle of the room, half a dozen near-naked Thai girls with long black hair hanging geometrically straight down their bare backs were jerking their limbs spasmodically in a weary semblance of Western disco dancing. All were bare-breasted and at the apex of their narrow thighs, each wore a small scrap of black material no bigger than a pirate's eye-patch, secured by bootlace-thin straps.

Plain wooden tables covered with empty and half-filled glasses were arranged on all sides of the stage. Around them were gathered groups of mainly male Thais ranging in age from their teens to paunchy, late middle-age. Most, Joceline could see, were drinking local beer and cheap Thai whisky and brandy. A few were accompanied by Thai women, who smoked and watched the stage with bored expressions while their men talked.

There were very few foreigners in the bar, which was situated above a lock-up garage in a poor area near the river, well away from the popular tourist areas of Bangkok. Two balding, overweight Germans were seated at a table in a far corner, identifiable by the guttural cadences of their language; their faces shone with perspiration and they stared unblinkingly towards the stage most of the time as they drank. Two younger, long-haired men in jeans and T-shirts, possibly American she decided, had taken up places close below the stage. More relaxed than the Germans, they grinned a lot and called out occasional provocative remarks in Thai to the girls as they danced. Like everybody else in the bar they knew the dancers were only filling in time and as the amplified music died away and the go-go girls hurried off-stage, an anticipatory buzz of conversation rose from the tables.

Ten minutes after Joceline arrived, the stage had been cleared, the lights had dimmed and a mattress had been dragged on to the dancing area. A scantily clad Thai woman who looked to be in her thirties had stepped unsmiling under a single spotlight with a young, muscular Thai male. Without grace or artifice, they had undressed one another; then they appeared to perform the sexual act with the tense, silent audience erupting every so often into ribald catcalling. Joceline, glad that she had taken a table in the shadows against the wall, had turned in her chair so that she no longer saw the stage and peered watchfully into the darkness around her, waiting on tenterhooks for an approach of some kind. But after ragged applause, the lights on the stage had gone up, the go-go dancers had returned and she had continued to wait vainly in the gloom. Unable to relax, she sat stiffly upright on her hard wooden chair; although the room was hot and her mouth was dry, she found she was unable to take even a sip of the cold beer on the table before her.

As the stage lights dimmed for the second time, Joceline felt the tension that had been growing steadily in the pit of her stomach become almost unbearable. Not for the first time, she regretted her rashness in insisting that she be allowed to come completely alone; she regretted, too, the unnecessary sharpness with which she had spoken to Ewington. He had become very alarmed on seeing she was determined to comply absolutely with the letter of the instructions in the note. He had tried to insist that he should either accompany her, or film her making the journey to the rendezvous in a *tuk-tuk* as an indirect form of protection. Their discussion had become heated and she had ungraciously cut it short by asserting that only she was qualified to decide how best to obtain information about her own father.

Remembering the moment, she realised just how foolhardy she had been. With her shoulders pressed against the grimy wall behind her, she felt very alone and vulnerable. She had fought down the impulse to hurry from the bar several times while the first pair of sad, spotlit bodies were writhing obscenely together on the tiny stage. Controlling her feelings of revulsion with difficulty, she had blotted out what was happening around her and concentrated hard on the implications of leaving the bar and giving up an important lead. The chance to discover something vital about the 'King's Death Case', she decided, was something she would have passed up, albeit reluctantly, because of the circumstances; in the end it had been the promise in the typewritten note of information about her father that had kept her in her seat.

Before setting out alone to keep the appointment, Joceline had spent an hour in her room, steeling herself to the ordeal. On her way back to the hotel after dining, she had checked with the *tuk-tuk* drivers in the road outside to see if they knew the address in the typewritten note. They had nodded eagerly and grinned in a way which left her in no doubt about the kind of place she would find. In her room she had pulled from her files the background briefs on Thailand prepared for her in London by Metropolitan researchers. One on organised crime and the country's burgeoning sex industry drew attention to the paradoxical growth of gun-law gangsterism in a country noted for its traditional gentleness and Buddhist pacifism. It also mentioned suspicions that there were possible connections between corrupt civilian and military figures and big-time criminals. With armed insurgencies in neighbouring Burma and Cambodia, weapons were easily and cheaply available everywhere, the briefs said. Dozens of murders were committed daily across the country and foreign tourists, businessmen and journalists from Asia and Europe had occasionally become victims.

Joceline remembered the details of the research briefs with an inward shudder as she glanced at the hard faces of the men seated around the adjoining tables. Her instinct told her that at least some of those present must be habitual criminals. When she had first arrived, many of the men present, including the two Germans and the Americans, had stared in surprise on seeing a European woman enter alone. From time to time she noticed other newcomers glancing in the direction of her table; some obviously murmured wisecracks which drew laughter from their companions and others had continued intermittently to dart curious glances at her. She tried to monitor those who had showed any obvious interest, watching them discreetly over the rim of her glass while pretending to sip the Singha beer. But still no individual approached or attempted to speak with her.

Then the lights dimmed and finally went out on the stage, leaving a single spot glowing. The return to near-darkness in the bar induced in her a feeling close to panic and she found herself wondering desperately what Ewington and the other members of the unit might be doing. They had probably gone to bed, she thought, wishing desperately that she, too, had stayed in the hotel. A loud cheer rose suddenly from the men at the tables as one of the slender go-go dancers stepped entirely naked into the spotlight. She was leading a well-built Thai with greying temples by the hand. At that moment an indistinct figure appeared beside Joceline and leaned over her table.

'You are Miss Joceline Hampson, yes?' asked a male Thai voice. 'You receive note?'

'Yes.' Joceline's voice was unsteady. 'Did the note come from you?'

'No – I take you to the man who send it. Please come with me.'

The man led the way to the door and Joceline rose quickly and followed him out just as the second pair of naked bodies began to grapple together on the shabby stage.

<h1 style="text-align:center">8</h1>

Michael Ewington raised his head cautiously above a low wall behind which he was hiding alongside his Scottish cameraman and the sound recordist. He peered for a moment along the unlit waterfront alley into which Joceline had turned more than half an hour earlier, then ducked his head down quickly out of sight again.

'Do you see anything?' demanded the cameraman in an urgent whisper.

Ewington nodded, his face tense. 'Somebody's just coming out of the bar – a Thai. He's heading this way.'

They all hunched lower behind the wall and the sound recordist quietly switched on his machine and held a microphone upright in his clenched fist to pick up the faint sound of footsteps that were growing louder.

'Do you want me to try and get a shot of him?' asked the cameraman in another fierce whisper, shifting to a position from which he could rise quickly to begin filming. 'Just a short burst?'

'No, for God's sake stay down, Mac,' whispered Ewington frantically. 'We can't risk it. Joceline nearly went hysterical when I suggested we should try and film her. If she knew what we'd done she'd be having kittens in there.'

'Mac' – Ian MacLachlan – frowned and shook his head in a gesture of frustration. 'This is getting crazier by the minute.'

The sound recordist held up his hand, looking irritable, and the three of them listened in silence as the footsteps approached, passed, then slowly died away. Ewington raised his head and looked towards the grimy neon sign that flickered outside the bar. The alley was deserted and he sank back into his position with a sigh.

'I know how you feel, Mac – but Joceline seemed to feel that the presence of cameras, if they were discovered, would put her life in greater danger than anything else. Do you want to be responsible for something terrible happening to her?'

The cameraman swore quietly to himself. 'We should never have been stupid enough to let her go in there alone.'

'Mac, it was absolutely impossible to dissuade her.' Ewington raked his hands through his hair in his agitation. 'She threw a lot of heavy moralising at me. "What right did I have to interfere with her finding out the truth about her own father?" – that sort of thing. She was very, very strung up by the note.'

'What reasons did she give?' asked the sound recordist quietly.

'She said if I tried to go along with her or film her, I'd be jeopardising her chances of discovering anything at all. She made it sound like the end of the world. I decided that the least I could do was to get some shots of her leaving the hotel and coming here in the *tuk-tuk*. I thought it might provide a minimum amount of "security" – and keep us close to the action . . .'

Ewington had ordered MacLachlan's assistant, Alan Eastwood, to set up the second camera discreetly on the balcony of his hotel room which overlooked the street. From there Eastwood had filmed Joceline from above as she left the hotel. Ewington and MacLachlan had been waiting in an ordinary taxi and had followed Joceline's *tuk-tuk* without her knowledge, filming her through the windscreen. Using portable telephones, they had kept in contact with the assistant cameraman, who had later driven the crew bus with the rest of the equipment to the riverside area. He had parked the bus and stayed with it, as instructed, several streets away so that they would have transport at hand when they finished filming. As soon as Joceline entered the bar, they had dismissed the taxi and Ewington and MacLachlan had concealed themselves behind the wall in sight of the front door of the bar. While they waited, the sound recordist had gone off to make a discreet survey of the area and on his return had reported that the rear of the bar faced open ground beside the river. It could be reached, he said, along the next alleyway. After agonising whether to try and cover the front or the back doors, Ewington had tossed a coin mentally and decided to remain in the hiding place behind the wall.

'If all this works,' continued Ewington, his voice anxious, 'it'll also give us a chance to edit in footage that pays some subtle tribute to Joceline's courage in the final film.' He shrugged and sighed loudly. 'But after what she said, it still feels like a gross act of betrayal . . .'

The urgent sound of approaching motorbike engines broke in on their whispered conversation and Ewington raised his head cautiously above the wall for a split second, then bobbed down again. The other two men looked at him expectantly.

'Five or six motorbikes – coming from the opposite direction.'

Without waiting for instructions, MacLachlan rose in a half crouch. His camera, held at his shoulder, was already running and he pointed it along the approach street, framing in his lens half a dozen gleaming Japanese motorcycles moving slowly in a group with two white-helmeted riders on each.

'What the hell are you doing, Mac?' demanded Ewington angrily. 'Get down or you'll be seen.'

'Relax – this is just a hunch,' breathed MacLachlan, filming the bikes and their riders steadily as they approached.

'Keep quiet both of you,' hissed the recordist, holding up his mike above the wall to pick up the engine noise. 'I'm getting your voices all over everywhere.'

Moving slowly, two and three abreast, the bikes slowed and turned in front of their hiding place without any of the riders apparently noticing the cameraman. MacLachlan could see the 'Suzuki' brand plates clearly on their petrol tanks and he continued to film them as the bikes moved steadily away from the camera, heading down the alley towards the bar. One of the rear riders was speaking into a two-way walkie-talkie or handphone that he carried: as he passed the hiding place, his words and the crackle of one sharp reply in Thai became clearly audible above the beat of the slowly revving engines.

'You probably didn't notice but there were two or three bikes like those buzzing behind us all the way from the hotel,' breathed MacLachlan, still filming. 'They kept changing places and passing us. I don't know what it means but it may well be worth something. Trust me.'

'Please shut up!' hissed the recordist, straining to pick up distant clean sound of the bikes, which were drawing to a halt outside the go-go bar.

Ewington raised his head to watch and saw two of the pillion passengers alight and run into the bar. The riders of the bikes from which they had leapt waited astride their machines, keeping their engines running. With a sudden roar of acceleration the other bikes shot away down the alley, heading fast towards the river.

'What the hell's going on?' breathed Ewington, wondering desperately whether they should abandon their hiding place and race down the alley to the bar itself. 'What do you think, Mac, shall we get down there now . . .?'

'I can go over to the 600 mm lens,' murmured MacLachlan, still filming. 'The light's not good but I'm using our fastest stock. We'll certainly be picking up something. It will be a bit grainy but very atmospheric.'

'Hell, I mean, shouldn't we get down there now for Joceline's sake?' said Ewington in a tense voice.

At that instant the unmistakable sounds of gunfire rang out from the direction of the bar. The first shots were isolated and sporadic, two or three single reports followed moments later by several more. Then they became more frequent as though other weapons were being fired.

'Oh my God,' gasped Ewington, deeply appalled. He turned to look at MacLachlan, who had stopped filming and raised his head to listen more carefully.

'It's coming from the back of the building, I'd say,' said MacLachlan, his face pale.

'We'd better get over there!' The recordist was rising to his feet, switching off his machine. 'She definitely needs help now.'

Hitching his tape machine up on his shoulder, he leapt over the wall and began running towards the alley which led down to the back of the bar. Ewington helped MacLachlan to gather up his equipment, then they too clambered over the wall and ran after him.

* * * * *

The door out of the bar led down a narrow flight of rickety wooden stairs. When Joceline reached the bottom and stepped through another door into the open air, the first thing she noticed was the damp, tangy smell of the Chao Phraya river. She was in a small yard littered with plastic beer-crates and broken furniture but in the darkness she could see very little. She never saw the man who stepped up behind her from outside the door. He pinioned her arms roughly to her sides with both his own while the first man produced a scarf and tied it around her head. She managed to cry out but not very loudly and the next moment a hand was clamped over her mouth.

Between them, the two men forced her forward through the darkness towards a car that was parked in the gloom beyond the littered yard. She heard the sounds of motorcycle engines approaching at the same instant that she became aware of other shadowy figures moving stealthily forward alongside her. The car was the first of three vehicles parked in a row and beside it other men were waiting, holding its doors open.

The two men restraining her used their strength to make her bend, trying to force her into the back seat of the first car; but a fierce surge of anger suddenly conquered her fright. She struggled hard against her molesters, lashing out backwards with her feet and twisting violently from side to side to free her arms. She succeeded in tearing her right hand from their grasp and swung her clenched fist by instinct into the face of the man holding her from behind. In response, he cursed and struck her heavily on the head, knocking her to the ground beside the open door of the car. All the time the noise of the motorbikes was becoming louder in her ears; then their headlights lit the scene as they squealed to a halt around the cars.

She heard shouts and more curses as the motorcycle riders flung down their machines and closed with the men about her. In the course of the struggle her blindfold had slipped and she saw the ugly glint of knives in the hands of some of the riders; then a pistol was fired by somebody close to her and its sound shocked her mind into a state of abnormal clarity. She heard a voice further away cry out in pain; other shots followed from different sources and she hugged the ground as she had done not so long ago in the snowy streets of Bucharest. Somebody bent over her, grunting and cursing, and tried to lift her bodily into the car. But again she struggled desperately, striking out blindly with both hands.

To her great relief a blow from elsewhere drove her attacker to his knees at her side. She saw his eyes widen with shock as several hands grabbed him and dragged him off. The next moment she felt herself lifted more gently to her feet. A supporting arm circled her waist and a Thai voice, muffled inside a crash helmet, encouraged her to walk away from the car. She responded, stumbling a little as she went, and was guided steadily out of the struggling group of men.

Beside one of the motorbikes, the tall, leather-jacketed Thai stopped and turned to face her. He released her experimentally and she stood swaying slightly. Tugging off the crash helmet, he held it out towards her.

'Do you think you're okay to ride behind me?' asked Prem in an urgent undertone.

She stared at him dazedly for a second, then nodded.

'Okay – put this on, quickly!'

He placed the helmet carefully over her head and fastened it. Then he helped her on to the pillion of his Suzuki. Climbing into the saddle, he took her arms and clamped them about his waist. Then he kicked the motor into life and she clung on to him hard as he sent the bike roaring away from the fighting.

9

'What do you think those thugs would have done?'

Joceline took a sip of hot ginger-root tea from a porcelain beaker that she held before her in both hands. She was sitting cross-legged on a cushion-pad laid on the worn flagstones of the candle-lit *viharn* at *Wat Kwan Kittima*; her voice still shook slightly as she spoke but she was otherwise beginning to recover from her fright.

'Where would I be now if you hadn't come along? Would I still be alive?'

Prem approached her, holding in his hands a small tin basin of warm water and a linen swab. For a moment he stood looking down at her with the same intensity of expression that she remembered from their previous meeting in London.

But this time in his eyes she could see a mixture of deep concern and relief.

'I don't know . . .' he said haltingly. '. . . The main thing is that you are safe.'

He knelt beside her and dabbed at a small cut on her forehead with a tenderness which surprised her. She had still been trembling with shock when he turned the Suzuki into the temple compound after a fast dash along the riverside and across Memorial Bridge into Thonburi. But his quiet, reassuring manner had quickly soothed her jangling nerves. Within moments of their arrival, a novice monk had appeared silently with the hot ginger tea. After she had drunk a little he had made her write a note to Michael Ewington, assuring him she was safe and well, and he had sent it by a motorcyclist to her hotel. He also said he had sent another motorcycle to fetch Surachai. Now, as she regained her composure, Prem's closeness beside her brought to mind again the curious feeling of intimacy that she had felt spontaneously at their first meeting. Then she had known only the merest outline of the strange bond of friendship between her father and Jutulak which in its turn linked them. Now, having read her father's detailed story many times, she suddenly felt that what joined them had grown even stronger.

'I'm very sorry, Joceline, about what happened tonight . . .' Prem drew back from her a little and studied her face. 'The injury on your forehead is only a graze – nothing serious. Are you sure you're feeling all right?'

Joceline smiled weakly. 'I'm feeling much better, thanks . . . I'm very grateful that you and your friends arrived when you did . . .'

'No, it was my duty,' said Prem hastily, rising and setting the bowl on a side table. 'It is because of me that you're here.'

In the vaulted chamber their voices echoed slightly and beyond the open doors in the shadowy courtyard Joceline could see the gnarled trunk and boughs of the kind of ancient bo-tree under which the Lord Buddha himself was believed to have meditated. After the horrors of the backstreet bar, the frightening attack on her and the gunfire, the ancient temple's atmosphere of enduring tranquillity made the events of the night seem like an unreal nightmare. From time to time she saw an oared boat with an oil lamp flickering on its bow slip silently by on the palm-fringed *klong* beyond the open temple gates; otherwise nothing broke the stillness of the compound.

'Who were they working for?' asked Joceline, sipping again from the beaker of tea. 'Who's behind this? They didn't seem like government security men.'

'No, they weren't *Santiban* agents of the government.' Prem came and sat down beside her on another cushion-pad but avoided her eyes. 'I'm almost sure the government agencies know nothing about this. If they did, they'd have found other ways to stop you filming. Those men were gangsters. I'm not sure who they were working for. But we will find out . . .'

As soon as he had helped her off the bike and settled her into the *viharn*, Prem had explained in an urgent tone that he and a group of sympathetic friends had been shadowing the film unit since its arrival, watching for signs of trouble. Former members of the seventies student movement who now worked in responsible positions in ministries and government departments in Bangkok had willingly provided information about the date of the film unit's impending arrival and its movements. Prem said he and his friends had followed her from the hotel that night because they expected further trouble after monitoring the incidents at the Grand Palace and the Erawan Shrine. One of his friends had slipped into the bar after her and alerted the other riders on a portable telephone when she made to leave. He had brought her to the *Wat Kwan Kittima* because the monks were sympathetic to him as a result of his father's past links with the temple. But the present monks knew nothing, he said, of her father's manuscript or the events surrounding it.

'This must be the very same *viharn* where my father waited to see the *acharn* on the night he was seized and interrogated,' said Joceline, gazing round at the painted panels of the *Jataka* with their stylised depictions of ancient Siamese life. 'And where Jutulak first saw these paintings as a boy.'

Prem nodded. 'Yes, that's right.'

Joceline's eyes widened. 'And is the jewelled betel box still lying by the altar in the *bot*?' she asked in an urgent whisper.

He shook his head. 'The *acharn* left and went to a northern forest monastery soon after your father came here in 1955. The other monks said he took the jewelled box with him. He died in the forest and the box was never found . . .' Prem hesitated and seemed about to say more; then he changed his mind and fell silent again.

For a time they sat and looked at one another without speaking. In the candle-light she could see that one side of his face was begrimed and possibly bruised. His hair, damp from the heat and the exertions of the fight, fell tousled over his forehead. He had removed his leather riding jacket and wore only a T-shirt with his jeans. During the frantic dash on the Suzuki, still weak with fright, she had been forced to cling to him in close physical intimacy. She had gained a clear impression of his physical self-confidence from the easy way he handled the motorbike at speed; now she could see clearly that he was strong, athletic, broad-shouldered and still youthful in his early thirties.

He sat very still, suggesting silently that he was the possessor of intelligent, controlled strength; the expression on his handsome face conveyed unusual determination and again, as she had done in London, Joceline felt a sense of attraction which seemed to be inextricably bound up with the accidents of fate that had brought them together. This time, however, the feeling was heightened by their surroundings: the eternal stillness of the temple which had already figured dramatically in the lives of both Jutulak and Adam Hampson seemed to invest the moment with a near-mystical quality. Suddenly she felt he might be on the point of reaching out to embrace her and she knew that she would have welcomed the comfort of his touch. Then with a slight sense of shock she realised her feelings were stronger: whether it was just from fear, anxiety or weariness she didn't know, but in that moment she longed desperately for him to put his arms around her.

Looking at him in the half-light, she wondered if he recognised what was in her mind; he was staring back with the familiar concentrated stillness in his gaze, as though something he had seen in her face had suddenly changed the entire direction of his thoughts. But to her surprise it was she who reached out and took one of his hands in both her own.

'I've got a thousand questions I need to ask you, Prem,' she said unsteadily. 'Some of them might prove awkward . . . But I want to say now, before we go any further, I don't regret coming back to Thailand – despite the awful things that happened tonight . . .'

His fingers tightened around hers and for a long moment he continued to gaze directly into her face. From the light in his eyes she saw suddenly that the feelings with which he was struggling were similar to her own.

'Joceline, week after week I sat in my room in London in agony,' he said in a low voice. 'Narong was dead and Penhaligon had committed suicide. I knew some day you would ask me many questions – but I didn't know how I would answer them. Many times I watched you reporting for "Perspective" from Berlin and Prague. I also saw you crouching beside tanks in Bucharest, hiding from the snipers . . . Journalists were being killed in Romania – I wondered whether you would come back.'

'All the time I was away,' she said quietly, 'I carried the manuscript with me. I couldn't forget the story my father had written – I read it constantly . . . Now you no longer seem like a stranger although we've only met once before . . .'

He lifted his free hand suddenly to cover both of hers. She shifted her position on the cushion, moving nearer, watching his face and listening intently. Gradually his grip on both her hands tightened, matching the intensity of his words.

'Night after night I saw countries that had been in chains for decades winning their freedom . . . It was like a dream. The world was changing before my eyes. And yet I knew that my own supposedly free country was not yet a proper democracy . . . It's still under the invisible control of the army – and deeply corrupt men who buy votes and make themselves rich on the proceeds . . .'

He paused, and drew in his breath sharply in agitation. Torn between saying everything he felt and staying silent, he shook his head helplessly from side to side; then he finally made up his mind.

'There's much to explain . . . I admit I knew it would be dangerous for you to come here . . . I agonised for a long time. Should I tell you to stay away – or not? In the end I decided to do nothing . . . And not just because I want to help my country . . .' He took another deep breath, looking at her with a troubled expression. 'I realise now I let you walk into danger partly because I knew I'd never see you again if I stopped you coming . . .'

He continued to hold her hands, watching her closely as

306

though anxious that his revelation might still provoke some kind of extreme reaction against him. After a moment Joceline smiled; freeing one hand, she reached up to touch his bruised cheek with the tips of her fingers.

'I didn't expect this, Prem,' she said softly. 'It just feels right, I don't know why . . . But I'd have come back anyway, no matter what you'd done.' She paused significantly. 'I have to find out the truth for myself . . .'

They continued to look at one another without moving; then he put his arms around her. She closed her eyes with a sigh, letting her cheek rest against his chest. She felt a sudden sense of ease and the tension drained out of her. But from outside the compound, the sound of approaching motorbike engines gradually intruded into the stillness of the temple. She felt Prem's body become tense and the next moment the bright, headlight beams of two bikes and a motor car swung through the gate and shone directly into the *viharn*. Then the car door banged and urgent footsteps sounded on the ancient flagstones. With a muffled exclamation he released her.

'It will be Surachai,' he said, rising to his feet.

Turning his back on her, he hurried away through the door of the *viharn* to greet the new arrivals in the courtyard outside.

10

Joceline sat motionless on the floor of the *viharn*. In one part of her mind she felt bewildered by the speed and unpredictability of her own emotions. At the same time another, more rational part of her was listening to the agitated murmur of voices speaking Thai in the quiet temple courtyard outside. For a short span of time the two sides of her nature warred with one another; then her professional instincts reasserted themselves. Dismissing everything else from her mind, she concentrated her whole attention on what she could hear.

The voices were low and guarded; she could understand nothing of the language itself but she closed her eyes and tried to measure the mood of the speakers. Ignoring their words, she listened only to the rhythm and intensity of what they said.

The conversation went on for several minutes. By the time it ended, she felt sure she had identified Prem's earnest speech patterns and the slower, sly-sounding tones of Surachai among two lighter, younger voices. Overall she thought she sensed pervasive anxiety, a tense uneasiness and lack of certainty – perhaps on how to proceed. When Prem led Surachai into the *viharn*, the tautness of their features seemed to confirm her suspicions. Surachai, however, fixed a practised smile on his face as he approached and before they seated themselves beside her on cushion-pads, the older Thai made an elaborate *wai* in Joceline's direction.

'I am very happy to see you in Thailand again, Miss Hampson,' he said quietly in English. 'I'm sorry you've had such an unpleasant experience tonight. It's a great credit to Prem that he was on hand to assist you . . .'

'The message we sent has reached your friends,' said Prem, cutting in quickly. 'Your producer says he's greatly relieved to know you're safe. We have a car and a driver waiting outside – you can be driven back to your hotel whenever you wish.'

He sat back, watching her very intently.

'Thank you, Prem.' Joceline held his gaze for a fraction of a second, then turned her head to smile formally at his companion. 'And thank you, Mr Surachai, for your welcome . . .'

'I've just learned that two of my friends suffered bad bullet wounds in the fighting outside the bar,' continued Prem grimly. 'They're both in a serious condition. Four of the men who tried to abduct you were severely injured, too. The police were called by people who heard the shooting. Unfortunately all the injured were taken to hospital.'

'I'm sorry about your friends.' Joceline looked at Prem in silence. 'Does this mean that the Bangkok police will now discover what lay behind the attack? Will the truth about my film come out?'

'I can assure you Prem's friends will say nothing,' replied Surachai smoothly before Prem could respond. 'And the hired gangsters may not even know who they were trying to abduct – or why.'

'Or for whom?' Joceline took a deep breath, focusing her full attention on the older Thai. 'Are you really asking me to believe those men wouldn't have known who wanted me kidnapped . . .?'

'Unfortunately, yes,' said Surachai with a mirthless smile.

'And do you know yourselves?' asked Joceline, continuing to watch him closely.

He hesitated; she could see that the older man's face was drawn and he appeared to have lost weight since she last saw him. Before answering her, he darted a quick sideways glance at Prem. 'We have certain suspicions – but they are no more than suspicions at present.'

As she looked at Surachai, Joceline remembered again the warning in Penhaligon's letter about his reputation as an unprincipled fixer. She recalled, too, the former diplomat's urgent exhortation to 'tackle him head-on as soon as possible' about the unscrupulous Chinese who was backing the project.

'Could the rich Chinese I met in Chiang Mai have been behind the attempt to kidnap me?' she asked abruptly.

Joceline saw shadows of unease flit across the faces of both men. Then Surachai laughed with relief. 'No – that is quite impossible. He wishes only to help us. Whatever could have made you think something like that, Miss Hampson?'

Joceline did not smile. 'In London the young man Narong was found dead on the same day that I was given the manuscript. He was involved in fighting when I came to meet you at the restaurant in London. And as soon as I arrive here to begin filming, there's more violence. You must have some idea why these things are happening – and you owe me an explanation.'

Surachai swallowed hard and dropped his eyes to the flag-stoned floor in front of him. 'We think Narong Chumto had foolishly involved himself with dangerous drug smugglers . . .'

'Isn't it possible that your mysterious Chinese patron might be an international drug criminal himself?' asked Joceline bluntly. 'Have you considered the possibility that you are being financed from the proceeds of illegal drug trafficking?'

Surachai's eyes narrowed uncomfortably. 'No, there's no question of that . . .' Prem was staring at him with a startled expression and Surachai turned towards the younger Thai and repeated his denial several times. 'It's not true – it's all lies!'

'And Nicholas Penhaligon's suicide,' said Joceline, pressing the question with an equal relentlessness. 'Was that just a coincidence?'

Surachai continued to look uneasy under her stare. 'We have no idea why Mr Penhaligon took his own life. Perhaps it was something very private from his past . . .' The Thai looked up at her, hollow-eyed. 'He was a good man – he tried to give us what help he could. We are very sorry he died . . .'

She looked at Prem. 'You told me Narong had paid others to help him steal my father's manuscript from you at the restaurant?'

Prem nodded, his expression apprehensive.

'Why did he do that?'

'To read it . . . As I told you before, he wanted to find out exactly what was going on. I hadn't taken him into my confidence.'

'Did he make any copies of the manuscript?' She looked from Prem to Surachai and back again, noting the older Thai's growing discomfort. 'Couldn't he have passed copies to other people here in Bangkok?'

Surachai began to shake his head quickly from side to side but Prem leaned forward suddenly towards her. 'I will be honest with you . . . Narong made one copy of the manuscript. I searched his room to make sure after he returned mine. I found a full photocopy – but it was intact . . .'

'We believe Narong was just naive,' broke in Surachai hurriedly. 'He didn't realise how dangerous his actions were. But we are almost sure he wasn't a paid informer – or a spy for somebody else.'

Joceline looked at the face of each man in turn; it was very clear that both felt themselves to be on shaky ground. She could sense, too, that they were far from being of one mind in their dealings with each other.

'Naive people are easily exploited, in my experience,' said Joceline evenly. 'Couldn't that have been possible in Narong's case?'

Again Surachai shook his head vigorously. 'No, we don't think so.'

Joceline looked at him in silence for a second or two. 'You said just now the Chinese could not have been responsible for the attack on me – then clearly some outsiders know why we are filming here . . .'

'It would be better to be completely honest now.' Prem spoke very quietly, staring down into his open hands but obviously addressing the man at his side. 'Narong had many Thai visitors to his room in London. He almost certainly showed the manuscript to others. Somebody without scruples may have managed to copy it again – and sold a copy or two here in Bangkok . . .'

'To whom?' demanded Joceline.

'We don't know,' insisted Surachai. 'We have no proof of this at all.'

'To the former Colonel Kasem Petcharat, perhaps?' asked Joceline quietly. 'The officer who interrogated my father in 1955?'

Both men looked up at her in surprise; but neither of them attempted to answer and she could see at once that her impulsive shot in the dark had struck home.

'Is Kasem Petcharat still alive?' she asked, looking at Surachai.

'Yes, he's still alive.' The Thai shifted uncomfortably under her gaze. 'But why should you think of him?'

'Apart from the "Butcher of Bangkok", Police-General Phao, Colonel Kasem Petcharat is the only Thai mentioned by name in my father's manuscript.' Joceline paused. 'What does he do now?'

The eyes of Surachai darted abstractedly round the walls as though he were looking for inspiration in the scenes from the *Jataka*. His whole demeanour suggested he was desperately seeking ways of turning the conversation in other directions; but Prem sat suddenly straighter on his mat and answered instead in a bitter undertone.

'*General* Kasem Petcharat is retired now – and he's enormously wealthy. His involvement in corruption dates right back to the time of Police-General Phao . . . Today he and three sons have wide business connections – vast logging concessions in the north and in Burma, big rice lands on the central plains . . . He owns tourist hotels in the south, sails a luxury yacht and has large real estate holdings in Bangkok.' Prem paused and his voice became harsher. 'He also likes the company of leading criminals – just as his old mentor Police-General Phao did . . .'

'So Kasem Petcharat could well have been behind tonight's

violence . . .' She broke off, her expression becoming puzzled. 'But why would such a powerful man worry about one brief mention of his name in the manuscript. Why would that merit so much alarm?'

Joceline saw Prem's face flex and become tense. Surachai had turned and was looking searchingly at him but Prem avoided his gaze. When he spoke there was an apologetic note in his voice. 'Joceline, I didn't, in the end, give you all of the manuscript in London . . . There are other chapters . . . They contain many incriminating references to Kasem Petcharat . . . But I felt they complicated the story unnecessarily for you when it was important to understand other essentials . . . I intended to give them to you here . . .'

'Were the extra chapters in the manuscript copied by Narong?'

Prem nodded miserably.

'So my life was threatened tonight because somebody was worried about me broadcasting incriminating allegations I've never even seen!'

Prem made no attempt to reply and Joceline felt a fierce knot of anger tighten inside her. Her earlier suspicion that she was the victim of elaborate and cynical manipulation returned more strongly than ever. When she spoke again, her anger showed immediately in her voice.

'What does the rest of the manuscript say about Kasem Petcharat . . .?'

Surachai's eyes glittered with an unnatural brightness. Joceline could see from his expression that the older Thai had not known about the withholding of part of the manuscript. Prem was staring at the flagstones in front of him, clearly unwilling to speak further at that moment. Surachai's gaze flickered back and forth between Joceline and Prem, then settled uneasily somewhere in space halfway between them.

'Colonel Kasem Petcharat was the local liaison officer with the KMT irregulars in the north in the mid-1950s . . . He was responsible for supervising the seizure of Jutulak on behalf of General Phao. Adam Hampson eventually discovered this and gave full details of his role in his manuscript . . .' Surachai paused, taking time to choose his words with great care. 'Later more evidence emerged, indicating that Kasem Petcharat was also responsible for the death of Jutulak . . . You see, Jutulak died violently at the hands of an assassin . . . All this and other details of Kasem Petcharat's corrupt life have been included in later parts of the manuscript.'

Joceline absorbed the information in silence. Then she shook her head incredulously. 'Knowing all this, how can you claim you don't know who my attackers were working for?'

'Before tonight we had no way of knowing if anybody here had received a copy of the manuscript,' said Surachai desperately. 'Now we can make suppositions – but we still lack proof . . . Don't you see, until you came to Bangkok with your crew and began filming . . .'

Surachai broke off, aware too late of the import of what he was saying. Joceline stared at him for a moment, then slowly stood up. Twin spots of colour appeared, burning in her cheeks, the only outward sign of her inner anger.

'Obviously my visit to Bangkok has already been of great assistance to your cause.' She turned and looked meaningfully at Prem. 'I can see all too clearly now the real reason you wanted me to come back. You needed me to help you flush out your enemies – and you didn't care what danger I might walk into doing it.'

They stared up at her wordlessly as she stood clenching and unclenching her fingers in an effort to control her anger. 'You've both lied deliberately. You've told so many lies already I won't be able to believe you again.' She stopped and looked at the older man. 'I don't even know your real name, "Mr Surachai". Like everything else, that smacks of the worst kind of deceit . . .'

'There were good reasons, I swear,' he protested. 'Until we knew whether we could trust one another . . .'

Joceline stopped listening. Looking down into Prem's handsome face she suddenly remembered the warning given to her by Nicholas Penhaligon in his poignant letter . . . 'Westerners fall under Thailand's spell very easily . . . You may discover that for yourself. But be on your guard . . . Failure to be on my guard at all times was one of the gravest mistakes I made in Thailand . . .' Turning away from them both, she folded her arms protectively about herself and paced back and forth once or twice beside the cushion-pads. Then she stopped and looked down again at Prem.

'I'd be a fool to rely on any of your "evidence" now. You

can't even agree on the untruths you're telling me . . . From the start I wondered whether the manuscript might have been tampered with. Now I'm certain it has.' She paused, her expression uncertain; then her face cleared. 'There's only one way to get to the bottom of all this – and I won't require your help.'

'What will you do?' asked Prem in consternation.

'I'll go north and find my father . . . I'm convinced he's still alive.'

In the tense silence that followed, the creak of an oar on a passing boat reached into the temple from the *klong*. Prem and Surachai exchanged uneasy glances. Then they turned to stare at her again.

'But you've seen his gravestone in the cemetery,' said Prem in a pleading voice. 'So have I . . . so has Surachai . . .'

'If necessary,' said Joceline, speaking with an icy calm, 'I'll go to Chiang Mai and exhume my father's grave with my own hands.'

Prem looked at her aghast. 'You mustn't try to do that.'

'Whatever happens, my film will be finished without your help,' she continued, ignoring his protest. 'Perhaps in the end it will be very different from what you had hoped.'

Without observing any formalities, she walked to the door and stepped out into the darkened courtyard. She could see a driver standing and smoking beside the waiting car and she walked quickly towards it. He opened a door on seeing her approach but Prem raced out of the *viharn* and caught her arm as she was about to get into the back seat.

'Joceline, I'm sorry! Everything's become distorted. Can we talk again as soon as you've recovered?'

Joceline looked at him levelly. 'I'm recovered already, Prem. A few minutes ago you had my complete trust . . . Now, I can see I was being very naive . . .'

He began speaking again but she ignored him and climbed into the back of the car. As soon as she relaxed, total weariness seemed to engulf her and she became aware of a throbbing ache in her head and all her limbs. As the driver pulled away through the temple gates, she relaxed against the seat. When the car was moving steadily, she closed her eyes and gave herself up to feelings of relief that washed through her like a warm wave.

'Why did you disobey instructions?'

Surachai asked the question furiously in Thai; shaking visibly, he rose from his cushion-pad and glared at Prem as he stepped back into the *viharn*.

'Why did you hold back the chapters that condemn Kasem Petcharat? Have you gone completely mad?'

Prem did not answer. Closing his eyes, he remained standing in the open doorway, listening distractedly to the fading sound of the car carrying Joceline away from the temple.

'Your foolishness has undermined the whole project!'

Surachai waddled quickly across the *viharn*. In front of Prem he stopped and looked up at him, his face dark with anger.

'I don't understand! Don't you wish any longer to expose the man responsible for the capture and murder of your father? Don't you want to help wake people up to reality? Have you given up all we're struggling for?'

Prem controlled himself with a visible effort. 'I haven't given up . . . I was trying to keep our hopes alive.'

'Keep our hopes alive?' Surachai's expression became incredulous. 'A very large sum of money was paid for those chapters to be composed in the style of Adam Hampson! Without consulting or telling anybody, you decided not to use them in our cause . . .'

'I felt there were very good reasons . . .'

Surachai's breathing quickened with his anger. 'Your actions alienated the television journalist. What do you think our Chinese patron will say? He's spent much money supporting us . . .'

Prem's calm expression became more animated. 'By ordering the murder of Narong and driving the Englishman Penhaligon to suicide, you mean? Was that the best support he could give?'

'There's no proof that he murdered Narong,' snapped Surachai. 'Nor can he be held responsible for the mental condition of an English homosexual . . .'

'It was the death of Narong and Penhaligon that aroused suspicion about our motives,' said Prem vehemently. 'Until then Joceline Hampson had great sympathy with us.'

'If you had given her the full manuscript, her suspicions would have been allayed.'

'No, you're wrong! After the trouble at the apartment, the false chapters looked even clumsier than before ... The Irish doctor McKenna had written exactly what he was told in Chiang Mai – but what he wrote was so different to what went before ... If Joceline Hampson had read the new material then, she would have become suspicious and cancelled her film at once. The manuscript changed abruptly from a revealing story to a witch-hunt against Kasem Petcharat ...'

Surachai's expression became defensive. 'If we'd refused the demand of our patron to include the new material, he wouldn't have financed and supported us.'

'That was our biggest mistake. Allowing "just a few additions" to the manuscript to please him didn't seem dangerous at first. Now I wish I'd never listened to you!' Prem's eyes glittered. 'And another thing ... Joceline Hampson asked you if our so-called patron was an international drug trafficker. Does she have any grounds for thinking that he is?'

Surachai walked slowly back to the cushion-pads and lowered himself to the floor. He sat cross-legged with his head bowed for a moment, then looked up at Prem with a shamefaced expression. 'I said nothing before because I knew you wouldn't agree to accept such help. I knew your ideals would get in the way.'

Prem cursed softly under his breath. 'So she was right! To bring freedom to our country we're using money that comes from selling drugs – drugs that wreck many lives in Europe and America.'

'Does it really matter where the money comes from so long as it serves a good end?'

'Yes, it matters very much to me!' Prem ran across the chamber and dropped to his knees in front of Surachai. 'If we want politics in our country to be open and honest, we must be open and honest ourselves!'

'Neither the world – nor Thailand – is that simple,' said Surachai quietly. 'Ideals alone were not enough after 1973.

There were too many idealists then. You must be ready to make practical compromises.'

'You can't compromise with truth and freedom,' said Prem fiercely. 'Your argument is an excuse for duplicity. It's our national disease!'

'But your brand of idealism will ensure that the disasters of the past are repeated,' replied Surachai in a warning tone. 'Unless you're very careful.'

'I'll be more careful from now on about trusting others,' said Prem heavily. 'I understand now why you've always seemed reluctant to talk about our "patron".' He sat down on a cushion-pad at Surachai's side. 'You must tell me everything you know about him.'

Surachai wiped perspiration from his brow with the back of his hand. 'Not much is known about him – he's very secretive. It's believed he fled across the border from China in 1949 when the Communists took over. He took command of one of the irregular Kuomintang military units that set up their bases inside Thailand. All the KMT troops became involved in opium smuggling in the Golden Triangle – so he would have dealt in opium from the earliest post-war days. He says he was jailed for nine or ten years in the mid-fifties – on a whim of Kasem Petcharat, whose word was law in the north. That's why he hates our military rulers . . . and that's why he wants revenge so badly against Kasem Petcharat.'

'Isn't it more likely that he and Petcharat were partners in opium smuggling – and fell out?'

'Perhaps – but to us it shouldn't matter. If his ambitions also serve our purpose, we should be glad.'

Prem let out an angry exclamation and stood up. 'My father would be deeply ashamed! I wanted to honour him and help to bring greater freedom in his name . . . But now we've been dragged into a sordid conflict between two of the worst kind of individuals in our society. Both of them are steeped in crime and corruption and they've tainted us . . .'

'You're not seeing things clearly,' said Surachai quietly. 'You're exhausted, you need to rest . . .'

Bright headlights swinging in through the temple gates lit the *viharn* suddenly, silencing them. Then a gleaming, elongated Mercedes limousine with a scarcely audible engine sighed to a halt outside. Prem and Surachai both looked expectantly towards the door; a moment later an immaculately dressed Chinese chauffeur in a cream uniform and cap appeared on the threshold. Behind him in the gloom they could see two tough-looking bodyguards dressed in dark suits. They had ranged themselves one on either side of the chauffeur and were staring into the *viharn* with watchful expressions on their dark, Chinese faces.

'Excuse me for interrupting, gentlemen,' said the chauffeur, bowing his head respectfully and joining his hands in a *wai*. 'My master has just heard about the disturbance. He wishes to speak with you both, most urgently . . . Will you please be kind enough to step into our vehicle.'

12

The outsize Mercedes limousine purred along a winding drive through a lush tropical garden and pulled up outside a two-storeyed traditional teak house. In front of the terrace, one of Bangkok's fashionable central *klongs* reflected the lights and carved gables of the house in its dark, unruffled water. As soon as the vehicle halted, the bodyguards sprang out and held open the doors. They watched Prem and Surachai with narrowed eyes as they climbed out, then escorted them to the lighted portico of the house.

A white-jacketed male servant appeared on the steps and led the way inside without bowing or greeting them. Still followed closely by the bodyguards, they passed quickly through a series of spacious rooms decorated with carved Chinese furniture and porcelain, Thai silk hangings, ancient Burmese statuary and Cambodian wooden figures. The floors and wall panels were made of polished teak and they glowed like bronze under artfully subdued lighting.

In a panelled drawing room, the Chinese was waiting for them; wearing black trousers, a blue smoking-jacket of embroidered brocade and his usual dark glasses, he was seated on a silk divan before a low table, smoking a cigarette in an ivory holder. When they stopped before the table, the Chinese made a peremptory gesture and the two bodyguards withdrew to take up positions outside in the hall, one on either side of the door.

'I've just heard that gangsters employed by Kasem Petcharat tried to kidnap the English journalist!' He spoke harshly in Thai, glaring at each of the men before him in turn. 'So I was right – the youth Narong must have sent a stolen copy of the manuscript to Bangkok.'

Prem and Surachai looked at one another, then Surachai nodded uneasily. 'We believe, General, that it's more likely that Narong was exploited by unscrupulous friends. We don't think . . .'

'It doesn't matter what you think!' The Chinese stood up and moved round the table to face Surachai. 'You were responsible for conveying the manuscript to the journalist – but you allowed it to be stolen . . .'

'There were *Santiban* agents in London,' protested Surachai, his face showing alarm. 'We took normal precautions – but we didn't expect . . .'

The Chinese waved an angry hand to silence him and moved closer. 'Your precautions were inadequate! A simple boy foiled them! Now Kasem Petcharat knows somebody is plotting against him . . .'

Surachai's face had become pale and he gazed speechlessly back at the Chinese. At his side, Prem watched both men closely. During the tense journey in the Mercedes he had been battling with a growing despondency that had descended on him at the temple. The threatening presence of the bodyguards had stifled all conversation and he had felt increasingly downcast as they neared the house. But in the intimidating presence of the Chinese he felt his despondency begin to give way to a growing anger at the manner in which he had been misled. The ferocity of the emotion surprised him and it blotted out any feelings of caution that might otherwise have prevailed.

'What do you think Petcharat will do now?' he asked in a firm voice. 'Will he go on trying to stop the film?'

The Chinese drew hard on his cigarette, still glaring at Surachai. 'Kasem Petcharat even today is still a very dangerous man. This new knowledge will make him more dangerous than ever. I think he will probably keep the information to himself – and he certainly won't give up his efforts to stop the film . . .'

'Where will the main danger come from?' asked Prem tersely.

'If he found out who was trying to disgrace him, he would act ruthlessly against all of us ... He will certainly employ criminals. But there might be officers in the police and army who still fear him ... So he could use uniformed men too.'

'Why don't you have Kasem Petcharat killed?' asked Prem bluntly. 'Wouldn't that solve the problem quickly ...?'

The unconcealed aggression in the question caused the Chinese to turn away from Surachai. Drawing thoughtfully on his cigarette, he subjected Prem to a long, careful scrutiny; then a flash of hatred showed in his eyes.

'The death of General Kasem Petcharat would not be sufficient revenge. I wish to see him dishonoured and humiliated before he dies ...'

The Chinese walked to a side-table covered with enlarged photographs in silver frames. He surveyed them carefully, selected one and picked it up. Still looking at the picture, he walked back to where the two men stood and held it towards them.

'Look at this,' he commanded.

Prem saw that it showed the Chinese himself posing on a formal Bangkok occasion among a group of the nation's best-known faces. The group included both Thai army leaders and leading politicians of the civilian coalition government. Pointing, the Chinese tapped the glass close to the face of a portly, silver-haired Thai in a double-breasted white suit, standing smiling at the side of the Chinese.

'Today General Kasem Petcharat has forgotten much of the past. He is growing old. Now he and I move in the same social circles – the highest. In a few days time, for instance, I will be one of the honoured guests on his luxury yacht. We will observe the spectacular royal barge ceremony on the Chao Phraya here in Bangkok ... There is nothing that Kasem Petcharat values more highly than his wealth and status ...' The Chinese paused and again Prem saw the light of a fierce hatred glow in his eyes. 'That's why nothing will give me greater satisfaction than to reduce his reputation to tatters!'

'Why do you hate him so much?' asked Prem in a quiet voice.

The Chinese studied the young Thai's face once more; then

his mouth twisted unpleasantly. 'He threw me into jail for ten long years! And every day I was given the worst kind of treatment on his specific orders.'

'Then he must know you hate him.'

The Chinese shook his head and his eyes narrowed. 'Since my release I've been careful never to show him any animosity. He assumes I fear his power and his connections. Many do. But I'm not afraid of him. I am wary . . . I respect his strength . . . Nobody forgets that he was a secret confidant of Police-General Phao during the Butcher's reign of terror . . .'

'And why did he throw you into prison? Did you fall out over the proceeds of opium smuggling?'

The Chinese walked slowly to Prem's side, eyeing him coldly. 'Your questions are very bold. I advise you to be more careful with your tongue. Unlike your companion you have plenty of spirit. But you're not very wise . . .'

'But am I right about the reasons for your imprisonment?' demanded Prem.

'Partly – but it may surprise you to learn that I was jailed soon after your own father was abducted. The abduction – or its failure – was an indirect cause.'

Prem stared at him in astonishment. 'How?'

'On Colonel Kasem Petcharat's urgent instructions I passed on radio orders to a mobile unit of KMT troops coming down from Burma. They were carrying a large consignment of opium which they had gathered from the mountain villages. They were commanded to seize your father from an elephant camp. I remained at a border post many miles away throughout. By a bizarre chance your father was set free, as you know . . .'

The Chinese paused to insert another cigarette in the holder. After lighting it, he exhaled slowly, watching Prem through the smoke.

'Kasem Petcharat was enraged. He blamed me personally as the officer in command of the KMT troops in the region. He sent his own troops to attack that unit and seized all of its opium without payment. Opium then was our only means of survival. So he left us without money, food or weapons. I withheld all other opium in my possession from that season's harvest and Kasem Petcharat sent in more of his troops to claim it. He used a numerically superior force. I was captured. He trumped up charges and I was imprisoned . . .'

'I've been told,' said Prem slowly, 'that you obtained information which showed that Kasem Petcharat later ordered my father's death. Is that reliable information – or did you manufacture that to further blacken his name?'

'It is quite true,' said the Chinese in a neutral tone. 'In those days I had close contacts with other high-ranking officers in Bangkok through the secret opium trade . . . After my release I set out to discover as much as I could about General Kasem Petcharat. As part of my quest for revenge, I've continued to keep dossiers on him and all other important leaders over the years. I've collected information of every kind. I've paid a great deal of money for information – to soldiers, peasants, civilians, politicians, people of all kinds, high and low. Even frightened people will talk if the price is high enough . . .'

'Who told you about my father?' asked Prem in a tense voice.

The Chinese frowned reflectively. 'I thought little of it at that time. But after the Hampson manuscript was brought to me I had a search made of my archives. I found testimony from a gunman involved in the killing of your father. He described the scene, the place and what happened there in great detail. Those are the papers I gave to the Irishman McKenna in Chiang Mai to help him compile the section on your father's death in the manuscript. That testimony made it very clear that the soldiers had been acting on the orders of Kasem Petcharat . . .'

'Why did he give such a command after all those years?' asked Prem with a bitter note in his voice. 'Did the gunman know?'

The Chinese shook his head. 'Many people had things to hide from the time of General Phao. Perhaps many different things were linked together – like a chain of explosives. If one link exploded, many more would certainly do so. All the gaps had to be closed . . . So you see, we have a common interest in the exposure and ruin of Kasem Petcharat.'

Prem did not reply; his expression was distracted and momentarily sad, his eyes unfocused.

'That's why,' added the Chinese, 'I intend to do everything necessary to ensure this film is completed successfully . . .'

'At the present moment it is very difficult,' cut in Surachai. 'We've run into bad trouble with the English reporter.'

'What?' The Chinese swung round suddenly, as though the

sound of the older Thai's voice had rekindled a momentarily forgotten anger. 'What sort of trouble?'

Surachai hesitated, glancing nervously at Prem. 'It was the violence in London that first aroused her suspicions . . .'

'Your stupidity made the violence in London unavoidable,' rasped the Chinese. 'If you had not behaved so incompetently, it would not have been necessary.'

Surachai, bewildered by the sudden change of mood, took a step backwards. 'Unfortunately, because of the difficulties raised by the deaths of Narong and the Englishman, parts of the manuscript were temporarily withheld in London . . .'

'Which parts?' demanded the Chinese in a menacing tone.

'The later stages – those parts dealing with the crimes of Kasem Petcharat.' Surachai glanced desperately at Prem.

'It was my decision,' said Prem quietly. 'In the circumstances they seemed too clumsy . . .'

'Prem intended to hand over the rest of the manuscript here when circumstances were more favourable . . .' Surachai swallowed hard. 'But after the attack on her tonight, the English journalist became distraught. She also said she was suspicious about the whole manuscript . . . In the end she told us she didn't want any further help from us . . .'

The Chinese became very still as he looked at Surachai. 'So what does she intend to do now . . .?'

'She said she would go north to try to find her father,' said Surachai nervously. 'She refused to believe he was dead. She said she would seek the truth about the manuscript from him . . .'

Without taking his eyes from Surachai's face, the Chinese shouted loudly to the bodyguards outside the door and they hurried obediently into the room. He barked rapid orders in Chinese and both of them grabbed Surachai by the arms. One raised his flattened hand high above his head and chopped down hard against the side of Surachai's neck. The Thai instantly buckled at the knees and went limp. The Chinese made an impatient gesture towards the door and the two bodyguards quickly dragged him out into the hall.

Prem stared at the Chinese. 'What have you done?' he asked in a horrified voice. 'Have you killed him?'

'It's unlikely,' said the Chinese flatly. He looked

calculatingly at Prem for a moment. 'But his fate is now entirely in your hands.'

'How can it be?' asked Prem, mystified.

'Go and correct the foolish errors that you have both made and he will remain alive. Find the English television reporter and persuade her she's wrong. You will have to hurry – and so will she. Kasem Petcharat will not give up.' The Chinese leaned over an ashtray to eject and stub out his cigarette with sudden, unnecessary force. 'If the reporter abandons the film or produces something unfavourable, you won't see your friend Surachai alive again . . .'

Prem started to protest but the Chinese waved him to silence.

'Go!' he commanded and strode quickly from the room.

13

Joceline slipped and slithered frequently on the muddy red track that snaked up the steep, jungle-covered mountainside. Sometimes she had to use her hands to stop herself falling; often, to save time, she clambered rapidly over rocks and tree roots on all fours to reach a higher section of the path without following its serpentine detours. The mid-afternoon temperature was hovering towards the usual hundred degree mark but despite the heat and the difficulties of the rain forest terrain, she refused to slacken the fast pace she had set since leaving their vehicle at the end of the nearest motor track over an hour earlier.

Alan Eastwood, who was filming her as he climbed fifty yards to the rear, was finding it difficult to hold her in the frame of his lens. Her safari shirt and trousers were already streaked with perspiration and red mud from the loam track; and whenever she turned and looked back at him, apparently to check how he was progressing with the heavy camera equipment, Eastwood could see daubs of the red mud on her cheeks and forehead.

Slung across her back in a small rucksack she carried the film recordist's second tape machine and a clapper-board so that between them they were compactly equipped to record images and sound. Like Eastwood, she also carried a water-bottle on a strap. Ahead of her an experienced Thai trekking guide whom they had hired in Chiang Mai was also occasionally slipping in mud that had been made more treacherous by a recent downpour of rain. Barefoot, wearing ragged trousers, a faded combat jacket and a cloth bandanna around his forehead, the guide carried a long jungle knife thrust through his belt. On his shoulder he was humping a duffle bag containing their spare film stock, blank sound tapes, microphones, other essential equipment and some food.

Somewhere near the ridge above their heads, the guide had assured them, there was an Akha hill-tribe village. They had already seen two or three groups of dark-faced Akha women and children in brightly embroidered tribal clothes and silvered head-dresses descending into the valley with wicker baskets of fruit on their backs. The guide had questioned each group briefly but they had only smiled shyly and shrugged in response before resuming their descent. From time to time they passed little spirit altars jutting from the undergrowth: the wooden platforms generally bore wilted flowers and banana-leaf plates of rice shrivelled by the heat but Joceline found there was something oddly moving in these simple expressions of reverence for the mystery and majesty of the mountain jungles.

On a flat rock at a bend in the track, she halted, unshouldered her rucksack and set up the tape machine. After calling to the guide to wait on the track above, she connected a microphone and began recording a minute or two of the jungle background sounds that could be laid against the film images of the climb if they were needed. Moving away from the microphone, she unslung her water-bottle and took a drink. When Eastwood arrived panting to join her, he eased the camera off his shoulder on to the rock and mopped his streaming face with the damp square of towelling that hung from his belt. His dishevelled blond hair was dark with sweat and blotches of the red mud covered his legs, shorts and T-shirt.

'You're certainly keeping up a cracking pace, Joceline,' gasped the young assistant cameraman after she had switched off the tape machine. He grinned at her and took a long swig from his own water-bottle. 'I'm not surprised you're looking back every few minutes to see if you've lost me.'

'It's not that, Alan,' replied Joceline, speaking quietly so that her voice did not reach the guide. 'I'm checking to see if we're being followed.'

Eastwood glanced uneasily back the way they had come. As much of the track as they could see winding down between the creeper-clad trees was deserted. The whirr of cicadas and the sharp cries of unseen jungle birds were the only sounds that broke the afternoon stillness and because his visibility was limited, Eastwood found himself straining his ears for evidence of stealthy movement or hushed voices. But he could detect nothing unnatural and, picking up his camera again, he forced a cheerful smile.

'Don't worry, we'll keep one step ahead of them – if they're there.'

She smiled appreciatively at his attempt to reassure her.

'I got some nice shots of the last group of Akha girls passing one of the spirit shrines,' said Eastwood enthusiastically. 'What's our guide asking them?'

'If they've ever heard of an English *farang* being trampled to death by a wild elephant in this area.'

'And have they?'

Joceline shook her head significantly. 'Not so far, no.'

She rose to her feet, repacked her bag carefully and lifted it on to her shoulder. 'How much further is it to the settlement?' she called to the guide as they began climbing again.

'Half a mile – no more.' He flashed her a friendly smile. 'We arrive at the Akha spirit gates in fifteen minutes.'

The guide, a wiry, light-skinned Thai of about thirty, was not an indigenous northerner. He had told them that as a student he had taken part in some of the Bangkok demonstrations in 1976 and had fled to the northern jungles to escape the bloodshed. Although others had returned south several years earlier when an amnesty was offered, he had decided to stay and had made a living guiding young foreign tourists on adventurous rafting and elephant trekking expeditions from Chiang Mai. Joceline had found him at one of the small trekking agencies in the main street after taking the first flight to Chiang Mai from Bangkok with Alan Eastwood on the morning after the attack at the riverside bar. She had called a crisis meeting of the whole crew in her room after returning from *Wat Kwan Kittima*; despite the obvious dangers they faced, every member of the unit had loyally supported her proposal that they should try to finish the film as fast as possible. Michael Ewington had agreed to stay in Bangkok with MacLachlan, Angela and the sound recordist to finish up the outstanding sequences of the temple, the king, the military and the Erawan Shrine, while she and Eastwood flew north to begin the hunt in the rain forests.

At the Foreign Cemetery in Chiang Mai on the day of their arrival, they had filmed a bland interview beside the Adam Hampson grave with the cemetery secretary, Arnold Davenport. Guarded, edgy and sweating profusely in the heat, he had declined to repeat on camera his suspicions about Adam Hampson's death. But, pressed by Joceline, he had taken them to the home of Dr Patrick McKenna and Joceline had persuaded the Irishman to allow them to film the spartan rooms inhabited by Adam Hampson when he lived in Chiang Mai. Dr McKenna himself had firmly declined to give a filmed interview. But under Joceline's persistent questioning off camera he had brusquely repeated the story first told by Arnold Davenport that he had gone up into the forests of the Golden Triangle to identify the body of Adam Hampson after he had been fatally trampled by an elephant. Joceline, producing a map, had asked him to identify the area and with some reluctance he had indicated a region some twenty miles west of the hub of the Golden Triangle where the borders of Burma, Thailand and Laos meet. On checking with the trekking guide, she had learned that there were Akha hill-tribe settlements in the vicinity and she immediately decided to make the area their starting point. After a restless night in a small Chiang Mai hotel, they had left at dawn, the guide driving them north with their equipment in a hired Toyota pick-up truck.

At Fang they had switched to a long-tailed boat and sped down the Khok river at high speed, shooting through spectacular white-water rapids to reach Chiang Rai. In Thailand's most northerly settlement of any size, they had hired another Toyota pick-up and driven to the foot of the mountain up which they were toiling. In the trucks and on the river Joceline had at all times kept a wary eye open for signs of pursuit; but she had seen nothing suspicious. As they climbed the last few hundred yards to the Akha settlement which straddled a high, sharp ridge, they came out into an open, rocky area and, looking back, she was able to see far below their red truck parked against a limestone bluff at the end of the narrow mountain track.

She felt relieved to see that the vehicle still stood alone. She glanced at her wristwatch and waited for Eastwood to catch up, intending to point out to him how high they had climbed in little more than an hour and a half. But before he reached her side, she saw two moving specks that turned out to be two vehicles driving swiftly up the same road through the foothills. They were slewing fast round corners, sometimes skidding professionally, then righting themselves, and immediately the speed and purpose with which they were being driven alarmed her. She was still gazing at them when Eastwood reached her side. Noticing her distracted expression, he turned at once to follow her eye.

'Who do you think that is?' he asked in an urgent whisper.

'I don't know – but let's get out of sight quickly and film them. I've got a nasty feeling they're going to be part of our story – if we survive to tell it.'

She waved urgently to the guide, who was fifty yards ahead, to join them; then all three of them dashed for cover behind a thorn thicket. Once they were concealed, Eastwood picked up the two speeding vehicles and held them in a long, travelling wide shot; then he stopped filming and took a carefully wrapped 600 mm telephoto lens from his backpack and fitted it. When he began running again he could see the two pick-up trucks greatly enlarged. Both were covered in canvas and as they lurched and spun around a hairpin bend, he saw into the rear of each of the vehicles in turn.

'There are men in the back of both of them,' he murmured, still holding the shot. 'They all look as if they might be holding weapons.'

Beside him, Joceline stiffened. Hardly breathing, she peered through the thorns, watching the two speeding vehicles race towards the rocky bluff where the road terminated. 'Keep filming when they reach our pick-up,' she urged him. 'What they do there should give us some idea of who they are and what they're up to.'

Crouching at their side, the Thai guide stared first at Joceline, then at Eastwood. 'What is going on?' he asked in a puzzled voice.

'We don't know yet,' replied Joceline tersely, not taking her eyes from the scene below. 'Somebody may want to stop our film.'

The faint sound of revving engines, squealing brakes and slamming doors reached them as the two vehicles shuddered to a halt on either side of the parked Toyota far below. Seven or eight dark-clad figures immediately swarmed out of them, carrying what looked like light machine-guns.

'I'd guess it's some kind of paramilitary outfit,' breathed Eastwood. 'They're wearing black battle fatigues and black jockey caps but no badges as far as I can tell ... They look like a private security force of some kind ...'

Suddenly all the men closed in an arc around the Toyota, holding their guns at the ready. They peered cautiously into its empty cab and the rear interior; then several quick bursts of firing echoed up the mountain and Eastwood cursed softly while continuing to hold the camera steady on the scene far below.

'They've just shot all our bloody tyres to ribbons!'

As Joceline, Eastwood and the guide continued to watch, the armed group gathered in a knot to talk. Some lifted their heads to look up the mountain and one pointed to the foot of the narrow track up which they had just climbed. While the talking continued, one of the men pulled out a pair of binoculars to make a slow sweep along the ridge. Joceline and the two men shrank down further behind their thorn bush, watching anxiously. They saw the man with the binoculars post a solo guard by the two vehicles. Then he waved an arm towards the mountain and the rest ran fast towards the foot of the track and disappeared beneath the overhead canopy of foliage.

Joceline glanced at her wristwatch, then rose to her feet, looking at the trekking guide. 'We've got an hour at the most before they can get up here – lead us to the Akha village quickly!'

The Akha chief sitting cross-legged on the veranda of his palm-thatch hut looked searchingly at Joceline but didn't speak. A squat, paunchy man dressed only in a turban and a breech clout, he had narrow eyes and flat features that suggested great natural cunning. He was sucking on a long-stemmed bamboo pipe that had gone out and in the smoky gloom of the hut behind him, Joceline could see half a dozen Akha women, presumably his wives. Naked to the waist, they were busying themselves around cooking pots that simmered in small hearths.

'Did the chief fully understand the question, do you think?' asked Joceline in a desperate whisper, turning enquiringly to the Thai trekking guide who stood at her side.

'Yes.' The guide nodded quickly. 'I'm sure he understands perfectly.'

Joceline glanced edgily at her watch, then peered over her shoulder towards the path by which they had entered the settlement. To her relief she saw only Akha women straggling into the village in twos and threes carrying wicker baskets on their heads. Less than half an hour had passed since they had watched the armed men arrive at the foot of the mountain and she knew it was impossible for them to have climbed to the ridge so soon. Nevertheless a feeling was growing inside her that time was quickly running out.

'Ask the chief the question again please,' she said, looking meaningfully at the guide. 'And say that we will reward him well with money for his tribespeople if his information is helpful.'

The Thai, speaking Akha slowly and clearly, complimented the chief on his numerous and beautiful wives and the general prosperity of the settlement, then said that if he could provide any information at all about a wild elephant trampling a *farang* to death in the area a year ago, the visitors would donate generously to the tribe's welfare funds.

The chief half closed his eyes and chewed thoughtfully

on the thin stem of his bamboo pipe. Then he murmured something in reply and Joceline looked expectantly at the guide.

'He asks who you are,' said the Thai quietly.

'Tell the chief I am the daughter of the man who is reported to have been killed by the wild elephant,' said Joceline tensely. 'Tell him I do not believe my father is dead. Tell him I'm trying to find him ... Say it is most important.'

The guide spoke again very slowly and for an instant Joceline thought she saw a spark of interest glow in the chief's rheumy eyes. He continued to suck the pipe stem reflectively and at length he muttered another short response.

'What was that?' asked Joceline anxiously.

The guide smiled apologetically. 'The chief said, "I cannot help the *farang* woman."'

'Is that all?'

He nodded. 'Yes, that's all he said. I'm sorry.'

The guide bowed towards the chief and joined his hands in a *wai*. Joceline smiled formally to thank him before stepping down from the veranda into the mud of the street that divided two lines of stilted, thatched huts. The chief's dwelling was perched almost on the crest of the ridge and Alan Eastwood was standing beside it, filming the wide panorama of jungle-clad hills that rolled away spectacularly beneath them into the distance. When she approached, he broke off and raised his eyebrows hopefully.

'Any luck?'

'No, none at all.' A hint of despondency crept into her voice. 'The chief was curiously evasive. He wouldn't answer any of my questions ...'

Eastwood grimaced in disappointment, then lifted his camera to his shoulder again to finish his panning shots.

'Have you seen something special, Alan?' she asked, turning to look in the direction that he was filming.

'No, I'm trying to capture some of this strange Golden Triangle atmosphere. These land formations are very rare – there's an incredible rock mountain over there with trees and vegetation sprouting from the top ... It looks a bit like a human head in outline.'

Joceline lifted her tilted hand to her brow to shade her eyes; haze shrouded the far distance but the moment she caught sight of the strangely weathered mountain that reared up abruptly out of the jungle, she felt a shivering sensation crawl slowly up her spine. She waited tensely until Eastwood stopped filming, then asked if she could look through the telephoto lens. He readily agreed and she inspected the mountain through the magnifying eye of the camera for a full minute.

'He was right,' she breathed, speaking almost to herself. 'It looks just like a human skull.'

Without taking her eye from the viewfinder, she called to the guide and when he came to her side she asked him the name of the weird rock mountain.

'It's called "The Black World of Lost Spirits". The tribespeople say at night the tormented screams of wandering souls trapped there can be heard for many miles . . .'

Joceline handed the camera back to Eastwood, her face becoming taut. 'Can you lead us there?'

The guide grinned a little uneasily. 'If you really want to go, yes.'

'How far is it?'

The sky was growing duller; against the background of distant jungle the rock mountain was standing out more starkly and the guide screwed up his eyes dubiously. 'Perhaps twenty-five miles. But it will take many hours on foot . . . And I think a bad storm is coming.'

'We can't go back the way we came,' said Joceline in an urgent undertone. She pointed down into the jungle below them. 'Is there a way down this side?'

'Yes – it leads to a road . . .'

He was interrupted suddenly by the loud, excited shouts of a gang of small Akha boys who were racing along the street towards the chief's house. They stopped below the veranda platform, calling to the chief and gesticulating towards the track up which Joceline and Eastwood had climbed earlier with the guide. Joceline saw that the boys were holding imaginary rifles to their shoulders, pretending to shoot, and although she understood nothing of the language, she realised with a start what they were miming.

'It looks as if our friends with the machine-guns are getting nearer,' said Joceline in a low voice. 'We must go.'

Picking up their bags and equipment from the ground, they

332

stepped over the edge of the escarpment and began hurrying down the mountain behind the guide.

15

The track descended steeply through dense bamboo thickets that rattled as they passed and over gnarled roots that seemed to clutch like living hands at Joceline's feet and ankles. Often she stumbled as she panted along behind the fleet-footed guide, who ran with an easy rhythm, looking left and right into the undergrowth. Beneath the dense foliage, the light grew thick and green and whenever Joceline caught sight of the sky, she saw that heavy banks of dark cloud were building up rapidly from the south.

Although the afternoon was wearing on, the heat had intensified because every breath of wind seemed to have disappeared. Her shirt was sticking to her back and Joceline followed the guide's example and tied a silk scarf around her forehead to help keep the perspiration out of her eyes. The equipment they were carrying seemed to get heavier by the minute and behind her she heard Alan Eastwood breathing raggedly as he ran as best he could with the heavy camera bag.

'Will the Akha chief tell the gunmen which route we've taken?' gasped Joceline as she caught up with the guide in a level stretch of forest.

'Yes – they'll probably be men from a drug baron's private army. They supervise collection of the opium harvest from the hill-tribe areas. So they are used to threatening and bribing the tribespeople . . .'

He cocked his head to listen for signs of pursuit and in the silence they heard the first roll of distant thunder. Almost at once the sky became blacker and the remaining light beneath the jungle canopy took on a dull, luminous glow. Then Joceline heard the distant thud of booted feet further up the track and the crash of underbrush being thrust aside.

'They're gaining on us!' said the guide. 'We must go faster.'

He led the way downward again at a run but almost

immediately Alan Eastwood, unbalanced by the camera bag, tripped and fell heavily. When he got back to his feet, he was limping and the guide took the bag from him and helped him along. A minute or two later the first heavy drops of rain began to splatter against the leaves above their heads and the sound of thunder grew louder. Joceline's breathing was becoming more laboured and every time she stopped to rest she heard the sounds of the men behind her grow louder.

'We shall have to try to hide off the path,' panted the guide, scanning the jungle on either side as he ran. 'We can't outdistance them.'

As they hurried on Joceline became aware that the combined effects of heat and the rough terrain were taking a great toll of her energy. She began to wonder whether their pursuers would try to shoot them on sight or take them captive. Then, on rounding a bend in the track where it ran alongside a steep drop to rocks below, they came face to face with two other armed men advancing towards them. One, like the trekking guide, was barefoot and dressed in a torn army flak jacket and faded jeans. He carried a knife in his belt and an old American Armalite AR-15 slung over one shoulder. The other, taller man wore faded khaki drabs and a soft hat. He held a light machine-gun before him with its muzzle pointing at the guide's chest and Joceline was astonished when the face beneath the hat brim broke into a broad grin.

'Prem!' She stared, scarcely able to believe her eyes. 'How in heavens name . . .?'

Prem let the weapon he was holding hang loose on its shoulder strap and he reached out to shake hands warmly with their guide. Both men spoke rapidly in Thai for a few moments, then Prem stared up the track with narrowed eyes, listening to the audible sounds of the approaching men.

'We must try to stop them with an ambush,' he said crisply and pointed to a tree twenty yards up the track.

His companion ran forward and climbed nimbly into its lower branches. Unslinging his weapon, Prem handed it to the trekking guide and indicated another broad-trunked tree growing amongst thick underbrush on the other side of the track. The guide ran swiftly to the hiding place and dropped into a comfortable crouch, cradling the weapon in his arms. Prem grabbed the camera bag from Eastwood's hand and turned down the track, gesturing for Joceline and the young camera-man to follow him.

'How on earth did you find us?' asked Joceline as she fell into step behind him.

'Michael Ewington told me you'd gone to Chiang Mai. I followed on a later plane and went straight to Arnold Daven-port and Doctor McKenna . . .'

'But how did you know we were here?'

'I checked the trekking agencies until I found which guide you'd hired. His office told me where he was taking you. Then I guessed you'd try the nearest Akha village first . . .'

A sudden volley of shots rang out from above and leaves torn from the trees by the fusillade of bullets fluttered down on them. Moments later they heard the stutter of guns close at hand as the guide and Prem's companion opened fire in reply. Prem urged them to move faster but another fusillade of shots followed and Joceline heard Eastwood cry out in pain behind her. Turning her head, she saw him slip and tumble off the track; he twisted as he fell through thorns and under-scrub and he grabbed vainly at trailing creepers, trying to save himself before the trunk of a tree halted his momentum twenty feet below. She heard more firing, then the heavens seemed to open and driving rain began to lash the mountainside.

Prem ran back, calling loudly for her to take cover; then he swung down the rocky slope hand over hand to where East-wood lay stunned by his fall. Hoisting him with difficulty on to his shoulders, Prem clambered back to the track and began moving downhill again, calling for Joceline to follow. Drenched and half-blinded by the fierce rain, she slithered after him, trying to close her ears to the growing volume of shots crashing through the trees above her.

16

A brilliant flash of lightning illuminated the interior of the tiny village temple for an instant as Joceline peeled off her saturated clothes. The broad, impassive face of the brass Buddha image that towered above her on its raised pedestal glowed brightly. Then as thunder crashed, it disappeared abruptly into the blackness again.

Dropping the clothes in a sodden heap on the flagstoned floor, she dried her naked body as best she could on a small, threadbare towel and wrapped herself quickly in one of a pair of rough blankets which the temple monks had also provided for her. She stood listening for a moment to the roar of the wind and the fast drum of the torrential rain on the curved roof of the tiny *viharn*. The storm seemed to be intensifying as it came nearer and although she felt grateful for the difficulties it was providing for their pursuers, she found its growing ferocity unnerving.

Despite her exhaustion, she found she could not sit down. The frantic flight down the mountain in the near-darkness and slashing rain had left her feeling dazed and light-headed. From time to time she shuddered inside the prickly blanket, although it was not cold, and the muscles of her arms and legs ached and tingled from the unusual exertion.

Stepping on to an area of rush matting that covered part of the flagstones, she picked up a tin mug of spiced soup which the monks had brought her with the towel and blankets. On taking a sip of the peppery liquid, she felt some vitality begin to flow back into her for the first time since reaching the temple. In an adjoining *sala* she had knelt for half an hour at Alan Eastwood's side, bathing his bruised and lacerated face until he insisted she get some rest. On arrival they had found to their relief that a bullet had passed through the flesh of his left shoulder without causing much bleeding. In the driving rain he had revived while Prem was carrying him down the mountain and had been able to hobble on foot with assistance to the spot where Prem had parked a battered truck.

They had driven nearly ten miles to the nearest village and three or four shaven-headed monks at its impoverished temple had granted Prem's request for shelter as soon as he drove into the compound. Without asking any questions, they had provided hot water, bowls and improvised dressings for Eastwood's injuries. After whispered consultations among themselves, they had suggested that Joceline rest in the small *viharn* itself since there was little space elsewhere. Having conducted her there by the light of a tiny oil lamp, they had returned minutes later wih the hot soup, blankets and towels.

They assured her that Eastwood was comfortable and that they would dry all their wet clothes for them in due course in the temple's rudimentary kitchen.

'Yes, Alan's sleeping now,' said Prem, appearing silently in the doorway a few moments after the monks had departed. 'All he needs is rest – he's fortunate, he escaped serious injury.'

'So far,' added Joceline with heavy irony.

A new flash of lightning lit the *viharn*, followed by a rapid roll of thunder. The note of the wind rose higher and the rain drove down more loudly on to the roofs and courtyards of the temple. In the feeble glow of the little oil lamp which the monks had left on the pedestal at the Buddha's feet, Joceline could see that Prem's face was grey with fatigue. The khaki drabs he wore clung wetly to his body and he stood looking at her with an uncertain expression in his eyes, as though dubious about whether he should speak at all.

'I'm concerned about your two friends,' said Joceline quietly. 'There was a lot of shooting behind us . . .'

Prem nodded, his expression grim. 'I think the rain came just at the right time. It probably helped them get away . . .'

'But they were outnumbered . . .'

'We were always outnumbered . . . Both of those men were with me in the jungles east of here for five years . . . I told the guide your film was important to our old cause. He didn't hesitate. He was glad to help . . .'

There was an awkward silence for a while, then Joceline picked up the spare blanket and held it out towards him. 'You'd better take off your wet clothes.'

She sat down on the rush matting and turned her head away as he stripped off the khaki drabs. But the lightning flashes were becoming longer and she had an indistinct, flickering impression of his nakedness as he towelled himself dry. Once he was swathed in the blanket he came and sat down opposite her. For a long time they looked at one another without speaking; then she handed him the tin mug of soup and watched him drink.

'Where were you heading when I met you?' he asked, wiping his lips.

She hesitated, watching his face closely. 'To the Black Mountain of Lost Spirits.'

His head shot up and a new flash of lightning illuminated the startled look in his eyes. 'Then you know?'

The answering thunder crashed again after a shorter interval and she waited until the rumbling echoes died away. 'I think I knew instinctively as soon as I saw the outline of the mountain from the Akha village . . . Now your reaction has confirmed it.'

His expression showed relief and regret mingled in equal measure. 'And are you still determined to go there?'

'Yes, as soon as the storm has passed, I'd like to go on. If we wait till daylight, we could be spotted again.'

'But what about your cameraman?'

'We'll leave Alan here and come back for him . . . I can operate the camera if necessary . . . Will you show me the way?'

'Yes, of course.' He looked searchingly at her. 'What sort of film will you make now? What will it say?'

'That depends a lot on what I find at the Black Mountain . . .'

She broke off as a longer flash of lightning again lit the inside of the *viharn*. Only a second or two later a sharp clap of thunder exploded with deafening force. The rain was rapidly flooding the dirt courtyard outside and cascading in sheets from the temple roofs. By constantly whipping the little clusters of bells suspended from the eaves, the wind was producing a frenzied high-pitched clamour that contrasted sharply with the deeper roar of the pounding rain.

'I'm very sorry, Joceline . . . I've deceived you in so many ways . . .' Prem hunched his shoulders and drew the blanket closer about himself. 'You were right about the Chinese – he's a big-time drug trafficker. Surachai lied about that . . . But I should have suspected . . . It was the Chinese who insisted we falsify the manuscript to incriminate Kasem Petcharat. He's hated him for many years . . .'

'Why did you go along with that?'

'Surachai was one of my old professors. He has suffered many times in jail and he was absolutely convinced we needed money to succeed. I let him persuade me . . . He arranged for the Irishman Patrick McKenna to do the extra writing. Because he and your father had been working on a book together about the Thai spirit world, he knew your father's style . . . McKenna was paid a lot of money.' Prem paused and sighed explosively.

'I should never have agreed to it – I've been such a fool!'

Despite her earlier misgivings, Joceline felt a sudden surge of sympathy for him. The lightning was becoming almost continuous and in its flickering glow Prem's handsome face plainly betrayed the inner torture he was suffering.

'How did your father die?' asked Joceline quietly.

Prem dropped his gaze. 'He was found dead in one of his rice fields with a bullet in his back when I was five years old. Nobody saw what happened. He had never told anybody about his past at the Grand Palace. My mother was a local woman and everybody thought he was just an ordinary farmer . . . The village gendarmes said it must have been the Communists. But there was no reason for the Communists to kill him . . . Not until I tracked down your father did I begin to understand . . .'

'Had my father heard of his death?'

Prem shook his head. 'No, he'd heard nothing since that night he went missing on the Black Mountain of Lost Spirits . . . When I appeared in the door of his hut in a hill-tribe village he looked at me as if I was a ghost. Because of the family resemblance he genuinely thought at first he was looking at my father again as a young man . . .'

Joceline stared at the face of the Thai, feeling deeply moved by his revelation. 'Why did my father write the manuscript?'

'He was very angry when he heard how Jutulak had died. He told the whole story then. It was me that asked him to write it all down -- so I could use it to right the injustices done to my father and my country . . .'

Another prolonged flash of lightning brightened the *viharn* like day. Deafening thunder followed almost instantaneously, indicating that the storm was arriving above the village. Separated by only a few feet, they sat wrapped in their blankets looking intently at one another.

'The worst lie I had to tell you was about your father's death,' he said in a voice that broke a little. 'But I really had no choice. Your father agreed that to protect him from reprisals we must pretend he had died. McKenna was paid more money to manufacture that verbal story . . .'

'So Doctor McKenna never came to the forest – to identify the body or for any other reason?'

Prem shook his head quickly. 'No, he didn't come, although

he knew this area well and chose it for the false story. Your father wasn't told about his manuscript being changed. And every time you asked me about him, I could see the emotion in your face . . .' He broke off and looked beseechingly at her. 'I longed to tell you the truth – but don't you see, I couldn't break the word I'd given to your father . . .'

'I understand now . . .'

Joceline uncovered one arm to reach out and touch his hand but at that moment a flash of light so bright that it hurt their eyes seemed to explode directly overhead in the darkness. A terrible searing, rushing sound filled their ears, making them ring, and they felt the temple foundations shudder under a terrible impact. A deafening boom of thunder seemed to split the heavens before rebounding to echo and re-echo repeatedly as it faded into the far distance.

A surge of wind carrying the smell of burnt earth blew in through the open door and at the same moment they both let their blankets fall away and moved forward until their naked bodies were pressed consolingly together. They embraced, their arms clasped tight around one another, trembling at first from the shock of the terrifying lightning strike so close outside in the temple garden. Then suddenly and simultaneously they felt the uprush of desire; she kissed him fiercely and strained against him, rejoicing in the frenzied movement of his hands and mouth upon her. More lightning flashed, brightening the face of the bronze Buddha that gazed fixedly into the darkness above their heads. The thunder that now roared unceasingly filled their ears, obliterating words they scarcely knew they were uttering.

Seeing the Buddha's face appearing and disappearing by turns in the blackness and hearing the frantic ringing of the tiny temple bells, Joceline wondered if some unseen, mystical force was directing the wild movements and rhythms of her body. Relief at surviving on the mountain and fear of the storm's elemental strength fired her passion, fanning and forcing it swiftly to an ecstatic peak. Her body tensed and arched, seemed to soar up towards the storm and they clung to one another with what she already knew deep in her heart was a fierce and absolute finality. In the continuing pandemonium of thunder, lightning, wind and rain, their indistinct cries swelled and multiplied – but even in their own ears they went unheard.

As they neared the top of the winding path, the black stream at the foot of the limestone cliff was turning to silver. Through drifting tendrils of mist Joceline watched it begin to glow in the half-light of the breaking dawn. They passed a shelf of jutting rock, discernible in shadowy outline, and Joceline wondered whether it sheltered the spot where her father had sat during the frighteningly dark night of Jutulak's rescue thirty-five years earlier.

Prem was trudging silently upwards in front of her. Slung across his broad back, he carried the bag containing Alan Eastwood's film camera, some spare film stock and the sound-recording tape machine. In the rear of Prem's covered pick-up truck several hundred feet below, Alan Eastwood was stretched out full-length on a bedroll, resting as best he could. His head and part of his face was swathed in bandages but a few hours of sleep had helped restore some of his strength.

On being wakened in the temple *sala* and told of their plans, Eastwood had become highly indignant at the idea of being left behind. If there was anything to film he would struggle out of the vehicle and get up the mountain somehow, he said. He had not come halfway across the world to miss the pay-off. During the jolting, hour-long journey over rough tracks in the muddy darkness, no complaint had escaped his lips and before they began the climb, he had extracted a firm promise from Prem to return and lead him up the rockface if camera work of any consequence became necessary.

Near the summit of the Black Mountain of Lost Spirits the dawn air was hushed and still; no birds called and the higher reaches of the path were still wreathed in impenetrable mist. Above the jungle canopy which spread across steep valleys and rolling hills far below, thinner wreaths of mist hung like smoke in the still, moist air. The downpour of the storm had left the vegetation and rocks darkly wet and Joceline found herself longing for the first warming rays of the morning sun:

but when the dense mists of the summit closed clammily around them, she began to shiver and could not stop.

At the top of the mountain the narrow path levelled out finally to lead in among stunted, leafless trees. One after another bare branches reached out of the mist towards them like the disfigured hands of silent ghosts. Now and again Prem looked round at Joceline, his expression a silent enquiry as to her well-being. Each time she nodded quickly, indicating he should continue. After the storm abated they had slept for an hour or two beneath the Buddha's pedestal; on waking, they had climbed into their dried clothes and quickly decided on the practical arrangements for their journey. Both of them instinctively put the urgency of their work before everything else and they were consciously avoiding all personal and sentimental gestures.

To Joceline's surprise the ground beneath her feet began suddenly to slope downwards and soften into what seemed to be a fertile, bowl-shaped valley. The withered tree skeletons at the rocky rim of the cliff gave way to thick jungle growth and tall grass that had not been visible at all from below. The dense mist heightened the eerie stillness that cloaked the mountaintop and Joceline realised that she was holding her breath as she followed Prem deeper into the hidden forest.

Although he was moving in front of her, Joceline was the first to notice the massive, shadowy shape shifting threateningly towards them through the white haze. Towering over them, seemingly broad and shapeless, it was moving without making any sound at all. Then a long, dark serpent and a pair of curved and pointed horns seemed to swim down towards her from out of the mist. Stifling a gasp of horror, she stood rooted to the spot, unable to move. Prem, who had been peering sideways, turned quickly upon hearing her smothered cry and looked up at the shape as it bore upon them.

'Don't make any sudden movement,' he said to her, speaking quietly over his shoulder. 'Just stand perfectly still.'

The writhing serpent came close to her face, its mouth open and searching; then above the long curved horns, large eyes appeared, staring unblinkingly at her. But in their brown depths there was no hostility, only a strange, gentle curiosity; two mighty ears flapped the air like wings and at last Joceline recognised the trunk and ivory tusks of the massive bull elephant for what they were.

The elephant had never ceased to move and now, seemingly satisfied with its inspection of her, it curled its trunk upwards in an arc and shifted noiselessly past her on its thickly padded feet. Before it had disappeared, another moving shadow materialised into the less threatening bulk of a tuskless female. At its side moved a calf less than half its size and as the young elephant came abreast of them, Prem let out an exclamation of surprise.

'How extraordinary – the calf is white!'

Joceline looked hard and saw that the small elephant's skin was unusually pale, a pinkish beige in places, as though it had been bleached or scrubbed. Its eyes and eyelashes were also light-coloured, giving the animal a rare and distinctive appearance. It passed them warily, shrinking against its mother's flank, and Joceline saw then that two human figures, a woman and a man, were walking solicitously behind the elephants.

The woman, slight and shy in her demeanour, wore the extravagantly decorated silver bonnet of the Akha tribe and Joceline was struck instantly by the serene beauty of her broad face. The man, much taller and broad in the shoulder, was barefoot and wore only a simple forest monk's robe, dyed brown with the juice of the jackfruit. His hair, which had been cropped very short against his head, was grizzled and the visible skin of his face and one shoulder left uncovered by the robe was weatherbeaten but still obviously European.

The moment they caught sight of Prem, both figures stopped and stood very still. For a moment there was an absolute silence in the mist. Joceline became aware that the elephants had also stopped and turned their heads to watch.

'You look more like your father than ever,' said the man, speaking to Prem quietly in English. 'Why have you come back?'

Prem made a *wai*, bowing his head very low over his hands in a token of the deepest respect. 'Please forgive my intrusion – but I've brought somebody who feels she must speak with you . . .'

Prem turned to gesture politely with an open palm in Joceline's direction and the man looked at her closely for the first time.

343

'Who are you?' he asked in a gentle voice.

Joceline found herself unable to speak and she gazed in silence at the man before her. Although she knew he was in his early sixties, she saw that his face was smooth and little-lined, his expression calm: in his eyes there was a lively spark of brightness and his face was still recognisably that of the much younger man in the photograph she had been given by his grave in the Chiang Mai cemetery.

Adam Hampson looked content and at ease with himself and for a second or two she felt illogically she should not intrude into the remoteness of his secret world by announcing her true identity. Then she saw that he was smiling faintly, as if he already knew what she would say and was prepared.

'I was told you were dead,' she said at last in a subdued voice. 'I had to find out for myself if it was true . . . I'm your daughter, Joceline . . .'

18

Adam led the way without speaking to a rough-hewn hut of palm thatch and bamboo. Before its stilted platform he invited Joceline and Prem to sit on sawn-off tree stumps. The Akha woman disappeared silently into the hut's dark interior while Adam seated himself cross-legged on the boards of its front veranda. The sun had just broken through the mist, the air was suddenly warmer and Joceline stopped shivering.

Unseen among the trees, birds began to call and squawk; cicadas too began to whirr and the ominous atmosphere of the rock mountain evaporated with the mist. On the veranda, Adam made no attempt to break the silence; he sat perfectly still, seemingly content to absorb, one by one, the sights and sounds of the new day.

Looking at her father, Joceline noticed that his expression, while not a smile, was contented and calm. He held himself firmly upright in what might have been a posture of meditation; yet the ease of his manner suggested he was savouring the uniqueness of the moment.

Countless times in past months she had wondered how she

344

would react if such a meeting ever occurred. She had expected to feel intensely emotional; now, to her surprise, she felt detached, almost like an outside observer, having no clear idea of what her true feelings were for the stranger sitting before her. In the hauntingly beautiful setting, even framing direct personal enquiries inside her head seemed an offence and she found herself struggling to find appropriate words.

'I feel I've got a thousand questions to ask,' said Joceline awkwardly. 'But I hardly know where to begin.'

'I hope,' replied Adam in a gently ironic tone, 'that I can find a thousand good answers for you.'

About a hundred yards beyond the hut at the foot of a gently sloping glade she could see a pool of water surrounded by trees. As she watched, the three elephants appeared from beneath distant shade and moved slowly towards the shining pool. At the same moment the Akha woman emerged briefly from the hut to place a woven basket of bananas and papayas at Adam's side. Although no longer young, she was still slender and graceful in her movements and her face, framed by the close-fitting Akha bonnet, had the smooth composure that Joceline associated with nuns.

'Thank you, Ladhya,' said Adam quietly, as the woman moved away. She did not reply or look at him directly, but Joceline became aware in that moment of the invisible harmony that existed between them.

'Did you know that I'd become a television journalist?' asked Joceline hesitantly when Ladhya had left them.

'I'd seen your name in the British newspapers which came to Chiang Mai . . . Reviews of your programmes, articles about you. And I once saw a photograph – so I had a good idea who you were.'

'Did you ever think I might investigate your manuscript?'

'No.'

'Will it seem offensive if I ask you questions about what you wrote?'

'You've come a very long way. You deserve answers to your questions.'

Joceline hesitated, feeling again that she had brought a discordant intrusiveness to the remote mountain. Curiosity about her father's feelings that she had scarcely ever admitted to herself welled up in a rush from somewhere deep in her subconscious. What were your real motives thirty-five years ago? . . . Was there any real love in that hasty, ill-starred marriage? . . . Did you later suffer regret? . . . But almost as soon as the questions rose to the surface of her mind, Joceline dismissed them as futile. Whether they would rebound harmlessly off his now implacable exterior or whether they would still visibly wound, she did not know. Perhaps, above all else, she decided, it was too late to ask.

While she was grappling with these thoughts, she saw Ladhya step down from the rear of the hut and begin walking through the trees towards the pool where the elephants had gathered. A moment later a much younger female figure, taller but similarly graceful in her movements, emerged to follow her. The younger woman, who was also wearing Akha tribal dress, turned her head quickly to look back in the direction of the hut. It was very obvious that Joceline was the object of her curiosity; and even at a distance Joceline could see that her skin was noticeably paler than Ladhya's and that her broad face was striking in its beauty. When Joceline turned her attention back to her father, she found he was watching her and his quizzical expression suggested he had read her unspoken thoughts.

'Yes, she is your half-sister,' he said very quietly. 'Perhaps two months older.'

Joceline looked again at the two female figures walking side by side towards the quiet pool. 'When did you find out about her?'

'Not until she was ten years old.'

Joceline glanced quickly at Prem, who was sitting tense and silent at her side listening to the exchanges. 'I haven't read all of your manuscript yet. I know nothing of what happened after you set out to walk along the Thames to the London docks in 1955 . . .'

'I took a passage to Malaya and found work in logging there. Every day for ten years I thought about the "King's Death Case" and Jutulak while I worked with elephants in the Malayan jungles . . . But even after Police-General Phao was overthrown, it would still have been dangerous for me to return to Thailand . . .'

'Didn't you ever work again in the forests here?'

Adam shook his head. 'The last foreign jungle wallahs left

after the Thai forests were nationalised in 1960 . . . But I never gave up hope. I was still determined to discover the truth about Jutulak and the king.'

'How did you get back here?'

'I lived very frugally in Malaya. I saved every penny I could so that I could come back one day. I got more capital when I sold the family manor house in Cheshire. In 1966 I returned quietly to Chiang Mai to start a new search. I taught a little at the university and because of my 1955 experiences I began writing a learned work with Doctor McKenna on the Thai spirit world.' He turned his head and looked towards the pool. 'Ladhya had waited, and never given up hope . . . I came to the mountains along the border many times before I found her village again.'

'Who was it who interrogated you in Bangkok in 1955?' asked Joceline suddenly.

Adam's forehead crinkled in puzzlement at the question. 'Didn't I describe that in the manuscript? It was Police-General Phao himself . . .'

'And did you write anything about Colonel Kasem Petcharat?'

Adam shook his head slowly. 'No, who is Kasem Petcharat? Why do you ask that question?'

Joceline glanced quickly at Prem, who was holding his head in his hands. 'Dubious evidence has been fed into the text of the manuscript without your knowledge. Different people have been trying to exploit your story for different ends. In my film I'll report this – but I shan't use any of the names.'

Adam was looking uncomprehendingly back and forth between them. 'I don't fully understand – but isn't it worth remembering the Lord Buddha's teaching that in the end evil is never overcome by evil?'

Prem stared at Adam for a second or two, then sprang to his feet. 'I've failed you both in different ways,' he said in a tortured voice. He faced Adam, his expression becoming anguished. 'I've betrayed your trust because I allowed others to add to what you wrote. And I've put Joceline in danger from Kasem Petcharat's gangsters . . .' He swung round to face her. 'There's only one thing I can do to make amends . . . I'll go to Kasem Petcharat – I'll make him call off his gunmen somehow . . .'

'Prem, wait!'

'No – none of us will be safe until I do that.' He moved off two or three paces, then stopped. 'I'll leave the truck at the foot of the mountain for you. I'll bring Alan up to film, first. Then I'll set out – I should be in Bangkok by morning.'

'Prem, please wait!'

Joceline tried to restrain him but he brushed past her. Breaking into a run, he disappeared quickly among the trees, heading for the path that led back down the rockface.

19

Alan Eastwood held his breath as he framed the white calf sporting and splashing in the jungle pool between the two adult elephants. He knew he was getting exclusive, high-impact film of a lifetime. Very likely the footage could make his name in the industry; fate seemed to have handed him a break beyond the wildest dreams of any assistant cameraman in his early twenties. As he worked he thanked God fervently that the bandages which covered the left side of his face had at least left free the eye he was pressing to his viewfinder.

Adjusting the lens to go into a close-up on the calf, his hands shook slightly. He reminded himself silently that the elephants, basking only thirty or forty yards from him, might decide to disappear into the forest any moment and there would be no second chances. Half concealed by trees, he was straining every nerve not to make a noise and disturb the animals. To his relief they showed no sign of leaving the pool. The calf was gambolling around the great gnarled bull, occasionally hosing his flanks playfully with water. The bull elephant, towering majestically above him, feigned annoyance and indifference by turns and sometimes swatted the calf gently with the tip of his trunk.

'Poo Tongkam has acquired great patience in his old age,' said Adam quietly, watching the scene beside Joceline from a distance.

Joceline's face lit up with an astonished smile. 'Is the bull Poo Tongkam?'

348

'Yes. Ladhya had found him by the time I returned. She'd searched the jungles for five years or more. When she found him she worked her magic on him and he stayed near her. He still had the old bullet in his shoulder and limped a little. After I came back, we gave him an anaesthetic and I dug it out. Since then he's been fine . . .'

Joceline watched Poo Tongkam move out of the pool, his movements stately and massively dignified. Ladhya and her daughter had appeared carrying something in their hands and Poo Tongkam approached them quietly, flapping his ears as though in welcome. Eastwood moved his tripod silently into the open to get a better angle and continued filming as Poo Tongkam, the female and the calf ate gently from the hands of the hill-tribe women.

'Do you think it will bring danger here if this film is shown?' asked Joceline in a concerned tone. 'You did agree to the subterfuge about your death to protect you before, didn't you?'

Adam watched the cameraman in silence for a while. 'Yes, but now that you've come here, perhaps we should let things take their course.' He looked round to where great stretches of distant jungle were visible below the mountain. 'We can move into Burma or Laos. There's still plenty of space for us to hide . . .'

'What's in your grave?' asked Joceline gently.

He smiled. 'A very large elephant's tusk – nothing more. Ladhya advised us it would ward off ill luck.'

'If I didn't show the mountain in long shot,' said Joceline slowly, voicing her thoughts aloud, 'my film wouldn't identify this place at all. It could be almost anywhere.'

'You must decide,' said her father simply. 'It might be best to avoid further deceit – we'll be ready to meet whatever comes.'

After Prem's sudden departure they had walked together for an hour or more in the hidden forest while Joceline explained in detail the reasons for Prem's anguish. She had recounted everything that had happened since her first visit to Chiang Mai and he had listened without interrupting. When Alan Eastwood appeared alone, having been brought to the top of the mountain path by Prem, Adam had welcomed him equably and offered no objections to his filming the calf or the surroundings.

'How in heaven's name did you succeed in breeding a *white* calf?' asked Joceline in an awed voice as they continued to watch Eastwood manoeuvring his camera around the young elephant and Poo Tongkam.

'It was not my doing – Ladhya must be given all the credit.' He paused, watching Tongkam kneel by the pool on Ladhya's instructions so that she and her daughter could climb into position on his head and back. 'I'm not sure she could explain how . . . She and her people live by instinct and intuition . . . Where intuition ends and the spirit world begins – if it truly exists outside of our minds – I still can't say.'

'But what did you do?'

'Hard-headed realism is an essential complement to insights into the spirit world.' A rare smile lit his face. 'That was my contribution. A British teak company bred a white calf by chance in 1926. I got hold of the records from their old archives and told Ladhya exactly what sort of elephants had been involved. Then she began selecting mates for Poo Tongkam . . .' He nodded towards the pool. 'That female was her tenth choice . . .'

'Is that what you were doing every time you disappeared from Chiang Mai . . . Helping her?'

Adam nodded slowly. 'Yes.'

'Why did you want to do it?'

They began walking slowly towards the pool but he did not answer at once. She saw him looking ahead towards the calf through narrowed eyes as though reflecting deeply on his motives.

'I can tell by your tone of voice,' he said at last, turning his head to smile at her again, 'that you want to know whether I believe, like the ancient Siamese, that white elephants are really messengers from God . . . Whether I believe the Lord Buddha became a white elephant in his last incarnation and circled his mother's bed three times with his trunk out-stretched before disappearing into her womb . . .'

Joceline smiled too. 'Yes, perhaps that's what I'm asking.'

They walked on again for a while without speaking. 'I don't think I ever embraced those ideas as the gospel truth – but what people *believe* is of enormous importance. Ancient beliefs may seem bizarre but they've stood the test of time . . . It may be coincidence but no white elephants were ever found anywhere in Thailand during the time King Ananda was on the throne.'

'Have any been found since the present king's coronation?'

'Yes, a number. You can see some of them in the Bangkok zoo – but as far as I know, nobody has ever succeeded in breeding one deliberately.' He smiled again. 'You might say that's our small invisible gift to Thailand for whatever it may be worth.'

Joceline considered what he had said in silence. 'These abstractions are very beguiling. But I set out to make this film hoping I might get at the real facts. When I was handed your manuscript in London I was also given old secret diplomatic papers retailing rumours that a member of the Thai royal household might have been accidentally responsible for Ananda's death. Do you think there could be any truth in such rumours . . .?'

'There are many rumours. And I think I've heard them all. People will tell you the families of the executed courtiers have received discreet financial help from somewhere . . . People will tell you many other things in confidence . . . But there's still no incontrovertible proof to support any of the stories. When I'd waded through all of that, I looked at how successful and popular Thailand's monarchy has been since the tragedy of 1946. An unbroken reign of nearly forty-four years is an answer of a kind in itself.' He paused and smiled again. 'In the end, I suppose you could say, my obsession to save Jutulak and find out what happened to King Ananda led me here to this hidden forest . . .'

'Why was that?'

'I became convinced that the truth of what really happened in 1946, if it were known, might cause more trouble . . . That it might hinder rather than help, divide rather than unite . . .'

'Why?'

'I can't say exactly. Perhaps we're moving into the area of intuition again. I reached that conclusion after spending several more years trying unsuccessfully to unravel it all . . . First I searched the villages around this mountain looking for Jutulak. Over about four years I moved out in an ever-widening radius – and found absolutely nothing and nobody who even slightly resembled Jutulak . . . So I stopped looking for him and started looking for the key to the mystery.'

'Where did you look for that?'

'I started at the *Wat Kwan Kittima* in Bangkok. I went to talk to the old *acharn*. I harboured a stubborn hope that there was something in the locked betel box which the king gave Jutulak. But the monks told me the *acharn* had gone to a forest monastery in the north-east – and taken the box with him.'

'Did they tell you which one?'

'Yes – and when I got there I found the *acharn* had died five years before. The box hadn't been found among his meagre belongings. So I stayed and became a forest monk . . . At first my only ambition was to try and find out what had happened to the box . . . The monks there barely spoke to one another. But after I'd been there nearly a year I talked with one very old man. He told me he had seen the *acharn* walk into the forest one day with a gilded box and a spade. He said he returned carrying only the spade which was damp with earth . . . I got him to show me which way the *acharn* had gone. And every day for the next two and a half years I went into the forest and dug in the earth beneath the trees for an hour or two . . .'

'But you never found anything after all that time?' asked Joceline in a hushed voice.

'Yes, I found something – something very important . . .'

Adam had stopped and was watching Poo Tongkam approach along the path towards them with Ladhya on his head. When the elephant saw Adam it lifted its trunk high into the air and trumpeted suddenly in an apparently joyous greeting; the long, loud roar echoed and re-echoed through the trees of the hidden forest and its primitive harshness sent a shiver up Joceline's spine.

'One day after I'd returned from another futile spell of digging, the very old monk came to my *kuti* smiling. He said, "I see you found something in the forest today." I was puzzled and he took me back to where I had been digging. He asked me to go and look into the hole . . . I thought I'd see the gilded box . . . But in the bottom of the hole there was water. And it hadn't rained for days . . .'

Joceline frowned. 'What did he mean?'

'He said: "The truth is like water underground – it's there for everybody to find if they look deeply enough." 'Adam waited for Poo Tongkam to come up to him. 'I stayed another year after that meditating and studying the Buddhist scriptures. I think it took me that long to understand properly what he meant . . .'

Adam reached into a pouch at his waist and pulled out a pressed ball of tamarind and boiled rice which he held out on the palm of his hand. Poo Tongkam waved his trunk over the delicacy once, then took it and curled it deftly into his mouth. Adam took out a second tamarind ball and passed it surreptitiously to Joceline. When she held it towards Poo Tongkam, he hesitated, his trunk weaving indecisively above her hand. Moving noiselessly, the calf stole quickly along his flank and whisked the tamarind ball away with a single movement of its trunk; once the food was safely inside his mouth he squealed loudly to celebrate his impertinence and backed away.

Ladhya and her daughter laughed at the calf's mischievousness. Then they exchanged words with Adam in their own language. After a few moments he turned to Joceline again.

'Ladhya reminded me to tell you of her dream . . . On my return from the forest monastery, she described a vivid dream she'd had several times during my absence. There were hundreds of pale-skinned elephants in her dream, she said – all the white elephants of history, it seemed. And riding amongst them a royal spirit who tried to tell her again and again something he found it difficult to say . . . She was never very sure, but she thought the spirit wanted to convey he was at peace . . . And was glad to have escaped at an early age from the responsibilities of his throne which had often seemed too great to bear.'

Joceline looked up at Ladhya and her daughter on the elephant. They had both been smiling with pleasure while Adam recounted the dream, although he had spoken in language they did not understand. As she smiled back at Ladhya and thanked her, Joceline was again struck by the aura of serenity which seemed to surround the two women; something rare was emanated by their presence which appeared to soften the very air about them. They continued to smile as Poo Tongkam shifted his great bulk again, carrying them onwards, and Joceline watched them go until they disappeared with the elephants round a bend in the track.

'Will you say some of the things you've told me to my camera?' she asked tentatively.

Adam nodded and smiled. 'If you think it would be of some use.'

'It would be very important indeed.' Joceline glanced up the track along which the elephants and Ladhya had walked and her voice softened. 'I think I understand better now what you meant when you wrote of angels in your manuscript. At first it seemed very odd ... but here, everything is different.'

Adam looked at her with a strange expression in his eyes, as though seeing her clearly for the first time. 'Perhaps I was more fortunate than I knew ... Perhaps there's always been more than one ...'

The sun was gaining strength rapidly and the heat and stillness of the hidden forest around them was suddenly more noticeable. As she looked at the stranger who was her father, Joceline felt a wild thought stray into her mind. Had she somehow come there under a mysterious compulsion to make amends for his past suffering? And might that explain why she had instinctively sympathised with his obsessive quest to help Jutulak and his family? Could that also account for her mystifying sympathy – and more – for Prem? Perhaps these same, unknown imperatives had even produced the inexplicable restlessness which had driven her abroad obsessively on her many other film journeys ... The questions chased one another through her mind and their very strangeness made her uneasy. Suddenly the mountaintop seemed faintly ominous again and she shuddered despite the heat. With a conscious effort she turned her thoughts in another direction.

'Will you send the white calf to the king in keeping with the old custom?' she asked, beginning to walk again.

Adam shook his head. 'No. By the same traditions, the king owns all the elephants in Thailand, wild or tamed. If white elephants can truly inspire auspicious events and bring peace and harmony, I hope they can do it anonymously from the depths of the jungle as well as from royal stables while being suckled by naked, nubile handmaidens ...'

The gentle, sane irony of his answer helped deflate her tension and she felt suddenly lighter. 'Have your forest meditations convinced you that the Buddhist way is nearest to the truth? Has it made you reject your own upbringing?'

Adam thought for a long time. When he spoke, his tone

was faintly apologetic, as though he uttered his conclusions reluctantly. 'I think the truth is like a well-cut diamond. It has many facets. Perhaps the great religions make the mistake of believing they've found an exclusive road to the truth. I think all of them see truth in part. But they should realise they only complement one another . . .' They walked silently side by side towards the pool. 'From the forest monastery I brought away one enduring image. The *acharn* is one of Thailand's famous sages . . . He said in meditating you should try to make your mind still like a forest pool. And when it's perfectly still, all manner of wondrous animals will come to drink there . . .'

His words fell quietly into the hot silence.

'That's very beautiful imagery . . .'

He looked at her and the rare smile again lit his face. 'It's not just imagery, it works. You've come here, haven't you, from the other side of the world?'

They walked on and ahead of them Alan Eastwood became visible. He was kneeling in the shade sorting his equipment and reloading his camera. His face was red and sweating from his exertions but on looking up and catching sight of Joceline he smiled triumphantly. Joceline went to him and patted his shoulder in congratulation.

'To finish off, I'd like you to film a few minutes of my father speaking alone to the camera by this pool . . . You won't need me, he knows exactly what he wants to say . . .'

'Okay, I'll get out the tripod again . . .'

Feeling suddenly drained of energy, Joceline left them and went to sit in the shade in sight of the water. She heard the gentle murmur of her father's voice drifting pleasantly across the water in the heat and felt the comforting warmth of the rock beneath her. She fell asleep for what seemed a minute or two, then opened her eyes to find Eastwood had already finished and packed away all his equipment. He was standing expectantly above her and in the moment that she awoke, she knew that she should leave the mountain at once.

When they were ready Adam walked with them to the top of the path that led down the rock-face. Eastwood immediately took his leave and began to descend, leaving them standing together. Joceline realised then that she and her father had neither used any familiarity nor touched one another and she suddenly felt that it was profoundly right that they had behaved that way.

As they stood alone on the lip of the high crag, looking at one another, she realised that she would never see him again. But that too, she knew suddenly, was also right. They had shared something profound that transcended normal expressions of affection. In some way she did not yet fully understand, she sensed she had unravelled a secret, although not the one she had expected.

From his unsmiling expression and his stillness as he looked at her, she could tell that he, too, felt it was right that way, and after a moment of silence she thanked him, then turned away to begin her descent. But after she had taken a few paces something stopped her and she looked back. She found that he was watching her with an unguarded softness in his gaze. The next moment they moved together and their arms went around one another. On the edge of the rock mountain they held each other close at last in an embrace that seemed to Joceline to last for ever.

20

Joceline glanced impatiently at her wristwatch. It was nearly 9.30 and the heat of the early day was already making the air shimmer above the *klong* beyond the courtyard of *Wat Kwan Kittima*. She had been waiting almost half an hour, sitting in the shade beneath the ancient bo-tree, but there was still no sign of Prem. Somewhere monks began chanting from the Buddhist scriptures and she listened for a moment; but sounds that she had found soothing in the past only fuelled her impatience. Part of her mind, she realised, was listening for the sounds of an approaching motorbike engine.

Prem had sent a note to the hotel at dawn asking her to meet him alone at the temple at nine o'clock. Tantalisingly, the message made no mention of his efforts to placate Kasem Petcharat. It merely said that despite a tight security ban, he could obtain a long-tailed boat from which they could film the king's river procession and she should come to finalise the arrangements. Although the contents of the note had seemed oblique, she had kept the appointment without hesitation. But as the empty minutes ticked by, she began to feel increasingly on edge.

Standing up, she strolled restlessly into the shady *viharn* where she had spoken with Prem and Surachai on her last visit. She looked idly at the painted *Jataka* panels and her eye fell again on the jewelled betel boxes. In her mind she heard her father's faintly ironic voice telling of his fruitless search for Jutulak's gift from the king, of his endless digging at the forest temple where the *acharn* had buried it. 'The truth is like water underground,' she heard him say again. 'It's there for everybody to find if they look deeply enough.' Wandering from one painting of the Buddha to another, she wondered if she really believed her father's words, or even if she yet understood them fully.

She had left The Black World of Lost Spirits feeling profoundly moved, but confused too. The images of her father and Ladhya living on the eerie, paradisial mountaintop, the memory of Poo Tongkam's huge bulk looming from the mist and the white calf sporting in the shimmering pool – all had haunted her mind, waking and sleeping, ever since. But thirty-six hours later she still felt overwhelmed by the experience. In addition, the tensions surrounding the unfinished film were continuing to affect her and the entire unit; significantly, there had been no signs of surveillance in the past two days and they assumed Prem had somehow convinced Kasem Petcharat that the documentary no longer presented any threat to him. Nevertheless, much of the time an underlying sense of anxiety still coloured her thoughts and she knew she would not be capable of assessing her real reactions to all the things that had happened in Thailand until she was able to reflect on them in tranquillity back in England.

Beside one of the painted panels she paused; a little set of lacquered drawers, each stamped with a number, stood on a table beneath the painting. A matching vase beside them contained numbered slivers of wood and out of curiosity Joceline opened one of the drawers. Inside she saw small squares of numbered paper printed with separate paragraphs of Thai script and Chinese characters. As she was closing the drawer she heard a soft footfall behind her. Turning, she saw standing in the open doorway the same young, shaven-headed monk who had welcomed her on arrival at the temple half an hour earlier. He advanced towards her, grave-faced and serious, and she saw that he carried in his hands a brass amulet of the Lord Buddha on a necklet. Halting before her, he indicated she should bow her head a little and when she did so he placed the amulet around her neck. Then, reaching out, he tied around her right wrist a protective twist of cotton the same colour as his saffron robe. Remembering that something similar had happened to her father there, she wondered whether his actions had been prompted by some sign of agitation in herself but the monk merely murmured a ritual blessing. Then, about to turn away, he smiled.

'I saw you inspect our *seeam see* – you like to know the future?'

Joceline smiled back politely, uncertain of his meaning, and he picked up the lacquered vase of numbered sticks. He made a little demonstration of shaking it at an angle, then handed it to her. When she shook the vase, one of the sticks quickly detached itself from the others and fell out on to the table. Picking it up, the monk showed her the number – two – and gestured towards the drawers. She opened the drawer with the number 'two' on it and took out one of the printed slips. She looked at the indecipherable Thai script, then smiled and handed it to the monk. She watched him as he read it, then he looked up at her and smiled again.

'It is very good for you. It says, "If you get Number Two, you will do all you wish in life. But it will come step by step ..."' He paused and read again. 'It also says, "You will find true happiness before long ... but you must have patience ..."'

He folded the slip and handed it to her as the sound of a revving motorcycle grew loud in the courtyard outside. Joceline thanked him perfunctorily, her mind already on the arrival of Prem, and he walked silently out of the *viharn* as Prem appeared in his riding leathers, carrying his crash helmet. Joceline could see as he came towards her that his face was set in tense lines.

'I've got a long-tailed boat for your camera crew,' he said quickly. 'I'm sorry for the delay. All civilian craft have been barred from the river – so it took longer than I thought ...'

'Thank you.' She began to smile in gratitude but his strained manner alarmed her suddenly. 'There's something else, isn't there? Something's wrong, I can tell.'

He nodded grimly. 'The Chinese has asked me to give you a message . . . He says he will kill Surachai unless you give him your personal guarantee that your film will condemn Kasem Petcharat. He says you must quote the false material in the manuscript in full . . .'

She stared at him in horror. 'Prem, that's impossible! A journalist can't give in to blackmail like that . . . Now, even if I don't name him, it's my duty to say in my commentary that these threats have been made . . . and explain why.'

'I tried to tell him that – but he believes everything can be achieved by force . . .'

'What can we do?' asked Joceline desperately.

Prem grimaced. 'There's only one thing left to do now.'

'What's that?'

He looked hard at her, his eyes glittering in a way that made her uneasy. 'Perhaps it's better not to ask . . .'

They were standing only two or three feet apart and his eye fell on the slip of folded paper she held in her hand. The drawer in the little *seeam see* cabinet from which it came was still open and on seeing this, his expression softened. 'Were you looking into the future while you waited for me?'

She nodded absently.

'What does it foretell?' The tension in his voice betrayed his interest and as he spoke, he reached out and took the prediction slip from her hand. He read it quickly, then looked at her again.

'You are promised good fortune,' he said softly. 'I'm very glad . . .' He paused and moved a step closer. 'Joceline, what happened in the north between us was the most beautiful experience in all my life . . . To me it was very important . . .' He hesitated, searching for the right words. 'Was it important for you?'

Joceline felt unable to look directly into his eyes. 'Prem, it was terrifying and wonderful all at the same time . . .' She lowered her voice and tried to summon a smile . . . 'I shall never forget that storm as long as I live . . . And what happened seemed . . . preordained in some strange way I can't explain . . .' She paused, feeling ill at ease, not knowing how to put the confusion she felt into words . . . 'But I've been through so much here . . . And we haven't finished yet . . . I can't answer that question honestly at the moment . . . I hope you understand . . .'

He had been watching her closely all the time she was speaking and with a sudden, almost violent movement he snatched up the vase of numbered sticks from the table. Sadness and suppressed anger showed in his face and he shook the vase with unnecessary force. Immediately one stick rose out of the very middle of the bundle and spurted on to the table.

'Tell me the number, Joceline, please?' he commanded.

She picked the stick and showed him. 'Number eleven.'

'Will you open the drawer for me?'

She pulled out the eleventh drawer and reached inside for the printed prediction. Then she turned to look at him, her expression becoming uneasy.

'What is it? What's wrong?'

'The drawer's empty.'

His eyes narrowed and some colour left his face. Then he tugged a ball-point pen from inside his leather jacket and scribbled something on her slip of paper from the *seeam see*.

'Be at this boat-house on the river by midday,' he said in an unsteady voice. 'Everything will be ready by then for you to film the king's river procession.'

He handed her the paper and started to turn away. Then he stopped and looked round at her, his expression betraying inner turmoil. Impulsively he came back and put both arms around her; he kissed her fiercely and she felt him tremble with the force of his passion. But this time some inexplicable barrier which seemed to have arisen between them prevented her from responding.

When he sensed this, he released her. Turning silently away, he hurried from the *viharn* without another glance. She heard him kick-start his Suzuki and a moment later he shot out of the temple courtyard, riding at an unnecessary and dangerously fast speed.

21

Skimming lightly over the surface of the broad Chao Phraya river like graceful, golden swans came the ancient flotilla of narrow, high-prowed, Siamese royal barges. Propelled by hundreds of scarlet-uniformed rowers who dipped and raised their gilded oars in perfect unison, fifty spectacular boats, spread out along the river for more than a kilometre, were speeding downstream in the direction of the Temple of the Dawn. Watched by tens of thousands of applauding people from the river banks, the revered King of Thailand was travelling at the heart of the procession.

Seated on a throne in a tiny gilded pavilion and dressed in full regalia, he was being carried by the most magnificent craft of all, the gold and purple *Suphannahongse* built by King Rama I. After nearly forty-four years on the throne, the longest-reigning monarch of the entire Chakri dynasty was acknowledging the affection and respect of the crowd as always with an outward show of shy modesty.

Conch shells wailed, drums throbbed and the sun glinted on the symbolic, multi-tiered umbrellas of kingship held aloft by uniformed canopy bearers. Taking their time from rhythm-keepers who tapped the butts of silver spears upon the decks, the oarsmen chanted lines of hallowed poetry as they rowed, praising all the kings of the dynasty. In a closed boatshed on the western bank of the river, Prem paused to wipe sweat from his brow and listen for a moment to the chanting. He had just positioned inside the bows of a long-tailed boat a twenty-pound package of what American explosive experts called 'black putty'. Rolled into cigar-sized strips each weighing half a pound and wrapped in brown, waterproof paper, the plastic high explosive designated PE 3A had originally been manufactured in an American arms factory. Now, having been bought by Prem on Bangkok's armaments black market, it was connected by two ordinary pieces of copper telephone wiring to a percussion detonator which Prem had fixed carefully to the prow of the long-tailed boat. Although he was stripped to the waist he was perspiring freely from the tension of handling the 'black putty'. Using a method he had learned from Communist guerrillas in the northern jungles, he had wired the plastic explosive to a torch battery which would provide the vital spark when the metal core of the percussion detonator closed the small electrical circuit on impacting with another vessel.

When he was satisfied with his work, Prem covered the explosive with a tarpaulin sheet. Then he moved to the boat-house doors opening on to the river to check that they were poised ready to swing open when he nosed the boat forward. Since the last security check by water-borne military units two hours earlier, he had cut painstakingly through three bolts on the outside with a tapering steel rasp file. Now, after testing them tentatively, he was satisfied that one thrust from the boat's throaty, sawn-down version of a lorry engine would push the pointed bows through the gap in the doors and send them crashing back on their hinges.

Peering out through a crack in the wood, he found he could see the flotilla approaching. The array of brilliant, red and gold craft spread across 'the River of Kings', with their slender prows and sterns curving magically skywards, looked unreal: what he saw resembled a scene from the ancient Siamese legends recounted by monks in the village temple school of his boyhood. The stylised rowing, perfected in the ancient capital of Ayutthaya, added to the impression that the boats, fashioned in the form of mythical birds, were skimming the water on glittering wings. As they lifted their blades skywards, the oarsmen paused as one man for an instant before sweeping them downwards once more. Each stroke, which he knew was called *nok bin* – 'birds flying' – was timed so perfectly that the individual oars on each boat appeared to form themselves into large, gossamer wings beating with a natural grace and rhythm.

On glimpsing the gilded pavilion on the *Suphannahongse* and the slight, regal figure seated rigidly upright in its shade, Prem formed his hands automatically into a *wai* and bowed his head over them. He remained like this for a long moment, with his eyes closed, as though seeking silent forgiveness for his forthcoming actions. Then he straightened up and his face clenched itself once more into a determined expression.

Tugging on a shirt, he ran to unfasten one of the rear doors. Easing it open a fraction, he peered out through the vertical opening. Less than a hundred yards away outside the empty boatshed to which he had deliberately misdirected them, he could see Joceline and the entire Metropolitan film unit. They were clustered around two cameras on tripods that were pointing upriver. Through a small window in the boatshed he had checked surreptitiously every few minutes while making his preparations to ensure they were still there. Even at a distance he had been able to register their impatience but now Ian MacLachlan was bent over one tripod filming the approaching royal barges.

As he watched, Prem saw Joceline look at her wrist and glance impatiently up and down the street as she had done many times during the previous half hour. A crowd ten-deep lined the very edge of the river but their attention was directed at the advancing pageant and nobody looked his way. Seizing his chance, he opened the door, stepped outside into full view and waved vigorously in Joceline's direction. When he was sure she had seen him, he beckoned urgently for her to join him. Joceline spoke hurriedly to the others, then started running in his direction, followed closely by the sound recordist and MacLachlan.

'What's going on Prem?' demanded Joceline breathlessly when she reached him. 'What happened to our boat?'

'It's in here – quickly.' He held the door open and motioned the three of them into the boatshed. Following them in, he slammed the door and locked it.

'It's a bit damned late,' began MacLachlan, staring distastefully at the shabby, long-tailed boat. 'And I'm not sure this is the best sort of thing to film from . . .'

'It's not for you – it's for me!' Prem leapt down into the boat and ran along it to where the high explosive lay covered by the tarpaulin.

'What do you mean, Prem?' asked Joceline in a puzzled tone.

Instead of answering, he pulled the tarpaulin aside. The dumpling-like blob of lethal material and its connected wires were fully exposed and Joceline and the two crew members stared in disbelief.

'Good God!' exclaimed MacLachlan quietly when he found his voice. 'It's a bloody floating bomb!'

'Yes!' Prem looked quickly from face to face. 'I don't want you to film from this boat – I want this boat filmed.'

'What in God's name are you going to do?' asked Joceline in a shocked tone.

'In thirty seconds from now I'm going to ram open those doors . . . and you'll be able to record every detail of what follows.'

Joceline glanced out of the grimy window through which the shimmering boats carrying the king and his entourage were visible. They were holding the centre of the stream as they neared the boatshed and she turned back to stare in horror at him.

'What can you possibly achieve by this, Prem?'

'I can show others the way . . .'

He ran to the rear of the boat, jerked the starting coil and stood back as the powerful engine roared into life, filling the boatshed with noise and acrid exhaust smoke. MacLachlan had stepped back to get a wider angle and was already filming Prem, the boat and the uncovered bomb; the sound recordist, too, was concentrating on adjusting the knobs on his tape machine in accordance with its flickering dials and what he was picking up through his headphones.

'For God's sake help me stop him!' yelled Joceline, jumping down into the boat.

Because of its narrowness, the craft rocked wildly as she rushed towards the stern where Prem had taken hold of the tiller to begin manoeuvring.

'Don't do it,' she pleaded, clutching him with both hands. 'Security is very heavy along both sides of the river . . .'

She broke off, staring; from his expressionless face she could see that he was fully aware of what he was doing and had made his fateful decision in cold blood.

'Get off the boat, Joceline!' Prem darted a glance through the boathouse window at the waterborne procession and opened the throttle warningly. 'The *Suphannahongse* is about to pass!'

She shook her head defiantly. 'No – killing the king and making yourself a martyr will achieve nothing at all . . . I won't let you . . .'

Instead of replying, he adjusted the engine controls and sent the boat nosing forward just enough to ease the doors open two or three feet. Crouching, he pointed straight out across the broad river.

'It's nothing to do with the king . . . He won't be harmed – Kasem Petcharat and the Chinese are on board Kasem's yacht together at this very moment . . .'

Joceline followed the line of his pointing finger. Moored opposite the boatshed on the far side of the river was a sleek, white, ocean-going yacht. Tiny figures were visible crowding its polished rails, looking towards the speeding royal barges.

'Prem, remember what my father said.' Her expression became beseeching. 'You'll never destroy evil with evil . . .'

He reached behind his back suddenly and an automatic pistol appeared in his right fist. 'Joceline, I'm sorry. You mustn't try to stop me . . .It's the only choice left for me – the drawer of the *seeam see* was empty, remember!'

'Prem, that needn't mean anything . . .'

She began moving towards him, reaching out with one hand, but he lifted the gun threateningly to halt her . . . 'My "failure" here, if that's what it turns out to be, will be noticed – it may inspire others to finish what I've tried to start . . .'

He fanned the pistol in an arc to cover MacLachlan and the recordist, who had put down their equipment and run forward to try to help her.

'Pick up your gear again and begin filming!' he commanded.

The two Englishmen stopped disconcertedly in their tracks. Seeing from Prem's implacable expression that he was in deadly earnest, they took up their equipment and MacLachlan stepped back to focus his camera on the long-tailed boat again. Still holding the pistol on Joceline, Prem gestured for her to disembark and she reluctantly obeyed.

As soon as she had climbed out, he engaged the clutch and opened the throttle wide. The long-tailed boat surged forward with a roar, smashing the boathouse doors apart and splintering their woodwork. As it hurtled out into the river Prem guided the craft with great skill, swerving and weaving through the minor royal barges that were carrying princes, princesses and other dignitaries in the wake of the king. The majestic *Suphannahongse* itself was already well downstream, gliding on smoothly and inperturbably under the power of its expert oarsmen.

As soon as Prem's craft entered the clear water on the far

side of the river, Joceline heard the ugly rattle of machine-gun fire. Coming from several different military security launches the heavy-calibre bullets kicked up long lines of converging spray around the racing longboat. Prem, standing high in the stern, continued to swing the tiller skilfully from side to side, curving the craft in a long arc towards the moored yacht.

Despite the growing volume of fire, it began to seem that against the odds, he would reach his target. Then in a patch of open water, the speeding boat dissolved without warning into a column of bright orange flame and a billow of black smoke. The roar of the explosive detonating sounded like thunder. Chunks of wood and metal rose high above the water in a spiralling shower and tumbled slowly down again. As the flames disappeared and the cloud of smoke thickened, pieces of debris continued to rain back into the river. Scanning the cluttered surface with desperate eyes, Joceline searched in vain for Prem. Like his hopes, the long-tailed boat had disintegrated into a thousand pieces. Amongst its wreckage there was no sign of a bobbing head. Nowhere on the surface of the river was there any indication that he had himself survived.

FINALE

1991

The buzzing audience of glamorous, bejewelled women and dinner-jacketed men seated at sumptuously laden tables in a Park Lane hotel fell abruptly silent. From the wings of a tiny stage the handsome figure of one of Britain's best-known television presenters emerged. Wearing black tie and a dinner jacket himself, he carried a gold-coloured envelope in one hand and he stopped before a small, central lectern to open it.

'Here are the nominations for the Tagman Television Documentary Prize for 1990,' he said, smiling professionally towards a camera that was broadcasting the proceedings of the English Annual Film and Television Awards live from London to the nation. 'Northern Television's "South Africa's Agony" by Roger Smythe; "Life on the Breadline in Britain" – Keith Middlemass for the BBC; Anglia TV's "Japan – Dilemma for the Western World" and finally . . .' The presenter paused long enough to send a subliminal, private smile in the direction of Joceline, who was seated at a table close to the podium . . . 'Metropolitan Television's "Perspective" Special "The Bangkok Secret – Story of an Investigation" by Joceline Hampson . . .'

The well-groomed audience gave a burst of enthusiastic applause to the four short-listed films and on to the screens of television viewers across the country flashed four simultaneous, side-by-side close-ups of the four individual documentary-makers who were in contention for this particular EAFTA award. Some were smiling self-consciously, others remained serious-faced as they sat at their respective tables, which like all the others in the great banqueting suite were covered with gleaming napery, sparkling glasses and expensive bottles of wine. At the Metropolitan table, Joceline fixed her attention on the starched, snowy-white cloth in front of her and avoided the lens of the hand-held camera being operated by one of several dinner-jacketed cameramen moving among the glittering throng. She wore a blue halter-neck dress which left her back and shoulders bare and viewers saw her looking stern and unsmiling in profile; when she glanced up briefly, Robert Lancaster, who was seated at the far end of the oval table, caught her eye. The programme controller smiled quickly and lifted his right hand just an inch or two to show her that he had crossed his fingers to wish her luck.

Beside Joceline, Angela Gladstone, resplendent in yellow chiffon, was gazing tensely towards the large screen suspended above the heads of the diners at one side of the saloon. The lights had already dimmed sufficiently to enhance the images on the screen. Brief clips of film and sound commentary had already begun to run for 'South Africa's Agony' and images of the bronze EAFTA awards in the shape of a Greek actor's mask were being superimposed intermittently on the screen to divide and link the disconnected images.

'Are you glad you came now, Joceline?' whispered a dinner-jacketed Ian MacLachlan, grinning at her from his seat two places along the table. 'I'm surprised you didn't find an excuse to dash off on your travels again somewhere tonight.'

Looking genuinely uncomfortable, she pulled a child's comic face and shot him a forced smile. 'I'd rather be anywhere in the world than here at this moment, Ian,' she replied in an undertone.

'Does that include the little go-go bar by the river in Bangkok?' asked the sound recordist in a satirical stage whisper from across the table.

'Well, *almost* anywhere else.'

She closed her eyes and raised her shoulders in a mock shudder as she corrected herself. In his chair on her other side, Michael Ewington, looking boyishly enthusiastic as always in a wine-coloured velvet jacket and frilled shirt, smiled ruefully at the recollection of the terrible night by the Chao Phraya.

She had agreed to attend the annual award ceremonies for the first time in her career after special pleading from the chairman of Metropolitan. She had won several nominations and two outright awards in past years but had always contrived deliberately to miss the presentation event because she doubted the value of competitive awards for television programmes. The Metropolitan chairman, a bald, hearty man, was smoking a very large cigar at the head of the table, with Robert Lancaster on his right hand, and from time to time he smiled broadly in her direction, holding up his cigar and making a Churchillian V-sign to give silent reassurance that Metropolitan would emerge victorious.

'Just relax, my dear, it's really a one-horse race,' he had said repeatedly before dining began, not realising that Joceline had no real regard for the little EAFTA statuettes. He had personally ordered that full-page advertisements be placed for the documentary in the national and provincial press, both before and after it had drawn record ratings at its autumn 1990 transmission on the national ITV network. On his specific instructions, copy-writers had extolled the film's unique merits in support of Metropolitan's claim to lead the nation's television companies in serious journalistic enterprise and endeavour. They cited it as a symbolic example of Metropolitan's concern to create high-quality programmes and offered it as one of the prime reasons why Metropolitan should retain the exclusive right to the lucrative independent franchise for the London region. Metropolitan, the advertisements added, had never ceased and would never cease to give the highest priority to serious international investigative documentaries. Domestic press coverage and foreign sales of the film had both been outstanding; but not surprisingly it had not been sold for transmission in Thailand.

On the elevated screen, a telling clip of a Tokyo geisha girl bowing to sheepish-looking British businessmen was bringing to a close the brief résumé of 'Japan – A Dilemma for the Western World'. From around the large room came a sharp burst of relieved applause. Many of the guests at the opulent gathering had watched uneasily moments before as the screen revealed close shots and snatches of interviews with derelict men and women living in cardboard boxes. Other scenes from 'Life on the Breadline in Britain' had left them feeling subdued and ill at ease and they were glad their minds had been transported quickly towards the more distant, exotic problems that Japan posed for the West. Then, without a break, 'The Bangkok Secret – Story of an Investigation' showed in white letters underneath a title close-up of a small, pale-skinned elephant calf.

Joceline stared at the baby elephant, lost for the briefest

moment in the poignancy of the discovery she had made on the jungle-covered mountain. Alan Eastwood's face shone with pride as he watched the film he had bravely obtained when physically wounded. Some of his facial scars were still visible but he was quietly proud of them as the honourable marks of battle. As the shots of the elephant calf gave way to a wider angle of Poo Tongkam, moving with majestic slowness across a jungle glade, Joceline reached quickly into the small evening handbag on the table in front of her. Ignoring the film, she pulled out a card and a pen and began to scribble a hurried note.

Other images and snatches of dialogue continued to chase one another across the screen: the slow-revving Suzuki motorcycles and their white-helmeted riders moving past MacLachlan's concealed camera and into the dingy, riverside alleyway in Bangkok; the sudden, sharp sound of gunfire, laid over dramatic, jerky camera shots of the bar and running motorcyclists; the exotic spires of the Grand Palace and the Temple of the Dawn, the crowded Erawan Shrine and its stone elephant guards seen through swimming clouds of incense. Then, finally, the audience hushed as they watched Prem climb grim-faced into the long-tailed boat beside the Chao Phraya.

The gilded royal barges and their scarlet-clad oarsmen became visible, approaching along the broad river. Prem, pale and tense in close-up, started the long-tailed boat's engine and it roared away from the wharf at great speed. The clip had already become famous because it had been rushed back to London and included in the ITN news bulletins the day after it was filmed. From the comfort of their tables, the whole audience watched, holding their breath for the dreadful moment they knew was coming.

MacLachlan had held the speeding boat brilliantly in a medium close shot as it careered into mid-river, swerving to avoid gunfire which began pouring towards it the moment it was spotted from military security launches. With a terrible suddenness, the long-tailed boat dissolved into a plume of orange flame and a giant fist of black smoke; the sound of the explosion came a split second later. Shards of flying wood and engine metal were hurled high in the air, then rained slowly down again into the water. The spectacular procession of golden barges, however, did not falter in its momentum. The ancient craft continued to move downriver, safely beyond the range of the explosion, and slowly the whole screen dimmed and faded to black.

The audience, deeply moved, did not, as was customary, applaud. For a second or two a tense silence held the room. On the tiny stage the celebrity male presenter lifted from the lectern another sealed envelope which contained the result of the ballot of members of EAFTA.

'And the winner of the Tagman Television Documentary Prize for 1990 is . . .' He fumbled in opening the envelope and darted a little, embarrassed smile of apology at the audience. Then he succeeded in extracting the card. After reading it, he glanced up smiling broadly at the cameras and the audience. 'The winner is . . . "The Bangkok Secret" by Joceline Hampson!'

Loud, sustained applause broke out and all heads turned in the direction of the Metropolitan table. The chairman began clapping delightedly, clenching his cigar between his teeth. A moment or two of elation passed before he and everyone else in the banqueting suite noticed that Joceline's chair at the end of the table was empty. Millions of viewers in their homes had known for slightly longer; the four live close-ups of the contending producers and presenters transmitted as the result was read out had not included Joceline. Instead, the Metropolitan frame had shown a wider view of the whole table and its occupants, with one important chair empty.

As the applause continued and the master of ceremonies waited disconcertedly on the stage holding the Tagman Award statuette, Angela Gladstone rose hastily from her seat holding the card written by Joceline. She hurried with it to Robert Lancaster at the head of the table; after a brief, whispered consultation she beckoned to Michael Ewington and the other members of the Thailand crew, as well as two home-based film editors, and led them quickly through the tables to the stage. While the applause continued she whispered a further explanation to the master of ceremonies, who nodded, and Angela stepped forward shyly to receive the EAFTA statuette from the hands of the smiling male presenter.

'Joceline has asked me to deputise for her – she claims last-minute stage fright,' said Angela, speaking diffidently into the microphone on the lectern as the applause faded. 'She specifically requested that the whole unit come up to receive this award, which all of us, especially Joceline, regard as the highest possible honour . . .'

She paused and glanced round at Ewington, the two cameramen, the sound recordist and the two film editors, who were standing in a ragged line across the stage, grinning broadly. On an impulse Angela handed over the statuette to Ewington and it was passed playfully from hand to hand down the line as though it was too hot to hold. This piece of pantomime produced a new round of applause and when it died away, Angela lifted into view the card on which Joceline had scribbled.

'Joceline asked me to say that perhaps this award and all documentary awards should not be given to us, the film-makers alone, but equally to the people who are the subjects, the people who appear in the films . . .' She hesitated, then glanced at the card again. 'Joceline believes that the best documentaries are always about people – and it's they more than us who strive against hardship, make sacrifices, suffer and endure . . . "Perhaps," she adds, "we should regard this award as having been made in that spirit to all concerned people in Thailand."'

The applause began again and continued as the members of the unit, flushed and smiling, made their way back to their places through back-slapping colleagues and friends. Robert Lancaster, who was on his feet at the table, shook each of them warmly by the hand; then while the next award was being introduced, he slipped away and hurried downstairs to the street-level exit which opened on to Park Lane. Coming out into the cold March night, he glanced anxiously up and down the pavement; but to his dismay he found it deserted in both directions. A continuous flow of taxis, buses and private cars was flashing past at high speed, heading down towards Hyde Park Corner, and he stood indecisively on the kerb, wondering whether Joceline had already flagged down a taxi. Then a movement attracted his attention nearly a hundred yards away and he screwed up his eyes to peer into the darkness.

Joceline's bare-shouldered figure, he could see, was just visible, hurrying northward along the raised, central reservation that divides the two broad carriageways of Park Lane. Even at a distance he could detect her agitation; she seemed to be searching for a break in the northward-flowing traffic and as he watched, she suddenly darted through a gap and ran towards the railings bordering Hyde Park. He cupped his hands to his mouth and called her name loudly; but she did not pause or turn. Breaking into a run, he dashed over the south-bound carriageway heedless of the oncoming rush of traffic.

The horns of fast-moving vehicles blared and wailed at him as he crossed the far carriageway in the same way. Joceline was walking quickly but he saw her stop suddenly and bend down to remove her high-heeled evening shoes. Holding them in one hand, she climbed nimbly over the low railings into the park and hurried on down an avenue of trees. He accelerated, calling her name again, this time very loudly. But although she was obviously near enough to hear, she still didn't turn. He scrambled over the fence himself and ran fast until he caught up with her. Gasping for breath, he moved in front of her, forcing her to stop; when he looked at her, he saw that tears were streaming down her cheeks.

She was shivering and he removed his dinner jacket to place it gently around her bare shoulders. Neither of them spoke and after a moment or two they began walking side by side in silence. Eventually he tugged a folded handkerchief from the breast pocket of the jacket and held it out to her. She took it without looking at him and dabbed abstractedly at her face.

A cold breeze was blowing, tossing the yellow heads of daffodils that had already sprouted around the tree trunks all along the avenue. By the light of the street lamps outside in Park Lane, he could see that on the bare branches above their heads, new leaves were also beginning to appear. Ahead of them a squirrel darted across the shadowy path and sprang up into a tree with one enormous bound.

'I'm sorry, Robert, I just had to get out of there,' said Joceline, touching her cheeks again with the handkerchief.

'Don't apologise . . .' He thrust his hands into his pockets. 'Angela was an excellent stand-in . . . She dragged the whole crew up with her as instructed. They enjoyed it and she said her piece – and yours – very prettily . . .'

They walked on again in silence for two or three minutes.

'You probably haven't noticed but I've given up cigars,' he

said, smiling wryly. 'I stopped well over a year ago – in the autumn of '89 ... The day after your scathing diatribe in my office about poor families in the Third World. Do you remember?'

She sniffed, dabbed a last time at her face, and nodded.

'But I believe diatribes are now a thing of the past with you, am I right? ... Everybody tells me you're much more at ease with yourself these days ...'

They walked on once more in silence. Close to Speakers Corner a sea of daffodils rippling in the night wind spread its glow across the dark of the greensward. In the darkness high above their heads, they heard a formation of geese calling in flight.

'My wife is divorcing me.'

The discordant, two-note siren of an ambulance or police car advancing along Park Lane grew louder suddenly, until it filled their ears. After it had passed, it faded just as quickly and the silence around them seemed enhanced.

'It's at my request. At long last I realised I should have done it five years ago ... I was a fool.'

He looked sideways at her but she was still staring expressionlessly ahead along the avenue of trees.

'I remember you making it clear on that memorable day that you wouldn't want to take up with me again "under any circumstances". So please don't think I harbour any illusions ... But your remarks about indecision also started me thinking. I went to see my lawyers the following week ... I moved out to a little mews house nearby about six months ago and we've kept it all very quiet ... Things will probably be finalised by the end of the summer.'

He dug his hands deeper into his pockets and hunched his shoulders against the wind.

'There isn't anybody else ... Very belatedly and very inadequately, I'm trying to pay some homage to those precious feelings we once shared ...'

Somewhere overhead a Jumbo jet heading down towards Heathrow reversed its engines with a dull roar. Looking up through the branches that were just coming into leaf, Joceline saw the gleam of the airliner's navigation lights floating slowly across the sky. For a time she walked on, watching them in silence; then she halted and turned to face him.

'Thank you, Robert,' she said in a quiet voice. 'I never dreamed I'd hear you say anything like that . . .'

She had stopped weeping and she smiled briefly. He was watching her face with an intentness that belied his earlier assertion that he harboured no illusions about the future. She could see that, despite all that had happened in the past, he felt sure that she had gone on caring for him. In the shadowy darkness he was waiting for her to open her arms to him again.

'I hope everything works out well, Robert,' she said softly, looking directly into his eyes. 'For you both.'

His brow knitted in puzzlement. 'What do you mean "for you both"?'

'You *and* Metropolitan.'

His frown deepened. 'Why do you say that?'

'Because I'm going to move on.'

Smiling again, she took off his jacket and handed it back to him. Although her shoulders were bare and the chill in the night air was becoming sharper, she no longer showed any sign that she felt the cold.

'And before you ask me, I'd better tell you. I haven't had any tempting offers. In fact, I've had no offers at all.'

He stared bemusedly at her. 'Then why on earth are you going?'

'It's intuition . . . I decided one minute ago . . . When you told me about your divorce.'

She reached out and replaced his folded handkerchief in the top pocket of his dinner jacket. Then she smiled at him a last time and started to turn away.

'But that's crazy.' Lancaster spoke in a disbelieving voice and caught at her arm to stop her. 'Where will you go?'

'I don't know yet – but it's not important.'

'I don't understand,' he said gruffly.

'Perhaps you're right about one thing – I *am* more at ease with the world now – and my place in it. I didn't solve the secret that lured me to Thailand. But I think I did learn something important there . . .'

'And what was that?'

'I can't really put it into words . . .'

In her mind's eye she saw the elephants drinking from the placid pool in the green mountain glade. Even a year later she could still remember the intense feeling of peace and serenity she had experienced during the hours she had spent there; but she knew the words would sound meaningless if she tried to describe the feeling to anyone else.

'I'm just going to follow my instinct and sit back quietly on my own here in London.' She shrugged. 'I'll just wait and see what comes to me.'

He shook his head in bewilderment. 'It doesn't make any sense.'

'Perhaps not to you, Robert. But I'm quite certain it's the right thing for me to do.'

Turning her back on him, she walked on alone once more along the shadowy avenue. Looking up, she saw the lights of the airliner again, sinking and diminishing ahead of her. The tiny pinpoints of moving radiance were shimmering and glowing like precious jewels in the quiet spring night and suddenly the everyday sight was strangely beautiful to her. In the brightness of the lights she seemed to see a new, undefined promise and she watched them in silence until they faded gently into the far darkness.